Stalin's Door

A Novel By

John St. Clair

Stalin's Door

Copyright © 2021 by John St. Clair

All rights reserved. No part of this book may be reproduced in any form by any electronic or mechanical means including photocopying, recording, or information storage and retrieval without permission in writing from the author.

Cover illustration of the woggle was hand drawn by my friend Matthew Soffe!

Cover artwork, interior design, and book layout by John St. Clair

My cover guru is Catlin Liliana Price!

You may give feedback on this novel at: jstclair@gmail.com

ISBN: 9798719441962 (paperback)

First Edition
09 March 2021
Alea iacta est

For Nancy

Contents

Acknowledgments

Russian Names Primer

Special Notes

The Novel

Zhenya's Tale................	Finding Stalin's Door........................	1
Sava's Tragedy..............	Behind Stalin's Door......................	77
Lera's Yarn....................	Beyond Stalin's Door....................	203
Zhenya's Allegory..........	Return To Stalin's Door..............	341

Glossary Of Transliterated Russian Words

Colophon

About The Author

Acknowledgments

I've been working on this novel for five years. It took me a lengthy period to write and an even longer period to revise and edit. I feel as if I set the bar high for myself starting this project: a culture I didn't grow up in, a language I don't speak, and a time I didn't live in. Writing is not a straightforward process. However, it is highly rewarding once there's a final product. This novel was a labor of love, and I can promise you I scrutinized and fussed over every single word.

I'd like to take a moment and give a gigantic thank you to all the wonderful people that have supported me in the beta-reading and review process. There are legions of you! Some have been with me from the very beginning, when *Stalin's Door* was merely a short story in 2016. Others joined up from its expansion to a novella in 2017, and many more when I completed the first draft of the novel in 2019. Now we're into 2021, and the arduous editing and revising process is finally complete! I am grateful to everyone that spent their precious time to read my words, and I am especially humbled at the suggestions, corrections, and excellent feedback provided to me. I am also thankful for your constant encouragement, good will, kind inquires, and support.

I am deeply indebted to the following individuals for their overwhelming assistance:

Alma Rosales	Frank Gifford	Kathryn St. Clair
Angie Roote	Graham Powell	L. Robert Fitch
Catlin Liliana Price	Jason Price	Rachael Rouleau
Colleen McGrath	Jeremy Spilker	Rick Anderson
Dennis Marti	Karen Warkentien	

The woggle, seen in the top center and back of my book cover, was hand drawn by my friend Matthew Soffe! I've commissioned several pieces of art from him over the years and highly endorse his services.

I owe an acknowledgment to the following works of non-fiction that helped me tremendously in my research into this traumatic time in Russian history. I can recommend them wholeheartedly!

The Great Terror: A Reassessment by Robert Conquest
Let History Judge by Roy Medvedev
Gulag: A History by Anne Applebaum

I owe a special acknowledgment to Nancy McAtee for putting up with me, for her endless motivation, and her unwavering inspiration!

John St. Clair
March 2021

Russian Names Primer

To ensure that my novel makes sense, I'd like to give you a crash course on the intricacies of how Russian names work. Russians can go by many names all at the same time! This can be naturally perplexing to an uninitiated reader. Depending on the social setting, circumstances, and the age of the person, the exact usage of one's name will often change without notice. So, let's figure it out together.

Fundamentally, all Russians have three names. A given name (GN), a patronymic (P), and a family surname (FS). The diminutive is a shortened form of the GN of a person and is meant to express affection. They are commonly used only within family situations. In exceptional circumstances, the double diminutive may be used. They are usually reserved for moments of tender sentimentality. On rare occasions they're even used in anger! The P is always derived from the GN of the father. Men's Ps will always end in -*ovich* or -*evich*, and women's Ps will always end in -*ovna* or -*evna*. The FS has a male & female version, with the female one ending in -*a*.

It is natural for acquaintances, co-workers, and even your boss to use your GN + P together when conversing. In formal ceremonial occasions, or when referring to someone in the third person, but never in conversations, all three names of GN + P + FS will be used together—in that order. In legal proceedings, official documents, and tombstones, all three names will be used, however the FS will be listed first, e.g., FS + GN + P. Of course, when to use the GN of a person, or their diminutive, the GN + P, or just the title of a person and their FS, are all dictated by what social situation you find yourself in. A supervisor may call you by your GN + P, but you would always use his or her title out of respect. Parents would naturally use your diminutive freely, but your co-worker would use your GN + P, unless they're a good friend, and then they'd just use your GN or a nickname. Lastly, one's age may also shape how names are used. Older Russians may be steeped in formal naming traditions. Younger Russians today may be more lax in following them, e.g. they might introduce themselves by their GN + FS together—just like in the West. They may also shun using the more traditional GN + P among co-workers or friends in large groups. It sounds complicated, but I promise it's not! Here are some examples of Russian names:

Given Name	Patronymic	Surname	Diminutive	Double Diminutive
Yevgeniya	Avksentyevna (daughter of Avksenty)	Kanadina	Zhenya	Zhenechka
Avksenty	Yemelyanovich (son of Yemelyan)	Kanadin	Senya	Senechka

Special Notes

British Spelling & Vocabulary

In the text of my novel, for every case of spelling and vocabulary, when I could choose between a version of an American English word and a version of a British English word, I went with the British English variant. Examples of these word choices include: colour, honour, rumour, defence, organisation, travelling, judgement, practise, acknowledgement, moustache, kilometre, waggon, and manoeuvre. This is merely a style preference of mine.

Disclaimer

This novel is a work of fiction. References to any historical events, real people, or real places are used in a purely fictitious manner by me. Other names, characters, places, and events are pure products of my imagination. Any resemblances to actual events, places, or persons, living or deceased, is entirely by coincidence. The role played by Stalin in this novel is entirely fictional, however my imagined Stalin does abide by the known facts of the real Stalin's life, and I occasionally have quoted him verbatim.

Stalin's Door

Zhenya's Tale

Finding Stalin's Door

Spring 1934

The luxurious ZiS limousine raced through the uncrowded streets of downtown Moskva. Our destination this evening filled me with anxiousness and excitement. Tonight would be my first visit to the House on the Embankment.

The remarkable speed at which we were travelling left my father with an unmistakable look of queasiness upon his face. His eyes were wide and his complexion was noticeably pallid.

"Oh, I say, driver?" My father rapped his knuckles on the thick etched glass partition that separated our passenger compartment from the front. "I say, would you care to slow down a tad?"

No one riding inside the automobile could mistake the chauffeur's reply.

"Nyet!"

Whether this meant our driver didn't mind taking it easier or whether he would not pay any notice to my father's request was immediately obvious to us all. The driver increased the speed of the car. Because I sat next to my mother and faced forward, we suddenly reeled backward into the stitched leather bench seating with substantial force. My father, who sat at the front of the passenger compartment and faced towards us, lurched out of his seat straightaway, as if he were flying. He promptly found himself facedown on the plush floor carpeting.

I remembered that I couldn't help but squeak out a laugh at the absurdity of it all.

"Zhenya! Shame on you!" My mother instantly scolded me.

My father then righted himself and reclined backwards to where he was only a moment ago. Papa looked no worse for wear as he brushed himself off. I detected an ever so slight hint of a smile on his face, and he desperately tried not to make eye contact with me for fear of bursting into laughter himself.

These are my memories. Today, I stand upon the famous Bolshoy Kamenny bridge, my gaze descending to the storied Moskva river. In my mind's eye I imagine I'm holding out an ornate spyglass, fully extended, and ready to peek into the deepest recesses of my brain. When I peer through, it's not into the small round eyepiece, but rather through the other larger end. I'm looking backwards in time, and everything I see appears tiny, distorted, and far away from me—at first. With some effort, I make things come into focus. Like the cold black waters of the river below, channels of time gently ebb and flow inside my mind, as I stare across the decades. I finally arrive at a crucial day. The day everything changed for me.

I can see myself then as a small child. I was uninformed and naïve to the truth of the actual world that lay outside of my insulated family cocoon. My world was one of privilege, of which I was just barely aware. How could I possibly have known what was to come in the years ahead? As I examine my physical body as it is today—frail, ancient, and failing me, I feel blessed that my mind is still an instrument; scalpel-like and razor sharp. Recollecting to that time in my young life, I can remember perfectly the events of what would be a remarkable and fateful night. The path I find myself on today began with the events from that evening.

As I stop and reminisce, I can't shake the feeling that I'm being followed. An old man follows me today, staying just out of my sight. For what reason, I cannot fathom. Perhaps he's been sent to prevent me from carrying out what I must do today.

However, I'm jumping too far ahead, dearest reader. Now, I must return you to the start.

My story begins with that treacherous journey inside the luxurious black ZiS limousine. It was a cool, beautiful spring evening in our capital city. As my tiny hands peeled back the curtains from the passenger compartment, I could see thousands of roses and dozens of glorious banners. The ornate displays from the International Workers' Day parade from only a few days ago still decorated the storied boulevard with pride. I felt exceptional tonight, imagining for a moment that I too was part of the venerable cavalcade. I felt excited—yes—however, I tried to contain my emotions and took my cue from my parents' demeanour. My usually serene mother and father looked unduly nervous.

Our host this evening was kind enough to send his personal car and driver to collect us at our cramped kommunalka. These flats—the ubiquitous communal apartments—peppered the capital like grains of sand on a beach. Our transportation left me with a refreshing feeling. I could easily grow fond of this utter luxuriousness, especially when compared to the loud, crowded, and noxious diesel trams we took everywhere downtown. I envisioned for a moment what a ride on the brand-new Moskva Metro might be like. Surely it would be even faster and more direct than anything available today? I couldn't wait for the subway to open next year, barring any more construction delays.

Our destination collected many names throughout the years. Some monikers were utterly mundane, whilst others were more exotic sounding:

The Government Building,

the Government House,

the House of the USSR,

the House of Preliminary Detention, and

the House of Secrets.

The House on the Embankment was perhaps its most famous name.

In time, I would call the House on the Embankment my home—if only for a little while. Nevertheless, tonight would be my inaugural visit there.

I caught my first glimpse of the building from the Bolshoy Moskvoretsky bridge many blocks away and found myself astonished at the sheer size of the complex. It was easily larger than any other I'd ever visited before. This block wide compound, in the centre of our capital city, was so enormous they said it eclipsed the sun in the early morning. Of that, I now knew!

As our car finally decelerated to take a turn right into the primary entrance, I could make out many impeccably dressed soldiers from the Soviet army standing watch outside. As we drove through the initial checkpoint, the sentries all snapped to attention, saluted us, and I heard them yell out in unison.

"Comrade Commissar!"

My father took my hand inside of his and looked sternly at me.

"Now, Zhenya, please understand that you must be on your absolute best behaviour this evening. Be polite and only speak when spoken to. Do you hear me?"

My mother chimed in after.

"Yes, honey. Please, this visit is critical to your papa's career. His boss is a very important man. We'll tolerate none of your usual nonsense tonight."

I stared at both of them and nodded.

"I agree."

Still, I felt strangely nervous as I recalled a conversation that I overheard earlier in the week. It made no sense to me.

"This invitation is baffling, Senya. What does it mean? And why do we need to bring Zhenya with us? Are you being dismissed from the commissariat? And another thing. Hosting a reception on a Friday of all days? It's not good luck. Not at all. You know this to be true." My mother pleaded.

"Please do not worry yourself. Stay calm, Shura. We don't want to alarm—her. I'm not being sacked, believe me. Everything will be all right—you can place your trust within me. My boss is an honourable gentleman. Please don't fret about it." My father replied with assurance.

The limousine parked in the centre of an enormous interior courtyard. We exited the vehicle quickly. I then immediately noticed how quiet it was all around us. Many hundreds of people, by the count of all the windows that looked down upon us, must live here—yet I heard nothing emanating from them. I could see lights from electric lamps inside the flats shining brightly out and noted several opened casements to let in the fresh spring evening air.

However, I detected no sounds of children playing, nor of conversations public or private, nor disagreements, nor lamentations or salutations.

It was as if we were walking through a graveyard. It felt solemn.

"Come—this way." Our driver growled as he motioned with his black-gloved hands.

I dutifully trailed behind my parents as they followed our driver onto a neatly constructed brick path that took us over to an enormous concrete staircase. Our chauffeur was a mountain of a man—his long black trench coat and black hat were like an impenetrable wall in front of us. We ascended the stairs slowly, which I noticed were unusually wide and lengthy. After counting to 26, we reached the landing.

Once we were inside the gigantic apartment building, I saw long fancy hallways to the left and to the right, with large black doors every few metres along the inner side. Directly in front of us stood another staircase, made of ornate marble. We proceeded up two winding flights, keeping ourselves in the centre. An expensive-looking carpet runner lay on top of the stone stairs, tacked down with thin brass rods at the joints. Once we were on the third floor, and turned around another corner, we finally arrived.

We all gathered around the large front door of our destination, flat No. 59. The black door looked heavy and strong. I noticed the decorative stained glass in the wide transom above. Our driver stepped up and depressed the doorbell, producing a loud buzzing sound. He then quickly moved aside.

A moment later, an older woman slowly opened the door. She scrutinised all of us in a drawn-out, deliberate manner before speaking.

"Da, he's been expecting you. Please come inside."

But, before we could proceed, the babushka insistently glanced at the floor, gazing at a small pile of slippers laying just to the right of the threshold. Hastily she pointed at them.

We hurriedly took off our shoes and donned the tapochki. My pair felt enormous over my feet, and I knew immediately that our host was not in the habit of entertaining any children here. The elderly matron then ushered us into the foyer.

Coming from up ahead of us in the drawing room, I could hear the melodious chimes of a grandfather clock ring out. When it finished striking six times, I knew that we were precisely on schedule. I gazed at my father and heard him as he let out a loud sigh of relief. He appeared blissful for the first time tonight.

Our host for the evening then presented himself in front of us, smiling broadly.

The initial characteristic I noticed about this man was just how aged he appeared to be. Even my own grandparents were not as elderly looking in appearance. The fellow was stout, distinguished, and impeccably dressed in an expensive black suit. Short grey hair adorned his head, and I detected just a whiff of cologne. Our host was my father's boss, a commissar, and he grinned at all of us, imparting an instant feeling of warmth and trust in me. Clasping his huge hands tightly together, he turned to the old woman standing beside us.

"Olesya Zakharovna, may I please introduce my excellent friend? This is Principal Deputy Commissar Kanadin, accompanied tonight by his winsome family." Our host said in a deep, commanding voice.

As the commissar was talking, he unclasped his fingers, and with his right hand palm up, he moved it along in a level motion pointing towards my mother and me. The commissar continued the introductions and turned to address us all now. He looked over to the senior zhenshchina standing across from us.

"And this is my resident housekeeper-cook. She's the best in our beautiful capital city! Just wait until you see what she's prepared for us this fine night."

"The commissar is far too kind." The old woman feigned some modesty, speaking in a gentle voice.

The commissar then took his large right hand and firmly grasped my father's, now extended out in friendship. He showered my father with praise.

"Thank you very much for your company tonight, Avksenty Yemelyanovich."

Their vigorous handshake went on for many seconds. My father nodded approvingly and then presented something to the short old man, held from within his other hand. The commissar appeared delighted as he studied the gift.

"Spasiba za padarak! My friend, really, you shouldn't have."

Our host gripped the expensive-looking bottle, cradling it for a moment, before he extended it outwards for everyone to see. The glass of the container took on the colour of the rich brown liquid inside of it. The striking printed label seemed regal and serious. I was unsure of the name of the spirit contained within. I knew it must be an unusual one based upon the positive reaction of my father's boss.

After the commissar pretended to push it away twice, he finally accepted the gift graciously as he beamed widely.

"I know this is scarce, and hard to find, good Sir. I am truly honoured."

The commissar then placed the present on a small side table alongside the wall, with some care. He then turned his attention to my mother, who was standing conscientiously behind my father, waiting patiently. The commissar gently shook her diminutive hand precisely three times—as required.

"It's so delightful to see you again, Aleksandra Vasilievna." He paused for a moment and touched his forefinger to his lips, his eyes looking upwards. "If I recall correctly, it was almost a year ago now at the Zux Harbour conference in Sevastopol, when we met last?"

"Da, that is correct, Sir." My mother smiled. "And these are for you, Comrade Commissar." She then handed our host a small bouquet of wildflowers.

"Why these are lovely!"

The commissar took the posy and held them out at his arm's length to admire the unique colours. After a moment or two he looked over to his domestic helper.

"Asya? Please put these in water and place them in the dining room so we may enjoy them all evening."

The housekeeper-cook removed the bundle of blooms from the commissar's grasp and then excused herself.

The commissar now leaned down towards me, with a broad grin. As he towered over my little frame, I couldn't help noticing his gleaming white teeth and deep blue eyes. The unmistakable odour of alcohol wafted into my nostrils as he placed one of his mammoth hands upon my thick head of hair, patting gently. His voice bellowed out.

"And whom do we have here? Hmmm? Why, this must be the charming Yevgeniya that I've been hearing so much about!

You wouldn't remember the last time I saw you. Don't you just look pretty in your fancy dress, my pet?"

"Yes, thank you Sir." I shyly replied.

My mother taught me to be weary of compliments from strangers.

"Excuse me, Comrade Commissar? Will he be joining us for supper this evening?" My father was glancing at our driver, as his hulking frame still blocked the entire front doorway.

"Oh, no. No, not at all." The commissar laughed. "Maxim Ilyich will wait faithfully outside for you. He can take care of himself. I'm sure that my housekeeper-cook made him some delicious pirozhki to eat later."

The driver tipped his right forefinger to the brim of his black cap and excused himself by closing the front door behind him.

The commissar then escorted us into the sizeable drawing room, which lay straight off the foyer.

"Please, my friends, make yourself comfortable. We have a few minutes to wait before supper is ready."

I immediately felt impressed at the size and complexity of the space. Warmth from the fire bathed my face, and its many electric lamps brightly lit up all the corners of the parlour. I could see there were endless places to sit down and relax in. I sat on one of the plush couches, adorned with plenty of soft pillows. My parents selected a divan next to me. I noted the commissar relaxing in what must have been his favourite armchair. I could hear music coming from the gramophone—pleasant and low sounding. The selection was no doubt one of the Russian masters, although I couldn't instantly place it. Crackles and pops emanating from the fireplace were random and delightful to listen to, whilst the constant rhythm of the ticking grandfather clock made me feel lethargic.

Stalin's Door

Of all the rich décor in this grand room, the one piece that stood out was the enormous colour portraiture of Comrade Stalin, that hung on the centre wall above the fireplace. Every flat I'd ever visited had a requisite study of our Union's supreme leader prominently displayed within. My mother informed me only deviants and criminals dared not have him watching over them.

Some residences even had one depiction of Comrade Stalin in every room!

This portrait I studied had exquisite detail in every respect. I could discern and count the individual hairs of his impressive bushy moustache. I could also make out the fine wood grain of the pipe he was holding. Almost every portrait I'd seen had the smoking implement in his hands, as if it extended naturally from his body. The sheer size of this portraiture made me feel as if Comrade Stalin himself was standing in the room with us, taller than a gigantic pine tree. It was beyond life sized. Our supreme leader appeared to stand over three metres in height. I thought it was just a little eerie, to be honest. From anywhere in the room, his beady eyeballs would constantly stare at you—never wavering—always seeing all. I could never escape those black within black eyes looking me over.

After a few moments of waiting quietly, the housekeeper-cook brought in a fancy silver tray which contained plates of white bread and a bowl of table salt in the middle. She placed the tray upon the low table in front of my parents. As is our tradition, my father tore off a small chunk of bread and dipped it into the fine white crystals. He then ate the morsel rapidly. My mother then repeated the ritual.

I looked at the commissar as he nodded in approval at my father and mother. I could see he was quite pleased. In an indistinct voice he spoke up.

"Da, very good. Now we may begin."

§

The supper was a torturous and intolerable affair with course after course of rich food. The commissar's housekeeper-cook served us so much that I couldn't possibly think of eating again. She must have been in the kitchen all day preparing. No one dared stop, however, for fear of insulting our generous host.

I felt embarrassed. With only the four of us dining tonight, it seemed like an awful waste of fare. As the evening wore on, and the level of alcohol consumption increased, naturally the degree of ambient noise shot straight upwards. The adults proposed endless toasts to people I'd never heard of—which only begat even more salutes and tributes.

Backslapping and laughing followed in a manner so deafening that I felt as if sticking my fingers into my ears could drown out the clangour.

Well sung patriotic songs rang out, one after the other. Then the stories of their work events and current affairs seemed to drag on endlessly, or for as long as their supply of vodka would hold out.

Vodka—I must confess that it's a strange drink. The name itself comes from the diminutive of voda. This so-called little water had become the preferred alcoholic beverage of all our countrymen in those days. I can remember one time years ago when I begged my father for a taste of his. I pressed the thin short glass to my lips for only a second, and quickly downed the clear liquid all in one go, just as I had seen the adults do countless times before me.

I instantaneously felt a crushing and burning sensation radiate throughout my chest, and I coughed powerfully for many seconds. I could have sworn my throat was closing up on me. My father laughed, pointed at me, and announced to everyone that curiosity had surely killed the kitten. I made sure never to make that mistake again.

That night of the supper in the old commissar's home, I was especially uncomfortable as I sat in the hard dining room chairs. My constant fidgeting and sighing histrionics caught the attention of my mother. She pleaded with me in a stern and whispering tone.

"Zhenya, you promised to behave tonight! Now sit still at once!"

When the pace of the food and drinks had slowed, and the conversations petered out, there came a pregnant pause. My father exchanged a curious glance with my mother. I wondered what this meant. Suddenly she stood up from the table.

"Let me help poor Olesya Zakharovna with the dishes in the kitchen. I would love to pick her brain on some of tonight's delicious recipes. Please excuse me, Comrade Commissar?"

I watched as the commissar's torso had come halfway out of his chair in politeness to my mother. He held his body there at that awkward angle for a moment. My mother looked towards my father, and he nodded ever so gently at her. She then turned to address me.

"Zhenya, please sit in the drawing room. Be a reverent girl and go on now. Let the men talk in private."

I demurred and pretended to show my reluctance to leave. However, I secretly felt relieved to get away from that table! Hours and hours of sitting were more than I could tolerate. I scampered quickly back to the comfortable couches from earlier that evening. As I laid my head down on the plush cushions, I couldn't remember ever feeling so tired before. Normally by this time in the night I would have already been in my bed, fast asleep. I rested peacefully for a few more moments and then picked up on the reverberations within the other areas of the flat. I could easily discern the clanking of dishes being washed in the kitchen, the gentle vibrations of the grandfather clock ticking reliably in the room's corner, and the occasional sounds of the automobile traffic on the street below. I looked over and saw someone had opened a window. If I really tried hard to, I could almost smell the unmistakable scent of the Moskva river as it wafted in from outside—even all the way up here.

Curiously, I recall that I could also perfectly hear my father and the commissar as they conferred in the adjacent dining room. I didn't mean to listen in at all and I knew it was a rude habit. It was however all very passive, and I wasn't even positive at the time what they were speaking to each other about. Their conversation came in spurts and whispers.

This is what I remember them saying:

"Avksenty Yemelyanovich, let us be frank on the actual reason I asked you here this evening."

"Da, Comrade Commissar?"

"How long have you worked for me now? Will it really be ten years next month? You know, I had to look it up. I couldn't believe it myself! I can still remember the day when you joined us, fresh from graduate university. Back in those days, the People's Transportation Commissariat hadn't divided into smaller directorates yet. Things were chaotic—and swift. I needed powerful men—who could get things done—asking no questions of me. What a time that was."

"Yes, they were Comrade Commissar."

"These are heady times we live in now, too. From what I heard, we might even soon be working for Comrade Kirov. Who can say for sure? They say nothing is as dangerous as an idea, when it's the only one you have. Without some effort, you won't pull a fish out of a pond. Do you understand what I'm trying to tell you? There are limitless possibilities ahead—you just need to be bold enough to take hold of them. The future is so bright."

The commissar sounded quite pensive now.

"Our first Five-Year Plan left us dizzy with success. But this business of continuing the Revolution is for the younger generation, Avksenty Yemelyanovich. Your generation. You're not only my hardest worker, you're also my most loyal confidant. So, I will tell you this, in the strictest of confidence. I'm getting too old and now must reluctantly—reluctantly step aside."

"No, no, Comrade Commissar. This cannot be! Please. But who will lead us?"

"Plainly speaking, the Boss has had his eye on you—for some time now. You're a rising star within the Communist Party. In fact, just earlier today I submitted with my highest recommendation your promotion to commissar, following my retirement. Your years of loyalty and hard work are now finally being rewarded.

"There will be a formal interview process, and the Boss has final approval. However, I have it on good authority that your ascension is all but assured. The winds of change are blowing my friend, don't go against them.

So, for now, let me be the first to offer you my congratulations, Commissar-designate!"

My eyes immediately glanced at the oversized portrait of Comrade Stalin hovering above me. Could this really be happening? Suddenly, Papa's voice was much louder now.

"Comrade Commissar, this is all too much. I do not know what to say!"

"You must accept, Avksenty Yemelyanovich. Don't even dare to think of turning this promotion down! I realise you'll be the youngest commissar in the entire Sovnarkom, however we're long overdue for some fresh blood in the place. Younger men, I mean. You will do glorious things. This I know."

After a minute of silence, their conversation continued.

"Do you have any thoughts on whom you'll name as your new number one?"

"Well to be honest Comrade Commissar, I was thinking of young Valerian Savelievich. He will make an excellent choice. I don't think the man ever leaves the office!"

"Da, that would have been my preference too. Well done. I can see that my commissariat will be in expert hands with you firmly at the helm."

Their conversation then grew much louder.

"Good man! Now call that lovely daughter of yours, Yevgeniya, in here. There's one more thing we have to do this evening."

I then heard my father call out for me.

"Zhenya? Please come in here now. Please hurry!"

I came running back into the dining room and noticed that my mother had rejoined my father. She now stood behind his chair with her hands placed upon his shoulders firmly.

Sitting at the head of the table, the commissar motioned for me to come over to him. I cautiously approached.

"Over here, young lady. Stand next to me. Wonderful girl. Now, my commissariat sources have informed me that your birthday was—only last week? Isn't that correct?"

"Yes, Sir." I quickly replied.

I wondered for a moment where this conversation would lead.

The commissar glanced towards my parents, who were smiling at me now. One of the commissar's enormous hands then reached into his trouser pocket and he palmed an item from within. Upon withdrawing his grip, he kept his fist closed tightly around the object for a moment.

"This is something I want you to have."

The commissar then cupped my diminutive right hand inside of his free one, turning my palm upwards. Something metallic and dense was then placed into the centre. As he slowly removed his beefy fingers, the present revealed itself for everyone to see.

As I gazed upon this wondrous treasure, I immediately noted its weight. It felt heavy, and I knew this was no toy I now possessed. While the gift rested inside my palm, its metal surface felt strong. The ball-shaped object was noticeably cold—almost icy to my touch. I found this to be odd considering where it had just come from.

Although I doubted it was made of solid gold, the item was bathed in paint to make it look that way. Ridges twisting and turning on the surface of the bulbous gadget were formed and implied that this was the heart of a great knot of cords.

Hollow throughout its middle, the prize was approximately the size of a champion walnut. Attached onto the front of the device was a large brilliant five-pointed red star outlined in gold. The ruby colours radiated out in all directions from its centre, and it looked shiny and reflective.

Contained within the red star were a gold hammer and sickle, and together they represented the official insignia of the Soviet Union.

I now knew what this sublime stunner was. I was holding a woggle, the traditional apparatus for fastening the red neckerchief of a Young Pioneers uniform.

"But, Sir, I cannot possibly accept this!" My hand pushed the astounding honour back towards the commissar.

"Zhenya! You forget yourself! Thank the commissar and be grateful." My father instantly chided me.

"Thank you, Sir. However, I'm only nine years old and belong to the Little Octobrists. I am not eligible to join the Young Pioneers until I'm ten years old." I corrected myself.

"I am confident you'll be a first stage pioneer by this time next year. Your father informed me you're an exemplary student, my dear. I am counting on your nomination within their first batch! In the meantime, please reflect upon their motto. Do you know what it is?"

"No, Sir."

"Be always ready!" The commissar smiled at me. "Now, make our Union proud, my pet."

Summer 1935

The House on the Embankment had been our home since the beginning of the year, on what is technically a massive holm in the capital's heart, known simply as the Island.

My new address was Two Ulitsa Serafimovicha, flat No. 137, in the venerable Bersenevka neighbourhood. My father's glorious promotion to People's Commissar for Water Transportation made me feel so proud. I'll never forget the tremendous ceremony to commemorate that day. Papa now presided over the entire Soviet merchant marine fleet, and he was critical to the success of our Union. Tens of thousands of men worked for him in his commissariat, and he reported directly to Comrade Stalin—as one of his most ardent and trusted commissars.

Our beautiful flat was straight across the way from the brilliantly lit up Moskva Kremlin, along the banks of Moskva river. Just on the other side of the Moskva Kremlin lay our world-famous Red Square, where we would gather to celebrate the International Workers' Day and the patriotic October Revolution.

Commensurate with my father's current rank and position, he now had the exclusive use of his own ZiS limousine—which came equipped with its own bodyguard-driver service. Papa told me he disdained the motorcar and preferred walking over to his Moskva Kremlin office every day instead.

The distance from the Government House to his workplace was merely several hundred metres—an easy jaunt via the newly renovated Bolshoy Moskvoretsky bridge.

Construction work comprising hundreds of men and heavy machinery proceeded on the closer Bolshoy Kamenny bridge, which when completed would shorten his commute!

Every morning, my mother lovingly packed my father a sandwich and a piece of fruit and kissed him goodbye before he left for his office. My father's loyal bodyguard-driver Radomir Yurievich, who was always waiting just outside our flat's front door, followed behind him at a discrete distance— ever on the lookout for trouble. While not a tall man, his frame was solid, and he possessed outsized hands that appeared as if they could snap a tree right in half. I never saw the bodyguard-driver without his signature black leather trench coat and black hat upon his person, even now in the warmth of the Russian summer.

By law, Radomir Yurievich could not step inside of our flat, so my mother would occasionally check on him after our supper. As a reward for his faithful service to my father, she would invariably tempt him with spicy tea and tasty biscuits. To my knowledge, he politely declined every time. Out of respect to my mother, Radomir Yurievich made it a point to consistently remove his black cap when speaking with her. No one could miss his frightening bald head embedded with deep scars, which resembled river channels. I shuddered to imagine what blunt force could have inflicted such traumas. Radomir Yurievich's appearance looked fearsome for certain. However, he would always grin broadly in my presence, revealing his gnarled yellow stained teeth. I customarily felt at ease when I would pass him in the hallway.

Stalin's Door

The upper crust of the Soviet elite and their families lived with us at the House of Secrets. There were 519 flats within this gargantuan complex. Some residences were large and extravagant, some others were modest, still all were luxurious when compared with the standard utilitarian apartments throughout the capital.

By official government decree, important Communist Party officials, commissars, military generals, along with other rising stars, all lived here. Comrade Stalin himself selected and approved only the first-rate from our Union.

Located downstairs, just outside the front gates, a permanently stationed platoon of regular Soviet army soldiers stood watch over us. These brave men dutifully guarded the entrances to the Government House, day and night. I suppose apart from a service base, or other official installation, this was by far the safest place to live in the entire metropolis.

Mama would often refer to the House on the Embankment as a city within a city. Anything we needed came included as a benefit of living here. We wanted for nothing. We enjoyed the convenience of our own private bakeshop, delicatessen, and butchery.

Contained within the expansive courtyard of the complex were exclusive markets for various goods and sundry services. A trio of fine dining restaurants of rotating seasonal cuisine were only steps away from our front door. We had our own medical facility, many recreational centres, a bank, a post office, a telegram station, and even a cinema where you could take in the latest approved moving pictures. The private library was enormous, with thousands of books and magazines to choose from. But my favorite amenity by far was the theatre, known colloquially as the House of Culture. It was the finest one in Moskva, and only the tenants who lived here, and their guests, could attend the magnificent stage plays, ballets, and symphonies.

My mother seemed ecstatic at having the use of her own kitchen, even though it was minuscule. Ensconced at the rear, a stout blue electric refrigerator came standard, and I marvelled at this modern convenience. I'd never seen one in person before. Mama informed me the USSR manufactured them for the first time, only this year. My mother enthusiastically instructed me in its usage.

A common icebox and gas-burning stove were here too. Cooking was one of her specialties, and my father was endlessly praising her for it.

Commensurate with my father's new rank and position, we could have eaten in the cafés or bistros on the property, or even hired a permanent cook. But my mother wouldn't agree to it. She said we should always strive to be as self-sufficient as possible. The future wasn't certain, and what was here today could easily disappear tomorrow. My mother was truly wise!

Although my father would never admit it, his new favourite haunt was the private water closet in our flat. Whenever there was an opportunity, he was in there along with a newspaper or book. It was like his own private refuge from life. After having lived in the kommunalki and having shared a WC for years and years with our neighbours, I could not blame him. What a blessing it was not to have to wait for another person to finish any longer.

My father's next favourite hangout was the picture palace, on the basement level. He invariably made it a point to watch the latest cines there. Frequently, my mother asked me to collect Papa from the cavernous auditorium right before supper. I noted that the plush seats were wide and comfortable, and I regularly captured my father napping there as he caught up on his much-needed sleep. I would poke and prod his chest with my fingers as I begged him to come upstairs and eat with us.

Papa would always say the same thing to me when he woke up with a start:

"We may go now. Anyway, this is the part where I came in."

Because the government provided everything for us in our new living arrangement, there was never any practical reason to leave the House on the Embankment.

In fact, the residents could not step outside the compound without written permission, I discovered. Except for going to my primary school, I never left the premises.

I felt appreciative of all our family had now. I recalled the day when we first arrived. Moving was especially easy because the flat they assigned us came fully furnished. We merely had to bring our clothes and personal items upon leaving our kommunalka.

Truth be told, I was not sad to leave those cramped communal apartments behind us. I couldn't have been happier. This was the absolute best time in my life that I could remember.

§

I first met Zinaida Valerievna the day she and her family moved into the apartment across the corridor from us. She lived in flat No. 140. Her father, a newly promoted Lt General, was a Soviet Army Corps Commander. As a towering fellow, he had to duck down walking through every door frame. Being short myself, I couldn't imagine what that must have been like. His uniform was always pristine and crisp in appearance, replete with medals, ribbons, and many honours. The large epaulettes of red and gold on his massive shoulders were unmistakably the grade of a senior general.

Since our household held the most seniority on the floor, it fell upon my mother to welcome them as recent residents to the Government House. It didn't take long for me to discover that Zina was an only child, like myself. I think this was the reason we became fast friends.

Earlier that morning, my mother collected some khvorost from the bakery downstairs. The Uzbek man who worked there was truly a magician of his craft.

And my mother already scolded me for helping myself prematurely.

"Zhenya! You know better than that!"

I sincerely apologised to her.

I just couldn't resist the heavenly deep-fried dough and powdered sugar. I considered it an uncommonly tasty treat. I was told I needed to wait for teatime, and then we'd welcome our new neighbours together. Only then, if I was still an obedient girl, could I have more of those delicious angel wings.

As Mama prepared the tea service, I remained patiently in the drawing room for our visitors to arrive. I couldn't wait to show Zina my bedroom, which sported an impressive, growing collection of dolls. The women would engage in small talk, no doubt gossiping on some trivial matter, whilst the men would lecture about the important business of the government and the Communist Party.

Our drawing room was sizeable, and comprised a pair of sofas, a couch, a lower table, a sideboard, tall bookcases, a desk, and many chairs. There was a rich and ornate Persian rug that covered the polished wooden floor. Instead of a fireplace for warming us all, this room had something I'd seen nowhere else. Along many of the walls, and close to the floor, I could see thin metal grates attached. Heated air would disperse from them, just like miniature radiators. I asked my mother, and she told me all about these new baseboard heaters. The entire room became pleasant and toasty on chilly evenings. There were also many fancy decorations in here too.

The requisite portrait of Comrade Stalin hung prominently with care on the back wall, keeping watch.

Papa was fond of saying that the Boss always had his eyes on me in this room. Of that, I knew for certain.

Mama reminded me countless times never to eat or drink anything in the drawing room—but this rule rarely applied to the adults of course. Our family spent more time here than in any of the others, it seemed. It was by far the largest in the flat, and just like the old commissar's home where I visited last year, the dining room was directly adjacent.

In the evenings concluding supper, my father would sip on his vodka drink and read the Pravda newspaper, or one of his endless work briefings. My mother would duteously attend to her embroidery, or help me out with my Young Pioneers exercises, whilst drinking cup after cup of strong black tea. If my parents judged me to have been especially gracious for that day, I might even get to listen to some classical music on the wireless receiver for a bit.

One tradition our family started soon after moving into the flat was our nightly council. This was a time for 20 minutes or so, when we would report to each other on our comings and goings, the news, and to reflect on the progress of the day. We normally did this directly after supper, and always in the drawing room. There were no exceptions.

Every family council would begin the same way, with my father praising Comrade Stalin. Our supreme leader was responsible for everything we had, and of our continued national success, so we thanked him endlessly. This adoration was normal and deserved for sure. My father seemed insistent in always facing into a particular corner of the room whilst speaking these honours.

Yes, it was true our requisite portrait of Comrade Stalin hung on that side of the room. The artist of this lifelike portraiture posed our supreme leader in a manner as if to convey a commanding regal presence, as he stood watch over our nation, looking to the east.

However, my father wasn't directly looking at Comrade Stalin's portrait. His head was askew. It took me weeks to notice this slight quirk, and once I saw it, it really stood out. Like a sore thumb.

Papa, normally a quiet man when speaking to us, made it a point to especially stand and talk in a stern tone of voice for these evening time family meetings. It bothered me when he used such booming and jarring words. I looked at his pale neck and could see the veins bulging and pulsing as he made each speech forcefully.

I always wondered why Papa did it in this way, when we were plainly sitting right next to him. Perhaps this was how he spoke when in his office, whilst commanding his men? I could imagine Papa barking out the official orders of the day, expecting them to be carried out with immediate speed and efficiency. My father's subordinates would scurry about trying to curry favour with him, as they themselves worked their way up that long ladder of power and responsibility. Rewards followed hard work and loyalty, however only the best would ever lead us.

This was the manner in which things were—the Comrade Stalin way.

After my father praised Comrade Stalin, he would bring us up to speed on the progress being made on the intricate projects his commissariat was undertaking. I was terribly proud of him. My father bore considerable responsibility in his position—it was almost too much for one man to handle alone. The Communist Party was lucky he was so dedicated to his job, and I knew that Comrade Stalin greatly depended upon him. This meant that he had to return to his office to work late into the night practically every evening.

My father also insisted on discussing the continuing investigation into the assassination of someone named Sergey Mironovich Kirov, a very important man within the Communist Party. It seemed this subject was all anyone ever wanted to talk about lately, even though Comrade Kirov's death was half a year ago now. An assassin shot Comrade Kirov dead under very mysterious circumstances at his office in Leningrad. The official inquiry was still front-page news in the Pravda newspaper.

After my father spoke, it would be my turn to speak. I really appreciated that my parents consistently focused on me during this time. It delighted me to recount what I had learned in school that day, or of the progress I made within the Young Pioneers.

Their leadership selected me to join up within the first batch—which was a tremendous distinction. My enthusiasm couldn't be dampened, and my goal was promotion to troop leader. Perhaps I'd even rate a brigade premier one day!

My parents were so happy for me. I wore my Young Pioneers uniform with pride—so much so that these days I could hardly be seen out of it. I made it a point to always keep my uniform in pristine shape and would allow nothing to soil it. My mother insisted that to be the best, I must look my best.

Finishing the nightly family council would be my mother's time to speak. Her announcement tonight took everyone by surprise.

"You know I was having tea downstairs with Madam Boguna today, and I heard some sad news. Commissar Zykin suddenly passed away last week. I think she said it was a heart attack or something. Zhenya, you remember when we had that lovely reception at his home last year—don't you? The commissar was especially fond of you as I recall."

"Yes, Mama." The news from my mother was unexpected, and so I tried desperately to find anything to say. "Papa, I am sorry to hear of this. I know he was your dear friend."

I clutched at the centre of my neckerchief with my thumb and forefinger, where the old commissar's generous gift now resided. It was the highlight of my uniform, and my most cherished possession. The neckerchief woggle was always hot to my touch, the heat of my body no doubt constantly warming the metal bundle.

"Yes, the old commissar has passed on." My father paused for a second and looked at the floor. "—Err away, I mean. But he was not my dear friend. I am sure of that. It is good that he is no longer at the commissariat, for sure. Yes, it is good, I say."

That my father would utter such a thing really mystified me. I was positive that they were excellent friends.

"How old was he, Papa?"

"Oh, let's see now. He was forty-five years old, my dear. Let us not speak of him again in this house."

And we never did.

§

Unlike our Capitalist rivals in the west, who took off this time of year for endless vacations and hours of leisure, the children of the Communist Party elite attended their classes all year around. I didn't mind at all and did very well in all my studies. I especially liked the classes in mathematics. Because of my stellar marks, I rated an advancement of three technical levels.

Walking to school was pleasant for me now, as my campus was just two kilometres down the ulitsa. We didn't even have to leave the Island. Most of my classmates also lived with us at the Government House, and we always walked as a group every day.

Our studies were important, of course. However, in the small hours after the lectures, right before homework, chores, and supper—we used these for our play!

Zina and I were constantly running around in the halls of the Government House and slipping on the carpet runners that were not properly tacked down onto the ornate floors. We discovered to our delight it was even more fun to gather up a tremendous amount of speed and slide in our stockings directly on to the cool marble, located to the right and left sides of the rugs. We could traverse many metres if we wished to—imagining ourselves as graceful figure skaters in an ice rink. By chance, when we accidentally glided down the slick staircases in the same manner, the outcome was both utterly treacherous and unforgiving. The poor elevator liftman, who witnessed us taking this plunge, must have cringed as we came to rest painfully upon the polished stone floor at the landing.

I stood up quickly and placed my hands around my hips. I looked down at Zina, still laying prone beneath me, and feigning injury. With all seriousness, I intoned my best imitation of my mother and used one of her favourite phrases:

"Do not worry. It will heal before your wedding."

Zina grinned broadly back at me as she brushed herself off. With much laughter, she immediately ran back upstairs to do it all over again!

Yes, we caused mischief—occasionally. That said, there were plenty of times when we felt civically minded, so we would go up to the roof level, to the crèche. It was always fun to cavort with the little ones, and the adults who worked there were grateful for all the help.

And it seemed as if there were so many preschoolers here now. Every family that lived in the Government House had three or four or five children each. Zina and I were in the minority because we had no siblings of our own.

One afternoon after our Young Pioneers convocation, I was playing dolls with Zina in the drawing room of our flat. Pivoting, I accidentally bumped into one armchair with some force. I noticed it didn't move at all. This puzzled me. The chair after all was not that heavy. As I bent over to look at the chair's legs at the bottom, I saw them affixed to the floor with bulky metal fasteners. Going around to examine each piece of furnishing in here yielded the same result. It definitely wasn't something I had considered until now, that the furniture was immovable. You couldn't rearrange anything, even if you wanted to. I thought that was odd and called my mother in to ask her about it.

"Be at ease, honey. We're just the caretakers in this generous home. This is the way it's done here." She answered.

"But Mama, what if we want to place the couch on this side of the room, and these chairs over here?" I gestured with my arms and pointed with my fingers all about.

"Oh, Zhenya, don't be silly! We will not do that. Now, don't forget about your chores! Your father arrives home from work shortly, and you must not disappoint him." She turned to my friend Zina with a stern look upon her face. "And you, young lady! I am sure you have things to do as well."

My mother stared at both of us for many more seconds, however Zina and I held firm in our conviction—not wanting our playtime to end. Finally, my mother caved into our demands. We had won out! She winked at us both, as if she was breaking a cardinal rule.

"Oh, all right, you two! You have fifteen more minutes of recess. Make them count!"

My mother left the room to work on her supper preparation, shaking her head in bemusement as we continued our rollicking. Later on, I would discover the genuine reason the furnishings couldn't move about. Curiously from out of nowhere, Zina stopped what she was doing with her dolls and stared over into the far end of the room. She looked into the corner for many minutes.

I peeked over to where Zina held her gaze and noted that between the end of the sofa on the far wall, and the low table on the adjoining wall, was a distinctive blank space. It was less than a metre wide, however looking at it from over here at this angle, the corner seemed oddly—empty. In every other corner and along every wall in this room were unique items of décor. Sofas, chairs, end tables, clocks, desks, and so forth. Every inch of space seemed filled with something, except for that one corner of the drawing room. I scratched my head and wondered why I hadn't noticed this before now.

"That's so neat!" Zina exclaimed.

"Excuse me, Zina, what's so neat?"

"You have a Stalin's door!" Zina pointed her finger toward the empty corner as she seemed transfixed by something over there.

"I am sorry Zina, a what kind of door?" I responded, taken aback.

It seemed as if Comrade Stalin had his likeness everywhere you looked these days, I admitted, however I had yet to see a door with his unmistakable visage blazoned upon it.

"Oh, I thought my family were the only ones that had this special door inside our flat! It's from where Comrade Stalin can watch us. Do you see that small slit that runs from the floor all the way to the ceiling, on the wood panelling? No? Well, I admit it's hard to distinguish—and it's easily missed. If you look closely however, you'll notice the panel is actually a door." Zina informed me.

As I walked closer to where Zina had been referring to, I examined the wall boards with my hands, moving them slowly over the coarse wood.

"Zina, all I see is a faint dark line that penetrates into the woodgrain, to the baseboards. There's no door of any kind here."

"Oh, yes, there is! The wall here is part of a door panel that slides this way—recessing into the corner." Zina motioned with her hands towards the right. "It's locked from the other side though, just in case you're thinking of opening it." She looked delighted as she described all of this.

I took a moment to let all this new information sink in.

"He is here? Watching us now? Comrade Stalin himself?" I was incredulous with Zina and couldn't believe what I was asking her.

"He is. Yes, right now. He watches us all the time." Zina said matter-of-factly, with a proud look upon her face.

I was still skeptical of my best friend. And just a little scared, too. What would be the purpose of putting a door there? I didn't even see a handle, although come to think of it, if Comrade Stalin was on the other side of the wall watching us, he would be in the perfect location to see everything inside of the drawing room.

As I stood in that corner and turned to face outwards, from my point of view I could clearly see every single item in the room. I even saw beyond into the dining room too! Since they fixed the locations of the furniture in place, one couldn't block the corner, or the view from it.

But this was all silly. If Comrade Stalin was always here watching us now, then how could he possibly watch Zina and her family too, when she returned to her flat? He couldn't be in both places at the same time, could he? I contemplated that thought for a moment.

Later that evening after supper, I asked my mother about this curious turn of events.

"Mama, is Comrade Stalin watching us?"

"My dearest, Comrade Stalin sees all." She then quickly followed up. "He hears everything too, so always take care of what you say!"

My mother was only half paying attention to me as she read one of her women's magazines.

"No, no, Mamushka. I meant to say, is Comrade Stalin watching us right now?"

My mother put her reading material down rather quickly now, and I heard the glossy paper as it loudly slapped against her knees. She then turned to glare at my father for a moment. I could see she was mouthing something to him silently.

"She gets this from you!" I read her lips.

"Shura, please calm her now." My father then whispered back.

After exchanging further glances, she looked down at where I was sitting and spoke to me slowly, in a firm collected voice.

"Um, well. My honey, you know Comrade Stalin is constantly swamped with all of his official duties. He carries tremendous responsibilities upon his shoulders. I am sure that he, or one of his loyal men, are always watching over us.

"Comrade Stalin keeps us safe and sound. Isn't that nice of him to do that for you? The finest thing one can do is to always think of what's best for our Union in everything you do and say—or he'll know about it. It's what's required to be a good compatriot."

I thought about a specific part my mother mentioned, for a moment to myself.

"Or one of his loyal men."

My father followed up immediately, speaking in an especially loud tone of voice again.

"Yes, Zhenya, we owe Comrade Stalin special thanks for all that we have here. Be thankful. His supreme guidance and leadership are unmatched. He works harder than anyone I know. Comrade Stalin is a genius for the ages! Why just look at his magnificence, standing there like a gigantic pine tree. May he lead us for many years to come."

I felt reassured. For now.

Autumn 1936

The leaves of this season turn so quickly on the trees up and down the boulevards in our capital, that the memories of the carefree summer days are soon long forgotten.

The dreary grey skies above are a constant suggestion of the imminent return of Ded Moroz, colloquially known as Grandfather Frost. And unlike his expected annual arrival, I would shortly greet another unforeseen elderly visitor to our home at the Government House. What should have been a brief family visit would develop into something more—permanent.

My mother's oldest aunt, Nyura Victorovna, moved into our flat that autumn following the abrupt passing of her husband in Leningrad. My grandaunt was elderly, grey, and enraptured by the pre-Revolutionary Russian traditions and ideas that she grew up with. She frequently reminded us of them on a recurring basis.

She had a habit of whispering in a low deliberate manner, the cadence perfectly matching the speed at which she would stroll about the place. As I would discover much later, she could be mobile and spry, when she wanted.

My grandaunt was always doting, pinching and hugging me, as you'd expect. However, she regularly referred to my mother as her favourite niece.

My tetushka constantly gazed upon my mother with much affection in her eyes and held her in the highest state of adoration. This fondness in no way extended to my father. Nyura Victorovna, like our current season, was chilly with her feelings towards Papa. She preferred outright ignoring him instead. I sensed that some trauma from long ago was at the root of their conflict.

My tetushka was shorter in stature than I was, so I never missed an opportunity in teasing her about it. And I would make every excuse to prove this fact to anyone who would care to see us standing back-to-back, comparing our heights with hands on our heads as I laughed. Her face wore a serious expression most of the time, and her green eyes had a way of looking right through you—as if she could instantly sense if there was any nonsense afoot.

"Zhenya, why in the world do you insist on wearing that dreadful utilitarian uniform at all times? You should act more like a young lady would and wear frilly dresses and such. Why, when I was your age...." Her voice trailed off as she stared into the distance. My grandaunt did not approve at all of my devotion to the Young Pioneers and showed much condescension towards my father for letting me serve. Her reluctance to understand one's obligation to the Revolution was no doubt a product of her generation. I received my comeuppance by frequently having to sit and listen to her endless tall tales and adventures of the old days gone by.

Because my tetushka was the eldest woman in our home now, custom required her to take over most of the cooking duties. This development immediately became a constant source of conflict between my parents.

"You can't understand, Senya. She's inflexible and set in her ways. I've got no choice in this matter! I must defer. Believe me, I'm not at all thrilled with this arrangement any more than you are." My mother pleaded with my father.

Regretfully my grandaunt was in nowhere the same culinary class as my mother. Our new meals were quite bland now. There were lots of plain soups and boiled things to eat. My auntie surely considered simple salt and pepper to be exotic spices—and far too risky to use. After being accustomed to my mother's wonderful feasts, my father now suffered terribly at supper.

"Couldn't you at least teach her your recipe for rassolnik? It's so easy, I doubt if even she could screw it up. You know it's my favourite." My father suggested as he looked expectantly towards my mother.

He held out his hands—cupped together—as if he was cradling a small bowl.

I too loved this superb pickle and barley soup, that Papa was begging for. I longed for it.

"I will try, Senya. But you know she never leaves the kitchen now, and there's barely enough room in there to manoeuvre for two people!" Mama glared at my father.

I sensed that my mother was on the verge of losing all patience with Papa.

The sudden clangour of the telephone interrupted their spirited discussion. My father constantly received calls at home nowadays—for emergencies and such from his commissariat. I always knew it was the Moskva Kremlin on the other end of the line, based upon the timbre of the ring.

"Da! Sir!" My father snapped to attention upon answering, standing in an uncomfortable and rigid fashion.

There was only one person in the entire world that he addressed as sir. His boss had a nasty habit of requiring Papa's presence at all hours, especially in the late evenings. There would be no discussion. No negotiation.

"At once, Comrade General Secretary!" My father hung up the receiver gently and went to fetch his coat.

While I was not happy that Papa would have to return to his office, he would at least snatch some actual food from the bistro downstairs on his way over. It had become a regular haunt of my father's since my grandaunt started doing all the cooking.

Having to share my bedroom with my auntie was another change that took some getting used to. After spending my earlier years in the kommunalki, I had now grown accustomed to having a bedroom to myself.

Personal space that was yours alone was a luxury few people would ever know. Believe me, I felt grateful. My bed was large and comfortable, and there was plenty of room for the both of us. Unfortunately, her perpetual snoring was almost too much for me to bear. Sawing logs in a mill would surely sound serene compared to what I heard each night. I felt as if I was way behind in my sleep, and I became irritable as of late.

§

One evening after supper, I joined my parents and my auntie in the drawing room. We continued the tradition of discussing events of the day, both serious and irreverent. I then remembered something strange that I'd seen earlier.

"Papa? May I ask you a question?"

"Yes, sweetie? What is it?" My father casually looked at me from over the top fold in his thick newspaper.

"This afternoon, Zina was helping me walk the young ones home from their pre-school classes. Along the way, I spotted a strange yellow-coloured bill affixed to the front door of one of the residences—in the centre. The notice was large and bright and had a bold black typeface. From what I recall, it said the flat was now officially sealed, and to not enter without permission from the NKVD. A Colonel Medvedkov signed the bill. What is the NKVD, Papa?"

"Where did you see this notice?" My father looked at me with a hint of panic in his eyes.

I was certain I had his full attention now as he sat upright in his easy chair, with his bulky broadsheet spilling into his lap.

"I believe they affixed it on the door across from flat number three three four. I could find out for sure if you wanted me to?"

"No, no, that's all right, honey. What you saw was nothing. I shouldn't be too concerned. Just put it out of your mind." My father then glanced at my mother for a moment, with a look of worry upon his face.

"You know I saw two of those yellow notices today. You should tell your daughter. She will find out soon enough." My grandaunt interjected suddenly.

My father squirmed around in his chair, and I knew that he felt agitated now. He glared at my grandaunt, and it was as if his eyes were shooting daggers at her. Papa folded his reading material up and slammed it down upon the side table.

After taking a deep breath, he turned to me and calmly spoke in a reassuring voice.

"The Narodnyy Komissariat Vnutrennikh Del are the People's Commissariat for Internal Affairs. Think of them as Comrade Stalin's special police force. You see honey, in this world that we live in, it's unfortunate there are many fellows who are the sworn enemies of our Communist State. Those evil men only wish harm and destruction to come to all of us. So, it's the job of the NKVD to root out these wreckers and saboteurs at all costs, to protect our beloved Comrade Stalin. I am sure you can understand that. Can't you, sweetie?"

I sat still for a while and tried to comprehend what Papa was telling me. I was quite shocked to hear that anybody could go against Comrade Stalin in the first place, considering the workers' paradise that he alone created for all and sundry. Who could not want to live the way we did? I just couldn't think of anyone. These so-called agitators and anarchists must truly be sick in their heads. I hoped that they were all caught and put on a path to reform—and quickly.

I asked a follow-up question of my father.

"The man who heads up the People's Internal Affairs Commissariat, is he like you?"

"Yes, Zhenya. In fact, they recently installed him as a commissar only last month. He's a curious fellow. Very short in stature. Comrade Stalin has a high opinion of him, however."

My father paused for a few seconds.

"I don't really know the man though."

"Oh really? What residence number does he live at?" I inquired.

Papa stroked his chin slowly with his right hand for a moment.

"If I recall correctly, my dearest, I don't believe Comrade Yezhov lives with us here at the Government House. That's eccentric, come to think of it. Oh well, I'm sure there's an official reason."

I reclined further into the comfortable sofa and wondered introspectively about the unusual yellow bills I saw earlier today and what they really meant. How was it that anyone who was against Comrade Stalin, be allowed to live in the Government House in the first place?

I recalled for a moment the extraordinary rumours my school friends had told me. Rumours of black windowless trucks that would come in the night to take men away—the men that had been bad.

They called these trucks voronki, because they resembled big black birds. Ravens. Once a black raven came for you—you disappeared forever. However, I put these fantastical tales out of my mind. I'd never even seen one before—these fearsome raptors. Frankly, I didn't believe in them. This was pure nonsense.

"Papa? Where do the families go to? I mean the women and children that used to live here?"

My father tried to calm me down, as he could tell I was becoming concerned.

"I should think they're taken away for their own protection. To a safe location. You needn't brood about them. They are fine."

I suddenly wasn't so sure. Recently, in our current events discussions at my school, we were examining the outcome of an important Communist State trial that had just concluded two months ago.

Some important men of the Revolution, Grigory Yevseyevich Zinoviev and Lev Borisovich Kamenev, went on trial along with 14 of their conspiring compatriots.

The court case, which became known colloquially as The Trial of the 16, exposed a cabal of old Bolsheviks. They were on trial for the assassination of Sergei Kirov at his Leningrad office in '34.

Comrade Kirov was a young, influential rising star within the Communist Party, who held great popularity within the proletariat.

These wreckers also stood accused of constructing plots to kill Comrade Stalin, of wanting to destroy the Communist State, and of fomenting chaos and terror throughout the USSR.

After being found guilty, they executed all of the defendants.

I continued to press my father on this matter that he was obviously so reticent to discuss further.

"Papa? The men taken away from the Government House, were they working with those corrupted men from the Trial of the Sixteen?"

"Sweetie, really, none of this should concern you." My father now was desperately trying to get me to drop this subject.

"It damn well should, Senechka! You know where all of this is going? You do. You're a part of that enormous machine. You may fool a naïve girl, but you can't fool me any longer!" My grandaunt exploded in indignation.

My tetushka was now up on her feet and was cursing loudly at my father. Specks of spittle flew from her mouth as she shouted. By invoking my father's double diminutive in the pejorative form, my grandaunt was imparting an extreme lack of respect towards him now.

My father stood up, his eyes locked in an infuriating gaze with the elderly matron. Being brazenly insulted in his own home was the match in the powder barrel. He howled back at my grandaunt now, as loud as I've ever heard him before.

"I've not heard any complaints about your current living situation, my dear tetya! You're lucky to even be here!"

"Oh, come off it!" My grandaunt retorted. "This gilded flat is a prison, and you know it. Before the Revolution, Tsar Nicholas' Okhrana secret policemen didn't arrest entire families when they rooted out traitorous subversives! Those fellows had honour and respect." My grandaunt got especially pensive. "That was a different time. Oh, the parties we threw."

Auntie now exploded again in anger.

"Now we must all bow down in worship to our new Red Tsar. Rot in hell!"

The venerable woman stuck a gnarled digit out from her hand and pointed at the conspicuous portraiture of Comrade Stalin that watched us all from above.

"You bitch! Take that back. You can't possibly mean that. You're drunk!" My father was shaking his fist wildly about my grandaunt's face, as if he might strike her.

"You're a miserable bastard! You and your turncoat father both!" My grandaunt pushed her fingertips into my father's chest.

"Zhenya, go to your room immediately!" My mother shouted at me.

"But what did I do?"

This family conflict left me feeling stunned. Still, I took some comfort in knowing that I couldn't possibly have caused its ignition.

"Now! Make haste, young lady!" My mother pointed towards my bedroom.

I started crying and fled from the blowup. Before I could shut my bedroom door, I listened to the last of their heated argument.

"They can come and take me away for all I care. I wish they'd just get it over with!" My grandaunt howled.

"You've buried us all, you old witch." My father lamented.

"Oh, Senya! How could you?" My mother cried.

Much later that night when I heard my grandaunt come to bed, she bent over to check on me. I pretended to be fast asleep, even though I knew it would be hours before I could wind down from the calamitous storm that evening.

"I am so sorry, Zhenya. Oh, my beloved Zhenechka." She whispered gently into my ear whilst stroking my overlong blonde hair.

§

A few days following that horrible evening, I found myself in the drawing room in the late afternoon after my classes. I was trying desperately to keep myself focused on my studies, as I discovered that this had a positive effect on my mood and demeanour. I was re-reading my Young Pioneers handbook for what must have been the millionth time. The manual, it seemed, was never far from my side, and was becoming quite dog-eared.

I recently received a promotion to Second Stage Pioneer and wanted above all to make my parents proud of me. This playing with the dolls and causing mischief with my friends had to be elements of the past now.

I became determined to put away those childish habits so I might fulfill my duty to be the best that I could be for our Union. It was just after four p.m. and my mother had run downstairs to do some shopping. I could hear my grandaunt puttering about in the kitchen as she argued with herself.

Stalin's Door

As I sat on the comfortable couch nearest the far corner of the room, I suddenly recalled what my friend Zina told me last year. About the Stalin's door. Could Comrade Stalin really be watching me from inside there? I mean, after all this time?

It didn't seem at all possible to me, however I always made sure I was on my best behaviour whenever I found myself in the drawing room. Especially now that I was climbing the ladder of the Young Pioneers. There was no sense in me taking any chances. I knew that what I did and said was being graded and classified for real now, and I wanted to be the best. Always.

Still, I recognised something peculiar going on in here. Whenever I was in this part of the apartment lately. I mean close to this back corner. When I inhaled deeply, I noticed the distinct odour of cigar smoke within my nostrils. This was not natural since no one in the flat was a smoker. My father gave up cigarettes years ago and my mother never caught the habit. As far as I knew my grandaunt didn't light up, and even if she did, I doubted she would choose stogies. Everyone knew that cigars were for the men.

I visited enough of my friends' apartments to know the difference too, between the odour of cigarette smoke, or of cigars, or a pipe. This aroma was definitely that of cigar fumes. It wasn't pervasive, however. If I took only a few steps away from that back corner, the stink would quickly dissipate to nothingness.

I sat there dumbfounded for a few minutes, trying to think this through logically. Did Comrade Stalin smoke? Why yes, he frequently enjoyed a pipe based upon all the photographs I came across. What was it that Zina said?

"It's where Comrade Stalin can watch us from."

The cigar vapours must have been coming from the other side of the wall—what Zina called a Stalin's door.

Upon further inspection in that corner, I saw a small slit in the wooden panelling about a metre from the corner. In fact, once you noticed it, it was hard not to see it again. The gap ran from the bottom of the floorboards to the ceiling. I found that if I stood in the corner and reached over, I could just depress my fingers into that tiny line on the wall, like so, and then I would notice a minuscule change.

I detected that the wall moved inwards, just ever so slightly. Did it, in fact, slide across like Zina said it did? I saw no obvious way of making this happen, as there was nothing to hold on to.

I placed my ear up to the wooden panelling next to the slit and listened intently. Maybe I could hear Comrade Stalin on the other side if I was especially quiet. I could definitely smell the odour of cigars much more intensely now.

I stood as still as I could. Focusing. I strained to hear anything at all. I caught the sound of my heartbeat in my chest—thump—thump—thump, however I didn't hear any noises coming from the opposite side. If I forced them to, I could just get my fingertips into that gap along the wall. If I just pulled a little, yes, like that, I could see it move a tad. I swear I could just make out something behind the panel, I could see a faint light and—

Abruptly, I overheard a loud screeching noise and the unmistakable reverberations of footsteps, as if someone was running up behind me.

"Why you little criminal! What do you think you're doing? Get away from there this instant! Do you hear me?"

My grandaunt, sounding furious, was closing in on me from the dining room with all deliberate speed. Her face held an expression, one that I'd never seen before. I felt horrified to see her visage all twisted like that.

I found myself instantly taken aback at this turn of events and could do nothing about it. I froze up in fear—unable to move at all. She terrified me. My body refused to budge. I was like a statue. Trapped.

My grandaunt grabbed me by the blouse of my uniform and dragged me towards the kitchen.

"I will teach you to spy! I will show you to Kuzka's mother now!"

I wasn't able to think straight and did not understand what was happening to me.

Still, I knew I was in deep trouble. On the rare occasions that I provoked my parents to beyond their limits, the mere threat of being taken to see Kuzka's mother was enough to get me to straighten out immediately. That idiom filled me with mortal terror, as it had done to children for generations.

I didn't believe I would get any lenience from my grandaunt this time.

It mystified me, though. What transgression had I committed? Abandoning all hope, I knew that a brutal punishment, taught as a lesson, was in store.

Once inside the tiny kitchen, my auntie retrieved a heavy wooden spoon from a drawer, waving it all about her person.

"Don't you ever go near there again. Do you hear me? Insolent child!"

And with that she beat me thrice upon the backsides of my bare legs, below the hem of my skirt. Her instrument of punishment inflicted a painful stinging sensation with every blow.

"Tetushka!" I tried using the dearest and tenderest diminutive I could think of for her. "Forgive me, please! I didn't know any better!"

I was crying by now, and my face felt hot and red. As the tears streamed down my cheeks, I experienced sadness mixed with fear. What could I have possibly done to make my grandaunt so angry?

"Now, go to your room, and don't come out. And there is no supper for you either! I'm telling your father all about it when he gets home. I can promise you his displeasure will eclipse my own!"

My grandaunt forcefully shoved me down the hallway and into our bedroom. She slammed the door behind her, which rattled the glass in the windows.

It would be weeks before I would feel comfortable being in the drawing room again.

§

On the second Friday of November, the thirteenth, an event took place that even now, years later, I cannot forget about.

For an entire week beforehand, my mother and I, along with Zina and her mother, prepared for a fabulous reception-party.

Our families shared hosting responsibilities for this soirée, simultaneously, since we lived right across the hall from one another. We intended our honoured guests to mingle freely in between both of our homes. There would be plenty of rich food to eat, and only the best quality vodka to drink. Important men from the government and military, and their wives, would attend. As the only children present, our mothers instructed Zina and me to exhibit the proper decorum at all times. Papa added his own commandment.

"Zhenya, you shall be seen and not heard."

I wasn't sure what the occasion for celebration was, so I asked Mama. She would only make cryptic comments back to me.

"It was high time we made some festivity around here. Considering these serious days we live in now."

That day of the reception-party, which was the end of the work week, seemed to fly by in an instant. The very moment that I came home from the academy, my mother pulled me aside.

"I'm cancelling all your home studies this afternoon, young lady. You and I have many chores to complete before our honoured guests arrive. You're my number one assistant. Come with me!" She decreed.

I could see extra chairs, delivered from the carpenter's shop in the basement, arranged nicely in the drawing room. These were not present when I departed for school. Lengthy wooden tables complete with pristine white tablecloths now hugged the walls too.

As the enticing prepared edibles arrived, lovingly made in the bakeshops and restaurants we frequented downstairs, my mother tasked me with ensuring everything went where it belonged. To aid me, my mother filled out little beige index cards beforehand, showing where each appetiser should go. I felt like a traffic policeman, pointing this way and that, at the frenzied deliverymen with their hands full of baskets and trays.

"I think we will run out of chafing dishes, and the party's not even started!" My mother sounded worried.

A tremendous array of fare lay proudly displayed before us. I marvelled at the small silver cans of pink paste placed under the pans. When set aflame, they could keep the hors d'oeuvres warmed for hours on end. My work assisting Mama seemed endless. Serving utensils and silverware needed unboxing, and fine china canapé plates needed wiping down and pre-staging. I came and went so quickly, pirouetting around such, that I must have looked like a ballet dancer performing in the Bolshoi Theatre. I imagined Zina going through the same rituals in her residence as our reception-party co-hosts.

When the candles were lit, I tuned the wireless receiver into a broadcast of classical music. I knew then that my mother's arrangements were at last concluded. My mother collapsed upon the divan, with her lithe fingertips pressing into her forehead.

"Blin! I never thought we'd make it!" She exclaimed.

At some point I saw that Papa had arrived home from his office, surveying our progress and eyeing the tasty treats with considerable delight. My mother scolded him out loud for nearly being late—and cutting it much too close! My father just grinned at her and said that she fretted too often.

"Everything looks lovely, Shura."

It didn't escape our notice that he'd already been drinking heavily. His breath reeked of alcohol. He then turned to address me.

"Zhenya, be quick like a hare and get yourself cleaned up and changed. Our reception-party guests will arrive in fifteen minutes." His index finger pointed directly at the grandfather clock faithfully ticking away in the room's corner.

I needed to make myself smartly dressed. So, I wasted no time changing into my Young Pioneers uniform. I would wear my very best white pressed blouse and finest pressed blue skirt—ones that I saved only for special occasions like this evening.

I selected my brightest red neckerchief and fastened it around my neck, as I had done hundreds of times. I felt reassured as I looped it through the keystone accoutrement to my uniform—my neckerchief woggle.

As was always the case, my woggle felt warm to the touch as it rested just below my throat. As I cinched the neckerchief up, I recalled the night the old commissar presented the woggle to me. It was truly a wondrous gift. Although it seemed like a lifetime ago now, it was only two-and-a-half years. I remembered my Papa's old boss was so kind to me the evening we visited him. I watched myself in the mirror and brushed my lengthy blonde hair, pulling it back neatly.

I knew I was ready. The reception-party that my mother had worked so hard to prepare for would soon be an enormous success. I just knew it.

As if in an instant, all of our reception-party guests arrived simultaneously. In no time at all, the ambient noise level of our normally serene flat suddenly transformed into a boisterous din. Our guests now filled the drawing room to the brim. There were dozens of adults I'd never met beforehand.

As I surveyed the visitors, I marvelled at the array of dark suits, colourful dresses, and sharp military uniforms on display in here. Everyone was wearing their best this evening, looking smart and formal. They left not a single square metre of space in the drawing room unfilled, and everyone stood shoulder to shoulder. A symphony of mingling, eating, and especially drinking was now in full swing. The reception-party was just beginning.

As I observed plate after plate of delicious smelling bite sized finger foods and sweet treats passing me by, I endeavoured to see if I could surreptitiously try each one without my mother noticing me. I also pocketed a slight amount of the appetisers and placed them inside my skirt pocket for a special delivery later. I then slinked through the bustling crowd and forced my way through to the front door, which stood open and welcoming.

Standing watch outside in the hallway was the redoubtable Radomir Yurievich. My father's steadfast bodyguard-driver was always on alert, inspecting each reception-party guest before he granted admittance into our home. I retrieved the small folded up napkin of morsels I managed to smuggle out and slipped them inside the pocket of his gigantic black leather trench coat without him noticing. He'd appreciate the opportunity to eat the snacks later.

I then made my way over to Zina's flat, where I witnessed a similar amount of people festively imbibing and stuffing their merry faces with treats. We made it a point to flit back and forth between each apartment to compare and contrast how the reception-party progressed.

As was my obligation, every time I passed near my father's orbit that night, he would deliberately stop his conversation and pull me aside for the umpteenth occasion to announce me to yet another important Communist Party official or fellow commissar.

I repeatedly made sure I conscientiously listened, smiled, and showed great respect towards our reception-party guests, before escaping to see what fun Zina was up to without me.

"Zhenya! There you are! Please come over here, my dear. I'd like you to meet an excellent friend of mine."

Papa could always spot me in the middle of a crowded room, despite my trying to remain inconspicuous.

I floated back over to him faithfully, as he introduced me. My father grinned from ear to ear.

"Fridrik Vsevolodovich, may I please proudly present my beautiful daughter, Yevgeniya. She received all of her lovely looks from her mother, don't you know?"

The man standing beside my father towered over everyone around him. He wore the dress uniform of a most senior Soviet naval officer. Large red and gold epaulettes with many golden stars adorned his shoulders, and his pristine dark blue uniform jacket was replete with dozens of service ribbons and medals.

His perfectly combed brunette hair had just the hint of future greys. The fellow smiled broadly, as he cradled an enormous glass of red wine within his hands.

As the admiral turned to gaze at me straight on, I tried desperately not to wince at the fearsome burn scars that disfigured the left side of his face. The raised reddish blotches of skin which ran from his temple, along his cheek, and down into his neck looked painful. My mother always told me that maintaining good eye contact was essential in being polite—so I ensured that my eyes remained locked with his. I shuddered to conceive what kind of calamity caused his hideous injury. I felt some assuagement when I was able to gyrate back to my father as he completed his introductions.

"Zhenya, this is my good friend Admiral Krayevsky. The admiral was recently promoted and now commands our entire Baltic fleet."

The navy principal inspected my appearance and admired my uniform as my father continued.

"Yevgeniya earned an early promotion to Second Stage Pioneer, as you know. And even ahead of the much older girls in her class. We're expecting exceptional things from her. I know she'll make us proud. Right, my honey?"

"Da, Papa."

"Your daughter is most impressive, Commissar Kanadin. Congratulations." The admiral then turned to address me. "That's quite a smart uniform you have on, Yevgeniya. I'm particularly impressed with your —your—"

The admiral used his forefinger to point at the knot of his own tie.

I mimicked the admiral's gesture.

"My neckerchief woggle, Sir." I felt delighted at receiving a compliment for it.

After a few more minutes of small talk with the admiral, my father could sense my restlessness, and released me from any further inquisitions.

Inevitably, whenever copious amounts of vodka were being consumed by the adults, the ambient noise level would escalate quickly from a din to an almost deafening uproar.

Laughing and cackles, followed by backslapping and shouting. Long chorused songs, both patriotic and frivolous broke out, and it was all I could do to just hear my own thoughts inside my head. Many men at the reception-party, well past the point of no return, were rapidly approaching the line at which they would become mean drunkards.

I recalled an adage that my mother was fond of saying:

"What's on a sober man's mind is on a drunk man's tongue."

I think I now know what she was talking about. I made it a point with Zina not to even walk close to those types of fellows.

By this point in the reception-party, Zina and I found ourselves exhausted from running around and playing spies as we watched all the adults slip deep into insobriety. We retreated into my bedroom and closed the door quickly behind us.

A dim electric lamp was lit beside the bed, and given how late it was in the evening, I was not at all surprised to see that my grandaunt had already put herself to bed. She was snoring loudly, yet it was as if we couldn't even hear her over the overflowing noise coming in from the drawing room.

Zina joined me as we sat on the floor, giggling at what a silly time the grownups were having. It was well past my bedtime, and I estimated it had to be after midnight by now.

Without warning, all the unceasing and boisterous clamour from the drawing room ended. All together—and all at once. It was quite startling not to hear even a peep coming from the dozens of adults any longer. I exchanged a worried glance with Zina as we both heard nothing—save for the heavy breathing of my grandaunt in bed. I leapt from the floor and motioned for Zina to follow me. I slowly opened the bedroom door for us to investigate the abrupt departure of noise. We crept down the long hallway on all fours and with deliberate stealth until we reached a point at which we could secretly peer around the corner to determine the cause of the sudden silence.

As I crouched down, I took a peek into the drawing room. What I saw there shocked me to my core.

Standing in the centre of the room was an uncommonly short man who wore an off-white military tunic with large front buttoned breast pockets and a wide down-turned collar. I could see his jacket buttons fastened all the way to the top. His dark trousers were plain, and he sported brown leather riding boots. Our visitor's hair was the colour of coal, and his bushy moustache unmistakable. The sea of reception-party guests had divided all around him. Everyone was just staring intensely at our recent guest, in silence, as if they were afraid to say or do anything at all. The man's entourage comprised a quartet of impossibly tall bodyguards, who were all dressed in black leather trench coats.

My father approached our new caller, cautiously. Papa struggled to engage this honoured surprise guest. I had only ever seen Comrade Stalin from afar, and now he was only a few metres away from me. In my home!

For a moment, I felt taken aback as I studied Comrade Stalin's visage. Shockingly, I observed dozens of pockmarks upon our supreme leader's skin. His complexion was grey and dull.

This was nothing like what I was used to seeing. It was in sharp contrast to the hundreds of portraits of him I'd looked at over the years, which always showed a flawless and glowing countenance. And his height—or the lack thereof! The man I saw here, our supreme leader, had been egregiously exaggerated in both paintings and sculptures.

"Comrade General Secretary! My—oh my goodness, no one informed me you were coming over this evening. It's a monumental privilege to welcome you into our home. I'm sure you recall meeting my wife?" My father's hands were visibly shaking as he gestured hurriedly for my mother to join him at his side.

Comrade Stalin stood with an expression of bemusement upon his face for a moment, and then spoke up in a muted, almost squeaky voice. Surely it would have been impossible to discern anything had it not been for the stony silence throughout the entire flat.

"What lovely quarters you have here, Avksenty Yemelyanovich. Yes, quite lovely indeed. This is truly a grand reception-party you have thrown together. Why look at all of your guests, happy and full, and drinking like fishes."

Comrade Stalin then paused for an instant, before gesturing at one of the windows that looked down upon the Moskva river.

"You all were making such a racket, that I could hear you all the way over on the Bolshoy Moskvoretsky bridge as I drove myself here. I was wondering where all my commissars and committee officials had gotten off to tonight. Looks as if I found my answer."

"If only I had the foresight to have invited you, Comrade General Secretary. It was my mistake. I take full responsibility. Of course I know of your habit of working late into the evening. I did not intend to disturb you." Papa's voice was breaking, and he was speaking slowly and deliberately, making sure not to slur any of his words whilst in his inebriated state.

"Yes, you are correct, Avksenty Yemelyanovich. I was working late tonight. There are so many duties to look after these days, don't you know? When I went looking for you in your office, would you venture to take a wild guess at who I found labouring after-hours, instead of you?"

Comrade Stalin now scrutinised my father's eyes and didn't even bother to wait for an answer from him.

"Why it was your number one—deputy—I think his name is young Valerian Savelievich, or some such? He was most helpful to me. Most helpful indeed."

"Oh, my goodness, Comrade General Secretary! Is there something I can help you out with here and now?" The expression on my father's face was one of sheer terror, and his complexion had become pallid with fright.

"Oh, no. Everything is fine. Or rather, I think it's fine. Or is it? It's so hard to tell."

"Let me return immediately to my commissariat. I'll get to the bottom of it right away, Comrade General Secretary!"

"Yes, I rather think that's a splendid idea, Avksenty Yemelyanovich."

My father then burst from Comrade Stalin's side and rushed towards the front door without even bothering to collect his hat and coat.

Comrade Stalin then turned to address my mother, who looked like she was ready to faint with panic.

"Sorry to intrude like this. I'm sure you can understand, Madam Kanadina? By the way, you have such a lovely home."

The majority of our reception-party guests took the hint from my father and were hurriedly donning their coats and gathering their belongings in a frenzy. There was a race to see who could get out the door and back to the Moskva Kremlin in the quickest amount of time.

Comrade Stalin soon departed our flat too. And with that, the reception-party was over.

Winter 1937

The last few days of '37 were gloomy and miserable. It would go down as the coldest week our capital city had seen in over a century. Everything felt frozen and slow. Hard packed down snow lay beneath my feet, which was past the point of shovelling. Everywhere I looked I could see ice embedded upon all the surfaces.

As I rode the municipal transit bus back home from the academy, I lamented that I always journeyed in the darkness now—even in the afternoons. It seemed as if I never got to see the sun any longer. The ancient electric heater inside our coach wasn't working today, and my four layers of dress couldn't ward off the bone chilling dankness.

Thank goodness I had my neckerchief woggle with me. I discovered by accident that if I held on to it in my clenched fist, it would remain remarkably hot to the touch—for hours on end. I never could reasonably explain why this was the case.

I wouldn't turn down the tremendous warming effect that it provided throughout my entire body, however. On the bitterest of days, this little radiator I possessed saved me from freezing.

I took notice that it was eerily quiet inside the charabanc today—no one dared speak to one another. People would sit quietly by themselves whilst conspicuously not making eye contact with anyone else. This was our routine now. Everybody felt terrified of saying anything at all.

We learned painfully, the hard way, that a wrong word—even one spoken in jest—could provoke a visit from the dreaded State secret police.

Their voronki, those black trucks that resembled giant ravens, were surely visiting us every night now. Everywhere I looked, entire floors within the House of Secrets were being emptied by the NKVD.

With so many people being arrested, a flat could have a new family move in at the start of the week, and by the end of the week that group could completely disappear. No one saw or heard from them again. It was as if they never existed. The process would then start anew.

Some flats rotated through unique families four or five times over by the end of '37. It didn't escape anyone's notice that those infamous yellow-coloured bills, signifying an out-of-bounds area, adorned half of the front doors at the Government House now. Why did the NKVD lock up those apartments, sealing them for all time? I wasn't brave enough to ask anyone.

When I arrived home that afternoon, I noticed that there were three suitcases arranged neatly just inside the front door of our foyer. Upon inspection, I saw they contained warm clothing. I discretely asked my mother about them.

"Oh, honey, don't worry. We may be going on a trip shortly. I'm just being helpful and looking ahead for us."

It dumbfounded me. Where could we possibly travel this time of year?

I took a moment and recalled the painful memory of my dearest friend Zina, who left me in early autumn. Why did she suddenly leave? Where did she go?

Stalin's Door

I remember coming home from school that aching day, wondering why I hadn't seen her in classes all week. I went to check on her. The loud buzzer at her flat's door echoed in the chilly hallway.

"Da? What do you need young lady?" A strange babushka answered the door.

It wasn't Zina's mother, or their housekeeper.

"Excuse me, Madam. Is Zina there? May I speak with her? I think she's sick. I brought her some soup." I showed the woman the steaming bowl of sustenance cradled within my hands.

"Nyet. There is no one here by that name. Are you sure you're in the right place?"

"Of course, I've been here many times. I live right over there." With my hand, I pointed towards my front door, over my shoulder. "I'm a friend of hers." I was insistent that I see Zina at once.

"I am sorry young one, but you must leave. No one here can help you." And with that, she slammed the heavy door into my face.

I promptly rushed back to my home to ask my mother about this.

"You must be mistaken, my honey."

"What do you mean, Mama? Zina's flat, it's just across the hall."

"No, Zhenya, I don't know who you're talking about."

"Number one four naught? Across the way!" I motioned frantically with my finger.

"No, no. There's a nice older couple that live there. It's Mister Osinov, the new People's Commissar of Finance, and his lovely wife who reside at number one four naught. They have no kids. You know this. We had them over for dinner just last week. Don't you remember, honey?"

§

    This period in my life was especially painful. Papa was hardly home any longer. The exorbitant number of hours he was working at his commissariat every day meant that I never got to see him. I calmed myself by thinking there must be important work that only my father could see to, and I was positive that Comrade Stalin still relied on him tremendously.

    On the occasions that Papa was at home, I noticed that his drinking of alcohol was frequent and excessive. My father was constantly fighting with my mother too, usually about silly and inconsequential things. Someone that I didn't know at all had replaced this happy and quiescent man. This frightened me tremendously, and I struggled to understand what was going on with him.

    Why was he acting this way? My father was curt with me, or preferred to say nothing at all, versus lashing out. Was it his lack of sobriety? I knew that being a dipsomaniac could surely cost him his important job—couldn't it? What would Comrade Stalin think of him behaving in this fashion? What was happening to Papa?

    Our nightly family councils hadn't taken place in so long that I nearly forgot that we used to meet at all every evening after supper. I missed hearing the comings and goings of what Papa was working on at his commissariat, or what new delicious recipe that Mama was dying to try out.

    My grandaunt passed away unexpectedly on the last day of summer, which ushered in a somber time for the household. I felt that whilst there were moments of great conflict when she lived with us, the importance of having our family stick together was paramount. There weren't many of us left now.

 Mamushka didn't run out any longer, nor did she do any cooking. She was slowly letting go of all the simple things in her life that brought her pleasure. She stopped shopping in the stores downstairs, nor did she take time for tea with any of her friends. In fact, she could pass several weeks without even leaving the flat. I could tell that something was dreadfully amiss, however I wasn't equipped to ask the proper questions that would bring me some resolution.

 One of the neighbour's housekeeper-cooks would occasionally come in at supper time to help us out, or more often than not my mother would merely arrange delivery from a restaurant or bistro downstairs.

 Absolute silence reigned as we ate our meals now. The clanking of knives and forks upon the china were the only sounds I heard. It was deathly quiet at all the other times. It was as if we lived within a mausoleum.

 My mother obviously wasn't herself, and it seemed like she didn't want to leave me out of her sight—ever.

§

 One day I found myself seated at the dining room table, whilst I laboured with my endless after-classes work. I reasoned that keeping myself busy and maintaining my perfect grades were the keys to getting admitted into our capital's most prestigious secondary school. I reminded myself that this was crucial to my future success at university and within the Communist Party.

My mother was not a drinker herself, except on social occasions. So it distressed me greatly that afternoon when I could see her inebriation. Her normally pristine appearance in dress and in makeup were all horribly awry. My mother's hair was messy, and her blouse wrinkled. A strong odour of alcohol permeated from her person, and she was most unkempt. I knew that something was dreadfully wrong with Mama.

From out of nowhere, my mother snatched the heavy book from out of my hands. She then pulled me upwards with deliberate force.

"Zhenya, I need you to come with me now."

"Where are we going, Mama?" I had to admit that it was a treat to leave the apartment, although I was more than a little worried for my mother in her present condition.

"Put your shoes and coat on quickly and follow me. Don't ask questions."

I could sense my mother was not in a mood for frivolity.

We walked for a while throughout the first floor of the Government House, until we descended another flight of stairs, and finally came to the basement level on the other side of the compound. I recalled that I'd only ever been over this way twice in the almost three years I'd lived here. Compared with the frigid temperatures outside, and the chilly hallways inside, I could feel that it was noticeably warmer down here in the basement. I could pick up the sounds from all the heavy machinery and all the apparatuses that powered the steam boilers—which provided the heat to everyone's flats. They were working overtime in this brutal winter cold. This area was perhaps the warmest I'd been in.

Down the way, through a long corridor, we ducked ourselves into the carpenter's department. This workshop was huge, with complicated machinery installed all about the place. I could see piles of freshly milled wood, and projects in various stages of completion, stacked everywhere from the floor to the ceiling. The ambient noise level in this room was deafening, and I placed my fingers into my ears to dampen out the cacophony.

After waiting a moment just inside the door, the nice junior apprentice Demian Antonovich, who was on duty, noticed us and immediately quit his work. The mammoth piece of equipment he operated, a lathe I believe it's called, spun down rhythmically. The boy snapped to attention and rapidly removed his cap out of respect, hurrying over to where we stood.

"Da, Madam? What may I do for you today?"

My mother asked the polite apprentice some question about a broken chair in our flat. I knew immediately that it was nonsense. She made some small talk, feigned annoyance, and demanded the learner fetch his master. The terrified youth ran hastily away from us to the manager's office door in the corner of the expansive room.

"Now Zhenya, please pay attention to me. This is strictly important."

"Yes, Mother?" I was listening intently now.

"Look over there. Do you see that door in the room's corner?"

"Da, I do."

"No, not the office door, the other one by those green lockers." My mother pointed frantically. "Run over quickly and tell me if it's unlocked, before the master carpenter comes over. Do it now! Don't ask questions!"

My mother stared at me with all seriousness. I ran as swiftly as I could to the door she wanted. I turned the cool doorknob in my hands, and I knew instantly that it was open. I rejoined her just as a man and boy were walking over from the other side of the room. They both had the same worried look upon their faces.

"Nyet! Never mind. Come, Zhenya. We are leaving." Mama spat the words out as if the pair had gravely insulted her.

We left the startled master carpenter and his second standing dumbfounded as we fled the workshop.

"Mother, what is going on here?"

I was not normally slow on the uptake, however I did not understand what just transpired. She pulled my arm hard as we darted to the end of the hallway, and out of sight of anyone.

"Now Zhenya, this is the most crucial thing I will ever tell you."

She was crouching down on her knees now, so that I was looking down at her. Her voice was gloomy and trembling.

"Something is happening, and we may not have much time left to live here. I don't think you've missed the fact that people are being arrested. Sometimes entire families, all at once. I need you to concentrate. That special door you tested. Remember it. Burn its location into your brain. Your life may depend on it.

"Now, there may be a time—tonight, tomorrow night, or even a month from now, when things will happen and happen quickly. It'll likely be late at night. When I tell you to, and only then, I need you to come down here and go through that special door and wait. It'll be safe and warm inside.

"You might see other women and children waiting in there with you. Don't be afraid. Be brave for me. I know you can do this. Someone will come for you. Are you listening? This is vitally important. Someone will come for you."

My mother was shaking my arm firmly now, and it was hurting me.

Stalin's Door

"Who will come for me, Mama? What are you talking about?" Her story made no sense, and I felt terribly confused.

"Listen to me, please. A man will come for you, understand? Look for a man, and obey him, however only if he calls you by your diminutive, all right? He will also give you a very personal item of yours, so you know you can trust him. Look for this item. Do you hear what I'm saying to you? Unless the man presents an individual article and addresses you as Zhenya, then do not leave with him. Wait in the special room for as long as it takes."

I was now weeping, and not fully comprehending what my mother was trying to say to me. She continued.

"Zhenya! Hey, now. Don't cry. Be a big girl. This will be all right, but only if you're a brave Young Pioneer. We can't have any whimpering. Wipe your tears away. Here, use my handkerchief."

My mother pulled out a fine white cloth and handed it over. I wiped my face and stood tall for her, trying to act courageously.

§

It was only a couple nights later that I awakened from my slumber, startled by a huge crashing sound coming from the front of the flat. The time had to be well after midnight.

I could hear lots of shouting and the barking of orders. I had absolutely no guess what could be happening.

I quickly put on my warm robe and slippers, and I rushed out into the drawing room.

What I witnessed was appalling. My parents were sitting on the sofa, still dressed in their nightclothes. A group of men, wearing military uniforms, were swarming around the suite.

Some fellows were standing watch, whilst yet others were busy rifling through the papers on my father's desk and looking into his books. I didn't recognise the regimentals they wore, however there appeared to be a professional looking leader and at least six rugged henchmen. All of them were lanky and appeared fearsome to me. None of these men had even bothered to remove their jackboots at the front door, and I thought this was particularly graceless. My mother was surely furious at what they'd tracked in with them.

Then I saw something I'd never seen before.

In the room's corner, near the Stalin's door, there now was an opening, not more than a metre wide. I could see a small chamber located behind the wall. A dim light breaking from an electric lamp inside the space captured my attention. If I stared as intently as I could, using all my powers of concentration, the edge of a modest desk became visible.

Suddenly I heard a loud thrashing noise which startled me. Immediately my eyes focused on my father's loyal bodyguard-driver, Radomir Yurievich, who was laying prone on the floor by the foyer. Our defender was moaning loudly and appeared to be in tremendous pain. I could see copious amounts of blood now dripping from his battered face.

One soldier had a pistol pointed directly at his large bald head.

"If he even moves a millimetre, then shoot the bastard!" The leader barked whilst pointing in Radomir Yurievich's direction.

"Yevgeniya Avksentyevna! Stand right where you are and don't move any closer!" My mother shrieked.

I could see her eyes were bloodshot, and her face appeared flushed. The tone of voice she was using with me was mortally serious.

I felt shocked. I wondered why was she suddenly called me by my given name and patronymic, and not by my beloved diminutive?

"Comrade Commissar! Your attention, please! My name is Major Chernobrovin."

The leader was now standing over my father and held a sizeable piece of beige paper in his black-gloved hands. He wore a field green uniform jacket, neatly pressed. A dark blue cap with a bright wide red band adorned his head.

As was the style for all military men these days, the leader's face sported a thick black mustache. The fellow spoke deliberately, and he seemed to choose his words wisely.

"Sir, I formally charge you with violating article number fifty-eight, subsections seven and fourteen, of the Russian Soviet Federative Socialist Republic penal code. You are under arrest. We will transport you forthwith to the Lubyanka building for interrogation."

My father became instantly incensed, waving his finger towards the face of his accuser.

"I'll have you flogged and jailed for this outrage! Get me your commanding officer on the telephone immediately, you contemptible halfwit! Do you even have any idea who I am?" Papa was slurring his words badly.

"Oh, yes, Comrade Commissar. We know exactly who you are. There will be no last-minute reprieve." The leader looked disgusted with my father.

One of the younger officers then spoke out of turn, and in a manner so swift and violent, he was like a rabid dog choking himself on his lead.

"Your wrecking crimes are finished, you traitor!"

"Silence! We'll have discipline in the ranks. No further outbursts, Junior Lieutenant!" The major commanded.

"My apologies, Comrade Major." The young lieutenant stared meekly at the floor now.

The major now looked towards my mother and continued with his indictment.

"Madam, you too are under arrest. I charge you as an accessory to your husband's crimes, under NKVD order number naught naught four eight six."

My mother then let out a loud screech, the likes of which I'd never heard from anyone before.

"Now, no more time wasting! Gather your warmest belongings. It's frigid outside tonight." The major folded up the large beige paper neatly and tucked it inside his jacket pocket.

An unexpected ear-splitting racket coming from the direction of the foyer captured everyone's attention in an instant. I turned my head to see a struggle ensue between two men.

Radomir Yurievich now had a hold of the pistol previously pointed at him. In an act of utter desperation, he was trying to dislodge it from his opponent's hand. A thunderous detonation erupted, which echoed into every corner of the room.

The bodyguard-driver then slumped onto the floor—dead. I caught sight of a pool of dark crimson blood pouring out of his gunshot wound, all over the expensive Persian rug.

No one in the flat dared move now, frozen in anticipation for a few seconds, and unsure of what would happen subsequently.

The major then motioned with his hands.

Stalin's Door

"Come over here, girl. Come and stand next to me."

My mother looked hopelessly into my eyes and screamed at the top of her lungs.

"Yevgeniya Avksentyevna! Run! Now!"

I felt frightened, but only for a fraction of a second. I did what my mother commanded and raced as swiftly as I could out the front door. As I descended the stairs, I heard one henchman ask a question.

"What do we do about the daughter, Major?"

"Oh, just let her go. We'll collect her later. She can't get too far. It's late anyway."

§

In an instant I found myself downstairs in the basement, inside the carpenter's department, and behind the special door in the back room that my mother had presented earlier that week. I waited.

Time passed in a painfully slow manner. It could have been hours since I escaped, I wasn't sure. I tried to get some sleep, however it just wouldn't come. I knew it was still in the middle of the night—for the shop master had not yet started his day. As I sat against the dry warm wall in the corner of this special room, and in the dark, I could see the lights from the workshop coming in from underneath the door in front of me. I could hear nothing save for the dull sounds of the boiler's pipes hissing and knocking about in the distance.

For a moment, I nodded off.

The sudden appearance of the figure of a man, standing in the open door frame, startled me awake. I placed my hands to my face, trying to block the light from his electric torch, shining directly on me. The luminescence hurt my eyes, and I struggled to focus.

"How—how long have you been watching me, Sir?" I exclaimed.

"Oh, for quite a while now, young lady." The stranger replied.

Once my sight cleared, I could see this outré man wore a uniform, identical to those of the arresting soldiers from only a few hours ago in my home. He was now inside the room and stood directly over me.

A morbid thought unexpectedly raced about inside my mind. Surely I am done for? The men who arrested my father and my mother had now tracked me down. They would take me away, just like my parents. I didn't know if I would see my family again. I didn't know what to think. I sat motionless, and my body felt paralysed with dread.

I was desperately trying to recall what my mother had told me about this special room. What she told me would happen? If only I could sort this all out immediately inside my head. But there was no time to think straight!

Curiously, my nose then caught a strong whiff of cigar smoke that was wafting from off of the man's rumpled uniform jacket. I had smelled this pungent fragrance before, I was sure of it. It was from that peculiar corner in the drawing room—near the Stalin's door. It was unmistakable. I felt taken aback for a few seconds.

"Yevgeniya, please, we have to leave here—urgently!" The fellow was barking his orders at me, just like the soldiers upstairs had done to my parents.

"Wait. What—what did you call me, Sir?"

"Zhenya, I meant Zhenya. We need to go. Now." The man now had a gentler tone in his voice.

Stalin's Door

The stranger then placed his electric torch upon the dirty floor and in an instant he stretched his left arm outwards and down towards me. He was offering his left hand to help me up.

With his right hand, I saw him retrieve something from within his jacket pocket. The man then held it out for me to see. In between his index finger and thumb he displayed a bright, golden, rounded object about the size of a champion walnut. A majestic red star was affixed to the front of the item —and it shined directly at me. The gold hammer and sickle inside the red star were unmistakable.

My eyes instantly dilated as I stared at the prize within his grasp. I experienced a deep feeling of befuddlement.

The soldier was holding my Young Pioneers neckerchief woggle.

Sava's Tragedy

◇◇

Behind Stalin's Door

Leningrad
28 February 1936

My dreams have always been vivid and colourful—they're full of sounds and smells that seem lifelike. In the vast majority of dreams, my experiences are so realistic that I am not even aware that I am asleep.

My nightmares—even more so.

These phenomena are not unique to me, and I know that many people dream in much the same manner. The dream I was having tonight was bizarre. I questioned myself. Was I dreaming?

I found myself aboard my old ship, the destroyer *Uritsky*. We were patrolling the dark frigid waters on the Baltic sea, and the time was well after 2400 hours. But how could this be? I knew I hadn't served aboard any ship in over three years. It shocked me to be back out on the endless water, and I could feel the harsh sea wind whip my bearded face about as I clung tightly to the cold metal railing on the main deck. The destroyer was underway at over 25 knots, and I felt the tremendous power from her steam turbines vibrating throughout the damp deck plates beneath my feet.

Because I normally didn't stand watch above deck, it mystified me how I could have ended up out here. Perhaps this was some discipline for an infraction I had committed?

However, I thought that was absurd because I held the ship's distinction of never going on report. I knew then this had to be a mistake. Perhaps I was dreaming, but I couldn't be certain. Everything looked so vivid.

Suddenly, from over my shoulder, I heard a loud commotion that included much shouting and screaming. The disturbance was coming from just inside the bridge. I turned immediately to investigate.

Once inside the control centre, I witnessed a horrifying sight. They had made my captain kneel upon the decking, and he had a pistol pointed at his head. The man holding the handgun was our first officer, Commander Sonin!

Standing beside my captain were many other officers from the bridge staff. Bright red blood dripped from my captain's face, and it was obvious there had been a monumental struggle in here.

"Oh good, Petty Officer Komolov, you're here." The first officer uncocked his sidearm and walked over to me. "I charge Comrade Captain Molchanov with sabotage and wrecking aboard this ship. There's only one punishment for his crimes. Summary execution." The first officer then held out his pistol backwards to me. "I'd like you to carry out the sentence. Now, P.O. If you please? Do your duty!"

This dream was the most terrifying nightmare I'd ever experienced.

Please allow me to tell you the story of my end. As I find myself adrift inside this dimensionless void, I look back upon my life with some bitter compunction. Time is meaningless here, and yet I am left with some bewilderment as to how I arrived. I'm floating in a black pool of ether, with no earthly body to speak of. My mind is disembodied and desperately in search of closure.

I feel old now and out-of-date. I wondered why I never took any chances in my life. I always played it safe and knew exactly what the cost of everything was well ahead of its purchase.

As my grandfather used to say, "Two deaths cannot happen, however one is inevitable." I never really understood what that meant until recently. I think he was telling me that you only live once, so why not make the most of a risk?

My life was at a crossroads, yes, and a new opportunity would present itself shortly. Should I continue to remain circumspect, or do I dare to try something new?

Returning to my nightmare, I cannot promise you a happy ending.

"No Sir, Comrade Commander. This is all highly irregular! I cannot be a party to murder." I protested.

"Then I'm afraid P.O. that you too will join your master!" The first officer was smirking at me now.

Without warning, powerful hands from behind pushed me down by the shoulders, and I came to kneel beside my captain. As I stared into his eyes, I felt disturbed. The man's irises had turned completely black—with his pupils fully dilated. My captain no longer appeared human to me, almost as if his face had been replaced with a fearsome rubber mask.

The first officer then stood behind us both and re-cocked his pistol. I heard a familiar clicking sound coming from behind my head.

"I will shoot you both myself, you disloyal bastards! First you, Petty Officer Komolov!"

A tremendous clap of thunder then rang out, and I saw a kaleydoskop of falling stars dance like a shower of fire flowers all around me.

The resounding reverberation of the gunshot from inside my dream shocked me wide awake, and I sat bolt upright in bed—in a panic. I saw the surrounding room was still completely pitch dark and I could feel the rapid beating of my heart within my chest. I dabbed at the cold and clammy sweat upon my face, my hands shaking uncontrollably. To calm myself, I took a long deep breath in, and then exhaled softly.

I looked over at my wife and hoped that I had not awakened her with my nightmare.

I wasn't positive what time it was, however, I wished that I could get at least a couple more hours of sleep tonight. As I reclined myself back under the covers, I thought of my day to come, and how I had been dreading it for some time.

§

Waking myself up on time, I started my day just as I had done for many years. Except I knew this day would be different. The sun was not yet up, and the inside of our one-room cottage was dark and noticeably silent. I could hear nothing save for the almost imperceptible crackling of the dying embers within the wood-burning stove. I shuffled out of the cold empty bed, noting that my wife had already begun her day ahead of mine. I took care and ignited my kerosene lamp. As I undressed myself, I silently thanked Lera for laying out my dress uniform from the night before.

I redressed quickly because the air felt biting and sharp on my bare skin. If I concentrated on my listening, I could just make out the dawn chorus of songbirds starting up outside on this late winter morning. I then made my way over to the warm wood-burning stove at the centre of the cabin. I stared at the brass samovar sitting on the top—awaiting its ignition. The glow from the gaslight cast exaggerated shadows on the wall in front of me. Silhouettes of outsized cast-iron pots and pans hanging from above came alive, dancing with the flickering flame from my light.

There was work to do, and I jumped right into it. After a moment of tinkering, a wave of relief came over me as I discovered that kindling the coal this morning within the heavy metal urn was unusually easy. I had the samovar all fired up and ready to brew on my very first attempt. This meant that shortly there would be tea, and all would be correct in the world.

I then took several pieces of fresh cordwood and fed them delicately into the maw of the furnace, noting an almost instantaneous increase in the ambient temperature around me.

The outside conditions were chilly this time of year, and we weren't through with winter's snow and ice—not even by a long shot. I felt fatigued today and knew I had not received a good night's rest. It must be the result from growing greyer, I told myself.

Our heirloom samovar was even older than I was—I couldn't remember a time when my family didn't own it. It may have been ancient, yet it was always reliable. I chuckled at that thought because I always thought of myself in that same way. I was now old, and still reliable.

I looked over at the small dining table and could just make out the profile of Uncle Tima sitting there in the shadowy light. His snow-white crown of hair stood out like a mountain peak spotted from a distance. I don't think the man ever slept. My uncle always sat there—it was his spot. I walked over to sit with him for a few minutes before departing, my lamp still in hand.

I watched as Dyadya Tima intently studied the positions of game pieces upon a chessboard, as he hunched over the edge of the table. I noticed his large, gnarled hands would carefully make their way over each of the chessmen, delicately feeling their contours within his fingertips. I could see him deliberately and precisely counting from the lower left side of the game board, stopping, and then making his way up the game board and towards the centre. Each unoccupied square had a small hole drilled into its middle, with every black square slightly elevated from the base. When my uncle located the chess piece he needed, he would gently feel all the way around its bottom, pausing for a moment before moving his fingers slowly up and down. My uncle was constantly contemplating 14 or 15 moves ahead in our games.

The chess pieces were endowed with little dowels that protruded from their undersides, so they fit into the chessboard securely.

This little innovation ensured the chessmen always stayed firmly on the board, even if the table jostled accidentally. I swear he had touched each of the wooden figurines over and over, tens of thousands of times, smoothing the grains completely off.

"Would you prefer the brooms, or the tea with an elephant this morning, Uncle Tima?" I inquired.

"I will have the brooms, please."

"We ran out of lemons yesterday, so I'm afraid we only have a little jam. Is that agreeable with you?"

"Da." My uncle answered dryly.

I looked over towards Lera, who was now dutifully standing at the wood-burning stove. With one hand I held up a finger to signal Dyadya Tima's choice, and with my other hand I held up two fingers to reveal my own. My wife nodded her head and tinkered with the samovar to begin its delicate infusing process.

That last question I asked of my uncle was a trite and recurring joke between us. There had been no lemons in our teas since late last summer. With the onset of spring, it would be delightful having fresh fruit once again.

A few minutes passed, and then my wife brought us over our steaming beverages. Lera placed my uncle's mug onto the table and into a neat depression which formed there over the years, from constant use. I noticed the steady resting of his hands built up their own impressions too. I sat opposite from my uncle and sipped gradually from my cup of heated goodness. My wife then returned to her duties at the oven.

I observed Dyadya Tima taking his mug in between his hands and raising it slowly up to his lips. He then sighed. I could see water vapour evaporating off the surface of the tea as it warmed his weathered face. With each sip, he smiled, and showed me his yellowed cracking teeth.

My uncle then gazed up at me. While the pupils in his eyes were cloudy, his expression was still soulful. My uncle took a few more swallows from his tea and returned the cup to its spot. He then resumed his exploration of the game board with his hands.

This was our morning routine. Our current match was stretching into its third month.

"I think you've got a big decision coming up." My uncle broke in, after several minutes of silence.

"I'm sure you're about to remind me that the endgame is the most critical time?"

"Nyet. I need not tell you that." My uncle's voice barely rose above the level of a whisper.

I recalled all the games we'd competed in. In over 30 years, I'd never defeated him. Even when I was first learning chess—when my uncle played without his queen—he bested me every single time. His knowledge of the pastime was well beyond my own. My uncle's rating was easily a master's level now, although I do not believe he was ever formally ranked. I knew of no one in our entire village with a greater ability at shakhmaty, however.

There was a time when we'd play several matches a day. Then, whenever I served aboard ship, we'd switch to playing by post. One of our most memorable competitions lasted four years. Our games of late featured one move per day. I would take my turn in the morning, before I headed out for duty. Dyadya Tima would follow supper with his response at the end of our day.

"Pawn to queen's bishop six." I secured the pawn firmly into its new square, producing a satisfying clicking sound.

My uncle finished his first cuppa and contemplated giving me some advice. Our fixtures of late were less about keeping score, and more the passing on of his game theory and wisdom, which he'd accumulated over a lifetime of studying and playing. The student never stops learning, and the teacher never ceases teaching.

"I would urge caution here, Sava, at this point in the match. When entering the endgame, you must beware. One king will surely be ahead of his rival in matériel. This persuades the lesser king, excessively, to press his pawns forward to promotion. Successfully performed, a promoted pawn becomes interesting, and could in fact turn the tide of the match.

"However, you must keep your eyes open. Pushing pawns too quickly without a plan can make them far too conspicuous. They are then easily picked off, making the lesser king even more desperate to attack."

"Thank you. I will await your move this evening, Dyadya. I need to go now." I stood up from the table and patted him gently upon his shoulders.

Uncle Tima took a deep breath and smiled back at me.

I shuffled over to the wood-burning stove where Lera was leaning over, dotingly cooking breakfast. The kasha and tvorog she was preparing smelled delicious. This simple peasant food, comprised of barley porridge, butter, and mild cheese curds, would really stick to your ribs on frosty winter mornings like today. Unfortunately, I was in no mood to eat anything. My stomach felt tied up in knots with anxiety.

My beautiful wife peered up from her boiling pots, and then broadly grinned at me.

"Don't you look handsome this morning? My beloved husband!"

"Thank you, Lera!" I hugged her warm body from behind.

I had not worn my full dress uniform in quite a while, and I was grateful to my wife for never complaining when it came time to do its ironing. I made it a point to always thank her for all the chores she did around the cottage—and for looking after our uncle. Because of her skill with that dense piece of metal, my dark blue striped uniform blouse, the fabled telnyashka, was crisp and free of wrinkles.

Our seamen had worn this outfit for centuries, and I always saved a special one for occasions like today. My dress uniform looked sharp and was in immaculate shape, given its age.

"I should be busy today, so I won't require a sandwich. Make sure Uncle Tima doesn't get into trouble, all right?"

"Shalom, Sava. I love you."

I kissed Lera goodbye and donned my greatcoat. I stepped speedily through the wooden door so as not to let out the heat and found myself in the brisk late winter morning.

The cold air filled my lungs instantly with a familiar burning sensation. Today was not as bitter as previous mornings, and I felt just the slightest change in seasons coming.

As I left the cabin behind, I hustled down the icy sidewalks of our quiet suburban village and towards its central square. There was only one diesel tram that ran into Leningrad every day, and I surely didn't want to miss it. Not today of all days.

I observed that there were the usual crowd of commuters already queued up at the stop in front of me. In the distance, I could hear the tram slowing down as it approached us all. Abruptly, I felt a potent tapping sensation upon my shoulder.

"Good morning, Saveliy Yegorovich! My, oh my, you're all dressed up today! Don't you look smart in your formals? What's the occasion, sailor?"

My conversationalist was Mme Yolkova, a friendly older woman that lived just a few streets away from us. I knew that she worked in an accounting office in the city, and we would frequently chat with one another on our commute. I demurred and felt uncomfortable explaining the formality of this day. Besides, I detested small talk because I wasn't any good at it.

"Oh, it's nothing. We've an important inspection at the shipyard, don't you know?" I lied to her.

With that we all climbed aboard the already crowded tram and prepared for the lengthy journey into the city. The choking smell of burning diesel fuel in winter was something I never quite got used to.

§

When I arrived at the department of my commanding officer, his harried-looking yeoman directed me to have a seat just outside his office door. This metal chair was practical, but not at all comfortable. As I waited patiently, I glanced up and down the cold and wide corridor. I spotted the designations of at least a dozen naval departments, all represented here at our headquarters building. Each office door contained an etched glass pane, with the rank and name of its occupant stenciled in bold black letters. All carried the ranks of captains and commanders. The door behind my right shoulder read as follows:

CAPT SONIN, PROJECT SEVEN, *GROZNY*

After a brief wait, I discerned my captain barking out his orders from within his room.

"Attend me, P.O."

I heard his fingers then produce a loud snapping noise, not unlike the sound a starter pistol makes at the beginning of a footrace. Capt Sonin was not a man who wasted any time.

I opened the door and walked into his modest sized office. It was utilitarian and contained a small wooden desk and one guest chair. Large metal drafting boards of various capacities took up most of the free space inside the room. There were stacks and stacks of ship schematics, plans, and blueprints on every surface.

Enclosed within a small glass case on the adjoining wall, I spotted a scaled ship model of a destroyer.

Overflowing ashtrays filled with stout cigarette butts littered the floor —like landmines waiting for a hapless victim to step upon them.

Tucked away in the room's corner, an unkempt bunk and mess kit suggested the man might live in here.

I couldn't help but notice the two outsized windows behind his desk that looked out onto cold grey skies above. Gigantic shipyards loomed in the near distance.

The captain's workspace was brightly lit with electric light. Stuffy stale smoke permeated all about me.

Capt Sonin sat at his efficient desk and didn't even bother to look up when I entered the room. His attention remained on the overflowing paperwork in front of him.

I found it impossible not to stare at his fingertips, stained in the colour of Prussian blue. This was the consequence of countless hours of handling the ship's plans and prints, no doubt.

Behind my captain hung two framed black-and-white photographs. On the left side General Secretary Stalin surveyed us all, and the on the right side was the commander of the Baltic Fleet, Admiral Glukhov.

"Good morning, Comrade Captain." I stood stiffly at attention with my service record folder tucked inside my left arm.

"You may sit down, P.O." My captain announced in an unmistakably glum manner.

As I sat in the office guest chair, I gingerly placed my documents upon the peak of papers in front of me. My captain then took the file and leafed casually through it.

My captain was easily ten years younger than myself, trim and fit with inky hair and a black beard. He was part of the first contingent of Soviet naval leadership installed just after the Revolution. I could not imagine he saw any action in the Great War. Disciplined, stern, and no-nonsense, my captain committed himself fully to the Communist Party. Capt Sonin suffered no fools gladly.

We served together on my old destroyer, the *Uritsky*, for many years. He was then her first officer. When the *Uritsky* transferred into the Northern Fleet in '33, they promoted him to captain and he took over the lead operational development of the new *Gnevny*-class destroyers, which were being built right here in the Zhdanov shipyard.

Although it's not as famous as her sister shipyard, the Baltiysky, it was just as crucial to the service. Regrettably, the shifting political winds would soon erase all traces of individuality and pride with both shipyards renamed with dull monikers. No. 189 and No. 190, respectively. I found myself formally attached to his command echelon, however I'd not worked in his organisation for over three years.

My captain closed my service record and studied me.

"So, today's the day, eh? I never thought I'd see it come, P.O." I heard him let out a loud harrumph as he continued. "As you know, I'm taking command of the *Grozny*, and we'll begin her sea trials in a few months. I can promise you she'll be the finest vessel in the fleet, even if I have to drag her out of the dry dock with my bare hands.

"I'm planning on rating a promotion to rear admiral by the time I'm forty, and I don't care who I have to step over to get there. Nothing at all will stop me now. This has been the goal from my days in the academy. There's a whole new regime taking over—maybe you've not noticed before now? Things are changing—for the better. We will finally make a difference. Thankfully, you'll not be a part of the glory to come."

Capt Sonin stared down his nose at me with an expression of disgust upon his face.

That last bit of news, whilst not unexpected, came delivered in a way that left me feeling dazed.

My captain continued speaking, rather quickly now.

"I have to be honest here. I never liked you P.O. Really, when I studied your dossier, it's clear as day to me. How are you not embarrassed with yourself? This is not at all acceptable—a man with your experience and education."

He then spent several minutes rifling through the bound sheets of paper within my folder. My captain took a moment to light a cigarette. His smoking was swift and deliberate. Capt Sonin shuffled each page in the packet, right to the very end. He then continued his harangue.

"I am rather thrilled with these new enlistment protocols, actually. They will let the younger petty officers advance in rank. The ones who want to prove themselves. They'll be no more waiting for the dead weight to die off and retire. And if you ask me, this new direction is something that should have occurred a while ago."

Exhaling loudly—he produced a prodigious plume of blue-white smoke.

"Frankly, I'm surprised you advanced this far. Trust me, the fleet is better off without you."

My captain now looked directly into my eyes, with a gaze of pure disdain etched upon his face. His look betrayed a genuine hatred that I'd not seen in him before now.

"I think this is a wonderful thing, P.O. One less person of your—kind—in our service."

I bit down upon my tongue with such force that I was positive I drew blood. My face felt fiery, and my cheeks turned crimson as blood surged into the capillaries. My breathing ballooned within my chest. These new enlistment protocols, as my captain eloquently put them, were the new naval regulations dictating ranks and promotions for a sailor's time in grade. My rank for the last 16 years was petty officer first class. Since I hadn't rated a promotion to chief petty officer, the new orders now required me to retire. I was being unceremoniously discharged. Today would be my final day serving in the Soviet navy.

I thought it fitting that the name of his new ship, the *Grozny*, matched his personality. For it was another word for fearsome, formidable, menacing, or most befitting—terrible. My captain then struck up a more conciliatory tone with me.

"I will admit some positive points about you, P.O. You never visited the sickbay onboard ship. And as far as the records show, they never cited you for any infractions either minor or major. Your work ethic was—well—I wish all my sailors were as dedicated and diligent as you are, old man. I am surprised they even have you attached to my command, and the *Grozny*. What with your special duties for the last three years—"

An abrupt double rap of knuckles upon the plate glass in the office door broke my captain's train of thought—followed by its opening and closing promptly thereafter. I watched as the startled captain looked up from his papers. His face wore an expression of aggravation for the interruption.

But, before he could dole out any verbal admonishment, his demeanour quickly shifted to shock and then into fright. As rapidly as I've ever seen anyone rise to attention, my captain was bolt upright and standing rigidly at his desk. Capt Sonin then blurted out.

"Comrade Vice Admiral!" A smart salute snapped to from his right hand.

With no time to think, I too was up from my seat and at attention. I locked my eyes forward into place. I knew this was a serious business. Nonetheless, it was a welcome break from the surliness of Capt Sonin.

"No one informed me of your visit today. Is anything the matter?" My captain's voice was breaking, with an expression of anxiety painted upon his face.

"Oh, good—you're still here. Captain, might we have the room?" A deep sounding voice asked from behind me.

"At once, Comrade Vice Admiral. Petty Officer Komolov, I dismiss you!" My captain ordered me away with urgency.

"No, no, Captain Sonin. You misunderstood me. I would like to speak with the petty officer—alone—if you don't mind?"

A wave of apprehension now filled my stomach. What in the world did a vice admiral want to talk to me about, especially on my last day?

Looking at my captain, I observed befuddlement all about his face.

"Um, well, of course Comrade Vice Admiral. By your leave."

Stalin's Door

Capt Sonin glared at me as he hurriedly withdrew. The plate glass in the door's frame hardly made a sound when he closed it behind himself.

I was still standing rigidly at attention, my gaze staring straight ahead. With my peripheral vision, I watched a stately man walk around the captain's desk.

Vice Admiral Krayevsky was the deputy commander of the entire Baltic fleet. He'd already established himself as a Soviet naval legend, and his meteoric rise within the ranks assured him of greatness far beyond the service, if he wished it. The vice admiral's dark blue uniform was impeccable, perfect, crisp, and without a stitch out of place. The thick golden braids on his sleeve jacket insignia alone must have cost a fortune. The brilliant red and gilded shoulder boards were the size of bricks. The number of service medal ribbons pinned upon his chest commanded immediate respect. The fellow was youthful, thin, and self-assured. One distinguishing feature the vice admiral carried couldn't be avoided.

A series of grim lesions, the colour of port-wine stains, covered the left side of the vice admiral's face, running from his hairline to below his collarbone. It was obvious that he'd been savagely burned in some kind of accident from his past.

Within the vice admiral's hands, I spotted a dark maroon envelope. He inspected me for a moment before starting up.

"I really am delighted that I could meet you before your separation from our service, P.O."

The vice admiral then seated himself casually and lit up a cigarette, retrieved from a slim gilt case inside his jacket. I watched his head swing about as his eyes surveyed the room intently. He noticed all the overflowing ashtrays scattered around and just shook his head in disbelief. The vice admiral then extinguished the matchstick and muttered to himself.

"And I thought I smoked too much!"

He took a long drag from the skinny cigarette, then paused and exhaled. The vice admiral seemed to sense my nervousness, so he offered me some much-needed relief.

"Won't you please have a seat Saveliy Yegorovich? Just relax now. All is well."

I quickly sat down again, still feeling baffled. I did not understand what was happening here. I had no earthly idea at all.

The vice admiral looked directly at me now and started speaking again.

"You know it's fascinating. I perused your service record earlier this week and discovered that we're the same age. We'll both be forty-four years of age next month. If my memory serves, your birthday is on the thirteenth, yes? Mine is on the fifteenth."

I couldn't believe it. The vice admiral was much older than he appeared to be. He still had a full head of neatly combed brunette hair. He didn't look anywhere near 43 years of age to me. My own weathered complexion, silver-grey hair, and white beard were in stark contrast to this younger-looking man seated across the desk. I must have appeared to him at least ten years his senior.

"Let's have an informal conversation, shall we Saveliy Yegorovich?" The vice admiral took his index finger and tapped the ash from his cigarette into the nearest ashtray. He then raised the cigarette to his lips and took another long drag. "For instance, what can you tell me of your brother Eduard Yegorovich?"

That question caught me off guard and I didn't know what to say in response. This wasn't at all what I expected to talk about today, of all days. I gathered my thoughts and replied.

"Edik? Why do you want to learn about him, Comrade Vice Admiral?"

"Just indulge me, won't you?"

"Well, Sir, he perished in the Great War." Whenever I thought of my brother, it always left me with a dull sadness.

"Did you get along with him? What I mean to ask is, did you know your brother well?"

"I never knew my brother well, as an adult that is to say, Comrade Vice Admiral. He left home for a life at sea when I was just eight years old."

"Your brother was what, ten years older than you—yes?" The vice admiral inquired.

"Yes, Sir."

"And he died whilst serving aboard the *Imperatritsa Mariya*, did he not?" The vice admiral's tone changed and was insistent now.

"How—how did you know that, Comrade Vice Admiral?"

"This may surprise you, Saveliy Yegorovich, however I knew your brother. We served together. In fact, I was there, on that fateful night in 'sixteen." I could see the vice admiral's throat contract for a moment as he gulped. "What can you recall about the circumstances of his death?"

I took a moment to collect my thoughts. I thought back to that calamitous time, just after the new year in '17. I was serving aboard a ship at sea during the Great War when I received word that my brother was dead. The thoughtful letter, written by Edik's captain, had first been sent to our mother, who then forwarded it on to me.

The post recounted what happened on the night of 20 October 1916, whilst the *Imperatritsa Mariya* was in port at Sevastopol. A terrifying fire had broken out near her forward powder magazines, which then caused a devastating explosion. The detonation was so tremendous that they said it lifted the bow of the battleship up and out of the water completely.

By some miracle, the hull of the battleship remained intact, and uncompromised. Unfortunately, the flames reached her torpedo bays 45 minutes later, sealing the fate of the grand floating fortress. A series of secondary explosions then ripped giant holes along the sides of the vessel and within no time, she capsized. Over 220 sailors died on that horrifying evening.

"Comrade Vice Admiral, my brother saved fourteen of his fellow sailors, who were all badly burned, and at the cost of his own life. Before the catastrophic final explosion, he dragged them out onto the dockside, one by one. His crewmates must have deliberately flooded the internal compartments—even knowing it doomed them—to forestall the spread of the fire. This gave my brother, and others, time to get some wounded out. Regrettably, he never made it off the ship before—" I paused so I could take a deep breath. I felt a wave of pain radiating within my chest. "—before it sank."

I bowed my head and stared down at the floor.

"Your brother was an authentic hero in the Great War, Saveliy Yegorovich." The vice admiral looked thankful and lit up another cigarette. After an interminable pause, he continued. "I can say I wouldn't be alive today, without him."

"You—you Sir? My brother rescued you?"

"That's precisely right."

As I gazed upon the vice admiral's burn scars again, I now understood. He then continued.

"I was a newly promoted first lieutenant and less than three years out of the Imperial academy. Did you know I graduated in the last class before the Great War? I had only been aboard the *Imperatritsa Mariya* for five months when the disaster struck. I confess I didn't know your brother intimately, however we had a pleasant working relationship.

"Your brother always impressed me with his professionalism and sense of commitment. Chief Komolov was always forthright and never afraid to call things as he saw them.

"Why, one time I saw him sternly berate a commissioned officer for falling asleep at his post during critical manoeuvres. Your brother commanded respect, on and off our ship."

The vice admiral paused and looked pensively at me.

"My apologies, P.O. This next portion is a particularly painful memory. I remember the first indications of the fire that horrid night. It was right before eight bells. I recall that the deadly black smoke was everywhere, all at once—seemingly from out of nowhere. A terrible confusion reigned supreme aboard ship, and I ran towards the bow to help get the blaze put out. It couldn't have been over two minutes later that the first explosion threw me right into the bulkhead. It knocked me unconscious.

"When I woke up, I was in hospital, in port, along with all the other casualties from the catastrophe. I inquired over and over about how I arrived there, and it was finally told to me that Chief Komolov himself rescued me on that fateful evening.

"One year later I read of the chief's formal recognition as a bona fide champion of the Russian Empire. Chief Komolov posthumously received our highest honour, the Cross of Saint George—First Class. Fleet Admiral Zhzhyonov himself presented the medal to the chief's grieving widow."

I knew the prestigious award to which the vice admiral referred and had seen it many times over the years. Lera treasured its possession above all others.

The vice admiral lit up yet another cigarette and took a minor break, finishing half of it before continuing.

"Now Saveliy Yegorovich, I want you to tell me of your story." The vice admiral glanced at my service file laying on my captain's desk. "I could re-read this dry paperwork, but I'd like to hear from you directly. For instance, how did you come to be in the Soviet navy for the last twenty-two years?"

Feeling more at ease now, I started up.

"Certainly, Comrade Vice Admiral. I had just graduated from uni in the spring of 'fourteen. Because I could not find employment that summer, I joined the Imperial navy the day after the war broke out that August."

"Refresh my memory, won't you? What was your particular field of study?" The vice admiral inquired.

"Economics theory."

"That's—that's unusual to say the least, P.O. Hmmm. So you then enlisted? With your formal education you could have been an officer." The vice admiral sounded puzzled.

"That really didn't interest me at the time—commanding men, Sir. Frankly, I felt bored, and I wanted to join the war action just as soon as possible. I was desperately hoping to reunite with my brother onboard his ship too. I'd only seen him twice since he left for sea, and one of those times was the somber funeral for our father. "Alas, they assigned me first to the

Poltava, then the *Leitenant Burakov,* the *Petropavlovsk,* and finally the *Zabiyaka.* As you know they renamed the *Zabiyaka* the *Uritsky* in 'twenty-two. She transferred into the Northern Fleet three years ago now."

The vice admiral looked quite intrigued with me as I told my story.

"Saveliy Yegorovich, you were at the—uprising? I'm sorry, I meant to say the—action—at Kronstadt? While you served aboard the *Petropavlovsk?"*

"No, Comrade Vice Admiral. I joined the *Zabiyaka* a month before the insurrection."

"Don't worry, P.O. That's not the reason I'm here today. Just to let you know, I was at the action at Kronstadt too. Of course I fought on the winning side. But I digress. What have you been doing as of late?"

"I've been working here in Leningrad for the Inspector General's office. I'm primarily a clerk and investigations assistant."

The vice admiral took his arms and folded them in front of him.

"I see. You know, I asked around earlier today. Your supervising officer said you have a keen eye for detail, and a passion for rooting out decadence and corruption."

"Thank you, Sir."

"Tell me, Saveliy Yegorovich, what are your intensions now that you're leaving the service?"

"To be honest Comrade Vice Admiral, I don't have any formal plans. I was dreading this day."

"You know I fought tooth and nail against these rotten new enlistment protocols. I believe the service is losing too much institutional knowledge with these forced retirements. Well, I can tell you we don't have need for economics theoreticians at the moment, whilst we're on the verge of successfully completing another Five-Year national economics plan. That said, I have a fresh opportunity you might just find interesting."

The vice admiral then handed me the dark red envelope that he walked in with.

With much curiosity, I carefully opened the sleeve and looked at the papers within. I studied his offer for many moments before answering.

"Comrade Vice Admiral, surely I am too old for acceptance?"

"You'll be fine. In fact, you have a couple years yet to go. However, don't worry. With my recommendation, your admittance won't be an issue. You might say I have some—pull—within the Communist Party.

"You know they have an all-officer corps, don't you? Once you successfully complete the officer cadet school, you'll hold the rank of junior lieutenant. I think you still have something to contribute to our Union, and you can consider this offer as a thank you for your family's sacrifice in the Great War."

"I am not sure what to say, Sir."

"Well, you don't have to decide right this very moment. Take a few days to consider." The vice admiral extinguished his cigarette and brushed his hands vigorously. "Discuss it with your family if you like. The OCS starts a few weeks from today, so you must contact my office with your decision, soonest."

"Yes, Sir! Thank you, Comrade Vice Admiral!"

§

During supper that evening I debated the vice admiral's new opportunity with Lera, and my uncle Tima.

"I don't like it, Sava. Not one bit. You've already done enough for your country. Why not take some time off? That—organisation—the NKVD. I don't like them one bit. They're nothing but a bunch of thugs if you ask me." My uncle acted animated, and in a manner I'd not seen before. His hands were waving all about frantically.

I reached out for another opinion.

"What about you Lera, what do you think?"

"I believe you should do what's right for you and not listen to anyone else. If this is something you desire, then pursue it. Dyadya Tima and I should not factor into this equation." My wife disarmed me with her sage advice.

"I didn't give the vice admiral a commitment today. I believe I need to sleep on it. All good decisions come with a proper night of rest, I say."

"Harrumph!" My uncle snorted. "The actual decision you have tonight is the move I'm about to make in our match. Ready for it? Knight to queen's rook three. Check! Think about that, Sava!"

"Yes, Dyadya."

Once our supper concluded, I brought the chessboard back to the dining room table so that my uncle could take his turn and study the new positions.

Instantaneously, I saw his crumpled hands work over the chess pieces for the millionth time. I'm sure he had known what move he would make tonight for over two weeks now.

I then walked over and crouched down beside a modest-sized strongbox that I kept stored in the corner of our cottage. The dusty metal box was ancient and had a locking mechanism that had failed quite some time ago. Still, this was a centralised place where we could store important documentation, my military dress uniform ribbons, our family photographs, assorted heirlooms, and so forth.

Off to one side I spotted a small, long brown rectangular box, made from the finest polished wood. Carved in a bas-relief upon the lid was an exquisite countenance of Tsar Alexander I.

I retrieved the container and opened it slowly.

Located inside was Edik's Cross of St George medal, still in its pristine state. A folded striped silk ribbon, in alternating colours of orange and black, lay attached to a cross pattée made from gilded silver. Within the centre of the cross was the visage of St George on horseback, as he slayed the famous dragon. With much irony, I thought for a moment about the colours in the ribbon. Orange and black represented fire and gunpowder. These colours were a fitting representation given the circumstances of my brother's death aboard his doomed battleship.

I joined my wife as she reclined in one of our two rockers arranged by the wood-burning stove to keep warm.

I sat down beside her. Lera was lovingly engaged in her knitting routine. The cozy wool mittens, scarves, and snoods she produced were much appreciated this time of year. Her umber coloured birchwood needles, burnished after thousands of hours of use, were like natural extensions of her fingers now.

A familiar soft clicking sound danced into my ears, which always made me feel at home.

"Talk to me, Lera."

I then ignited my after-supper cigar. It was my one and only indulgence.

"Yes, my husband? What would you like to speak with me about?"

"Tell me—" My voice trailed off for a second, and I was lost in my own thoughts. "—tonight, let's reminisce about Edik."

I showed my wife the open ornate box so she could see his golden award again.

"Edik's medal!" Lera smiled at me, and I saw her bright white teeth gleaming by the light of the kerosene lamp.

As I looked into her crystal blue eyes, I saw them welled up with tears. I knew she was proud of my brother and still missed him tremendously. I continued.

"Can you please tell me about your life with Edik after you two were first married? For instance, I seem to recall you mentioning one time before that you travelled to Sochi for your honeymoon?"

Lera then regaled me of the details about her month-long holiday with Edik, which she said flew by like a whirlwind at that storied seaside resort town—back in the summer of '13 before the Great War.

I was pleased to hear of the good cheer they experienced and all the rich food they ate whilst visiting there.

Sadly, because of circumstances I couldn't control, I didn't take Lera on a proper honeymoon myself when we were wedded. They arranged our levirate marriage the day after Russia signed her peace treaty with Germany in the spring of '18. My union with Lera was bourne by decree, and she was a decade my senior. I certainly didn't love her any less because of it.

In a few days from now, we'd celebrate our eighteenth wedding anniversary together.

Outside Moskva
29 July 1936

Graduation day at the officer cadet school was here at last. I had just endured 13 weeks of struggle and now could finally revel in my triumph.

"Congratulations, Junior Lieutenant Komolov!" I silently repeated to myself as I looked into a mirror and practised my first salute as an officer, snapping to attention.

In a few hours I would recite the officer's commissioning oath for the Narodnyi Komissariat Vnutrennikh Del, better known by its acronym, the NKVD. The People's Commissariat for Internal Affairs was the official name of our organisation. Unofficially, General Secretary Stalin referred to us as his secret police agency, although I felt perplexed as to the secret part. We did in fact wear uniforms.

As I dressed for the ceremony that morning, I still couldn't believe I made it. I examined each part of my uniform one last time to ensure everything was correct. The officer's epaulettes felt strange upon my shoulders.

There were other accessories I needed to get used to. The medal boards on my left breast, the red and gold rank insignia, the thin red piping on my pressed blue slacks, and the bright gold buttons on my jacket. My vivid red and blue officer's cap was striking and distinctive. I would be the first commissioned officer in my family's lineage. Lera would be so proud when she next saw me in my smart officer's uniform!

As I looked back for a moment, I couldn't forget that first day when I arrived here at the officer cadet school. I had taken the lengthy journey by passenger train from Leningrad to Moskva in just over two days' time. The last leg of my trip took me another half day by diesel tram to reach the far suburbs of Moskva.

It was the initial Monday following International Workers' Day, and I estimated there were at least 100 candidates with me, give or take a dozen men. Our enrollment paperwork strictly ordered not to bring anything with us. The OCS would provide everything we needed.

Upon our arrival at the tram station, it shocked me that no one greeted us. A dilapidated sign explained that NKVD recruits were to proceed a kilometre down the road, to the Damir Innokentievich Gorlov recreational field, for formal intake processing. There didn't seem to be a soul around in this backwater rural village to make an inquiry of, so we marched down the street, almost in a single file, towards the unknown destination.

I felt mild bafflement at the situation.

In no time, we came to a grassy pitch—which accommodated a well maintained and vast oval clay track along its periphery. Another sign instructed us to form a line and stand by for our instructor. We dutifully stood shoulder to shoulder at the edge of the field. Many of the recruits laughed and joked with their new comrades. I too felt some excitement. Everyone around me appeared eager and enthusiastic, waiting in the fresh spring air. As I peeked at our surroundings, I could see there were dormitories on the premises, and what looked like out-buildings that contained classrooms. This facility must have been a secondary school in its past life.

Suddenly I heard a clock tower in the distance strike nine times melodically. We were all punctual.

Out of curiosity, I spied up and down our lengthy formation. I could see the ages of the other cadets ranged from just out of university to a few years older than that. I didn't see anyone who appeared even nearly as ancient as I must have looked to them.

After a few minutes more of standing, a stout older gentleman turned up, as if from nowhere.

As he approached our line, I examined his appearance. He wore brown trousers and a simple white kosovorotka, the traditional peasant shirt. The old chap looked to be about 60 years of age and would have fit right in attending to the expansive fields of wheat behind us in the distance. He had dark grey hair and a fair complexion. He walked with an exaggerated limp and showed curiosity about what we were doing here. Perhaps this fellow was just coming to see us off, before starting his work for the day?

The interloper slowly wandered up and down our group, whilst stopping to stare at each of us briefly. Along the way I could see him counting the number in our cadre.

"I say, gentlemen!" The grandfather's voice now boomed out. "All of you look impatient. As if you're waiting for something to happen. Something important? What are you doing here? Hmmm?"

Many of the cadets looked nervously around themselves and at each other. One of the bolder cadets then spoke up, acting for the group.

"What do you want, Sir? We're awaiting our instructor as ordered. You've lost your way to work, obviously. Please go about your business. Go on now."

"Well, at least I have one that can talk!" The elderly man rushed over to the cadet, who spoke out and stared up into his eyes. "What's your name, son?"

"Who wants to know, old chum?" The cadet sounded supremely annoyed at our outsider.

"You should think of me as a nemesis. That's the best advice you'll ever get from me. I—am—I am the enemy. Your worst adversary, in fact." The old man grinned at us frighteningly.

As we all exchanged glances with one another, it became readily obvious to everyone that this person was our instructor—in a disguise!

"I'm not what you expected, am I? That's excellent. You must expect the unexpected here at this school. Remember this, your enemies won't always wear a uniform. He might be anyone and might look like anybody. How would you know? You won't! You should suspect everything! You should accuse everyone! You must let go of your assumptions. Assumptions will kill you just as surely as a gunshot to the head—and more rapidly!

"In tight situations, I will require men that can think their way out, not punch their way out. All of you graduated from university, so I already know you're intelligent. What I intend to learn over the next few weeks is which of you can think! Now listen carefully. I always choose my words wisely. Remember that."

Our instructor paused for a moment, before continuing.

"I shall now declare that the NKVD Officer Cadet School, class number nine nine six, began its first day with one hundred and nineteen—"

The fellow paused momentarily, and looked us over again. "—I shall say, hopefuls. I say hopefuls because I can promise that not all of you will graduate from here. Not even by a long shot. In fact, I know many of you won't even make it past this first day. Should we meet again tomorrow, I will address you as cadets. But not yet. Not now. You're still hopefuls to me at the moment. Now, let's see what we have here."

Our instructor marched from one end of the formation to the other end, as he continued his initiations.

"A typical class will graduate between forty and fifty officers. This means that more than half of you won't be here in three months. Of that I can guarantee."

The short man made his way over to me and looked up into my eyes. I stared straight ahead, not wanting to draw unwanted attention to myself.

"You there, hopeful. Are you sure you're in the right place? We don't see too many hopefuls your age here."

Our instructor was centimetres from my face now. I continued staring forward and kept my composure about me.

"Yes, Sir! I'm precisely where I'm supposed to be."

"Well, Grandfather Frost, assuming you're still here the next morning, I'll need you to take that white beard off. Am I understood? I don't allow my cadets to wear them here."

"Da, Sir!" I acknowledged.

While the fellow continued with a few more of his inspections, one of the cadet-hopefuls piped in with a good question.

"Sir? Excuse my inquiry. How shall we address you?"

"You may call me—you may address me as Mister Kalagin."

I felt perplexed. Our instructor wasn't even an officer here? This seemed rather bizarre.

Mr Kalagin finished his review and then clapped his hands together five times, calling for our attention.

"Now we shall move right into screening number one. Are you ready? This examination is simple. And I promise you, they will get harder as we go along in the next thirteen weeks. I now require that everyone get yourselves out and around this oval track. That's it. Straightforward. Just move yourselves." Mr Kalagin urgently waved his hands towards the clay lanes right behind us. "Let me see what you're made of. Get out there hopefuls!"

The bulk of our formation then started a frenetic competition inside the earthen ellipse. I watched the bodies of men flying and jockeying for the coveted pole position. Many of them wanted to be first in this premier test, and at any expense necessary. I sensed a real urgency as the formal evaluations had begun. The instructors in this school were surely keeping score.

For myself, I just sauntered along the dried path as if in no hurry. I witnessed a few of the other cadet-hopefuls doing the same.

Mr Kalagin stationed himself near the edge of the ovoid, busily surveying my classmates during the race. He timed them with a pocket watch and made notes into a small notebook, accounting for our progress.

After everyone had completed a few laps around the track, I realised there were a pack of leaders, and then there were those just trying to keep up with them. Significantly to the rear were the laggards in my group, strolling deliberately. We casually exchanged smiles amongst ourselves, as if we all shared a great secret.

Mr Kalagin let this go on for a few more minutes and then gathered everyone back together where we started. He lined us up in the exact order that we finished the impromptu contest.

"Now, hopefuls. Were you paying attention? I don't think you were."

Mr Kalagin walked over and focused on the winner of the race, who was standing at the head of our new formation. The victor looked proud of himself and grinned broadly.

Mr Kalagin then shook his hand firmly.

"Congratulations, hopeful! I can see you're a man that wants to be first no matter the cost."

"Thank you, Sir!" The youthful man couldn't contain his excitement as he desperately tried to catch his breath.

"Congratulations. Apparently you have a room full of smarts, but alas, the key is lost!" Mr Kalagin then spat upon the cadet-hopeful's boots in utter disgust.

He had just called the man an idiot. The cadet-hopeful looked aghast and confused—as did most everyone else.

"I suppose all of you who were running are proud of yourselves, eh? Well, you shouldn't be."

Mr Kalagin walked down the line to the end, and over to our small group, towards the fellows that were simply walking on the track.

"See these hopefuls down here?" He pointed at us, making sure everyone took note. "They're the wise ones!"

Mr Kalagin then approached me.

"You there, Grandfather Frost! Explain it to me. Why weren't you running with the rest of the hopefuls?"

I answered him instantly and with just a hint of snark in my voice.

"Because you never said to run, Sir!"

I heard some cadet-hopefuls sighing loudly as they protested my answer. I watched as they placed their hands upon their hips, shifting their weight in place.

"That's sharp thinking, gentlemen! Exactly what I need from you. Grandfather Frost here is precisely right. I never said to run. I just said to move yourselves around the track. Most of you just assumed it was a timed competition. Well, I hope you're thoroughly rested after your warm-up, because you will need all of your strength now. I need you to walk. Just walk. Just walk around the track here. Keep moving at your own pace. Pick a direction and stick to it. It's up to you.

"This evaluation will not measure who is most physically capable, but who is the most mentally fervent. But beware! If you stop moving for any reason, I'll immediately discharge you. You'll be out of this school and on the next train back to Moskva, or wherever the hell you hail from. Being an exemplary officer in the NKVD won't depend on how physically fit you are—it will depend on how mentally tough you are. Start walking. Move it! This is the real deal, hopefuls."

I joined everyone as we started making our way around the oval again, in the traditional counterclockwise fashion. A few near the end of our line walked in the opposite direction. Nobody seemed to be in any sort of a rush this time.

"Mister Kalagin, how long shall we walk for?" One of the cadet-hopefuls shouted at him.

"Oh good! Another excellent question from the hopefuls.

I like questions. You will all walk until I dismiss ten of you. If you keep moving, you'll get to stay and have the privilege of taking screening number two. Understood?"

I instantly saw the logic in this examination. If our instructor could make any of the cadet-hopefuls drop out on the very first day, with something as simple as this, then that should quickly weed out the mentally infirm.

I ambled around and around and tried to conserve my energy. I felt positive this test would take a while.

§

Some 17 hours later, we were all finally allowed to stop and rest. I dropped to the hard clay surface of the oval, and my old body experienced the feeling of utter exhaustion.

Mr Kalagin clapped his hands together and signaled that he'd just discharged the tenth cadet-hopeful. I was victorious! I had completed the first examination—thank goodness!

Truth be told, I was not sure how much longer I would have been able to hold out. I couldn't see straight, nor could I feel my legs and feet. My bones felt done in.

Mr Kalagin achieved his required discharge quota just in time. We later learned that five cadet-hopefuls passed out and collapsed from fatigue, four quit out of what I guessed was sheer boredom and frustration, and one simply walked off into the darkness on his own—and never returned!

I had made it past the first day and into the next morning. But what had I gotten myself into here?

I surely hoped that our next examination was more cerebral, and less physical.

The nickname Grandfather Frost stuck with me for the entire time I was in the OCS.

§

The officer cadet school comprised rigorous class schedules that strengthened the mind and the body. We performed calisthenics every morning before breakfast, and every afternoon before dinner. In between those times we all had a full course load of academic studies, with weekly assessments ensuring knowledge retention.

Our coursework spanned a multitude of topics: Soviet political theory, intelligence, counterintelligence, interrogation techniques, security basics, small arms tactics and firearms proficiency, code breaking, surveillance, and other secret spy tradecraft.

Once every third day, Mr Kalagin would give us all another one of his fiendish screenings, designed to whittle down our cadre even further. This ensured he fulfilled his graduation quota. Each test was more intense and complex than the one before it.

During the free hour allotted to the cadets following supper, Mr Kalagin expected us to do laundry, cleaning, and other chores related to the upkeep of the dormitories.

I frequently used this time to write letters to Lera. I knew instinctively that all our correspondence was being censored and always kept things light and positive for her. Receiving correspondence from my wife proved nonexistent—which seemed peculiar to me. I wanted to get back to the chess match that my uncle and I began before I left for the OCS.

Every week Mr Kalagin graded each cadet on all aspects of his individual class performance and physical fitness prowess. The aggregation of one's grades produced an integer which then became a unique identifier for each cadet—for the following seven days. The higher your aggregate scores, the lower your class ranking, with the ranking of number one being the finest at the school. Rankings could fluctuate from week to week, and only those cadets with the correct trajectory could stay on at the OCS.

Standing orders required us to wear the number of our class ranking on an orange-coloured badge affixed to our fatigues. I used this integer in all challenges and challenge-responses given at the OCS. Everyone knew your number, and you would know theirs. With this status system, all the cadets had knowledge of where they stood at all times, compared with his peers.

So far, I was more than holding my own in the official class ranks. Any cadet privileged to have earned a number containing a single digit commanded immediate respect. Cadet Number One achieved a god-like status and enjoyed much admiration, and jealousy, amongst the cadets. My cadet class ranking started out in the lower 30s. However, within a few weeks I worked assiduously to pull myself up into the top ten of all cadets. By the beginning of the thirteenth week at the OCS, Mr Kalagin ranked me as Cadet Number Two.

§

Screening number 31 was the final examination of our OCS training, although I didn't know it yet.

I reported to a special door inside the classroom wing and Mr Kalagin was already there waiting for me, with a look of seriousness upon his face.

"Comrade Cadet Komolov, welcome to your next examination. I congratulate you on making it this far. This test is for you, and you alone. Individual achievement is paramount, and time is a factor here. Behind this simple door is a modest room with basic everyday items within. What I need you to do is make a thorough investigation.

"Make notes of everything you see inside, no matter how insignificant. You'll have up to sixty minutes to work. If you feel you have completed this assessment proficiently, then you may leave the room early, however, know that once you depart, the test is over. Do not discuss the mechanics of this examination with any of the other cadets. Do you understand? Do you have questions?"

"I have no questions, Sir. I am ready to proceed, Mr Kalagin."

"Good luck, Cadet Number Two. Here are your writing implements. You may begin."

My instructor handed me several sheets of writing paper and a pencil. He opened the door and watched me walk through. I then heard a soft clicking sound behind me. I expected that this exam would be nefarious. I'd soon find out if I was correct.

Stalin's Door

My surveillance training kicked in immediately, now that it was a habit. I could see that this chamber was compact and brightly illuminated, estimating it to be three metres by five metres in size. A wooden writing desk arranged on one side of the room, paired with its metal chair in front, were the only pieces of furniture. An electric lamp on top of the desk was the only source of light here. I noted there were various items scattered randomly upon the work surface.

Utilising my classroom instruction, I took a quick inventory of everything I could discern in here, recording them with my mind. There were three books, a newspaper, ten coins, an empty glass bottle with a cork stuck at the top of the neck, and a desk blotter.

I pulled out the cork and sniffed inside the bottle. I smelled an interesting fragrance. I replaced the cork.

I then used a technique we'd learned in one of our tradecraft classes to memorise the titles and authors of the books, the date of the newspaper—which was today's date—and the denominations and strike dates of the kopeck coins.

I looked in each of the cubbyholes above the desk and discovered them empty.

It didn't surprise me to see a tiny portrait of General Secretary Stalin hung respectfully above the desk. Instinctively, I took hold of the picture and looked upon the reverse side. I detected a minuscule stencil of the number eight there.

I gently replaced our supreme leader's picture upon the wall. I hastily completed my mental inventory. There was also a calendar here—which showed this month—but it was for the following year of '37, not '36. Why was this? I thought it bizarre.

The walls of the room were flat concrete and painted green, except along the far side. Curiously, there were unfinished wooden beams standing from floor to ceiling, placed every metre there.

I walked over and confirmed that the construction comprised white plasterwork on the back wall in the room, and in between the beams. The floor was a bare dull grey coloured concrete. As far as I could see there were no other remarkable things about this room.

I guessed that there had to be more to this exam than met the eye, however to save time I concluded I had better record what I observed first. After I finished that task, I could use all remaining time to uncover the secrets of this place.

I placed my writing paper upon the desk, and I took a seat in the utilitarian chair to make my notes.

Except that I didn't get very far. The pencil turned out to be unsharpened.

"How could I be so stupid?" I angrily cursed myself under my breath.

I recalled Mr Kalagin's frequent warning:

"Expect the unexpected!"

I couldn't leave the room to ask for a replacement writing utensil, or my exam would be over. I needed to find something else to write with—and quickly!

I then looked in all six of the drawers on the sides of the desk again, hoping I'd missed something. They were all empty.

I stood up and walked to the door. I turned myself around and searched about the chamber again. I thought there must be something missing! I told myself it was time to clear my head and reset myself, as I had learned in my training here.

Stalin's Door

I spotted a small and recessed area on the wall that housed a light switch with a dull metal cover plate. I kicked myself for not noticing it earlier. Did this light switch control the electric lamp sitting on the desk? I reached over and depressed the switch. The room suddenly grew pitch dark. I pulled the switch upwards and the electric desk lamp came on again.

I then arrested myself.

"Wait. What was that?"

I flicked the switch again and waited until my eyes grew accustomed to the blackness. Over on the far side of the room, and in between two of the wooden beams, I saw what looked like the faintest sliver of light all the way from the floor to the ceiling. I could just make out the illumination from over on this side of the room, however I was certain it was there.

I kept the light switch off, and I made my way carefully over and examined it more closely. I placed my head gingerly between the beams and moved my eyes as close to the slit of light as I could. I was abruptly astounded. From the angle of my head, I could now see into the chamber that lay behind this one. I wondered if what I was looking at was part of the test. I found it hard to believe that anything I discovered here was by accident.

With nothing to make notes with, I stared as intently as I could, memorising all the contents in the other room.

Without warning, a deafening alarm coming from outside the door of this examination room filled my eardrums. The loud klaxon warned of a fire, and on instinct I sprinted for the door to escape.

Upon opening it, I was at once blinded and choked by thick black smoke. The smog seemed to be everywhere all at once, and all around me. Feeling temporarily stunned for a moment, I reached up to rub my eyes, which stung painfully from the hot fumes.

I sensed a hand grabbing my arm and yanking it forwards.

"Comrade Cadet! Quickly, come with me!" I caught the voice of Mr Kalagin yelling out.

I did not understand and felt frustrated as he ushered me hurriedly down the hall and into another room. As I heard the door slamming behind us, I tried to catch my breath. My chest ached from violent coughing. I tried to expel the noxious gas from my lungs.

I opened my eyes and discovered that this room was pitch dark too.

"Mister Kalagin, the fire! We must evacuate!" I pleaded with my instructor with all urgency.

"You're not going anywhere, Cadet Number Two! What did you see?"

I thought to myself that this was a terribly silly question under the circumstances.

"What did I see?" With the smoke still stinging my eyes and the klaxon alarm ringing urgently, I blurted out. "Sir! Why aren't we withdrawing?"

"What did you see, Cadet Number Two? Answer me at once!" Mr Kalagin barked into my ear.

"I couldn't make any notes, Sir!"

"Damn your notes! Let's take it from the top. Who are the authors of the three books? Think Cadet, think!"

"Malikov, Pomelnikov, and Bezborodov."

"What were the strike dates on the kopecks?"

"All were 'thirty-six, except for one which was 'thirty-three."

"What is General Secretary Stalin's number?"

"Eight."

"What year is it in the room?"

"If you go by the date on the newspaper, it's this year, however the calendar shows next year, 'thirty-seven."

"What is in the glass bottle?"

"A disinfectant. I don't know which kind."

"And that's everything then?"

"No, Sir! There was another room, I could see it from a slit in the wall."

"Describe what's in the other room. Quickly!"

I listed all the contents of the other chamber that I had spied on. I hoped I remembered it all correctly.

When I finished speaking, the lights in this room came on all at once without warning. The smoke from the fire was missing, and the fire klaxon had ceased.

As I re-focused my eyes, I saw Mr Kalagin standing beside me and grinning.

He now wore the uniform of a full colonel in the NKVD. I felt overwhelmed and taken by surprise. I could only think to salute as quickly as I could.

"Comrade Colonel!"

"I always told you to expect the unexpected, didn't I? Congratulations, Cadet Number One. You just passed your final examination."

Moskva
20 October 1936

The Government House was the location of my official duty station in our capital city, Moskva. Because I scored so well in Col Kalagin's examinations, they selected me for the NKVD Special Assignment Directorate—officially attached to the Five Hundred Seventeenth Regiment, Twelfth Special Installation Security Division.

The Government House was a vast square-blocks wide compound in the centre of the metropolis, on an enormous island in-between the forks of the city's river. The Government House lay about a kilometre away from the Moskva Kremlin and Red Square.

I learned that General Secretary Stalin commissioned the construction of this rezidentsiya especially for the elite within the Communist Party. The logic followed that by putting all the stars, and rising stars in one central location, it would then make it easier for the NKVD to keep tabs on hundreds of top government officials by watching, listening, and recording everything they did there.

Our supreme leader even made suggestions during the planning of the building, right down to the tiniest of details. The House of Secrets was the unofficial nickname the NKVD gave to the Government House, however for the residents who made it their home, they knew it as the House on the Embankment.

Comrade Stalin hand-selected each one of the building's residents from the Soviet ruling class. Crucially, this honour was unworthy of even the slightest consideration.

One never said no to Comrade Stalin—if you valued your health.

Living at the Government House became a terrific status symbol for the over 500 families that made their homes within the luxurious flats. The lavish amenities were plentiful, and the residences were spacious and modern—replete with all the latest appliances and conveniences. The Politburo furnished everything for their tenants. Provisions, entertainment, and transportation were liberal, which stood out in stark contrast to the shortages experienced by the ordinary Moskvichi.

Yet some that lived in comfort openly complained that it was akin to living inside a gilded cage. The regular Soviet army had an entire battalion of soldiers permanently stationed around the compound providing physical security. No one got into the Government House without authorisation—and conversely no one left there without approval either.

My daily commute to the Government House was a pleasant one from our kommunalka in the suburbs, located ten kilometres outside downtown Moskva. The new Moskva Metro had opened to great fanfare only 18 months prior, and I was lucky enough to take the Sokolnicheskaya line directly to the Dzerzhinskaya station, beneath Dzerzhinsky Square. The headquarters building of the NKVD, named the Lubyanka, was here too. From the Lubyanka it was a decent three point two kilometre walk over to the Government House.

Stalin's Door

My wife and I found that the move to Moskva took some getting used to. Our kommunalka, the ubiquitous communal flats that everyone but the elite lived in, were far less—private—than our quaint little cottage in the suburbs of Leningrad.

I never once heard Lera complain to me about it, however. They allocated us a small one room space on the sixth floor of our apartment building. We shared a kitchen and WC with five other families there.

At first, learning our place within the communal pecking order of the kommunalka was difficult for us. It felt alien. There were nuances and rituals to follow here. For instance, the joint use of pots and pans in the kitchen was universal, whilst mugs, glasses, and cutlery remained exclusive. Seniority within the kommunalka determined one's seating arrangements at the common table during mealtimes. We learned quickly and adapted to these new customs.

Because of my new duty schedule, eating breakfast was the only time I got to share with Lera.

I was delighted to see Lera as she stayed busy. She contributed by helping with the cooking and cleaning chores within the kommunalka kitchen. I know that the other younger women, who were less experienced than she was, were grateful to her for that.

Everyone was respectful towards us, especially when I was wearing my NKVD uniform.

Whenever we ate meals together, our fellow flatmates from the sixth floor showed natural curiosity about me, and so I fielded lots of questions about my work. Since the regulations forbade me to discuss the details of my assignment, I quickly went from polite deferral to inventing fanciful stories of my work.

I single-handedly defended our Union from a plethora of spies and saboteurs, and other anecdotes of extravagant heroics. These tall tales bore little relation to reality—but they made for some entertaining conversations.

A perplexing incident from this morning was still at the forefront of my mind. As I refreshed my tea at the coal-burning stove, after an excellent meal of hot kasha, I could see an older woman approach our communal table. I'd not seen this zhenshchina before and wondered if she was here to visit someone.

After a moment, I heard an eruption of raised voices.

"I don't know Madam Ipatyeva! But I wouldn't recommend bugging Lieutenant Komolov about it." Osip Yurievich from next door said, pleading with the stranger.

"Ask me what?" As I returned to the take my place at the end of the bench.

"I'm sure it's nothing, Lieutenant. This is Madam Ipatyeva who lives downstairs. She was just leaving us." Osip Yurievich glared now at the old woman and tried to push her away.

Mme Ipatyeva exploded in anger and came to face me directly.

"I will not! I will not leave until I have answers! You must tell me what happened to them!"

"Slow down there, kind woman. What is the matter? Please tell me what has upset you so." I did my best to defuse this escalating confrontation.

"It's my son and my daughter-in-law. I hadn't heard from them in over a week, so I went to visit their flat on the other side of the city last night. When I arrived, I found that someone had sealed the front door to their apartment shut with finishing nails and carpentry. A posted yellow bill signed by officers of the NKVD warned everyone never to enter."

"Oh, I see. Well, I regret I cannot help you in this matter."

"But you don't understand, Lieutenant! I asked my son's neighbours, and they said the secret police took them away some days ago. No one has seen them since. And my poor grandson, Rodya! The NKVD left him behind all alone. He's just an infant! The residents next door could hear him screaming and crying for three days, before he fell silent. My grandson is dead thanks to you!"

The poor woman then stormed out of the communal area and went back downstairs.

I tried to make some discrete inquiries with my fellow secret policemen, about how to trace the whereabouts of someone recently arrested.

They politely advised me not to carry on with such nonsense, and to concentrate on my assigned duties.

As the year wore on, I noticed that what was once innocent nosiness from our neighbours over breakfast turned into fear and contempt.

Fear of me personally. Fear of the uniform I wore. Lera and I found ourselves ostracised and then ignored completely.

§

Whenever I arrived at, and departed from the Government House, my commanders ordered me to only use the rear entrance to the compound, at No. 11, located down a blind alley. This covert ingress was for the exclusive use of the NKVD Special Assignment Directorate and was strictly out-of-bounds to all the residents.

A cover story circulated that this disused area would soon be under renovation. Those repairs never came to pass. The inhabitants learned quickly not to ask too many questions here.

My first post was inside an elite unit in the prestigious Alfa Company, comprising 20 two-man units. As there were over 500 apartments under surveillance here, the total number of NKVD officers assigned to the Government House exceeded 1,000 men—the equivalent of a full-strength regiment. We kept watch day and night, seven days a week. We never stopped—for any reason.

The master was the senior officer in each two-man unit and was in charge of the team, specifically instructing the junior officer, known as the student.

My first master was a youthful man, 26 years of age, named Lt Pervak. Recently promoted, he was already bucking for an elevation to the rank of senior lieutenant. A similar work ethic however did not match his ambition for advancement. Because of this, all the administrative duties fell upon me—as the student in training. Lt Pervak would invent elaborate excuses for dodging work and told me regularly that the extra jobs he assigned were appropriate for me.

When we were first introduced, he confessed I wasn't at all what he was expecting. I easily explained my disparate age was because of the 22 years of service in the Soviet navy. Lt Pervak told me he'd been in the NKVD for two years now, and that he had graduated from the OCS in Class No. 902, directly after finishing his studies at university.

The 24-hour surveillance the NKVD conducted on all of the flats within the House of Secrets meant we each took a 12-hour shift every day. Depending upon the circumstances, there might be a little overlap for training and educational purposes. Because I was the junior member of the squad, my master took the quieter 0000 hours to 1200 hours shift, which left me with the 1200 hours to 2400 hours duties. He reasoned that most of the action inside the flat took place during waking hours, and that I needed the surveillance practise. My inherent intuition told me that he was merely acting lazy, and that he just wanted the easier shift. It was of no consequence to me. I was cheerful and made no complaints.

For all Lt Pervak's ambitions within the service, his time management skills were abhorrent. I don't believe there was a single shift where he arrived to relieve me on time. On the other hand, I made it a point to always arrive at least a quarter hour early to spell him.

Our duty station inside the Government House was called the struchok, colloquially known within the surveillance squads as the pod. I accessed the pod via a system of hidden interior corridors riddled within the bowels of this enormous building. The pod was a compact chamber no larger than 16 square metres in size, built next to each of the flats here. Our pod was No. 137 because the NKVD assigned it to surveil flat No. 137. The pod sat directly behind the back corner of the flat's drawing room, concealed from detection by the residents.

I soon discovered that the architects conceived this pod system with the goal of observation right from the very beginning of the Government House's construction.

When I looked through special slats on the far wall of the pod, it provided me with an unobstructed view of the sizeable drawing room beyond. Behind the drawing room was the dining room, which I also had an unobstructed witness of.

Unique building materials in the walls of these flats amplified all conversations within towards the front of the pod. I could easily hear everything said in those two rooms with crystal clear acuity.

If extraordinary circumstances required it, the wall at the far end of the pod, facing the drawing room, could detach and open like a sliding door. Constructing it in this manner ensured that the NKVD would always have access to the apartment, no matter what obstructions the residents placed at their front doors.

Our commander strictly ordered us never to enter any apartment on our own, nor do anything that might give away our position within the pod. Doing so accidentally or deliberately, they explained, would tip off the residents that they were constantly being watched. Working by stealth was our prime directive here. Silence was as good as gold. While I highly doubted that the tenants knew of the existence of our surveillance system, I sometimes had to wonder. I observed curious behaviours from time to time.

But I'm getting ahead of myself.

Regrettably, I discovered that the architects of the House on the Embankment forgot to equip the pods with proper heating or ventilation. My shifts here to date in autumn didn't prove too cold for me. Now, with the onset of an early winter, I feared that the conditions within the pod would become miserable. Lt Pervak already informed me I just missed a stiflingly hot summer season.

My singular mission whilst on duty within the pod was to transcribe everything said by the family that lived in flat No. 137. I was also to record their movements, any visitors received, and their telephone conversations. We recorded it all—no matter how inconsequential.

The pod came equipped with a small work desk on which sat a tiny electric lamp. I doubted if the bulb was over 15 watts. It was dim. My eyes grew accustomed to the twilight-like conditions pretty rapidly, however. The logic was that I must keep all light to a minimum, accentuating my observations through the slats in the wall. We didn't want to give away our position with any illuminations that the residents inside the flat might detect.

Above the desk hung two small framed black and white photographs. On the traditional left side was General Secretary Stalin, our supreme leader. On the right side was the NKVD Commissar, Nikolai Ivanovich Yezhov.

Comrade Yezhov was just appointed to lead the secret police less than a month ago. A terrible scandal engulfed his predecessor, Genrikh Grigoryevich Yagoda, which deeply disappointed General Secretary Stalin in some fashion. The result was a demotion. Comrade Yagoda took over leadership of the People's Commissariat for Post and Telegraph.

The drawers of the desk inside the pod contained plenty of writing materials—pencils and erasers and such—blank typing paper and notebooks. A special typewriter sat front and centre atop the workspace with which to make my formal notes of all the activities and conversations within the flat.

My commander ordered me to file typed reports, which were due at the end of my shift—with no acceptable delay!

The NKVD senior leadership was most interested in any conversations that even hinted at disloyalty, or traitorous activities—but especially unfavourable utterances involving General Secretary Stalin, the Communist Party, or the Soviet Politburo.

We transcribed everything we observed and heard within the Government House, however it wasn't up to Alfa Company to interpret or judge. That job fell to the legion of NKVD analysts that dissected our daily reports into infinite details.

I was already proficient in using typewriters from my experiences serving in the Naval Inspector General's office. Even so, I noticed that the one I used in the pod was remarkably different. No matter how hard I depressed the keys, the mechanism remained utterly silent in its operation.

I noted the brand name: Krasnoperov, made in the city of Perm. This one became even more inaudible because they also removed the carriage-return bell. The machine represented a marvel of Soviet engineering!

Modern technology aside, I found that it was more expeditious to make my notes with a pencil and paper, and then transcribe them via the special typewriter at the end of my shift, once the family had gone to sleep for the night. The vast majority of activity within the flat took place between 1800 hours and 2200 hours.

I nicknamed one unique feature in the pod the panic button. There was an electric switch on the side of the work desk, that when flipped, signaled the regimental headquarters at entrance No. 11 of a dire emergency. My supervisors never explained what exact circumstances would legitimise its use. They provided no example conditions in which to follow. I discretely tried to inquire a few more times about it, before I was told to drop the matter.

For any good it would do anyway, I discovered that the walk along the back-room corridors from entrance No. 11 to our pod at flat No. 137 took me well over 15 minutes to complete. I considered myself reasonably fit, and estimated that even at full speed, someone would still need ten minutes to reach me.

If there really was a catastrophic emergency, I couldn't expect help with any true immediacy. I was on my own.

I began each shift by familiarising myself with whom I was surveilling within the flat. I opened the thin red-coloured origins file and scanned the formal biographical notes inside. The breadth of the family living in flat No. 137 was modest, compared with typical families in Moskva.

There was just a father, mother, daughter, and an older woman who was the aunt of the mother.

Kanadin Avksenty Yemelyanovich, aged 35, was the head of the household. He served as General Secretary Stalin's youngest commissar in the Sovnarkom and was chief of the People's Commissariat for Water Transportation. Commissar Kanadin's political loyalty index stood at 94%. The NKVD deemed him Party reliable, ambitious, and dedicated to the Revolution. Considered a rising star within the Communist Party, he was perhaps on a trajectory towards the Politburo. A studious and brilliant man, Commissar Kanadin held advanced degrees in engineering and management. His interests included going to the cinema and listening to classical music. Commissar Kanadin was incumbent in his current position since 01 July 1935.

Kanadina Aleksandra Vasilievna, aged 32, was the lady of the household. She frequently showed support for her husband and was a loyal wife. Mme Kanadina held no known political ambitions. Her guests reported hospitality and graciousness at regular reception-party functions. Considered an independent thinker, she rarely spoke in opposition to her husband. Mme Kanadina was engaged and supportive of her daughter's education and extra-curricular activities. She occasionally played the peacemaker between her husband and her aunt. Mme Kanadina married her husband on 21 June 1924.

    Kanadina Yevgeniya Avksentyevna, aged 11, was the daughter. She held the rank of Second Stage in the Young Pioneers. State standardised testing placed her within the exceptional range in intelligence. Observed as studious and serious. The NKVD flagged her politically as a potential. She had no siblings.

    Loskutnikova Nyura Victorovna, aged 64, was the aunt of Mme Kanadina. She recently moved in with the commissar and his family on 09 October 1936. Mme Loskutnikova's political loyalty index stood at 12%. The NKVD did not rate her as Party reliable. She'd been flagged as a suspected Anti-Communist White Movement sympathiser and known Tsarist. Her husband was the Tsar's Minister of Finance before the Great War and had died suddenly on 26 September 1936. She was stern and had a strict personality. She frequently picked fights with the commissar borne out of a previous conflict with the commissar's father.

    Feeling peckish, I put down my reading materials and took a quick break to investigate my dinner this afternoon.

    Lera always lovingly sent a sandwich, or some of the leftovers from the previous night's supper, with me to eat every day. My duties inside the pod prevented me from any opportunity of leaving for dinner or supper.

    Upon finishing dinner, I would habitually smoke one cigar, which was an indulgence I'd enjoyed for many years now. If it was an especially quiet day, I would think about the chess match with my uncle. We reverted to playing by post ever since I began my duty assignment in Moskva.

Moskva
13 November 1936

My shift this day would prove one of dominant interest to the NKVD analysts and interpreters. When they poured over the accounting presented at the end of my shift this evening, I was confident that the amount of intelligence gathered would keep them busy for weeks to come.

The family I was surveilling from the pod in flat No. 137 was hosting a fancy reception-party tonight, for crucial government officials. Commissar Kanadin invited a veritable laundry list of the Soviet elite to visit. Central Committee Party leaders, fellow commissars, generals, and admirals would all be in attendance. My daily briefings this week detailed all the planning that had already occurred, with the lion's share of the work falling to the commissar's wife, Mme Kanadina, to oversee.

That afternoon I watched as deliverymen brought supplementary tables on which expensive looking tablecloths were unfolded. Wooden folding chairs from the carpentry shop in the basement provided extra places to sit for their guests. The seats looked freshly painted in white.

I observed an amount of prepared food, dispatched from the restaurants and bistros on the ground floor, appear with such consistency that I feared everyone else in the House of Secrets would surely starve this evening! These appetisers, warmed from silver cans lighted from beneath, could feed an army. The baked goods, finger foods, and hors d'oeuvres smelled delicious.

Yes, I inhaled their heavenly aromas even from my hidden position within the pod. My mouth was watering. Oh, what I would do for just a nibble! One principal delivery then turned up that I knew would guarantee a successful reception-party. Sweaty looking porters hauled six enormous cases of quality vodka up three flights and deposited them upon the floor in the drawing room with a resounding thud. With that volume of lubrication available, this would be a night to remember!

Mme Kanadina supervised all of this preparation with a never-ending look of worry upon her face. She even enlisted the help of her studious adolescent daughter, Yevgeniya. They were rushing about the apartment—in every which way imaginable—making certain that everything was perfect, and shipshape.

When I spoke with my shift commander about the reception-party for tonight, he gave me a special briefing on what to pay attention to, and how to make sure I could identify everyone that attended. It was key that I properly recorded all the names and ranks of the guests and not to overlook anything said.

To ensure the Special Assignment Directorate didn't miss bugger all this evening, I would require help. The bosses ordered my master, Lt Pervak, to report hours before his regular shift started, to assist me—a fact that he bemoaned for the entire night. Another man on temporary duty, Jr Lt Andryukhin, also joined us for this extraordinary occasion. One thing was certain, the space within the pod became quite cramped.

To help us with the identifications of all the visitors, they gave us an enormously overstuffed red binder. This document case contained the names and ranks of important Communist Party officials, along with a current black-and-white photograph and a brief biography.

For the identities of the guest's spouses, they instructed us to watch who stood by whom—and to make logical deductions.

To properly attribute who was speaking in the hundreds of conversations that would take place tonight, it was vital to match names with faces. I felt terribly worried I might miss something significant. If the Special Assignment Directorate assigned 20 additional officers this evening, I knew it would not be enough to get the job done!

The bosses informed us that the pod attached to flat No. 140 was also watching all the guests tonight, because Lt General Strelnikov and his wife were co-hosts of the reception-party. The men and women visiting this evening would float back and forth between the two flats all night long.

Because of the technical difficulty level of tonight's assignment, the shift commander naturally added a little extra incentive for us—to keep things sporting. The NKVD analysts would judge the formal reports from pods No. 137 and No. 140 on this night's activities, and the one deemed to be the most replete in intelligence would win their team a special achievement medal to commemorate the victory.

The pressure was surely on, however I knew our squad would be victorious!

John St. Clair

§

After five hours of intense surveillance, the reception-party showed no signs of abatement. Our triumvirate working inside the pod was nearing the point of pure exhaustion. The furious pace of jotting down notes, which recorded the infinite number of conversations this evening, seemed to fly by as if in a blur.

When two of us were at the front of the pod performing our observations, the third member of the squad tonight would flip through the heavy photographic binder hoping to match faces with names.

One guest at the reception-party tonight I recognised immediately! It was the man from Leningrad who set me upon the path I followed today— Admiral Krayevsky! He was engaged in a serious conversation with Commissar Kanadin.

I hadn't seen the admiral since our fateful meeting earlier this year in the office of my old captain. I took notice that he now wore the rank of a four-star admiral, which had meant promotion and command of the entire Baltic Fleet. This prestigious position was a gargantuan responsibility. The commissar spoke with the admiral for many minutes and it appeared to become heated and distressed.

The commissar was motioning with his hands fervently, whilst the admiral kept his poise and tried desperately to calm the commissar down. I wished I had the ability to pick up the entirety of their spirited exchange. I caught bits and pieces and made my notes frantically.

What I overheard for certain made no sense to me. Words like: cage, dangerous, uncoöperative, succession, and fantasy. Alas, it wasn't our job to interpret—that was for the multitude of our NKVD analysts to complete. I thought for a moment that the argument might come to blows until the commissar regained his composure and called over his daughter Yevgeniya for a formal introduction to the admiral.

Whenever we came across a positive match within the binder, we all observed a silent show of unity. Our trio would simultaneously lift a clenched fist skyward, signaling a victory. Our prime directive was to keep mum and undetected whilst we performed our duties.

However, truth be told, even if we had our own little reception-party inside the pod and made an excessive amount of racket, it likely wouldn't have mattered. For the noise level within the drawing room and dining room inside the apartment was at such an uproarious level that nothing we did in here mattered.

The copious amounts of vodka being consumed turned the normally stuffy and serious senior leadership of the Communist Party into outright hooligans. There were waves of long songs sung at the top of their lungs. The laughing, cackling, and shouting of the guests drowned out the patriotic themed music playing on the wireless receiver. It had become nearly impossible to even hear a coherent word spoken, and all the inappropriate behaviour I witnessed from grown men, who should know better, absolutely embarrassed me.

Men that couldn't hold their liquour were acting rudely and stirring up trouble. Some lay passed out on the couches, whilst yet others were drinking everything in sight and starting arguments. The reception-party had gone from cheerful drunkenness to infuriation and intoxication. Many of the wives appeared absolutely mortified by their husband's rude behaviour this evening. We noted the names of the troublemakers and were more than delighted to do our duty by reporting them to our higher-ups.

Since it was now after 2400 hours, my master Lt Pervak noted with great derision that his day was just beginning. But just like the lieutenant who had to come in early to start his shift, I couldn't leave now, just because my shift was technically over. Not by a long shot. The reception-party was far from finished, and I still had the honour of typing up the formal report. I wouldn't be leaving for hours yet.

I had barely started my typing at the desk, with Lt Pervak compiling all of our notes, when we both heard Jr Lt Andryukhin shout out.

"Holy shit! You'll never guess who just walked in!"

This outburst was uncharacteristic of him. Before I could admonish his carelessness, total silence reigned from within the flat—where there had been a deafening din not a moment before. My master and I both rushed to the wall at the front of the pod to peer inside the apartment.

A man of insignificant height, wearing an off-white colour military tunic, stood in the middle of the drawing room. His distinctive jacket, buttoned to the top, sported large breast pockets and a wide turned-down collar. The fellow wore dark trousers and brown riding boots. His black hair and even blacker bushy mustache were instantly recognisable.

General Secretary Stalin himself was standing practically in front of us with his contingent of towering bodyguards, dressed in leather trench coats the colour of coal.

Lt Pervak placed his index finger perpendicular to his lips and motioned for the junior lieutenant and me to join him at the work desk—immediately!

The lieutenant grabbed a blank piece of paper and wrote three words with his pencil, as quickly and as quietly as he could:

Red Notice Protocol

I had never seen or heard of a Red Notice Protocol being invoked before now. In fact, it was so rare that it took me a moment to recall what it commanded us to do.

In a nutshell, the NKVD commanders put out a standing order that if we ever came across General Secretary Stalin in performance of our duties, we were to not record that evidence under any circumstances. We must not acknowledge his presence in our notes, nor were we to transcribe the conversations of anything he might say. It would be as if a ghost appeared at the reception-party and we couldn't see or hear him. We all nodded in agreement and stopped our recorded surveillance, for as long as our supreme leader was inside the flat.

The Red Notice Protocol didn't forbid us from watching, however, and this is exactly what we did for the next few minutes.

General Secretary Stalin engaged Commissar Kanadin about some kind of emergency transpiring at his commissariat.

Commissar Kanadin looked as white as a sheet when he spoke to the general secretary, and no one else in the room dared utter a word out of turn.

Within a moment's time, the commissar appeared to be frantically making his way to the front door without even grabbing his hat and coat first. Many of the guests followed suit.

General Secretary Stalin then said his goodbyes to the lady of the household and departed just as quickly as he'd come. And with that, we saw the conclusion of the reception-party. A quick time after, only Mme Kanadina and her daughter remained in the flat, with quite the mess to clean up.

It was the most bizarre thing I'd ever witnessed in my service in the NKVD, and we couldn't report a word of it to anyone!

Moskva
23 November 1937

On the final Tuesday of every month, I reported to the NKVD headquarters at the Lubyanka to brief our deputy battalion commander. The Lubyanka was a stately neo-baroque building that served as the principal offices for an insurance company during the time of the Tsar. During the Revolution, the Soviet secret police—then known as the Cheka—had seized it for their de facto HQ. The premises sat centre in Dzerzhinsky Square and was a respectable three point two kilometre walk from my duty station at the Government House.

On days when the weather was pleasurable, the sojourn over felt especially good. I relished the fresh air and sun—a luxury that 12 hours a day inside the pod could not provide. Invariably, I'd find some excuse to extend my stroll. But this was not one of those days. The conditions outside were cold and mauling on this late autumn day. I hurried with utmost efficiency, making the journey in fewer than 30 minutes. Thankfully, the thick wool in my greatcoat kept the howling winds somewhat at bay.

This meeting took place in the morning before my shift began at the Government House, ensuring a protracted day for me.

The once cavernous offices inside the Lubyanka were now bursting at the seams with personnel and activities in these hectic days. NKVD officers and support staff were practically working on top of one another in departments that had become cramped and uncomfortable. It was now a rarity to find anyone with an office just to themselves.

To conserve capital expenses, they had not turned the central heating units on for the season—which made for drafty hallways and chilly workrooms. Because I was wearing my dress uniform today for inspection and debriefing, I felt comfortable.

Per the standing orders of our leader, all business conducted within HQ were to be by the book and formal. Comrade Commissar Yezhov expected all officers to comport themselves accordingly. The commissar's toady senior staff would sulk about the place, meting out on-the-spot fines and levying poppycock punishments for even the slightest rules infraction—real and imagined. Therefore, I ensured my appearances at HQ were always shipshape.

The bureaucracy here reigned supreme.

At precisely 1000 hours, I found myself inside Major Chupalov's fourth floor office. I stood at attention before him, as I heard the door behind me close. The major had just transferred in from the NKVD Corrections and Labour Camps Directorate only two weeks ago. Today was our first meeting in person.

"Please, please sit down, Lieutenant Komolov."

The major was younger in age than me, as almost everyone was in the service. He took a slight double take and stared at my face, before he returned his attention to the prodigious amount of paperwork that lay upon his desk.

I saw the major's workspace had no more room left. It was overflowing with folders, briefs, reports, and other assorted pieces of paper. We seemed to drown in it these days. I sat down in his office guest chair, after gently removing a large stack of documents by placing them upon the floor.

The major started right into our meeting, skipping any pretense of formal introductions.

"Yes, I was just catching up on all the recent reports. I must confess, Lieutenant, I've become entirely fond of reading yours. Your daily transcriptions are always complete with all the requisite details, and they're well written too.

"Oh, and before I forget, let me offer you my congratulations on your promotion last quarter! As you can see, this directorate values attention to detail and dedication. Qualities that you have in abundance."

The major then took notice of my service ribbon board on the left side of my dress uniform—focusing for a few seconds on the new medal featured prominently in its centre. He pointed to it with a look of jealousy in his eyes.

"That's quite an achievement, Lieutenant. Well done!"

"Thank you, Comrade Major."

I received the award at the start of this year for my outstanding performance that night Commissar Kanadin, and his wife, hosted the reception-party at flat No. 137 back in '36. The same one in which General Secretary Stalin had made a surprise appearance at the end. Per the regulations, I wasn't able to include that last part in the briefing.

My work at the Government House had been demanding, and commensurate with my promotion, I was now the master within pod No. 137.

For the last three months I was breaking in a new junior lieutenant as my student.

Because I had become accustomed to it, I kept the 1200 hours to 2400 hours shift for myself. Besides—the bulk of the activities inside the flat transpired in that timeframe, and I frankly didn't think my brand-new apprentice was up for their technical demands yet.

"Your station at the Government House—it's been just over a year now, yes?"

"Da, Comrade Major."

Most of our meeting then focused on Commissar Kanadin. The major asked pointed and directed questions, probing around the subjects of loyalty and dissent. Everyone these days seemed to walk on eggshells, not wanting to draw any accusations related to one's devotion to our Communist State or General Secretary Stalin.

Our briefing took just over the allotted time of one hour. We ended with some small talk, and truthfully I was just looking forward to getting back to my regular work.

"Oh, Lieutenant, I nearly forgot to tell you. We're a few men short for staffing the troikas today. I'll need you to report at once to Senior Lieutenant Rokossovsky downstairs. Young Lukyan Igorevich just outside my office can direct you there."

I shuddered at the thought of this temporary assignment and did all I could to relieve myself from it.

"Pardon me, Comrade Major. I'm expected over at the Government House to start my duties in less than an hour."

"Yes, yes, I am aware. But don't worry Lieutenant, I already telephoned your shift commander and got you excused for the day."

The major then returned his attention to his paperwork, which signaled the adjournment of the meeting. I was positive that my student would hop mad when he found out he'd have to serve a double shift in the pod today. I wouldn't have it any easier here, however.

The troikas that the major referred to were a new institution implemented by the NKVD this past July. The number of cases related to violations of Article No. 58, specifically counter-revolutionary activities, had absolutely exploded in volume over the last few months. Hundreds of people daily were being arrested for crimes ranging from the petty to the extreme—in a paroxysm of terror.

To expedite these legal proceedings, the NKVD convened an exclusive special court at the Lubyanka. By decree, the defendants—these saboteurs and wreckers—did not receive any statutory aid. A presumption of guilt hung around their necks, like an albatross. These trials were merely a formality in our justice system. The word troika meant a group of three. These were the number of NKVD officers required for each hearing. I'd be sitting in on the troika today as one of those officers.

Some 20 minutes after having left the briefing in the major's office, I waited impatiently on the first basement level of the Lubyanka, outside the designated room as ordered. The environment smelled musty down here, and I wasn't looking forward to this departure from my routine. A modest sign covered with brown rust hung in the middle of the heavy steel door.

No. 22
NKVD SPECIAL COURT
MAINTAIN SILENCE

A lanky uniformed man rapidly approached me from down the hallway. I presumed it had to be Sr Lt Rokossovsky. To my astonishment, and considering we were in the HQ of our agency, his arrival did not impress me. I couldn't help but notice the terrible wrinkles in the man's uniform, and his overall slovenly appearance. This was not at all up to our usual lofty standards.

The senior lieutenant's hands waved back and forth manically, and the blood vessels in his eyes were notably red and irritated. His neck and cheeks contained fresh nicks from a recent shave, one in which he'd attempted to clot with tiny pieces of loo roll.

"Lieutenant Komolov, good. You're not late. Here, take this and put it on."

The senior lieutenant handed me a black armband.

"What exactly am I to do here, Sir?" I felt eager for a crash course on my duties for today.

The senior lieutenant studied the special assignment badge on my uniform, below my medal board. He then snorted at me derisively.

"Don't worry, Comrade. Just follow my lead. But by all means, say nothing. The judge major is a hard ass. Don't cross him. Understand me?"

After I fumbled about for a few seconds with the new uniform apparatus, the senior lieutenant lost his patience. He huffed noisily.

"Hang on, I'll do it for you."

He then curtly grabbed the black armband and started adjusting it on my left bicep.

When the senior lieutenant stood in close to me, a shocking sensation flooded throughout my body. In all of his exaggerated ministrations, I definitely caught the strong whiff of an alarming odour.

Stalin's Door

"Excuse me, Comrade?" I made sure I had his full attention as I whispered. "Is that alcohol I smell on your breath?"

Sr Lt Rokossovsky turned and chuckled. I could see within his eyes however that he held me in contempt for even asking such a daring question.

"Did you expect we perform this obligation soberly? Listen, you incompetent fool. You idiots in the Special Assignment Directorate have it so easy, don't you? Do you honestly have any idea what we do over here? Well, you're about to find out. Get the hell in there you psikh!"

He then pushed me hard in my back, ushering me into the courtroom.

I stepped into the cramped and windowless room, constructed with unfinished grey cinder blocks. A long black table with three metal chairs sat along the far wall directly in front of us. In the exact centre of the room stood a lone aluminum chair. Heavy metal bolts affixed to its feet kept it securely in place upon the dusty concrete. Holes drilled right through the seat led to a small drain below, recessed into the floor.

My eyes squinted from the harsh electric light bathing the chamber. Overhead, large mercury-vapour lamps hung from the low ceiling, radiating out a painful glow.

On the table I noticed metal ashtrays at every corner, with a full carafe of water sitting in the middle. There were various administrative items here—pens, blotters, pencils, and a single small ornate brass call bell. Along one side in the room stood a stout ashcan made of tin. Next to that was an industrial centrifugal fan—which was not operating. The requisite black-and-white photograph of General Secretary Stalin hung on the wall behind the table, with Comrade Commissar Yezhov next to him. The ventilation was poor in here. Everything felt stuffy.

The excessive humidity had nowhere to discharge, and the concrete masonry in the walls almost seemed to drip with sweat. I truly hoped this temporary assignment would be brief. This was a miserable place.

A member of the NKVD administrative staff sat in the room's corner, with her hands at a stenography machine hastily making adjustments to the clunky apparatus. She did not acknowledge our presence.

The senior lieutenant trudged behind the table and stood at his seat —on the right. He then pointed at my seat on the far left. I stepped over and remained standing just as he did. The middle chair remained empty.

"What now, Comrade?" I inquired.

"Judge Major Maksimushkin will arrive in a moment. Be quiet."

After a few moments of waiting nervously, two more uniformed men joined us in the courtroom.

The first was a short man, who was the leader of our troika. The judge major's face held a demeanour as if he'd just drank sour milk—he didn't look at all physically well. His rounded eyeglasses were commonplace, except for the shaded right eyepiece. He sported a bright red armband upon his left bicep, and his dress uniform looked freshly pressed and impeccable.

Trailing behind the judge major was a sergeant from the national police service, who I presumed served as his administrative aide. The sergeant pulled a wooden cart containing an excessive amount of overflowing bound papers inside black-coloured sleeves. There were dozens and dozens— perhaps hundreds?

The administrative aide parked the waggon next to our table and retrieved the first batch of documents, placing them directly in front of me. He then stepped discretely away, standing to the side.

Stalin's Door

The judge major seated himself between the senior lieutenant and me. Retrieving a cigarette from a thin white ceramic case from inside his jacket, he lit up. As he extinguished the matchstick in a violent shaking motion, he commanded us.

"You may sit now, gentlemen."

We promptly settled ourselves. When I pulled in my chair, I heard a loud scraping sound on the hard, dirty floor that echoed all around this dismal space.

Sr Lt Rokossovsky wasted no time copying the judge major's smoking habit—to excess. He made it a point to always light up his next coffin nail before the conclusion of his current one. I wondered how many packets he carried upon his person. A dense white fog soon hung over the table, refracting in the jarring electric glare.

The judge major took out a silver pocket watch, opened it, and placed it in front of him. The ornate chain of the timepiece pooled neatly to the side. He then snapped his fingers. After a few seconds had passed, he turned his head to the left and glared.

"Well, Lieutenant? I'm waiting on you."

Thankfully, the sergeant standing behind me realised my plight. He leaned over to whisper into my ear, in assistance.

"You take the case folder from the top of the stack, peruse the charges rapidly, and then sign at the bottom. You then give it to the judge major."

I acted immediately on the sergeant's advice. I removed several bound sheets of neatly typed beige paper from the first black-coloured sleeve. Inside I studied the meticulous documentation regarding the accusation, arrest, and interrogation of a man who appeared to be an ordinary Moskvichi.

Suddenly, a gruff voice to my right rudely interrupted me.

"How long shall I linger for the wonderful weather by the sea, Lieutenant? I have a full docket today. Speed things along, if you please!"

I signed on the bottom dotted line, as the first troika witness. I then slid over the folder to the exasperated judge major. I felt a temporary relief then come over me.

"Now we may finally begin." The judge major grumbled.

He took the palm of his hand and smacked the top of the brass call bell firmly. A mellifluous timbre rang all about, echoing for many seconds inside the cramped chamber. In the pit of my stomach, a pain replaced my temporary respite. I experienced a grim feeling for what was about to happen.

The heavy steel door opened rapidly, and a civilian man dressed in simple clothes appeared. The fellow wore bulky iron handcuffs upon his wrists, which pinned his hands to his rumpled jacket.

Plodding behind were his escorts, two national police service guards, who each held the rank of corporal.

The prisoner looked terrified as they directed him to sit down in the aluminum chair—in the centre of the room. One of the bright lights affixed in the ceiling shone straight onto his grimacing, wrinkled face. The thick cloud of cigarette vapour now drifted over to the fellow like a gloomy incoming tide.

The prisoner's companions stood discreetly at the rear of the room, their expressions blank and emotionless—like automatons. The man's fists didn't escape my notice, as they clenched and unclenched incessantly within his lap. The fear radiating from this individual was utterly palpable.

I noted that sweat was dripping profusely from the fellow's temples. His ears were the colour of coppery red beets.

Judge Major Maksimushkin then started in with his ruling, with no hesitation. His voice was powerful and unwavering.

"This court affirms that—" He glanced down at the open folder. "—that Polichev Leontiy Yanovich receive a sentence of death for high treason and other violations of article number fifty-eight."

The judge major continued, almost as if he had repeated this same verdict countless times before.

"This judgement is absolute. You have no entitlement of appeal. We shall implement the decision with immediate effect. I discharge you. Guards, you may remand the convicted to the termination cell forthwith."

The judge major signed his name at the bottom of the papers and slid them over for the senior lieutenant to sign.

I affixed my eyes on the prisoner as the judge major read out the adjudication. The fellow held his head downwards the entire time.

When the pronouncement of his death sentence came, the convict exhaled loudly and let out an ear-piercing screeching cry that I was not expecting. In a fit of sheer panic, the newly convicted man lost control of his bladder, revealing the need for the pre-drilled holes in the chair's seat, and the drain built into the floor below. The prisoner's guards quickly dragged the doomed fellow out of the room whilst his legs flailed wildly about in protest.

"Next!" The judge major bellowed as he hit the call bell.

I grabbed the succeeding folder from the stack and continued a process that would repeat itself ad nauseam.

I studied the defendant's information contained within these black folders, using as much time as I thought I could get away with. I had to read and digest everything within rapidly because I didn't have much more than a moment or two with each document—before I had to sign and pass them along. Bureaucracies bred quotas, and these quotas had voracious appetites.

Curiously, in all the proceedings, the same pre-typed NKVD forms appeared inside detailing the arrests and interrogations, yet they recorded only the briefest of details into their accusations—the crimes committed against the Communist State. Without fail they always prominently documented the paramount piece of evidence, the signature of the defendant admitting to their guilt.

In four of the folders, I noticed something perplexing. The endorsement of the defendant was conspicuously missing. This omission of guilt irritated their interrogators to no end. Not confessing wouldn't save them, however. The same homogenous death sentence was inevitable.

In eight of the folders, I discovered something so preposterous I couldn't fathom any reason for it. In the section that recorded the felony of the defendant, a blank space remained, yet it still included a signature declaring their guilt at the bottom of the page. To what exactly the accused were admitting to confused me.

I presumed someone would type their high crimes and misdemeanors into the forms at a later date of the NKVD's choosing. Or maybe not at all.

If there was one common thread all the cases in this troika shared, it was the impossibly brief timeline from arrest, until the sentence of death. Rarely did this measure over 48 hours.

I also observed that the apprehended hailed from all walks of life in society. There were bakers, teachers, poets, writers, factory workers, accountants, nannies, nurses, cobblers, middle managers, tram drivers, firemen, jewelers, midwives, office clerks, and pipelayers.

How in the world Moskva could have so many wreckers and saboteurs working against the Communist State baffled me. It defied all logic. I shook my head in utter disbelief.

After six hours of slogging through the bulk of the proceedings—perhaps 100 cases—the judge major called for a much-needed recess.

During this time, the administrative woman handling the stenography machine in the room's corner attentively refreshed the carafe of water on our table and emptied all the ashtrays. She also refilled the paper rolls onto her apparatus and examined the transcriptions for errors.

I pondered why she flatly refused to acknowledge any of us, or even look us in the eyes. Sr Lt Rokossovsky stood up from his seat and stretched his legs. He then performed an impromptu calisthenics drill. I heard his shallow breathing—heavy and deliberate—and chuckled at the absurdity of the lit cigarette dangling from his lips.

Judge Major Maksimushkin didn't get up from his chair and seemed to concentrate on something important, staring blankly into space and blinking his eyes rapidly. Suddenly he was conscious of his surroundings and extinguished his cigarette. The judge major reached for another matchstick. He angrily barked out an order to the woman in the corner.

"Irisha Rostislavovna, get that damned fan operating! I can't even breathe in here." The judge major turned and shouted to his assistant. "Comrade Sergeant! Prop that door open!"

The silent woman hurried over to the centrifugal poklonnik and knelt down beside it. She adjusted the controls, and I watched as her hands trembled and fumbled about. Soon after, the hulking machine came to life and provided us with a surfeit of blowing air. The judge major's aide held the heavy steel door ajar. The stale cigarette smoke dissipated from the room after a brief time.

I sensed an opportunity to understand what was really going on here, so I engaged my superior with a question.

"Excuse me, Comrade Major?"

"Yes, what could you possibly need now, Lieutenant?"

The judge major stared at me with an expression of supreme irritation upon his face, for even bothering him in conversation.

"Pardon me for inquiring, Sir. This is my first time that I've served on a troika. Could you please advise me? Is every citizen guilty of these terrible crimes of which they're accused?"

Judge Major Maksimushkin appeared incredulous.

"Yes, of course they are. They wouldn't be here if they weren't culpable, would they? Plus, they—" His voice trailed off for a moment and he sat quiescent. "Well, most of them signed a confession, didn't they?"

The judge major now looked perturbed with me again.

"I'll give you a bit of advice for the future, Lieutenant." He drew a deep drag from his cigarette and then deliberately exhaled a prodigious amount of smoke directly into my face. "Mind your business!"

After our break concluded, the proceedings resumed. The sergeant now took several distinctive thick gold-coloured folders from the cart and placed them in front of me. Upon opening the initial one, I noted these documents were officially stamped with the following words along the top of each page:

HIGH VALUE INTERROGATION DETAINEE

These new cases were obviously unlike the civilian ones in the black-coloured folders from before.

These indictments contained extensive formal documentation on each prisoner. Each one had a full dossier, which comprised photographs of the captive, and a complete biographical history. The descriptions of the crimes committed by each one of the accused were replete with details—down to the nth degree.

Fully typed transcripts of the prisoner's interrogations and everything spoken within stretched on for dozens of pages. Protracted timelines existed between the arrest of these detainees and their troikas, sometimes on the order of months. These so-called HVIDs came from the highest military ranks, or they were executives at Soviet state-run companies —senior managers, or the equivalents.

I realised their interrogators spent a substantial amount of time and effort to extract an admission of guilt—no matter how long that process took. In 100 percent of these cases, the deposition included a signed confession from the prisoner. Special enclosed notes stipulated that new physical methods of influence were now authorised. I shuddered, imagining what horrible tortures these novel techniques entailed.

These fresh batches of prisoners came and went as before, the only sizeable difference being that the judge major took time to go into greater detail of their crimes in the sentencing phase. I noticed that the general physical demeanour and appearance of each of these detainees was markedly for the worse, after having been in custody for some time.

When there were no more folders to process, I naïvely thought we had finally finished for the day.

The judge major ordered the attention of the senior lieutenant and me.

"Be cheerful, gentlemen. We've almost completed our duty. There's just one more adjudication for this evening, comrades."

Judge Major Maksimushkin hit the call bell thrice now. The heavy steel door then opened, and I watched as the just sentenced convict, from what would be our penultimate trial, make his way for the exit with his police escort in tow.

I felt astonished as I watched our final detainee for the day enter the room. He was wearing an NKVD uniform! This was most unusual. As the two prisoners passed each other in the doorway, the condemned man from a moment ago couldn't help but take note too. In a proud yet derisive manner, he exclaimed something.

"Well, well. Even in this hellhole the damned jackals devour one of their own!"

The police guard, annoyed at this delay, then struck the newly convicted prisoner roughly over the head with the butt of his rifle. A shriek of pain rang out and they quickly exited the courtroom.

Everyone in the chamber could not help but notice that this final captive was struggling to stand up. His two guards all but carried him over to the lone aluminum chair. The prisoner kept his head lowered into his chest the entire time, and it wasn't easy to get a proper look at his face.

Nevertheless, the fellow was quite the sight to behold. Jarring electric illumination revealed his immaculate uniform, replete with all the accoutrements of a senior colonel in our directorate.

The man then let out an audible moan as they shoved him down onto the metal seat. While the prisoner's attire looked pristine, the condition of the body wearing it was far from perfect.

Before any of this could sink into my brain, I watched the judge major suddenly bolt upright from the table. I wasted no time in following suit, standing rigidly at attention. The senior lieutenant nearly spilled water over himself as he rose from his chair too.

A trio of colonels from the NKVD entered the room all at once. They ensconced themselves in the back of the chamber behind us, with their collective gazes firmly affixed on the prisoner.

They seemed to converse amongst themselves and paid no attention to our troika. The sergeant then walked over to the senior officers and retrieved a thick, bright red folder from one colonel. The sergeant hustled back over to me and handed over this special documentation.

Judge Major Maksimushkin looked over to the colonel who had carried in the crimson folder—for his approval. The senior officer nodded at him subtly. The judge major took his seat again, and the senior lieutenant and I then followed.

I opened the cover to this exceptional file. Revealed was an overabundance of typed beige paperwork, which had to be ten centimetres thick. The black-and-white photograph at the front of the dossier showed a dark-haired, good looking man who appeared to be about my own age.

The prisoner's name was NKVD Sr Col Tredyakovsky—one of the most experienced leaders we had—and a rising star within the Soviet state security directorate. This same person mysteriously disappeared six months ago and was the subject of rampant rumours and speculation. Some said he spied for the Germans, and that he'd defected. Others insisted that was impossible because Comrade Commissar Yezhov had chosen him for promotion to major general, which was a magnificent honour.

My own colleagues almost convinced me his vanishing was the result of some secret mission he'd been sent on.

Predictably, our commanders hushed everything up, and the colonel's office at the Lubyanka remained untouched to this day.

When his family turned up missing too, no one knew what to believe any longer. I immediately sensed the gravity of the situation, so I quickly signed at the bottom of the form as required and handed the bulky folder over to the judge major.

Taking advantage of the respite, I now examined the pitiful prisoner seated in front of us. The senior colonel looked pathetic and weak. With his head still lowered into his chest, I could see that his hair colour was bright white—which was a far cry from what I had seen in the photograph from his dossier. I studied his hands—swollen and gnarled—as they shook within their handcuffs.

After a signal from the judge major, one guard standing behind the senior colonel took his hand and slapped the back of the prisoner's skull brutally. As the senior colonel raised his head up slowly in response, I overheard a blood-curdling scream coming from the room's corner.

I quickly turned to see the administrative woman pointing her index finger at the captive's face. She shrieked for many seconds in utter horror.

I returned my gaze over to the senior colonel. An ill-fitted uniform covered his emaciated pale-grey body, now several measurements too big.

He'd lost a tremendous amount of weight during his disappearance. Bloody cracked teeth were all that remained within his swollen mouth, as he struggled to speak.

Most shocking of all were the dark black hollow spaces where healthy eyes should have resided. His eye sockets were empty—the eyeballs gouged out.

I sat in astonished silence. I couldn't understand how this person was even still alive. If his face and hands had endured this much trauma, the rest of his body must have been in dreadful shape.

"Order! I will have order inside this courtroom! Irisha Rostislavovna, you're dismissed!" The judge major barked. The poor woman was almost delirious—now sobbing. "Sergeant, take over the stenography machine at once."

After waiting a moment for the room to settle, the judge major cleared his throat, looked at the red folder, and began speaking.

"This court declares that Senior Colonel—" The judge major abruptly caught himself. "—correction, Citizen—"

I observed that in these desperate days, filled with terror and torture, the filthiest insult imaginable was addressing anyone in the military by the title of citizen—instead of loyal comrade.

"—Citizen Tredyakovsky Matvey Semyonovich confessed to the following violations of article number fifty-eight, which I shall read out for the official record. Wrecking crimes, fomenting anti-Communist insurrections, right-Trotskyite activities, counter-revolutionary agitation, spying for the German State, and most notably, plotting to assassinate General Secretary Stalin. This court affirms that Citizen Tredyakovsky receive a sentence of death. This judgement is absolute. You have no entitlement of—"

Suddenly an intense outcry that emanated from the prisoner cut off the judge major in mid-sentence. Everyone in the room appeared momentarily frozen at the disruption.

A tirade from the disgraced senior colonel quickly followed.

"I am trickily fucked then, yes? Bastards! You're all useless pussies!"

The convict then let loose with a string of feculent profanities the likes of which shocked even me. In all my years having served in the Soviet navy, I'd never heard such sordid language.

The judge major interrupted and tried to re-establish order, pounding his fists rapidly upon the metal table.

"Silence! This tribunal will have discipline! I will tolerate no further outbursts from the prisoner! Guards, restrain that man!"

"Go ahead! There's nothing more you can do to me." The broken man, broken in body but not in spirit, interjected.

One of the NKVD colonels standing behind us started laughing maniacally. The chamber grew deathly silent again. This colonel, who was at one time a deputy to the man in the chair, shouted out to him.

"You fucking traitor!" He then spat on the floor. "What I find impossible to reconcile, Matvey Semyonovich, is that you're not even sorry for your betrayal against General Secretary Stalin!"

"Oh, I say, is that Eugeni Nikitovich in here with us? I'm surprised you had the guts to be here in person. Well, you're in for a surprise, my friend." The goner tried to turn his head in the direction that he heard the colonel speaking from. "Listen to me carefully. Can you hear me?" I watched as the man's shackled hands rested just beneath where his eyes used to be. "I have no more tears to give you."

The judge major then swiftly completed his pronouncement of capital punishment.

"This judgement is absolute. You have no entitlement of appeal. We shall implement the decision with immediate effect. I discharge you. Guards, you may remand the convicted to the termination cell forthwith."

The policemen then dragged the former senior colonel from the room —to his death.

The judge major now released us from the troika, which felt like a relief the likes of which I'd never known before.

One thing had been bothering me all day, so I discretely pulled the senior lieutenant aside for one last question.

"Excuse me, Comrade?"

"Da, what in the hell do you want now Lieutenant Komolov?" The senior lieutenant acted as if he was beyond the point of being merely agitated with me. "I just want to go home and get drunk. Can't this wait until tomorrow?"

"My deepest apologies, Sir. I will be brief. Upon assignment to this troika this morning, Major Chupalov said that they were a few men short for the trials today. However, I didn't see any of the other replacements?"

"What is that you're saying, Lieutenant?"

"The replacements. Where were all the other men assigned for today? Everyone in the courtroom today was in his proper duty station."

"So?"

"So—I guess I'm confused. Where were the other temporary officers?"

"In the other courtrooms, of course. Is there anything else? I really need to get to the Metro before I miss the last train home."

"Sorry? What other courtrooms? I thought this was the only one?"

"The only one?! Oh, you ignorant fool. Go back to your personal cocoon in Special Assignment. I hope I never see you again! This is one of eleven courtrooms down here in the basement. We run these trials each day. Day after day. Do the math, simpleton! Over one thousand citizens are being shot every twenty-four hours. Don't you understand now?"

Moskva
28 December 1937

These were the terrible days. The Great Terror had extended its lethal grip around all of Moskva. The end of '37 couldn't come quick enough.

The deadly winter season had only been upon us for a few weeks, and already our capital city had recorded the coldest temperatures in over a century. It was minus 27 degrees centigrade tonight. When the biting wind ripped at my face, it felt even icier, like tiny daggers all about my skin.

The ambient conditions working inside the pod were unbearable because there was no direct source of heat in here. When the commissar used the drawing room, I could feel the warmth from the baseboard heaters as it leeched into my crawl space. That feeling was glorious! Unfortunately, it wasn't nearly enough to stay comfortable for an entire 12-hour shift. I made sure to always wear my wool greatcoat over my uniform and keep my gloves and ushanka—my fur-lined cap—nearby me.

With their only daughter Yevgeniya in middle school now, and the mother's aunt Nyura Victorovna having passed away over the summer, that left only Mme Kanadina inside the flat during the day. I could tell from her erratic behaviour she felt deeply disturbed—as of late.

She didn't think twice about the consequences of imbibing strong alcoholic beverages—morning or evening. I knew that this wasn't healthy, however I could do nothing about it.

I reported time after time that the commissar was never at home any longer and spent all of his time working at his office in the Moskva Kremlin. Sometimes he even finished the entire night there.

Because of these circumstances, I filed diminished formal reports to the directorate of the family's activities. I didn't want to distort the truth, so I took it upon myself to—shall we say—embellish with significant detail the subtle nuances of everything I observed inside the apartment.

For instance, highlighting the incidentals about the entrees served for supper. Or I could describe the intricacies of some film from the cinema that the commissar was recalling for his wife and daughter.

I always completed my assignments on time, even if they were in fact a little thinner on the political drama the legion of NKVD analysts were constantly hungering for.

With over half of the flats in the residence sealed, pending the end of their investigations, an oversubscription of officers in the Special Assignment Directorate clamoured for duty at the House of Secrets. There were never any problems getting time off or looking for last-minute replacements. It got so bad, that there were hundreds of men who just sat around the entrance at No. 11 whilst they awaited their work appointments. The senior commanders loaned out the idled officers to other duties within the NKVD, including the arrest and interrogation work groups. New families that had recently moved into the Government House were being arrested en masse daily. No one felt protected any longer.

Stalin's Door

I could already see that Mme Kanadina was in a fine form this afternoon. I observed her finishing a bottle of vodka, which she then promptly discarded onto the messy floor. She was moving swiftly from room to room in a frantic and undisciplined manner. I knew that no one else was with her inside the flat, yet she had this habit of muttering to herself as she flitted about.

Mme Kanadina used to take pride in her appearance, but as of late she let herself descend into quite a slovenly state. She never ironed her clothes, and her hair was unkempt and unruly. Except for rare occasions, she hardly departed the confines of the apartment. I really hated to include these personal details in my daily reports, however I was afraid not to just in case my student reported them, and I didn't.

From out of nowhere the lady of the household stood right in front of me, directly on the other side of the surveillance wall. Her voice bellowed at the top of her lungs.

"Open this door at once! I know you're in there! Open up, goddamnit!"

My body became instantly frozen in fear. This turn of events left me completely startled and unprepared. I could now hear my heart beating within my chest, and I felt an enormous rush of hot blood pooling inside my face. No one ever addressed me in this way. Nothing like this happened before. Our extensive training had not prepared me for this contingency. My mind raced with ideas of how I could proceed.

"Come out here and deal with me, you miserable bastard!" Mme Kanadina was now pounding her fists firmly on the wall just centimetres from my head.

With the added acuity enhancements built into the pod, it sounded like bombs were exploding all around me. I was panting and tried to concentrate. I had to think! I needed a moment to reset myself, as I had done countless times in stressful conditions.

I speculated and considered my options. Should I hit the panic-button? Or even try to? In all the scenarios that I could have imagined for its use, this situation might have qualified. Still, I did not know how long it would take to receive assistance, or in what manner the help would come. Matters within the flat could surely get more unpleasant in the meantime.

Mme Kanadina's tirade then continued.

"I will scream, and report that you attacked me! Do you hear me, soldier? Your superiors will hold you in disgrace. Comrade Stalin can have you locked up in the corrective labour camps. I shall make this happen! Just you test me! Now open this door at once, I say!"

There's an old saying my grandmother used frequently:

"Don't wake the monster whilst it slumbers."

Well, my beast was glaringly awake! I considered myself in a full panic. What in the world was I going to do now? Even just the mere accusation from her would mean the end of my career within the NKVD, regardless of the truth in the matter.

For this entire year, I had observed people being arrested and executed for considerably less. I knew I was on the horns of the devil. If I did nothing, I would inevitably face some unpleasant consequences, much questioning, or worse. Or I could open the partition and try to engage with her. But in doing so, I would break our cardinal rule of surveillance here.

Either decision surely posed a significant risk to me.

I made my judgement to open the barrier.

Stalin's Door

I carefully unhooked the two catches at the top and bottom of the wall panel and revealed a small handle that I could use to slide the door to the right. Slowly, so as not to cause any damage, I opened the portal. Years of accumulated dust knocked themselves loose from around the underside of the frame—as the door slid gently open. Within five seconds I had it broad enough to meet my challenger on the other side. I could see an expression of pure horror upon the face of the woman now. The lady of the household was so taken aback by my sudden appearance, that she nearly tripped on the thick carpet runners as she retreated from the Stalin's door. Her cheeks were ashen, and her mouth trembled.

I considered my next steps labouriously. For a moment I thought about withdrawing. However, I'd come this far and perceived it was impossible for me to turn back now.

I stepped through the threshold, and into the apartment's drawing room. Instinctively, I removed the ushanka from my head, and held it out in my bare hands—as a gesture of peace. I felt like Caesar must have, when he crossed over the Rubicon.

"Madam Kanadina, I can understand that you're quite distressed. Please, there's no need for empty threats and false accusations. Let us take a moment and de-escalate all of this." I spoke in a consulting and mild manner, as I was doing my best to defuse the tense situation.

Mme Kanadina stood solemnly for a minute. By pushing the folds of her dress downward with her tiny hands, she regained her composure. She then wiped off her face and straightened her unkempt hair. As she stayed upright and faced me, she became further confident. Automatically, and out of habit, she regressed into the style in which she felt most comfortable—that of acting as a hostess for visitors.

"Would you like some tea, Lieutenant? Please allow me to get you something to eat."

My principal consideration at the moment revolved around a single thought. If the commissar should suddenly arrive home now, he'd surely make a porridge of me. For that matter, if anyone saw me in here, my NKVD commanders would have me immediately remanded into custody.

"Thank you, no, Madam Kanadina, I respectfully require nothing from you."

"Forgive me, Lieutenant, as I am quite unnerved. It's not escaped my attention that everyone around us is getting arrested and taken away from here. It's just beyond my capacity to comprehend. I cannot explain what is happening any longer." The lady of the household started wringing her hands frantically and was breathing heavily again.

The drawing room felt toasty to me now, and I debated for a time whether it was prudent to shed my heavy greatcoat. I decided it was better if I remained on guard and vigilant.

"Won't you sit down for a moment, Lieutenant?" She looked at me with approval.

The lady could sense my calm demeanour, so she arranged herself onto the sofa closest to her.

"No, Madam Kanadina, I will stand right here." I considered this wise, so I could leave if suddenly required to.

"What will happen to my husband when he's finally arrested? Please, you must tell me!"

I remained reticent and looked soberly towards the floor. Having served on the troikas not six weeks ago, I knew the answer to her question. It wasn't suitable. It wasn't something she was prepared to hear—to comprehend—in her present condition.

"Wait a moment. What—what about poor Zhenya?" She looked horrified as the question left her mouth. "Please! You can't place Zhenya into the State orphanages. She'd never survive it. She's exceptional. Please Sir, don't do that! I beg you not to! Take me if you must, however, kindly spare my daughter!"

The lady of the household was correct in the concern for the girl, and herself. Since this past August, a new NKVD directive—No. 00486—permitted the arrest of the spouses and children of criminal conspirators. The wives not executed with their husbands would typically go to corrective labour camps for a term of ten years. The juveniles would live with their politically reliable relatives, or in the orphanages operated by the Communist State, if they could locate no next of kin.

Mme Kanadina was back to twisting her hands again. She appealed to me.

"I know the arrest of my husband is imminent. He has told me this himself. I realise I won't be able to live here any longer with my daughter when that day comes. What will we do? Where shall we go?"

I passed along some intelligence that I learned recently, hoping it would help her.

"Madam Kanadina, located down in the basement and behind the master carpenter's department, is a special room. I've read reports that they allow the families of the arrested husbands to remain there—for a short while. The wives and children can wait in there until the arrangements with their relatives work themselves out. Think of the special room as an informal way station on the journey away from here."

"But Lieutenant, we have no living relations! What shall become of us? We've nowhere else to go!" The lady of the household was becoming rather agitated with me. "Tell me, Sir. You must have children of your own. What would you do in my situation?"

I remained at attention and silent. I stared downwards towards the carpeting again.

"Wait—you don't have any kids, do you? Why this—this is perfect." Mme Kanadina contemplated her words for a moment and then pointed her right forefinger directly to me. "You there." Her eyes held an expression of deadly seriousness.

"Me?" I looked at her, feeling incredulous at the mere thought of what was coming my way.

"Yes, you. You must see to our Zhenya. Take her in and keep her safe. Please! My plan is flawless. No one will ever suspect it was you. You appear kind and honourable. A gentleman. Please, you have to help us. You wouldn't be speaking with me now if you didn't care!"

I shook my head briskly.

"Nyet! This is not possible. What you ask is not even remotely viable. I'd never get away with it. Besides, your daughter doesn't know me. She's never seen my face."

"I will tell her about the unique room in the basement. No, in fact I will take her there when she comes home from school today. I will then instruct her to go there, when they come to arrest my husband and take us away. I will advise her to wait until you collect her."

"But Madam Kanadina, why would she trust me, even after everything you tell her? How will she know it's me, and not another member of the secret police?"

The lady of the household rose quickly from her seat.

"Wait here for a minute. I'll be right back."

She was out of the drawing room for a moment and then returned, appearing out of breath. She stuck out her hand towards me.

"Here, take this." Mme Kanadina handed me a small, rounded object.

As the item rested in the palm of my hand—it felt cold—as if made of solid ice. The heavy item was globe-shaped, and about the size of a quail's egg. Its maker used a dense metal in the orb's construction and painted it gold. The surface appeared irregular, and it gave me the impression of a twisted sphere of hawsers.

The middle of the gadget was hollow on two sides, just as though it intended to allow something to pass through it. Connected to the front of the object was a bright crimson, shining star with a gilded border. In the middle of the red star, I saw the representation of the two common tools of proletarian solidarity—a golden sickle crossed atop of a hammer.

This marvellous object was a sight to behold, and I couldn't stop gawking at it.

Mme Kanadina then pointed at the bauble.

"That is Zhenya's Young Pioneers neckerchief woggle. If you have that within your possession, she will certainly trust you."

I stood motionless for several moments, before I reached a decision.

It was now or never.

"I will do as you ask, Madam Kanadina. Perhaps what this world needs is a bit of hope amongst the chaos and despair." At the time I spoke the words, it hadn't quite sunk in what I was signing up for.

"You must swear to me, Lieutenant. I must have your solemn oath."

"I will give you my tooth for it."

"Thank you, Lieutenant! Thank God for you! It's a miracle." The lady of the household was positively radiant with joy now and profusely wiped the tears streaming down upon her face.

I suddenly started thinking about the hundreds of innocent men and women that were being arrested and shot every day by the reign of terror that gripped our metropolis. Who would save them all?

"What—what God, Madam Kanadina? Where will we find him?"

"Perhaps in heaven?" She proffered.

"My people have no heaven."

Moskva
30 December 1937

It was shortly before midnight, and my long shift was coming to a close. The air within the pod was frigid this evening, and my only source of warmth was the small wattage bulb of the electric lamp on my desk.

Even whilst wearing my wool greatcoat over my uniform, and with my gloves and ushanka fully covering my hands and head, it didn't keep out the bone chilling raw temperatures of this miserable winter night. With every exhalation, my breath would cloud around me in a ghostly mist, before dissipating throughout this cramped enclosure.

If the thermometer read minus 40 degrees centigrade in here, it wouldn't have surprised me. However, soon my student would arrive for his duties, and I could look forward to catching the last Metro train out of the Dzerzhinskaya station for home, and a cozy bed.

As I reviewed my notes from this evening's surveillance, they proved to be much too short compared to my usually verbose standards. Commissar Kanadin arrived home late again—heavily inebriated—missing his supper. I detested putting these kinds of embarrassing personal details into my formal reports, but I knew I needed to be honest and perform my duty to the best of my abilities. The commissar was surely not himself as of late. Who could be in these horrible days?

Undoubtedly my superiors were aware of what was happening here. Why wasn't anything being done about it?

Truth be told, my performance this year left me exhausted and mentally drained. They say that work is no wolf, it won't run away into the woods. So, I found myself with no choice but to carry on.

As I sat and contemplated everything I saw going wrong in flat No. 137, I couldn't help recalling the encounter I had with Mme Kanadina 48 hours ago. I had an enormous amount of thinking to do. Just then, I heard a rustling sound behind me, and turned to see a shadowy figure approaching from the twisty conduit of passages buried deep within the recesses of the Government House. My eyes detected a dancing, shimmering light that emanated from an electric torch. The man was as stealthy as a spectre.

"Good evening, Comrade Lieutenant." My student whispered at me.

He was on time for his shift, for once.

"Good evening, Lukyan Innokentievich. What news do you bring me from the outside world?"

We had repeated this standard challenge and response between us since he started working for me in the autumn.

"Oh, I promise you'll find this particularly interesting, Sir. I just spoke with the shift commander in number eleven. They signed the commissar's arrest warrant only two hours ago! Apparently General Secretary Stalin even delayed going to the cinema tonight to ensure all the paperwork was in its proper order. Our boys in jackboots will kick in the door to this flat shortly. The commissar's wife is being arrested too.

Stalin's Door

"Looks like you'll be getting some time off from this assignment, you lucky bastard! Do you think they'll assign you another pod, Sir? They might decide to just keep us here—until the next family moves in. But still again, they could seal up the apartment. Do you have any ideas about what may happen? Anyway, you'll surely want to wait around for the evening's festivities, yes? This apprehension has been planned for a while, from what I've heard."

This intelligence from my student was not unexpected, however I just didn't expect it would be tonight of all nights. I instantly thought of the promise I made to Mme Kanadina. Inside my front blouse breast pocket was the Young Pioneers neckerchief woggle that belonged to Yevgeniya.

Her uniform implement felt icy cold next to my body, and I was constantly aware of its presence. What had I gotten myself into?

I took a deep breath and concentrated. Things were flashing before my eyes in rapid succession. There was no time to think properly any longer. Would she be able to arrive at the refuge behind the carpenter's department in the basement on time? Where would I take her? Would she even come with me? Perhaps showing her the woggle would make all the difference.

"Thank you for that announcement, Comrade. I am exhausted tonight and think I will skip the arrest proceedings. You'll want to make sure and document it for the nightly report, however. Try to remember everything I taught you. Use direct language. Good luck and stay warm, my friend."

"Be safe, Sir." My student was settling into the chair and prepared his notes for the evening shift.

Since I was not cognisant which exact moment the arrest squad would come for the commissar and his wife, I would just have to wait it out, if I had any chance of hoping to rescue their daughter. I zigzagged my way back through the protracted black corridors to entrance No. 11, which gave me a little more time to consider. What would I tell my wife? How would I resolve all this with her? What would happen in the long run with Yevgeniya? These questions were moot if Yevgeniya didn't go to where she'd been told.

Once I reached No. 11, I signed out of my shift with the commander on duty and put on the pretence of leaving quickly to catch the last Metro train out of the Dzerzhinskaya station. Before I exited outside however, I ducked downstairs to the huge connecting basement level. I made a gigantic assumption that Mme Kanadina had already imparted the crucial information to her daughter. I slowly traversed these warm catacombs over to my confidential destination this evening.

The carpenter's department was an enormous room filled with all the machines necessary to support the residents in a building of this size. There were electric jigsaws, lathes, drill presses, jointers, and sanders of various ranges throughout the workshop. I could see diverse projects in hundreds of states of completion stacked neatly against the sides of the walls. Because it was well after 2400 hours now, there were no construction workers anywhere around. This was a positive for me—a stroke of perfect luck. Massive electric lights hung from the ceiling still doused the factory in a harsh yellow-white light. Their rhythmic humming broke the silence in this place. I could feel the heat dissipating from the steam boilers operating on this level. Finally, I felt warm for once.

It wasn't yet 0100 hours, so I was positive that Yevgeniya couldn't have ensconced herself inside the secret back room yet. I found a quiet spot out of sight from everything. I took off my gloves, heavy greatcoat, and ushanka. As I sat on the cold concrete floor, I waited patiently for Yevgeniya to arrive. Sleep soon overcame me—and I passed out.

Stalin's Door

§

 Something startled me, and I woke myself up in a panic. I immediately checked the time on my pocket watch. It was now 30 minutes past 0300 hours. I felt certain that the NKVD arrest squad had completed its duty of taking the commissar and his wife into custody.

 I stood up and brushed my uniform off. I left my outerwear behind me and proceeded as noiselessly as I could over to the back of the workshop. I approached the secret back office and saw no one in sight. I then placed my hands on the doorknob and turned it to the right. I heard a soft clicking noise directly, knowing it was unlocked. I opened the door gradually and stepped into the frame. I retrieved my electric torch and switched it on to full intensity.

 A bright spotlight illuminated the inside of the office as I panned the beam slowly from side to side until I came across an adolescent girl curled up in the far corner.

 She still wore her night robe and slippers, which seemed out-of-place in here. Her face looked flushed, and her hair was messy.

 I caught her in a deep slumber. I stood there for a brief time. This was unquestionably the commissar's daughter, Yevgeniya. I'd know her from anywhere. I had been observing her entire family for well over a year now.

 Instantly the girl awoke in a panic. She raised her tiny hands to her face to block out the brilliant glare.

 "How—how long have you been watching me, Sir?" She uttered.

 I replied in such a way as to ease any worry she might be experiencing.

"Oh, for quite a while now, young lady."

I slowly walked over in her direction until I was standing next to her. Her face carried an expression of near frenzy and she inhaled deeply. She held her breath intently. I had her totally off guard. She studied my uniform intensely, her eyes rapidly darting up and down. The girl then bit down forcefully on her bottom lip, with her eyes squinting, as if she was trying to recall some bit of vital information.

"Yevgeniya, please, we have to leave here—urgently!" I knew time was of the essence, so I used a firm and commanding tone with her.

"Wait. What—what did you call me, Sir?" She now looked petrified.

"Zhenya, I meant Zhenya. We need to go. Now." I urgently sensed her distress, so I spoke to her in a much calmer and pleasant voice.

Carefully I sat the electric torch upon the dusty floor so I could assist the girl in standing up. I stretched out my left arm towards Zhenya, with my open palm turned up. With my right hand I reached into my uniform jacket and retrieved an item from within my front blouse breast pocket. I held the golden metal orb out for her to see, in between my thumb and forefinger.

Zhenya gazed upon her Young Pioneers neckerchief woggle, her eyes as wide as saucers. She glanced at me as if to tell me she now instantly understood who I was. Zhenya retrieved her property from my hand and closed her small fist around it securely.

"Oh my, it feels so cold!" She exclaimed with some astonishment.

Stalin's Door

§

I cursed myself under my breath. Removing Zhenya out of the Government House this morning would not be easy. I should have taken more time to plan what I needed to do. Alas, it was too late now for any more self-incrimination. I centred myself and attacked the problem step-by-step.

First, since it was well after midnight, I had missed the last Metro train out to our kommunalka in the suburbs. I conceded it might have been too conspicuous for us anyway, as you never knew who was watching. Ordinary citizens I could spot readily, and they were of no concern. The inordinate number of my fellow NKVD officers skulking about day and night all over the capital worried me to no end. I would have a hard time explaining why Zhenya was in my company.

Second, Zhenya didn't plan either. The frighteningly frigid weather outside was no place for nightclothes, a robe, and the decorative house tapochki on her tiny feet.

I felt a tugging on my jacket sleeve.

"You, Sir. You're the fellow behind the Stalin's door, aren't you? You've been watching our family and reporting to Comrade Stalin. Isn't that right? I know it must be you because of that smell of cigars coming from your uniform jacket. I've sniffed that distinctive odour for quite a time."

I thought to myself that Zhenya is a clever girl! That level of scrutiny impressed me greatly.

"Yes, Zhenya, I have been observing you all this time. Now, we have to figure out a way to get you properly dressed. You won't make it very far in your robe and slippers, I'm afraid. It is well below freezing outside."

"Where are we going, Sir? My mother said you'd be coming for me, however I'd like to know if she's safe. And what about my poor Papa?" Zhenya looked at me with mortal distress about her face. "I almost forgot! My father's bodyguard-driver. They shot him dead right in front of me!"

Abruptly, I felt taken aback. I could not imagine what in the world transpired during the arrest of the commissar tonight. I made a mental note to grab a copy of my student's notes for review.

"Zhenya, I'm taking you to our kommunalka where you'll stay with my wife Lera for a bit. Our apartment is far away from here. Your parents are being interviewed by the secret police, and I'm afraid they won't permit you to see them for some time. I made a promise to your mother to watch after you in the interim. Now, we have to figure out a way to get you out of here. We can't have you strolling around downtown Moskva dressed like you're ready for bedtime."

I could see that Zhenya absorbed this information and speedily worked everything out.

"But Sir, you're wearing the same uniform as the men that arrested my parents!"

"Yes, I am, Zhenya. I know all of this is perplexing to you. Be brave for me, and all will be satisfactory—I promise."

"Sir, what is your name?"

"For the time being, you may call me Mister Komolov. Now, we have the issue of getting you some warmer clothes."

"Mister Komolov, in the front foyer of our flat there are three suitcases. My mother said we had to pack them, just in case we needed to leave suddenly. Everything I need should be there."

"Wonderful girl! You stay put right here whilst I recover them. Don't move from this spot, and I'll return in fifteen minutes."

The procedure was nearly perfect. Going back to flat No. 137 should be relatively straightforward. Because I was wearing my uniform, none of the residents of the House of Secrets would dare stop me at this hour. And any of my kinsmen in the NKVD would be in their pods, surveilling their various residences, if they were even awake. Should my student be in our pod working on his notes, he wouldn't be able to see me in the flat's foyer. And, if they sealed the residence with a yellow bill, the front door would be still be unlocked. I could just retrieve the suitcase with Zhenya's things and be off before anyone realised I was in there.

§

I had Zhenya don all the clothes that her mother packed for her. Not only would that keep her warm, but it also meant neither of us would have to carry anything. Her winter jacket looked snug about her body with all the layers of clothing beneath. Her boots, gloves, and ushanka were in excellent shape.

Because of the early hour, it was painfully obvious that Zhenya and I would have to trudge back to the kommunalka—ten kilometres distance from here.

It was possible and would not be easy. We had to do it. We had no choice. I knew we'd better get started. I instructed Zhenya that we would need to hurry, and to walk as fast as she could, following behind me. If she stayed right inside my path, in lockstep, then my body could act as a shield against the biting and brutal winter winds.

After we'd walked through the deserted city streets for nearly two hours in the savage cold, I knew we were just a few more blocks from home.

I heard a hopeless voice cry out and a hand tug meekly on my greatcoat.

"Please, Mister Komolov! I cannot take another step. My feet are frostbitten. I won't make it."

"Don't be absurd, Zhenya. I will carry you. I made a pledge to your mother."

I desperately picked up her limp body, steadying myself for the rest of the journey. The hint of comfort and shelter was a great incentive to keep going. I tried as hard as I could to move swiftly towards the refuge that awaited us both.

Once I arrived at our apartment building, I ascended the six flights up to the front door to our room with Zhenya draped over my shoulder, like a rag doll. Her body felt like a dead weight, and it took all the remaining strength I had left to climb the 78 stairs. Thankfully, everyone on our floor was still fast asleep. The common areas were desolate.

Once we were at our front door, I put Zhenya down tenderly, and made her stand behind me. I turned the decrepit metal knob to our flat slowly and gave the door a slight push inwards. We crept inside. The warmth from the wood-burning stove upon my frozen face instantly felt like a blessed relief. We were finally home, safe and sound.

Suddenly, I could see a kerosene lamp ignite from a few metres away and move towards us.

I heard Lera whisper to me with a tone of fevered intensity.

"Where have you been Sava? It's nearly sunrise. Your absence worried me sick! Is everything all right?"

Without warning, the frozen and shivering girl stepped out from the rear of my greatcoat. She looked pathetic as she turned to intently stare at my wife—her eyes blinking from the brightness of the lamp.

My beloved wife brought the illumination closer, which perfectly lighted the face of our petite visitor.

I then introduced our guest.

"Lera, this is Zhenya."

Moskva
13 January 1938?

The icy brackish water blasted my face, producing an exquisitely painful stinging sensation, as if a thousand tiny needles had pierced my soul. I instantly awakened in a state of panic. Had I just passed out again—for a minute or for an hour? The lack of sleep kept me from knowing. Time became immaterial.

The interrogation cell I found myself in was dimly lit from a puny electric lamp in the ceiling. The room did not contain a heat source.

I could see a foggy mist race out in front of me with every exhalation. The cold metal chair they shackled me to was rigid and unforgiving.

I could no longer feel my legs after sitting for so long. My dingy wet clothes weighed me down, like a soggy blanket, as I lost control of my body, shivering with convulsions.

"Wake up, Citizen!" I heard one jailer scream out.

He hurled the wooden water bucket against the cell wall, crushing it to bits.

My imprisonment in this dank chamber was approaching its third day. After the NKVD arrested me at our apartment, they blindfolded me and drove to this location. I presumed I was on the prison level of the Lubyanka. But I couldn't be sure of anything.

Following classic NKVD inquisition procedures, I was smack in the middle of what we colloquially called the conveyor.

A rapid-fire series of queries asked over and over, sometimes hundreds of times per day—with no breaks. I had to remember that in this place, I was guilty until proven innocent.

After I had endured 12 straight hours of interrogation, trying to remain cognisant felt beyond painful.

After I had held out for 48 hours, I thought it would be nearly impossible not to give in. A sickening fatigue invaded my body, and I could feel myself being poisoned from the inside out.

By design, the conveyor would wear down and break a prisoner so the NKVD could extract the truth. If the facts weren't forthcoming rapidly enough to meet the demands of the truth seekers, they would then use other —methods—at their disposal. A new internal NKVD order authorised the use of harsh physical forms of influence during an inquisition, solely at the discretion of the questioners.

These new techniques had another name—torture. Extracting a confession from the guilty was of paramount importance to the truth seekers, and by any means necessary.

Rotating teams of men, working in paired units, conducted a standard examination of me. Two junior NKVD lieutenants presided over my interrogation at the moment.

Their questions and accusations followed a now familiar pattern:

"How long have you been spying for the British?"

"No, no, Lavr Larionovich, this mole already stated the Germans enlisted him to spy on us."

"Did you really think you'd get away with it all?"

"How much did they pay you for your betrayal?"

"You miserable bastard! I have the authority to shoot you myself—right now!"

"Who recruited you? What is his code name?"

"Where did you hide all the evidence?"

"Give us the names of your accomplices and we might let you live."

"Confess now and you can go home—we promise."

"When did you first violate your oath for commissioned officers?"

"We will break you—no matter the time it takes."

"Why did you betray the Communist Party?"

"How long have you been plotting to assassinate General Secretary Stalin?"

"Tell us the extent of your sabotage."

"What does your wife know? Should we bring her in for an interrogation too?"

"What Soviet state plans have you wrecked with your schemes?"

"At what time does the bomb you planted explode?"

"We have signed confessions from ten of your associates swearing to your wrecking crimes."

"Sign this confession. Sign quickly, or we'll beat you so badly you won't be able to sign anything ever again."

And on, and on, and on like this—for hours. No breaks. No stops. No hope of a reprieve.

One of the interrogators lost his temper with me and ripped off the epaulettes from my uniform.

"You're not a lieutenant in the NKVD any longer. You're a cowardly citizen now. Do you hear me? You're a worthless citizen!"

The man then violently punched me in the back of the skull. My vision faded to black for a few moments, and it was a struggle now to even keep my head raised.

"Give it up, Lavrentiy Valeryevich, this fucker isn't going to sign anything, and we're behind on our quotas. Just put the standard confession form in his file. It doesn't matter, anyway."

Abruptly the cell door opened, and an unfamiliar face entered. The fellow wore the uniform of an NKVD major.

"Stand down, lieutenants. I'll be taking over now."

The junior lieutenants quickly stood to the side of the major as he walked over, pulling a wooden stool behind him. The peculiar individual seated himself so close that the sharp creases in his uniform might have wounded me. The major clutched a bright, red-coloured folder within his hands. His rapid breathing only ceased once he lit up a cigarette. He then started in.

"You're a curious case, Citizen Komolov. I can sincerely say you're the most interesting man I've seen today." The major took a deep drag on his cigarette and exhaled forcefully. "We were just going to classify you as a conventional prisoner, but some newly uncovered intelligence puts you on the path to being classified as a high value interrogation detainee. Want me to reveal what we found out? I'll wager you do, Citizen. You've got quite the family history, it turns out. Oh yes, we always check on these things. You never know what you will find out. Well, I didn't suspect it myself. For starters, it appears your entire household are nothing but traitors, wreckers, and saboteurs. Sounds familiar, doesn't it?"

I calmly explained I didn't understand what he was accusing me of.

The major leafed through the crimson folder, stopping to read every few pages.

"We checked the NKVD archives, and believe it or not, we uncovered a nasty rumour that's been floating around for years. It was your older brother Eduard Yegorovich who deliberately set that disastrous fire aboard the battleship *Imperatritsa Mariya* back in 'sixteen. Apparently this was in some vain attempt at heroics. Your brother planned to rescue all his poor fellow sailors single handedly. Instant admiration, yes? But fate stepped in and had other plans for your deplorable moron of a brother. Eduard Yegorovich burned himself up, along with two hundred other men that night. Tsk tsk. Charring oneself to a crisp—not a pleasant way to go—if you ask me." The major shook his head in faked admonishment.

"That's impossible!" I screamed.

"And let's now look at your uncle—correction, your wife's uncle, Timofey Tarasovich? Do you know what his livelihood was?"

"Of course. He was a master carpenter."

"Wrong! He was a lifelong agent for the Okhrana! It's incredible that a secret policeman for the Tsar was living with you for years, and you never knew? I'll make you a wager. I think you realised it all along!"

"That's fiction, you mudozvon!" I yelled at my interrogator.

"Oh, I'm no buggerer, Citizen." The major then extracted a small, white-coloured envelope from within the folder and held it out for me to see. "And look at what we have here. We just intercepted a post from your wife's uncle today. Aren't you dying to know what it says?" The major unfolded the beige writing paper.

My eyes tried to focus on the evidence gripped tightly in the man's hands, however I was having trouble keeping them open.

"Yes, here it is. Your dyadya wrote to you—something about moving a rook to king's bishop one, and checkmate? What is that exactly? Some kind of coded system alerting you when to carry out your assassination scheme against General Secretary Stalin? I'm sure glad we detained you in time. This could have been terrible."

These rapid-fire accusations against my family were too much to bear. The major was obviously just taking something from the ceiling now. That is to say he was making these charges up, without any real evidence.

My interrogator now looked at me with a supremely smug smile upon his face.

"Haven't you realised the genuine reason I came in here tonight? Oh, I know you will want to hear this! We have a signed admission from someone known to you personally. He swore upon pain of death that he recruited you to join and infiltrate the NKVD, and spy for the Germans. Oh yes, yours was the premier name emphasised within his confession, although I must say it took—"

The major snuffed out his cigarette butt upon the leg of his stool, and then lit up a fresh one.

"—it took more time than I thought was necessary to extract his statement given the level of influence we applied. But, alas, he confessed at the end. Everyone does."

"To whom are you referring, Comrade Major?" I genuinely felt intrigued for the answer.

"Your best friend and mentor, Admiral Krayevsky from the Soviet navy. Remember him? Fellow with the half-burned face? You know once we zeroed in on his fear of the flames, we merely had to torch the other side of his litso and he sang like a canary. You should have heard the screams as his skin melted off.

"He immediately signed a confession saying it was his idea to recruit you into his German spy network and infiltrate our beloved security service. On his personal recommendation, he got you admitted into the Officer Cadet School in 'thirty-six. It's truly an amazing story if you ask me. So, just so you understand, you need to mark your own acknowledgement soon. Things are fucking awful for you now. Do yourself a favour and let it all end."

The major stood up, preparing to leave, when he abruptly turned back.

"Just one more question, Citizen Komolov. Something that I don't follow. After your brother Eduard Yegorovich perished on his battleship, you married his widow the day after our peace treaty with Germany was signed. Now why was that?"

"It's called a levirate marriage. It is the way of our people. I wouldn't expect you to understand."

"Is that some religious—thing, Citizen?"

"Da."

The major then exploded in anger and spit into my face.

"Religion is not permitted in our society! There is only room for General Secretary Stalin!"

After a brief 15-minute respite, a fresh group of interrogators entered the cell with me. I was desperately trying to fight off sleep and fatigue.

I noted that these men dressed in the uniforms of the national police service. There would be no interrogation. Perhaps I was being moved.

"On your feet, Citizen!" One of them barked at me.

Rising slowly from the cold metal chair, I felt an excruciating pain radiate throughout my back and legs, after having sat for so many hours straight.

I cried out in pure misery.

"Stop your belly-aching and put your wrists together, out in front of you."

I did as he instructed, and the policeman slapped hard metal handcuffs on me.

"Now move!"

They marched me out of the dank room, and I saw a unique view for the first time in over 72 hours.

As I walked down the lengthy corridor, everything I could look at seemed awfully familiar.

I was definitely within the bowels of the Lubyanka HQ building. I had seen this part of the basement before—many weeks ago.

Trudging down the hallway, I could hear the pitiful shrieks and wails of the other prisoner's as they were being interrogated and tortured within the other cells. Their cries for help would surely haunt me for the rest of my life.

We rounded two more corners and approached our destination.

"Hold it up here!" The policeman yanked me to a stop, and I planted myself up against the chilly wall of the hallway to rest.

My eyes were having trouble staying focused, however I could swear I had previously been here.

My escorts' faces appeared expressionless and with some effort I studied the sign at the steel door across from me and read its grim knowledge:

No. 23
NKVD SPECIAL COURT
MAINTAIN SILENCE

I waited for a brief while and then heard the door across from us open up. A prisoner in handcuffs emerged, followed by two identically dressed guards coming up from behind him. The convict's ashen face betrayed a tremendous expression of terror. He didn't make eye contact with me.

Suddenly they firmly grabbed the collar of my uniform blouse and shoved me forward into the chamber. They spoke no words to me. I was being delivered into courtroom No. 23.

Once I stepped inside, everything here appeared identical to when I officiated on the troika, only eight weeks ago. A lonely metal chair sat in the middle of the chilly room. Overhead were the requisite mercury-vapour lamps, shining their harsh electric light all about. The non-commissioned officers from the national police service directed me to sit—quickly. They then stood watch behind me, and not once did they break out of their automaton-like gesticulations.

As I examined the men seated at the long metal table in front of me, I studied their features hoping to recognise someone familiar. Two junior ranking NKVD officers sat on either side of the presiding judge major. I didn't know their names. They made no special note of me either. This was not Judge Major Maksimushkin from the previous troika.

I saw the junior officer to the right of the judge major take the next folder from the top of the stack and open it. He skimmed the top page in the file and signed it. He then passed the paperwork over to the man in centre chair.

I then heard the booming voice of the judge major start up as he pronounced my fate. His speech was flat and mechanical.

"This court affirms that Komolov Saveliy Yegorovich receive a sentence of death for high treason and other violations of article number fifty-eight. This judgement is absolute. You have no entitlement of appeal. We shall implement the decision with immediate effect. I discharge you. Guards, you may remand the convicted to the termination cell forthwith."

I could not accept what was transpiring. My body and mind were numb with shock and I remained for a moment—not processing what had just ensued.

A sharp blow to the back of my head from the butt of a guard's rifle got me up on my feet.

As I was being led out, I noticed a strange man standing by the side wall. He wore the uniform of an NKVD senior colonel. As my vision cleared, I could barely make out that it was Col Kalagin—my instructor from the OCS.

He glared at me with much derision in his eyes. His head shook back and forth in disgust.

"I'm very disappointed in you, Cadet Number One."

But, I wasn't 100 percent positive it was really him. I couldn't be certain of anything any longer.

Stalin's Door

As I left the sentencing chamber, the next condemned prisoner awaiting his destiny came into view. It was Col Bobr, one of the officers from the day I worked on the other side of the table. His uniform was crisp and ironed—and in splendid condition. The colonel, however, was in a far from perfect state of being. His expression betrayed a broken shell of a man. He looked at me—as if he wanted to say something—but he couldn't form the words.

My guards then escorted me from the courtroom, to the end of a long corridor. The atmosphere here was deathly quiet, and the light quite dim. As I spun to the right, they pushed me into an adjoining alcove cut squarely into the damp concrete.

"Wait here, dead man." The guards then unlocked the handcuffs and took them off my distended wrists.

They then turned their backs to me and walked off.

In a moment an unfamiliar face appeared. It was a junior lieutenant from the NKVD. He tossed me a white cotton bundle.

"Strip out of all your clothes and put that on. Do it rapidly." His voice was stringent in tone.

I did as he instructed, removing my now soiled uniform. Of what use it was to anyone else was unknowable. The air felt especially bitter right here, and it burned my lungs when I inhaled. I hastily donned the plain white cotton undergarments given to me—momentarily warming up. My feet however remained bare, pressing into the frigid, hard floor beneath me.

The junior lieutenant then took me by the arm as we marched around the corner.

I observed a small desk arranged just outside a thick metal door, painted black. A senior lieutenant from the NKVD sat there idle, smoking a cigarette. On the desk were piles and piles of black and gold folders.

"Come over!" The man shouted to me.

I walked over with the junior lieutenant still behind me.

"Name?"

"Excuse me, Comrade?"

"What is your accursed name, convict?" The senior lieutenant looked more than agitated.

"My name is Lieutenant Komolov."

"Harrumph! Of course you are. Hold his head up, Isaak Larionovich, let's get a last look at him."

The junior lieutenant grabbed the back of my hair viciously as he directed my face to an electric torch the senior lieutenant held up, shining it into my eyes. The pain I felt was excruciating, and I continued to see spots for many moments afterwards. They both examined paperwork from another folder.

A small square black-and-white photograph in the corner of the page was their focal point. It was my photograph. It was my face.

My captor released me for a minute whilst both men signed and counter-signed the death warrant. The senior lieutenant then barked out.

"Cleared for debarkation. You may proceed."

I heard a faint electric buzzing sound, and the heavy metal black door opened slowly inwards. The junior lieutenant standing behind me pushed me forcefully inside.

The shadowy compact chamber I was now in looked utilitarian, save for the pair of industrial-sized fans on each side of the room. They pointed upwards and produced a low-pitched humming din. Icy cobblestones beneath me felt wet upon my bare feet—as if they were recently doused in water.

A large grey tarpaulin lay flat out in front of me, and I could see the floor sloped downwards towards the opposite wall. The illumination in this chamber was faint, and the air smelled stale. I could hear the door closing behind me now. It made a loud scraping noise against the threshold.

"Kneel!" A voice commanded—coming from behind me.

A brace of muscular hands pushed me down by the shoulders, as my knees buckled. I winced in pain when they hit the damp rocks below.

"Don't even move." The vocalisation added.

I then heard a loud clicking sound behind my right ear, like the hammer of a revolver being pulled back into place.

With my head pointing forward, my eyes looked up as far as I could manage towards the ceiling.

"Shalom, Lera, my love. I am sorry that I failed you." I whispered.

An explosion erupted, and I felt a tremendous concussion upon the back of my skull. In a millisecond, the bullet from the revolver entered my brain at a speed exceeding 2,700 kilometres per hour. My life had come to an end.

Lera's Yarn

◇◇◇

Beyond Stalin's Door

Year Of Paper

Daylight filtered through the wooden slats on the sides of this industrial cattle waggon, and the glow reminded me of a moving picture projection.

Beams of luminescence alternating from black to white, and white to black, for hours on end. When I concentrated, I could see particulates of dust and filth floating effortlessly in the glowing refractions of light. The illusion made me believe it was snowing inside here.

Time seemed to move in slow motion, even as our transportation relentlessly barrelled upon the railroad tracks at a formidable speed. I snapped out of my stupor and recognised this predicament was fatally serious. Thankfully, my infrangible positive attitude kept me alive. And as long as I carried that hope, the person who was now wholly reliant upon me would survive too. For I dared not fail her.

The living conditions inside this converted stock car, now serving solely as transportation for people, were nothing short of disgusting. A thin layer of mouldy straw covered the rickety wooden floorboards. The ventilation in here was unsatisfactory, and because of the freezing temperatures outside, everyone could see their own breath with each exhalation. The humidity felt rampant and collectively all the breathing caused showers of fine ice crystals to spray down upon our heads. We suffered in pure agony. Ever since I was a teenager, I always detested travelling by rail.

The floor space inside this railcar measured a dozen metres long, by three metres wide. An ancient wood-burning stove lay bolted into the centre and showed signs of an inferior installation. The amount of warmth it provided for all of us was scarcely noticeable, and no one could evade the discharge of its belching noxious white smoke. Choking rapidly replaced breathing. I peeked behind the log burner and noticed an ever-dwindling stack of green wood laying haphazardly about. That fuel would have to last us a good amount of time, for I had the feeling our journey was far from over.

The bulk of the adult occupants stood solemnly in place and tried desperately to keep warm. The NKVD guards had us packed together like so many sardines in a tin, and it was virtually impossible to move about. No one made eye contact with me, as I'm sure they were just as miserable as I was and could do nothing for it. Everyone carried on as best they could in this terrible spot. As the hours wore on, I noted a peculiar rite that came about—by necessity—if not by accident. All the women next to me held their arms tightly folded together and stamped their feet in unison upon the decking. This dance produced a distinctive beat whose rhythm starkly contrasted with the clacking sounds the railcar trucks in the undercarriage made against the railway ties. It was hypnotic and terrifying at the same time.

Words were useless here, and yet I could just make out the whimpering diatribe of some poor sister nearby. To save my sanity, I tried desperately to gaze outside upon the raw conditions of the wilderness. I pressed my nose up against the pitifully thin slats of frozen milled lumber, peering through to catch a glimpse. What lay not a meagre metre beyond my dismal face blinded me. A harrowing pain radiated from the back of my eyes, after having long grown accustomed to the perpetual twilight. I couldn't fathom the impossibly brilliant white landscapes that lay under dull grey skies, extending out endlessly into eternity. Kilometre after kilometre, we travelled into a frozen and barren wasteland of ice and misery.

Pain. I feel nothing but excruciation when I think about travelling by rail. It was just after my fourteenth birthday, in May 1896, when my father and mother took me to our glorious capital city of Moskva via the western Imperial railway. We left our home in Sankt-Petersburg to attend the fabulous coronation ceremonies for the last Emperor of Russia, His Imperial Majesty Nicholas II. On the morning of the eighteenth, just a few days after our new Tsar placed the crown upon his head for the first time, an enormous gathering of people attended a public celebration at the military fields of Khodynka, in the northwestern district of the capital. To augment the festivities, the Tsar provided a plethora of music, rich food, and drinks for his festive revelers.

Of course my parents forbade me any of the delicious smelling sausages and pelmeni, however I did manage to sneak a bite or two of the appetising cakes and gingerbread when my mother wasn't watching. These spicy victuals were my favourite! I spotted giant pretzels larger than the size of my head weave themselves about on lanky metal poles, as they were distributed to the happy bacchants. By the number of tapped barrels of beer I counted, this was guaranteed to be a day to remember. No one was worried that by some estimates, several hundred thousand subjects jammed themselves into a space not designed to accommodate such humungous crowds.

As a memento of the celebration, the Tsar promised a spectacular commemorative cup to everyone in attendance, the likes of which no one had ever seen before. These fabulously enameled mugs,

with a rich gold leaf, sported distinctive royal designs and imagery. I knew trouble would follow when wild rumours began circulating that the exhaustion of the lavish refreshments was imminent. Even more astonishing was the near frenzy of tittle-tattle that purported some of the chashki contained a solid gold kopek hidden on their undersides.
This news riled up the attendees, and unpredictably a terrible stampede ensued.

The screams. Suddenly the blood-curdling screaming was everywhere, and all around us.

I'll never forget hearing that high-pitched howl as hundreds of our fellow countrymen squashed themselves together, unable to restrain the force of thousands of people pressing forwards into them. Tighter and tighter they crammed, until their very last breaths were literally squeezed out from their compressed lungs, and their eyes faded to black—like a doll's. The police force on duty, in an effort to quell the rush, began to frantically fire their rifles into the air. What should have dispersed the crowds had the opposite effect, as the wave of human bodies were actually pushed into the policemen, until they themselves were smothered too.

I became separated from my parents at one point and was impelled into a direction where at least the people still moved to. A stranger took my hand and guided me to safety. I desperately looked around for the whereabouts of my kin, my head spinning in the cataclysm.

In the mass panic that followed, over 1,400 men, women, and children died from the ghastly crush. A myriad more sustained permanent injury. Instead of a day filled with triumph and celebration for HIM Tsar Nicholas II, today we now call that event the Khodynka

Tragedy. The catastrophe dogged Nicholas II's ominous reign for years to come, and our new monarch gained the nickname Bloody Nicholas.

My father and mother were amongst the many who lost their lives that terrible day. In a fit of grief, I later smashed the kruzhka, the commemorative cup of sorrows, onto the cobblestones in the streets of Moskva.

I felt a pain so abominable, so overwhelming, that I never fully recovered from it.

The journey on the train back to my home, without my parents, was the saddest moment of my life.

This was day number eight into our lamentable journey eastward. How long it would take us to arrive was anyone's guess. If I was correct, our destination lay thousands of kilometres away from Moskva. The northeastern regions of Siberia, colloquially named the sleeping land, would be our new home. I scanned the faces of the wretched occupants sharing my terrifying travail.

Their disparate ages ranged from an adolescent girl almost 13 years old, all the way to elderly women well into their 70s. I carried out a detailed census of all the denizens here and counted 54 souls. We were all women—now.

We started our persecuted trek with 69 aboard this cursed conveyance. Most of us that remained had the tremendous fortune—or just the prescience—to gather and wear numerous layers of clothing for this journey. As many as we could manage upon the pronouncements of our collective arrests and sentences. Those that didn't, or weren't able to, perished in the first couple of days of this peregrination.

The frigid temperatures we all experienced were—evil. There was just no other term to describe this icy hell. As the ambient air inside dipped to minus 20 degrees centigrade, everything became frozen solid. Our bones became brittle, and our joints constantly ached. Restful sleep was impossible, as nightmares and tortured dreams were the best that we could hope for.

The merciless gnawing of hunger was constant, however, thirst was a needling want we could never quench. We'd already long ago consumed the water provided for us during our one and only stop every day.

The more enterprising occupants here discovered they could manoeuvre their tiny hands above the transom in the carriage's rear and break off the thick icicles that formed there. These were tainted stalactites, because the exhaust of the coal furnaces powering the train covered everything outside in a thick layer of black soot. This inky frozen glaze they retrieved proved both useless and disgusting. The women now far beyond their wits devoured them with aplomb, revealing frightening caliginous stains inside their teeth as they grinned.

I wasn't that thirsty—yet—and prayed I wouldn't become that desperate.

With an abrupt jolt, I could feel us decelerating rapidly. Our train's engines had 48 railcars in tow and breaking took many minutes to complete. Our daily layover anticipated a now familiar routine. The refuelling of coal and water for our iron horses, the restocking of stores, and a much-needed respite outside for all of us away from our hellish confinement.

Once we came to a stop, I heard a familiar thrashing cadence, as the NKVD guards began unlocking the heavy metal latches that held the sliding doors of the cattle waggons closed. I overheard orders being yelled out, and then immediately repeated in acknowledgement. The steam from the train's engines, as it cooled down, produced a tremendous hissing racket. It was as if a giant beast now relaxed, catching its laboured breath.

We were all starving. Haltingly and painfully. We couldn't think of anything except our next meal.

As if right on schedule, I heard a loud crash come from outside and watched as the massive wooden door of the railcar opened forcefully. A blinding light seared my eyes, and I felt a stiff frozen wind blast me in the nose and mouth. I put my hands to my face, shielding myself temporarily from the elements. Inside my eyes I saw small blinking black spots, and my head felt woozy. Ramps built into the undercarriages deployed themselves forwards after much yanking and pulling from the uniformed men below. Supervisory NKVD guards yelled at us to disembark with utmost urgency. I could hear the repetitions of sharp whistles up and down the line.

"I'm so hungry, Grandmother." A diminutive voice crackled in front of me.

"I know, I know, my solnyshka. Our supper will be here shortly. Please stay strong for me."

I smiled, and instinctively grabbed Zhenya's tiny hand, clinging to it tightly. She assuredly was my small sun. The wool from her mitten felt stiff, yet I could immediately feel its warmth as it permeated into my bare palm. She squeezed my hand back, securely. We only had one pair of mittens to share between us, so we ended up alternating hands. For all the reasons that she should complain and whine, I was especially proud that she didn't excessively do so. Zhenya was special.

We all shuffled down the rickety wooden inclines in paired columns —deliberately. No one was in any hurry to trip and fall into the snow and ice. An injury in this place was a certain death sentence. To my left and right I could see all the miserable denizens of our caravan being discharged simultaneously. Hundreds of women were all exiting the confines of their filthy transports, trudging forwards, into the pristine white icepack.

My boots hit the harsh surface, making an all too familiar crunching sound. I looked over my shoulder and caught a familiar sight. Several women were making a direct dash to the undercarriages as best they could. This was because they desperately needed to relieve themselves. Our railcar had a pit cut directly into the floorboards, near the rear of the compartment. This is what we used as a WC. However, we promptly learned to keep the area clear —as it had the unfortunate tendency to ice itself over, rendering it useless. I guessed this had occurred inside the other cars.

§

In all our previous stops, we'd always arrived at the local train station of whatever town or village that synced to the invariable schedule we were now all following. This break allowed the NKVD guards the opportunity to feed us.

The more affluent prisoners in our caravan would seek out the neighbourhood residents to exchange their hard currency for extra rations or supplies.

I noticed right away that certain women in our caravan would scarf up any available eggs from the locals—as they were naturally kosher.

This practise was more of a luxury, and I had long concluded that staying alive by consuming everything served to us was more desirable than following the letter of religious law in this place.

As our convoy moved eastward day by day, cash became less advantageous, and a millennia old tradition of bartering naturally took its place. As neither Zhenya nor I had anything of value to trade, this severely diminished our chances of procuring anything extra. I thanked Yahweh that we both wore warm clothes, coats, and boots. And we had each other. We were the fortunate ones.

The locale we paused at today was nothing more than a distant supply depot, carved into the snowpack. I highly suspected it wasn't even on any official Soviet maps yet. There would be no trading in this desolate place.

A long single storey storage warehouse, painted black, lay near the railway tracks and served as the only sign of civilisation for hundreds of kilometres. The storehouse operated as a garrison for the NKVD and a predicable waypoint at which to refuel and resupply the dozens of trains making their way into the outlands of Siberia every month.

The NKVD guards had placed a series of colossal pots upon impromptu stands near the entrance of the repository. The steam from the liquids within bathed the entire area in an otherworldly thick grey fog. Whatever they stewed today smelled atrocious—like rotten cabbages, oatmeal, and some kind of meat they'd boiled into submission. But it would at least be a hot meal on this late wintry afternoon.

"Hold my hand, Zhenya. Let's get some food into you."

On the second day of our journey we all learned, to our collective horror, that being served last ran an enormous risk. The NKVD guards only made so many servings, and if you brought up the rear of the queue, then you'd likely go hungry when they inevitably ran out of foodstuffs. Whether this shortfall was because of mismanagement, human error, or the genuine possibility of the men withholding it for themselves—it was all academic.

It would be a long 24 hours until you ate anything again. We made sure to always get into position as soon as we arrived anywhere now. Zhenya and I stood near the head of a giant column of famished prisoners.

"Walk right up, ladies! We've not got all damned day."

I approached the dour man standing at the noxious cauldron and held out my cold metal bowl. A modest slop of piping hot soupy gruel, followed by a few chunky bits of solid matter, splashed inside. Another fellow then placed an insignificant piece of light-yellow hardtack on top.

"Bless you, kind sirs." I always offered gratitude for what they provided us and made sure Zhenya followed suit.

I couldn't imagine what was actually in our mazers, and frankly I didn't want to know. I studied the impossibly sullen faces of the NKVD guards attending us today. These youthful fellows looked bored and disdainful, as if we were nothing more than regrettable impositions. They plainly didn't want to be out here in the elements any more than we did.

"Let's move it along, Mother! One leg is here, another leg is there!" A supervisory NKVD guard barked, attempting to keep the queue in motion.

Zhenya and I found a quiet spot in which to dine. As if by some form of muscle memory, I took half of my hardtack and pocketed it for later. I discovered that even a slight morsel on these dismal numbing nights was enough to stave off the hunger pangs. At least for a limited while.

Dipping the rest of the frozen biscuit into the boiling broth made them somewhat edible—and provided an ancillary benefit too. These so-called army crackers occasionally had the unfortunate hitchhiker living within, so dunking them into our soups allowed any parasites to float up to the top. They were then easily skimmed right off.

I devoured the wicked swill with dispatch and felt a pleasant warming sensation radiate from inside me—even as I endured a wave of nausea. Zhenya didn't look delighted with her supper and merely held it in her hands with an expression of disgust. I admonished her.

"We don't know when or if we'll nosh again my dear, so down the hatch, if you please. And look sharp. Your starving sisters await right behind us. Besides, if you don't finish up, you can't have any dessert."

My attempt at some ironic humour fell flat with Zhenya. After a few more minutes, we finished our gruel.

Several hundred women remained eager for their turn to eat. A predictable shortage of serving bowls meant that the protracted procession was further impeded. Those in the formation's front had to inhale their skimpy helpings with swiftness. We would then pass the small metal dishes on to the individuals trailing us, who would then do the same to those who'd not eaten. The NKVD guards in charge of distributing our pitiful sustenance voiced their displeasure at all the delays—with much bemoaning and whining.

Zhenya and I then joined a lengthy column at the depot water station, which gave us an opportunity to fill whatever we could carry water with.

"Ensure you drink as much as you can manage, dearest. Dehydration can be a dangerous ailment in these arid conditions."

Thankfully, access to drinking water had not been an issue whilst we stopped each day. We felt temporarily human again as we stood next to a behemoth metal cistern.

This crucial storage tank sat raised upon a lattice of steel girders and contained a roaring bonfire underneath it to keep the only available water around from freezing. Should that have occurred, the endless procession of trains moving eastward would grind to a halt—paralysed—and no doubt many men at this way station would find themselves arrested and shot.

We idled in the snow and ice, for perhaps another hour, watching as the other women finished their suppers. My demeanour remained rosy, under the circumstances, and this had a practical effect on Zhenya's mood.

Naturally, I always stood near her to shield her from the elements. There was an unstoppable stiff wind coming from the north, and it made everything around us raw and miserable. I then held Zhenya even closer and turned her away from our transportation. On the ramps of our cursed conveyances, an all-familiar ritual now ran its course. The NKVD guards that weren't busy feeding the multitudes were engaged by offloading the poor souls that had passed away since our last stopover.

I didn't want Zhenya to witness any of this.

On board the nearest railcar to where we stood, two uniformed men were removing a corpse, frozen completely solid. The body of the lamentable woman lay in an unforgiving state, with a horrifying scowl caught forever upon her face.

I then overheard much griping and protesting of this serious duty by the NKVD guards. As I watched them take the pathetic deceased away, I couldn't help but think they treated her no differently than they would the carcass of a slaughtered animal. It was disgraceful behaviour.

As the duo passed nearby, hoisting the frostbitten body by the arms and legs, I noticed that they just disposed of the cadaver on top of an ever-growing pile situated directly away from the warehouse—like so much stacked cordwood.

A surly voice from one of them grumbled loudly.

"Oh, fuck me! They'll be here till summer. These damned zechkas are impossible to bury in winter, with the ground iced over."

"Have you no respect for the deceased, Comrade? Come and see." His companion replied. The fellow held a rigid appendage from one poor soul in his hands, up and into the frosty air. "Your sweet talk has her bored stiff!"

Both NKVD guards burst out laughing in unison.

The callous nature of this sacrilege disturbed me beyond words, and I pivoted away. I positioned Zhenya's back to all of it so that I protected her.

§

A short time later, as Zhenya and I remained standing solemnly in the bitter winter weather, I spied a troika of NKVD guards approaching us. I instantly noticed they all walked somewhat carelessly, which I thought quite out of character for soldiers on duty. These fellows wore shabby, ill-fitting light green field jackets, along with distressed black leather boots. In place of the traditional NKVD officers' blue felt cap with the Soviet star and red piping, these men wore green caps with a thin red outline, on their heads.

I could discern no obvious ranks or insignias, and suspected that unlike the all-officer corps my beloved Sava worked for, these chaps were some kind of new enlisted auxiliary guards unit. Perhaps they were even conscripts? With so many Russians being arrested and deported into the far east of Siberia these days, it would be unlikely that the entire NKVD were the officer elite any longer. None of them appeared to be carrying rifles.

Upon further examination, these men were not so much men, as they were boys. They appeared not much older than 18 or 19 years of age.

I knew from the expressions within their eyes they were intent on making a porridge—that is to say they had nothing but trouble on their minds. I'd seen these mannerisms before, during my nursing services in the Great War. I would require all of my wits to counter what I suspected their genuine intention to be.

The apparent leader of the trio sauntered up to where I stood and looked me over with much disdain. I held Zhenya in front of me, with both of my hands gripping tightly onto her shoulders. I tugged her in close with his approach.

This non-commissioned officer smirked at his comrades and then addressed me sternly.

"Why hello there, Mother. It's such a chilly afternoon here. I am particularly concerned with the constitution of your—"

The young, enlisted boy—a hooligan really—studied Zhenya intently for a moment. The lower part of his jaw was slightly agape and moved from side to side in a gradual and deliberate manner. It was impossible to miss the pungent smell of vodka upon his breath. The lad then looked up and scrutinised me all over again.

"—surely not your daughter? She must be your granddaughter, yes?"

"This is my granddaughter, and you Sir are away from your duties." I then firmed up my defencive position, ensuring that I solidified my feet into the shallow snowpack.

"Whoa now, Mother! Slow down. We just want to take your grand—daughter away for just a wee while. She is freezing, and we'd just like to warm her up for a bit. Let us take her somewhere cozy. We wouldn't be friendly hosts if we let her health deteriorate out here on the ice, now would we? It feels so bitter just standing idly around. Don't you want what's best for your vnuchka?" The leader sniggered at me and then turned to peer at his companions for a second. "If you prefer, I am sure we can give you something, as compensation for her time."

I knew precisely what they had in mind with Zhenya. Now was the moment for fight or flight.

The very prospect of making a dash for it was inconceivable in this environment. There wasn't anywhere to run to. And even if we tried, it was easily a distance of at least 100 kilometres to the nearest village. We'd surely freeze to death within hours of escaping or succumb to even worse fates. No, I rightly concluded I'd have to force my way out of this quandary.

"Why you should all be ashamed of yourselves!" I screamed as vehemently as I could muster, so I might attract some attention to this altercation. I was practically spitting in the boy's face as I shrieked out the words. "You're a disgrace to your unit, the lot of you!" I hesitated for a moment and watched the moon-eyed leader. His bloodshot eyes blinked rapidly at me, as if I surprised him with the sudden protest. "What would your wives and girlfriends think of this lecherous behaviour?"

One of the hooligan's companions chimed in to try and broker peace.

"C'mon Lavrentiy Valeryevich, this one's not worth it. There are so many others to choose from. You know? What with an extra slice of bread, or a piece of pirozhok, we can easily get another girl. And even if not, there will be additional trains tomorrow."

"Shut your mouth, Gavril Rodionovich!" The intoxicated fellow barked out. "I'm not going anywhere. This one's got a little—pluck. I intend to dissever the bitch for her insolence."

With that, the leader then produced a short carving knife from beneath his dingy jacket. Clasping it inside his left hand, he waved it slowly up and down, as it severed the air. I could see that the edge was dull, and the blade looked well used, and not in excellent condition. Its handle was thick wood, worn smooth from years of use. This nozh was still a fearsome weapon in the right hands, however. I didn't relish finding out the hard way just how sharp this cutter still was.

"Holy shit, Lavrentiy Valeryevich! What are you doing? You're not in your saucer! If Lieutenant Kalashnik sees that blade, we're finished! Stop this nonsense at once!"

A scuffle broke out between the two boys, with the dissenter trying desperately to dislodge the shank from his leader's determined grip.

The drunken hooligan quickly won out, standing his ground undeterred. The bullying schmuck then rebuffed his colleagues and took another step forward, bringing the point of his dagger closer to Zhenya's face.

I gasped and immediately took my hands to cover Zhenya's head as best as I could. I pulled her into my chest. I was positive that even through the many layers of blouses, and over the thickness of my coat, Zhenya could feel my heartbeat as it pounded inside my left breast.

As if by a miracle, a loud series of whistles followed by the eruptions of men shouting and barking came from behind us, startling everyone. The first required headcount was beginning, and its completion would be necessary before we'd embark back aboard the train. A full accounting of women, alive and otherwise, took place at periodic intervals. Leave it to the rigid NKVD regulations to save our day.

The deranged youth stopped—frozen in place. His pursed lips forced his breathing to make a distinctive wheezing sound.

A maniacal laugh then erupted from his companions.

"This game isn't worth the candles, eh? Better luck next time, Lavrentiy Valeryevich. C'mon, let's get out of here."

The boys then spun around and sprinted back to join the rest of their cadre. My utter relief was palpable.

§

Day number 17 on our hellish journey into the far northeast of Russia would be our last by rail, although we didn't know it at first. Our regular stopover for refuelling the train and distributing rations to the women came in the afternoon, right on schedule.

Yet, something felt peculiar after we waited an unusually long while for the cattle waggon door to open. I heard the sounds of an abundance of activities just outside, and I worried something was amiss. Whatever was taking so long? I lost consciousness whilst still on my feet. But only for a moment.

When the intense sunlight struck my poor eyes and the biting Siberian wind whipped my face, I knew disembarkation was finally upon us. I reached for Zhenya as we dragged ourselves from the smog and the stuffiness inside. I squinted my eyes and beheld a perfectly clear pale-blue sky above which joined an incredibly white, snowy landscape—stretching into infinity. I took in several lungfuls of the crisp, clean air to clear my pounding head. The lack of food and sleep left me featherbrained. We made our way down the wooden ramp, carefully and deliberately.

To everyone's horror, we discovered that there was nothing waiting for us here. I listened as much crying and lamentation followed. Several women were openly weeping. We were all beyond malnourished by this time and had been desperately looking forward to eating something—anything at all—for hours. The NKVD guards, who were out in force with their rifles drawn upon us, shouted orders. Their barking and tone were distinctly terrifying today.

Over and over we all heard the same deafening message:

"Get in that line over there! Follow the woman in front of you, single file if you please! Do not stop for any reason! Move quickly! No talking!"

They also instructed us thusly:

"If you have any difficulties or bother, arrange yourselves over this way—towards me! We will provide transportation for you!"

I could see a smattering of horse-drawn waggons, and some NKVD guards carrying the women that couldn't walk. Their gaunt bodies were then lifted up and into the conveyances.

As a further incentive, the men informed us that a hot meal and tea awaited when we arrived at the camp. And what a mighty incentive that was. I couldn't wait to get started.

A lonely icy road, recently cleared of drifting snow, snaked out in front of us. Its path lay directly away from the railway tracks, to the horizon. I knew we had a tedious trudge ahead of us.

I took Zhenya by the arm and we briskly joined the end of the queue, following our sisters who started out before us. One by one, we placed one foot in front of the other, and plodded along. We traversed a fairly tamped down snowpack, so the purchase of our feet was secure.

Left foot, right foot. Up, down. I smiled at Zhenya and urged her forward. I felt that it was crucial to always set an exemplary example.

Stalin's Door

The pace set by the women in front of us was agonisingly sluggish however, which given the circumstances was not that surprising. In less than an hour of marching, I estimated we had travelled fewer than three kilometres. Looking into the distance, I could see the ridgeline of an immense snowy forest. I reasoned the location of our encampment must be somewhere within. As we approached the periphery, the trees that once looked huge from afar now stood out like gigantic sentries guarding a national treasure. By the hundreds I recognised majestic pines, spruces, and larches. This was an ancient forest we travelled into. If someone had told me the trees were 50 metres in height, I would not have believed them, had I not seen them for myself.

We were now deep inside the interior of the Siberian taiga. I wondered how people could possibly live in such a remote and desolate place. Except for the occasional burst of wind from the north, and the sounds of the women in front of us making their way, an eerie silence engulfed us. After having experienced the sounds of a roaring train with no respite for days, the contrast was striking and beautiful.

A moderate snow fell. The snowflakes looked voluminous and ornate. Within just a few minutes, the precipitation began sticking to our coats and hats.

Was this the first sign of a buran to come? Those legendary blizzards of Siberia were fearsome, and being caught outside would surely merit a death sentence.

Just as the queue of our sisters in front of us was about to penetrate the forest border, I spotted a commotion ahead. A horse-drawn flat open waggon appeared stuck into the snowbank, off to the side of the path we were on. As we drew closer, it was clear this was a transport that carried some women unable to walk on their own—the afflicted and the elderly. This extended wide, wooden caisson appeared as if a rear wheel had come off its axle.

The pair of NKVD guards driving this sorry hauler were desperately trying to carry out repairs, and there was much cursing and shouting about. The disabled women, who remained inside the transport, lay frozen and catatonic. Others were now sitting on the ground, covered in fresh snow, just to the side of the trail. They looked up at us, helpless and afraid. Their eyes of anguish haunted me. To have made it this far was a miracle. To perish out in the open was inhumane.

"Grandmother?" Zhenya whispered. "We've got to help them, if we can. Don't you think? At least one? I'm sure it's not that much further before we arrive at the camp."

I smiled in adoration at her.

"You're so brave, my dearest."

I explained to Zhenya that my father had taught me an important proverb.

"Whoever destroys a single life is as guilty as though he had destroyed the entire world. And whoever rescues a single life earns as much merit as though he had rescued the entire world."

"Come, give me a hand." I urged Zhenya to help with the babushka closest to us.

"We may not be saving the world, Grandmother, however I would say that we're at least saving her world." Zhenya spoke with a wisdom far beyond her youth.

Spurred on and inspired by our example of charity, I observed other able women now following our lead. Any of our sisters able to stand up just received a lifebuoy. How much more time to live any of us had from this point forward was unknowable.

I braced my feet into the snowpack, along with Zhenya, and the elderly mother stood up with some effort. We placed each of her arms around our shoulders and braced her body in between our own. We grimaced as she cried out in agony with each step.

"You'll be all right, sister." I confided to her, not wanting to provoke the wrath of the NKVD guards. "We don't have far to go. You're doing a magnificent job! That's it, one foot forward, and then the other." I wished my words of encouragement provided some sustained benefit.

We slowly made our way and rejoined the endless procession travelling to the campsite.

As we moved past the horses at the front of the disabled carriage, it was obvious they were both in ghastly shape. These were not the local indigenous Siberian ponies, who'd grown used to these severe winter conditions—no. These poor chaps likely came from a more urban environment and were a wretched sight to behold. The stallions were nothing now but loose skin and bones borne from a punishing programme of overwork and abuse. Their proud heads hung low as I strode by. One horse was kneeling on his front legs, and he appeared to be in great discomfort. I speculated he might have a fractured metacarpal.

I overheard the two fellows as they considered a way out of their predicament.

"We will have to unhook Mishka and Polina and trek back to our brethren, Comrade. There's no hope of fixing that wheel now. We've lost the waggon! If we start out right away, we should be able to reach the train depot by nightfall."

"I'm sorry, who did you just say?"

"Mishka and Polina? The horses you fresh dolt!"

"Oh, you moron! You didn't go ahead and name them, did you? Now it'll be impossible for me to put them down! Which is what we should have done weeks ago! They hardly have any meat left on them, anyway. I cannot comprehend what we'll do now."

As we got out of sight of the disaster, a shot from a rifle pierced the silence, followed by a pause. A second shot then followed suit. The clamour was deafening.

After slogging our way into the forest, and following a well-marked trail inwards, we finally approached our destination. We had just hiked a further four kilometres from the catastrophe with the horses. With our disabled sister in tow, it had not been straightforward. Zhenya couldn't catch her breath, and I felt drained of all my remaining strength.

It was at this point that I first caught sight of what was to be our new home—for many years to come. An immense encampment, like a fortified compound, lay spread out in front of us. There appeared a mammoth clearing, carved out in the middle of this primaeval forest, and it was so substantial that the far side was not visible. Massive wooden posts, sourced from the indigenous trees, lay spaced every few metres, with a rudimentary barbed wire strung up between them.

A wide gate stood open in the centre of the path with tall watchtowers on each end of the entrance. It was not possible to miss the words on the enormous sign strung up above the gatehouse:

My Debt To The USSR Will Be Reimbursed By My Hard Work

Fearsome looking uniformed men gazed down upon us from the belvederes as we drew closer, with their rifles drawn and trained. I could see more NKVD guards manning the front gate and snapping harsh orders as everyone entered. They handed out beige pieces of paper to each woman as she crossed the threshold. When it was our turn, we each took a flyer and listened to the commands.

"Take these papers and proceed to your assigned huts immediately! No talking! Move! Keep this line going!"

Zhenya, our companion, and I all studied these thin sheets simultaneously. In a big bold typeface, we saw the number 31 printed. There were no other words or instructions. It seemed we were to proceed with all quickness to hut No. 31.

The construction of the compound's interior mirrored a giant square. Our new living quarters, the huts, were simple wooden buildings made of logs that dotted and lined the edges of the campground. The space in the middle of the campground remained clear. In typical Soviet style, the even numbered huts were on the left-hand side, and the odd-numbered ones were on the right. As we limped down the central thoroughfare of the complex, I could discern a small metal plaque attached to the door of each hut, with a solitary number embossed there. The numbers of the huts slowly increased in value as we made our way deeper into the compound. The footing felt solid in here. Dense snow piled itself onto the ground, creating a frozen solid surface.

I could see that these cabins were rudimentary, with earthen insulation packed between the large cut, wooden timbers. Corrugated metal roofing, formed in the shape of a delta, reached its way to a central chimney on top. These huts must contain wood-burning stoves, because each chimney belched thick columns of blue and white smoke skyward. The distance between each hut was four metres, or so. Women all around us were going into their own assigned huts, with much haste. Our hut, No. 31, lay much further ahead.

Some huts didn't seem to receive any new occupants, I noticed. I spotted tired and haggard looking women staring at us as we shuffled by. These women must have arrived well before us, and they stood from the porches built out from the front door of each hut. I distinctly heard one of them call us ryba. I wondered. Did they mean the aquatic animal, or the act of trawling?

As we passed huts No. 19 and No. 20, an expansive break opened up into a gigantic clearing in the very centre of the campground. I reasoned the distant side of the compound contained the remaining 20 cabins, including No. 31. A series of skillfully built freshwater wells became the natural focal point of the entire complex. Finding a spring for drinking water was crucial and likely factored into the decision of where to start construction of this remote outpost in the Siberian taiga.

To my left I could see administrative shacks, open workshops, various tools, and machinery of all kinds laid out in an orderly fashion. None of the tools or machinery had collected any snow today, which had meant their regular use before our arrival.

Stalin's Door

To my right I saw something unimaginable—a spectacle I'll not soon forget. I instantly stopped, motionless in my tracks, out of fear. The NKVD guards had constructed a steep, wide wooden structure, whose function was impossible to mistake for anything else. A gallows, built up from finely cut lumber, stood here. Its conspicuous placement within the camp assured maximum visibility. Much care went into the creation of this instrument of capital punishment, all but assuring its survival in the elements of this harsh place.

"Oh, Zhenya, honey, don't look at it. Please, just shut your eyes."

I hopelessly begged her to turn away, however it was too late. She caught sight of the macabre display, and I instantly felt sick to my stomach. With Zhenya assisting me as we held up the poor disabled woman between us, I wasn't in any position to pull Zhenya close, to avert her eyes from the scene.

This was a situation where I wished I could have turned back time, if only for a few seconds. I heard an audible gasp from our companion, and the sucking in of air through her teeth.

From up on the gallows, I watched as seven women hung helplessly. Thick nooses made of spun rope expedited their departures from this Earth. I could see their fragile hands bound tightly behind their backs. The simultaneous drop snapped their collective necks in a split second. The grimaces on their mutual faces did nothing to belie their last seconds of pain and suffering. In this brutally frigid weather, it didn't take long for their bodies to freeze completely solid, leaving them to twist in the vicious northern Russian winds—endlessly.

The gruesome exhibit left me with no doubts as to the severity of discipline in this forsaken place.

Just below the blackened and purple necks of the deceased, I spotted small wooden boards which lay draped upon their chests. An inscription of their crimes accompanied each plank and used just a single term. Fraternisation and thievery were their capital offences, for which they'd paid the ultimate price.

The women were all left there hanging—naked.

§

We continued walking over to the other side of the compound and arrived at hut No. 31. Except for the numbering, each cabin looked precisely the same to me. A large log of cut wood lay on the threshold of the door, propping it open, and we filed inside as quickly as we could manage. As I transitioned from the daylight, I instantly discerned how dim it was inside the hut. The huts didn't have any windows, or any other apparent means of outside illumination.

It took more than a few minutes for my eyes to adjust properly in here. The ambient temperature inside the hut was pleasant. The warmth emanating from the large iron wood-burning stove, installed in the centre of the lodge, washed over us like water, as if we were submerging into a decadent bath for the first time.

My demeanour improved at once.

Large black-coloured latches on the stove, with ringed metal handles on the ends, attached themselves to the central door of the furnace. An expansive flat area on its top held many pots and pans, and a fat metal exhaust pipe snaked its way into the ceiling above us. Slats built into the sides of the oven allowed for the regulation of heat and light.

I noted the large stack of cordwood piled nearly to the ceiling—directly opposite from the stove.

The inescapable aroma of delicious smelling food being prepared had my undivided attention. A pair of women, who were not in our group from the train procession, were attending to the outsized cauldrons. They rhythmically stirred the heavenly scented goodness with enormous wooden spoons. I could see steam rising from the pots, which filled the cabin in a savoury thick fog.

Not having eaten for over 24 hours, combined with not having any proper meals for well over 17 days, had taken its toll. My condition was not unlike all the women in here, I desperately needed something to devour—straightaway.

A positive voice then spoke up, yet I couldn't see who it was.

"Please, please, just find somewhere to sit for now. Hurry, please. One spot is as good as the next!"

Two lengthy narrow communal wooden tables, with accompanying benches made from the same timber, ran lengthwise down the centre of the hut, bisected by the wood-burning stove. As we all filed inside, I sat down near the end of the row, where we could find space.

Once settled, and with Zhenya right next to me, I took a moment to survey the contents of the shelter. Apart from the communal tables, the oven, a food preparation area, and the woodpile, the remaining space contained the bunks. Assembled along the sides of the hut, each bunk contained four berths, erected from the floor to the ceiling.

I counted five bunks on each side of the room, which meant 40 women could live in this hut. At the rear of the hut I saw a wooden partition that lead to an area in the back. I didn't yet know what was back there.

After a few more minutes had passed, and the last of the new No. 31's from our train found their seats, I watched a short woman walk over to the hut's door to remove the brace, closing it firmly behind her. She then skirted her way back over to the wood-burning stove and crouched down beside it. With some deft manoeuvres, she opened the slats on all sides of the iron behemoth—near the top. Once completed, it filled the hut with a rich amber light from the combustion within. I studied our apparent host intently.

The woman dressed plainly, wearing a traditional balakhon, which no doubt covered many layers of clothing beneath it. The pattern on her overgarment ran from an ordinary beige colour to a striking crimson. The material was thick, warm, and looked well cared for. I examined her weathered face and could see a demeanour of cautious friendliness that imparted trust. Under her headscarf, long locks of silver and grey hair flowed well past her shoulders. If I had to venture a guess, I thought her age close to my own.

The woman then stood upon a small wooden crate and turned to face all of us. Speaking with authority, she began.

"May I have your attention, please? My name is Madam Rokossovskaya, and I am the matron of hut number thirty-one. I bid you welcome after your interminable journey here. You are now all internees of Gulag camp Mytininsk twenty-three. This is a brand-new corrective labour camp for women. You've all received sentences and transportation to this camp to serve out your time. You must have many questions—and many concerns.

"Let us put a bookmark in that conversation for now and get you all something to eat first. Trust me, I know you're hungry. Let us all also thank Comrade Stalin for the generous meal we are about to consume."

Mme Rokossovskaya then pointed to a modest portraiture of our dearest leader that hung high on one of the timbered support columns in the centre of the cabin. Ironically, even whilst incarcerated here in the Gulag, we were still under his ever-watchful black within black eyes.

With that, she turned her attention to the women working at the wood-burning stove. The cooks started filling small metal bowls with the contents from their steaming pots. They then began distributing the wonderfully smelling nourishment to all the prisoners sitting at the communal tables. I felt a slight tugging sensation on my winter coat.

"What does Gulag mean, Grandmother?" Zhenya asked.

"The term Gulag is merely the informal name for the NKVD bureau of prison-camp administration. Now, please be silent!" I whispered to her.

The Main Directorate of Camps, the Glavnoe upravlenie lagerei, was abbreviated to form its infamous name—Gulag. Over the last three years, just hearing the word Gulag would strike utter terror into the hearts of even the bravest of Soviet comrades. Our arrested husbands and brothers not shot under the auspices of Article No. 58, became political prisoners: the politicheskiye. The wives and older children of the men caught up in this horror found themselves in a precarious legal situation. Guilt by association became de rigueur, and the NKVD arrested entire families en masse, deporting them to the Gulag labour camps of far northeastern Russia. Anyone, and at any time, might find themselves accused of a veritable laundry list of felonies, real and imaginary.

Friends denounced their friends, and neighbours turned against their neighbours. Even the act of speaking with strangers became precarious. NKVD informants were everywhere!

The only saving grace we experienced in this camp was the fact that we were being held with the other politicals, and not the common and hardcore criminals also swept up in the purges.

I sat patiently and urged Zhenya to stop her fidgeting. When my supper arrived, I immediately gave the bowl to Zhenya, and awaited another delivery.

"Please, Zhenya, eat now. Make sure you eat everything given to you and remember to always be thankful." I had no doubts that she would shortly devour everything in front of her.

"Yes, Grandmother."

When my allotment of sustenance arrived, I verbally thanked the woman who provided it to me and dug into it with all abandon. The stew in my bowl was hot and nourishing, and quite conceivably the most splendid tasting meal I'd ever eaten. From the very first bite, my taste buds experienced an overwhelming intensity of flavour and delight, as if a mighty explosion of joy had just gone off from within my mouth.

From that point forward, it was a monumental struggle between wanting to inhale all the contents within the dish as rapidly as possible, or to relax and try to savour the life-giving nutrition for a while. The former won out, and I was confident that I wouldn't have endured another day without eating. This meal was little more than some boiled meat in a thick broth, however it instantaneously improved my welfare.

When I finished my repast, and licked the metal bowl clean, I bowed my head and closed my eyes for a moment. On the inside of my eyelids I could still make out an afterimage from having watched the fires inside the wood-burning stove. Yellows faded into oranges, and oranges into ethereal blackness. I slowed my breathing.

Because I finally found some time, I followed my traditions and began to pray.

I said a silent blessing, the Birkat Hamazon, to the Lord. I also gave thanks for being able to continue to look after and protect Zhenya. She was the reason I must persevere in this place. I knew that Soviet law had forbidden all religion, yet I vowed never to be ungrateful.

"What was that you were just doing, Grandmother?" I noticed that Zhenya had finished her portion faster than I did and had been watching me pray.

"Oh, dear—now listen to me." I bent down and whispered to Zhenya. "I was just being thankful to the Lord for the food that he provided. I will teach you all about it."

After our supper, we saw Mme Rokossovskaya resume her place on top of the crate. She began speaking again.

"Now that you've eaten a proper meal, let me see if I can address some rules and protocols expected of you whilst you're here in this camp. First, if you remember nothing else, remember this. Your durability in this place depends on you adhering to a code. The code is simple: work is food, and food is life. This is a corrective labour camp and I expect everyone to work. Everyone. There are no exceptions. If you work every day, you will eat every day. It's that straightforward.

"Not everyone will have the same duties or responsibilities, however collectively we will always rise to meet our levied work quotas. Through hard work we shall pay off our debt to society. Achieving this goal is paramount to our survival."

She slowed her cadence and looked pensive.

"Allow me to offer you some sage advice. Please forget who you were back in the actual world—that life means nothing now. Here is all that matters. This place is all you should concern yourselves with. Take every day, one at a time, and be thankful you're still alive—for there are multitudes who are not.

"We are all cleansed, pure, and honourable in the crucible of work. Work well, stay strong, and your time in this camp will pass swiftly."

The matron now climbed down from the box and walked around the communal tables to study us. She was headstrong, confident in her speech, and kept constant eye contact with all of us.

"A few other policies to mention, if you don't mind. The bowl in front of you is now yours. Keep it with you at all times. If you cannot meet your daily work quota, or I place you on administrative punishment, then you'll receive a bowl one half the size of the one you possess. Please trust in me when I tell you you'll not last long on half-rations in this place.

"They say that hunger is no auntie, it will not give you a pie. Don't put yourself into that position, I beg of you. If you lose your bowl, or it's stolen, then you may not eat. Your bowl is now your most prized possession."

I noticed a thin wide slot punched into the side, near the lip of the bowl nearest the edge. I thought ahead and theorised this was so we could attach the bowls to our outer garments.

"If my information is reliable, you've all travelled here from our glorious capital Moskva. It's a beautiful city, I'm told, and one that I'd like to visit one day."

The matron returned to her crate, stood beside it, and continued addressing us.

"In case you're wondering, I too am incarcerated here. The NKVD gave me a ten-year sentence, just like all of you received. I've been in the Gulag for three years now. It's not been easy—I won't sugarcoat that fact at all. However, I'm a survivor, and I mean to keep you all alive too. I only ask that you work with me, and not against me.

"My original matron told me when I first arrived in the camps that we can make this situation for the best or deteriorate into pettiness and misery. Well, I choose the former, and I hope you do too. We're all equal in this place. We all have equal stations, equal responsibilities, and equal chances. Ironically, here in the Gulag, we might just be the last vestige of true Communism."

That last thought made me take a pause in contemplation. She might just have a point there.

When the matron finished speaking, we washed our bowls and dried them off. We then presented ourselves for bunk selections.

Seniority determined whom the matron assigned to each specific berth, with one's arrest date dictating seniority. The longer the NKVD had incarcerated you within the Gulag system, the more seniority you possessed.

As I'd already observed, there were 20 berths, across five bunks on each side of the hut. It was immediately obvious that being closer to the wood-burning stove, and higher off of the cabin floor, would be more desirable. Warmer and dryer for certain.

The matron attacked the sorting process logically.

"All right, let's make this as elementary as we can. I need the 'thirty-eights on this side with me, and the 'thirty-sevens, and before, over on that side." She motioned with her hands.

She requested that we sort ourselves according to the year they arrested us in.

The surrounding women began shuffling to their required sides. The NKVD arrested Zhenya and I on the tenth of January, so we remained with the matron in the 1938 group.

With everyone on either side of the room, the matron began inquiring as to our specific arrest dates. The vast majority were on the 1937 side. This process didn't take long, however. With a tie—women apprehended on the same day—then we would sort alphabetically by patronymic. They arrested no other women on the day Zhenya and I were, however we had a relatively recent date when compared to everyone else, and the matron placed us in the second furthest bunk on the right side of the room. I had the second berth, and Zhenya took the third, right above me.

My hands took hold on each of Zhenya's sides along her slight frame, and I boosted her up and into her berth. Then I bent down to squeeze myself into mine. Thankfully my berth, unlike the first position in the bunks, was not resting directly on the floor of the hut.

A note on the bunks here, if I may? These were the strangest beds I'd ever come across. Constructed from the same wood as everything around us, and stacked four berths high, they contained fully upright side panels. As I descended into my berth for the first time, I felt as if I were laying myself into a coffin. A thick layer of straw covered the bottom wooden part of the berth. The matron provided no blankets nor any covers. I supposed the sides of the berth were an attempt at insulation. Or maybe it would act like a railing so we wouldn't roll ourselves out in the middle of the night. I rested my head down upon the straw and felt instantly fatigued, in a way that I'd never felt before. But now was not the time for sleep.

I took the knuckles of my right hand and knocked them thrice upon the wood ceiling above me.

"Hey there, my solnyshka, how are you doing up there? How do you like your berth?"

"I am fine, Grandmother. I have plenty of room up here. It's cozy." A disembodied voice answered from above.

"Make sure you sleep on your back, so you won't squash your nose!" I joked with her.

§

Once we all completed the sorting of the bunks, we climbed back down, and joined the rest of the ladies at the common tables. The matron continued with her introductions.

"Now that you all have a place to rest your heads each night, it's time to finish up with all the finer points of camp administration. We will have an early evening. Our work begins first thing tomorrow morning. Over the next few days, I will interview all of you so I can best match up your skills and abilities against the myriad of jobs we have here."

I peered over at Zhenya to ensure she was still listening, as the matron spoke.

"One last note on the rules. I'm sure I don't have to dwell on what you all witnessed in the camp's quad this afternoon. Stealing property of any kind is forbidden—especially food. Also, we never permit fraternisation with the camp guards—ever. Do not speak or engage with any of them.

"If a camp guard approaches you, or otherwise communicates with you, report him to me, or any other matron at once! Failure to report any contact will have severe repercussions."

The matron paused and lowered her voice.

"If you're naïve enough to break these regulations—well, you've already seen justice meted out in this place. You will take your direction only from the matrons. This is our system, which has proved the most prosperous. Believe me when I tell you that any distractions that jeopardise our production quotas will be fatal to you, one way, or the other."

A feeling of dejection gripped me when I relived the sighting of those poor sisters as they hung from the gallows—stripped, frozen, and twisting in the never-ending harsh winds of Siberia.

The thought of execution for fraternisation or theft was most unpleasant.

Conversely, being slowly starved to death for not meeting your levied work quota sounded wholly painful.

I would continuously have to navigate a narrow channel of rules and regulations here to ensure the safety of Zhenya and myself.

The matron finished up with her speech.

"Oh, there's a partition you may have noticed in the hut's rear. That is the area that leads to our latrine and a washing nook. This time of year it's too cold for showers, so I'm afraid it will be sponge baths for the next few months."

Everyone collectively sighed at that news.

Not soon after the matron concluded, and when my head hit the hay inside my berth that first night in the camp, I fell asleep straightaway and dreamt.

§

It's been said that the stings from a swarm of shershni, the fierce indigenous breed of hornets that inhabit western Russia, can be agonisingly painful. Sometimes they were even fatal. I heard their angry din and witnessed these fearsome yellow and black flying insects all around me.

They darted in and out, dive-bombing my head in waves. I felt mystified by what I could have done to provoke such an attack. I tried waving my hands all about me to chase them away, which only seemed to make them more incensed. Their rhythmic humming sounded brassier now—until it was all that I could perceive. I was certain the shershni would prick me at any moment, and braced for the suffering to come, my eyes now shut tight.

Awakening myself in a panic, I took a deep breath and held it inside. Something had woken me. The reverberations of my beating heart echoed all around until I calmed myself. Now I could hear a harsh electric buzzing emanating from the common area. The sequence abruptly ended, a brief pause ensued, and then it started again. I counted to six this time. Somebody on this floor had a visitor. Who in the world called at this hour? Less than a minute later, the sound of fists pounding on our door shook us both wide awake.

"Sava! Who is it? What is going on? Is everything ok?" I urgently pleaded with my husband for answers.

"I am not sure dearest, however, I cannot think this is pleasant news. Let me open up before they start up again."

"Try to not disturb Zhenya, if you can help it." I begged him.

Sava lit a candle from the side table and then donned his robe. I watched as he gently peeled back the curtain that separated our bedroom nook from the rest of the one-room flat.

I heard him pad over to the entryway and throw free the bolt. The metal door opened, and I could discern the footsteps of several men. A tense conversation started up. There was a deliberately hushed tone and the beginnings of an argument ensued.

Feeling alarmed, I fumbled for my glasses, putting them on speedily. I then felt around for Sava's naval pocket watch on the nightstand and retrieved it. When I placed the face of the ticker near my eyes, I could make out little green specks of radium paint. The colourant illuminated the hour and minute hands, along with the ship's watchstanding periods.

If I looked sharp, and didn't blink, I'd swear the flecks were—dancing. Their performance was beautiful, like an ornate kaleydoskop of small fireworks exploding from within. Whenever I had trouble sleeping at night, I'd stare at this glowing light show for what seemed like hours on end. My own private mediation followed, with the ticking of the timepiece matching my heartbeat.

The moment was precisely three o'clock in the morning. Sava hadn't even been home for two hours this morning. What could this possibly be about, I wondered. I felt my heart racing from inside my chest.

"Stay calm." I silently told myself. "This is nothing, just relax."

Even so, I couldn't stay composed. We lived in dangerous times. I waited 60 seconds and decided against my better judgement to investigate our dead of night callers. I couldn't sleep now, anyway. I quickly put my night robe and slippers on, and I wandered out to join my husband.

At our door I saw two junior lieutenants and a captain from the NKVD huddling around Sava's glowing yellow candle. I immediately knew that Sava was deep into a dispute about some urgent departmental matter. I approached them gradually.

All four men simultaneously stopped their whispered conversations when they saw me. Just before they ceased their deliberations, I heard my husband say something.

"Yes, damn you—and what of our agreement?"

I waved my hands about, invitingly.

"Sava—may I put the kettle on and make you and your guests some hot tea?" I peered over at our visitants and pleaded with them too. "Why you officers have to be freezing! Where are your greatcoats? It has to be twenty-five below naught outside. Come, let me get you something?"

Our callers just wore their regular uniforms—and that seemed irregular to me.

Sava glanced towards me with reassurance.

"No, no, my dearest. There's no time for that. These men came directly to fetch me. There's a crisis at the Lubyanka, don't you know? Won't you try to understand? Now, be a darling and let me change my clothes. I've got to get into my uniform with all due dispatch."

With that, I saw Sava run behind our bedroom curtain to don his official dress. I stole a glance over at Zhenya, who was still fast asleep on her cot near the wood-burning stove. She appeared tranquil.

As I attended to our trio of guests, I noticed that they were merely adolescents. My husband was decades older than they were. Ah, if only youth would know, if only old age were able, I thought whimsically.

"Are you sure I can't make you a spiced brew, young sirs?"

"No, Madam, thank you positively." The captain tipped his forefinger to the brim of his thick, red banded blue cap. "We've got to get back to our headquarters immediately. Our colonel is waiting upon us to all return. It's an emergency, you see. We drove straight here."

I demurred and suddenly felt anxious.

In no time flat my husband returned, wearing his lieutenant's uniform, neatly pressed and crisp. He always made it a habit to iron his uniform when he arrived home from his duties, so he wouldn't have to do it the next morning. I had volunteered many times to help him with it, however he said it helped him to unwind after an endless day.

With my husband's hair now freshly combed, and his shoes shined, Sava was an authentic example of how an officer should comport himself. He stepped over to where I was standing and smiled. My husband then kissed me on the forehead. Sava looked soulfully into my eyes.

"Lera? Please don't forget that we need milk. See if you can get some from the kosher market in the morning, won't you? You know the one we like to go to?"

I felt my throat contract suddenly. I swallowed hard, and I could feel a litre of blood as it rushed into my cheeks. I meekly answered him.

"Yes, my husband. Goodbye." I gazed longingly at him, and our eyes met again—for just a moment. I would have done anything to hold that glance for an eternity.

In that brief instant, I understood—everything.

Stalin's Door

As the men departed the flat, I closed the door behind them. I felt my hands trembling on the doorknob, and I couldn't help myself. I inhaled a giant lungful of air and held it inside me for many seconds before exhaling forcefully.

My husband had just given me a coded message—one that I prayed I would never hear.

Previously, we arranged that if Sava ever told me in person, or over the telephone, to get some milk at the local kosher market, it meant he was being placed under arrest.

Sava confided in me many times before now that just because he worked for Comrade Stalin's secret police force, it didn't exempt him from the fearful suspicions of its leadership—not by a long shot. He constantly reminded me that the enemies of the people were everywhere!

Sava confessed that he suspected those within the NKVD were under even more intense scrutiny than ordinary people.

Comrade Stalin was deathly paranoid about an uprising, or coup d'état, formed organically from within the Communist Party. Therefore, Comrade Stalin did everything to prevent his unseating of absolute power. Our supreme leader believed that the only logical solution was to grind all threats into dust—no matter what the cost. No one was safe. Everyone was suspect. Arrest, deportation, execution, and death became commonplace.

I realised my husband wasn't coming back to me. I also suspected that another team of NKVD officers were, even now, on their way over.

My apprehension was possibly only moments away. With all deliberate speed, I rushed over to the closet and began throwing on clothing.

I put on as many garments as I could manage, regardless of comfort. I then hurriedly awakened the girl who was still asleep near the wood-burning stove.

"Move quickly, Zhenya! They are coming to arrest us next."

§

That first night inside the frigid basement prison cell was a horrific experience. I wasn't sure exactly where we were being detained. The police van in which they transported us had its windows sealed shut and blacked out. Because it was still in the middle of the night, I wouldn't have been able to see anything, anyway. We could have been anywhere within the metropolis.

The temperature outside was easily minus 30 degrees centigrade tonight, and to my dismay, I discovered our detention area lacked any semblance of proper heat or ventilation. I estimated the ambient air in here to be the freezing point of water. Thank goodness I insisted Zhenya put on every piece of clothing she owned before we left our communal apartment! A dim electric lamp installed into the high ceiling of this dungeon bathed us all in a kind of perpetual twilight. This place was the very definition of the word gloomy. A thick metal cage surrounded our only source of illumination, lest anyone get any ideas of trying to break it.

As I scanned all around this dank environment, I counted no fewer than 50 women jammed into this modest-sized room with Zhenya and me. Only a dozen men at a time would have reasonably fit in here—under normal circumstances. With so many people incarcerated these days, the overcrowding ensured we stood shoulder to shoulder. There was hardly any space to even turn around in place. I peered down at Zhenya, who was standing in front of me. She was more appropriately attired than many other women I saw here.

It saddened me to learn, much later, about a common tactic used by the NKVD arresting officers. To pacify those being apprehended, they informed the accused they were merely being picked up for the briefest of questioning. The prisoners were told they'd be back to their homes in only an hour's time—and to not worry at all. That it was all just standard operating procedure. The unfortunate women that believed those cruel lies were now in terrible shape for what awaited us all. Some women had nothing more with them than the nightclothes on their backs. I reasoned they'd be lucky just to survive the night. If any of us saw the morning sun again, what a welcome relief that would be.

Yes, the girl and I were in relatively decent shape in comparison, except in the rush of our arrests, I only grabbed one pair of mittens. I silently cursed myself at this forgetfulness. I must be more careful from now on. Our lives depended on it.

I tried to hand over the pair of thick wool rukavitsy for Zhenya to use, however she informed me that her hands were already rather warm. We could easily trade off when required.

I knew that getting any sleep tonight would be futile. Throughout the cell I could hear women crying and sobbing emotionally as they lamented their new circumstances. I felt horrible, as there was nothing I could do for them.

In one corner of this holding cell I spied a lone metal bucket, which I presumed was there for us to relieve ourselves into. Truth be told, I was not looking forward to that experience.

Mostly everyone kept to themselves—trying to make the best of this horrendous fate.

Along the wall I noticed one solitary woman, who found herself in a spot of bother. She was violently smashing her head into the thick stone. The noise it made with every impact—a distinctive squelching—nauseated me.

"Now Zhenya. Look at me, honey." I knelt down to ensure I was staring up into her fervent eyes. "What I'm about to tell you is critically important. Are you listening?"

"Yes, Madam Komolova, I am."

"When the NKVD guards come to interview us, you must declare you're related to me." I paused for a moment and contemplated what to do. "I don't think I can pass you off as my daughter. I'm much too mature for that. So you'll be my granddaughter instead, all right? Do you understand me? From this point forward, and for all the time we have left in this world, you must address me as grandmother." I kept my voice low, and I felt myself trembling ever so slightly.

Sensing Zhenya's confusion, I explained further.

"If the NKVD determine we're not family, they will separate us forever. It's my primary responsibility to keep you safe, and I can't do that if you're not with me."

"I think I understand—Grandmother." Zhenya wore a brave face now, and as I considered the dire conditions we found ourselves in, I felt immensely proud of her.

"There's another urgent matter, my dearest. I know your birthday is in late April. You'll be how old—thirteen this year—isn't that correct? Take heed of my advice. You're already thirteen years old. Do you hear me? You're thirteen years old today and you'll be turning fourteen in April."

"What? Why is that?"

"Because children aren't allowed where I suspect we're headed to. If the police discover you are only twelve years old, they won't let you go with me. Please repeat after me—I am thirteen years old."

"I'm—I'm thirteen years old."

"What year were you born in?"

"I was born in 'twenty-five. Wait." Zhenya thought for a moment and immediately corrected herself. "I mean 'twenty-four. Yes, I was born on the twenty-seventh of April, nineteen twenty-four. I'll be fourteen in three months."

"Superb, Zhenya. Now, one last thing. We've got to change your name. You can't be Yevgeniya Avksentyevna Kanadina any longer. Remember, when the NKVD arrested your parents, you escaped. I am confident those men are still searching for you.

"We need to come up with a new patronymic, so you'll be secure with me. If you were my real granddaughter, I'd think you'd have made a fine daughter for my son Ivan. In that case, your given name and patronymic would be Yevgeniya Ivanovna.

"We'll keep Komolova as the family surname to keep things simplified."

"So you and Mister Komolov have a son?"

"No, my dear. Little Ivan died when he was just an infant."

"Oh, I am sad about that."

"Now please give me your undivideds and reiterate exactly what I say. My name is Yevgeniya Ivanovna Komolova, and I was born on the twenty-seventh of April, nineteen twenty-four."

Zhenya repeated her alternative name and birthdate with no hesitation this time.

"That's excellent Zhenya. Now please say that to yourself as many times as is necessary. You must quickly learn this by rote. If you slip up and forget it—it will be miserable for both of us."

§

After a few more wretched hours of just standing in place and waiting, the NKVD officers abruptly opened the heavy metal cell door. Many of the women screamed out, as if frightened to death, and their screeching painfully pierced my ears. A dull ringing persisted with me for many seconds. The jailers then began yelling out new orders for us.

"Attention! Attention! Gather your belongings and proceed upstairs for processing and embarkation. No talking! Move now!"

One man used his truncheon, beating upon the frame multiple times. The reverberations were louder than thunder in this confined enclosure. I knew I surely wouldn't want to be on the receiving end of his baton. Everyone filed out of the dungeon—slowly.

I assumed it was now in the early morning, perhaps seven o'clock. I squeezed Zhenya's hand firmly, ensuring I didn't let go.

Stalin's Door

To guarantee our collective compliance, they promised us all hot tea and biscuits. Many hours had elapsed since we last ate or drank anything, and everyone felt fatigued from missing sleep in that miserable basement.

We soon joined a long procession of women, who were funneling out from all the other prison cells. A single file formed and snaked all around the dismal hallways of the detention complex. Once we finally made it to the main level, we formed ourselves into queues inside a large spacious auditorium. Looking near the top of the ceiling, I spotted tiny clerestory windows that let in brilliant sunlight which painfully blinded my eyes. The sensation felt jarring after I'd grown accustomed to the darkness from the last several hours, and it took me a few moments to acclimatise.

After I regained my composure, I studied our unfamiliar environment. Each lengthy line of women prisoners ended at a long table on the far side, which sat perpendicular to all of us. Several uniformed men sat there working. These NKVD guards appeared to be conducting interrogations whilst simultaneously recording the answers into giant red ledgers.

No one appeared overjoyed to be here, especially the fellows asking the questions. Except for the voices coming from the front of this assembly hall, it was deathly silent. I was not at all surprised to spy a surfeit of official looking documentation and mountains of papers upon the surface of the work areas.

In every totalitarian government, its lifeblood was the inevitability of endless administration. Filing and paperwork were as automatic here as breathing.

I suddenly chuckled at the thought of the Soviet Union suddenly collapsing one day because it ran out of letterhead in which to document everything.

After what seemed to be quite a tedious delay, it was now our turn for the men to debrief us. I walked up to the edge of the table with Zhenya as we presented ourselves to an NKVD guard seated directly in front. By his looks, he couldn't have been a year beyond the age of majority. The boyish man stared up at me with a surly expression of boredom upon his face and queried, not even bothering to remove the coffin nail from his lips.

"Papers?"

"We have no official identification, Sir."

"Of course you don't. You miserable zechkas! Name then? Family surname first, then given name and patronymic."

"Komolova Valeriya Timurovna."

"Date of birth?" The man scribbled furiously into the pages of the outsized book.

"I was born on the third of May, eighteen eighty-two."

"Place of birth?"

"Sankt-Petersburg." I answered as if speaking out of habit. I quickly caught myself before he could make an incident. "Correction, Sir. Leningrad. I was born in Leningrad."

The NKVD officer now glowered at me and flicked the ash of his cigarette forcefully into the overflowing receptacle to his right. He'd gracefully piled the extinguished butts high inside the tray, like a pyramid.

The fellow completed jotting down his accounting notes as he took hold of a small round rubber stamp. In a procedure he must have already performed dozens of times today, he made a quick two-step motion with the stamp. Stamp to ink, then stamp to paper.

"And who do we have here?"

"This is my granddaughter."

The sullen functionary took a lengthy drag from his cigarette and studied Zhenya intently, his eyes darting up and down. She stood beside me on the tips of her toes, as tall as she could present herself.

"How old are you, young lady?" He cocked an eyebrow as if to show he was positive something wasn't quite correct here.

"She's thir—"

The man cut me off mid-sentence.

"Excuse me, Mother. I was asking her."

"I am thirteen years old, Sir." Zhenya repeated confidently.

"Hmmmm, you don't look thirteen to me. Perhaps we should send you to the State orphanages to live? Where you're headed to shortly is no place for little girls."

"Please, Sir. She is all I have now. Please let her stay with me." I begged and pleaded with the officer.

After a few seconds of deliberation, the NKVD officer just shook his head in defeat and asked Zhenya for her vital information.

"Very well, as you wish."

"Komolova Yevgeniya Ivanovna. I was born on the twenty-seventh of April, nineteen twenty-four, in our capital city Moskva, Sir." Zhenya smartly declared.

After repeating the bit with the notes in the ledger and the rubber stamping, the youthful fellow reached behind his chair. From a large wooden box, he retrieved two small round metal discs. He studied the discs for a minute and wrote more information into his files.

He then took each disc, and by forcefully grabbing the edges and making a twisting motion, he split them in half along their middles. He handed us the now semicircle pieces of metal and then placed the other two halves into a bin underneath the table.

"These are your identification tags. Don't lose them, ever. Next!"

Zhenya and I took our badges, and proceeded into the next room over, with the others that had completed their processing. This area was much smaller and didn't have any windows. I saw a large metal sliding door at the front of the room.

When I had a minute to stop, I unclasped my hand and surveyed the thin metal tag inside. Embossed within the dark grey metal was the word Gulag. Below that was a six-digit number.

Mine read No. 069033. I made Zhenya show me hers, No. 069034.

I flipped over the tag and looked on the reverse side.

There I saw letters which looked like they had been pre-printed directly onto the alloy:

FEM POL

I was unsure what that meant.

Within a few minutes of our arrival, this new waiting area reached its capacity, and I heard the door we came in through as it closed violently. I estimated that there were over 100 women standing with us here, of all ages and generations.

A senior officer of the NKVD angrily barged his way through the throng of prisoners, and up to the front of the chamber. He turned around and addressed us is a loud booming voice.

"Attention! Attention! I am addressing the arrested wives and daughters of the traitors to the Motherland! As of today, under the authority of General Order number naught naught four eight six, we incarcerate you into the custody of the NKVD prison-camp administration bureau. In a few moments you will all board trains where we will then transport you to corrective labour camps within Siberia."

Siberia. I silently lamented this revelation of our ultimate destination, knowing it was many thousands of kilometres away from here. The territory was so far away in fact that it might as well have been on the horns of the devil himself.

The announcement continued.

"Each one of you will serve out a sentence of ten years. At the end of ten years, we will consider your debt to the Motherland paid in full. As political prisoners, we will not give you the right to correspondence, nor of appeal. Make sure and take a respectful look around our noble capital city upon your departure. You won't be seeing it ever again. Upon your release we will not allow you to live within one hundred kilometers of Moskva."

Although I was positive that neither Zhenya nor I had committed any of the crimes against the Communist State they had just levied against us, just being related to those arrested could prove no less fortunate in one's adjudication.

Once Stalin's secret police arrested one family member, the remainder of the household would soon follow suit. Guilt by association was in full effect, and the order of the day. One good apple could find its way into the whole rotten barrel—too easily, in fact. A spoonful of tar spoils a barrel of honey.

The NKVD officer then threw open the large metal latch on the sliding door in front of us. With a loud grunt he pulled the door towards his left side. A loud metal on metal grinding racket nearly deafened us. Instantly a crisp blast of winter air rushed into the room and filled my lungs—which produced a burning sensation. I squinted my eyes into the bright daylight and looked out upon an endless series of cattle waggons lined up one after the other. The cars that rode upon these giant iron railway tracks led all the way to the other side of the country—a half a planet distance from here.

"Honey, look at me now." I crouched down to address Zhenya.

"Yes, Grandmother?" Zhenya's bright eyes looked directly at me.

"Do you know what a Matryoshka doll is?"

"I do. My father gave me a set of the nesting dolls for my birthday when I was six years old. Six dolls, one for each year of my life." Zhenya's smile beamed as she recalled that happy memory for me.

"Splendid, my dear. That's superb. Now listen to me carefully. Shortly we'll be leaving Moskva, never to return. I don't know exactly what lies ahead of us, so I need you to be courageous. Think of all the enjoyable times you had with your parents, your friends, and your schoolmates. Think of every happy memory you had growing up.

"I need you to put them all into the recesses of your mind—now. Think of the innermost wooden doll in your set. Small and needing protection from the larger dolls outside of her. That's what I need you to construct inside your mind. Put layers and layers on top of the joyful thoughts you had when you were growing up. Keep them tucked away and safe.

"And remember to look in upon them, from time to time. They need you, and you will need them. Where we're headed, you must protect yourself in this way. No one can take your remembrances from you. Ever. Do you understand what I'm saying, my sheifale?" I watched as Zhenya desperately tried to comprehend me.

As Zhenya's eyes started to well up with tears, I sensed a great trepidation, and her lips trembled ever so slightly.

"Oh, hey now. Let's have none of that. You're a strong young zhenshchina now." I took a finger and rested it beneath her chin. "Be my big brave Matryona. You can do it. I'll be with you—always. I promise."

A voice from one NKVD guard on top of a tall watchtower in front of us delivered a sonorous message.

"Climb aboard now! Do this quickly! Move!" A series of whistles rang out, and everyone left our vestibule, shuffling forward into lengthy lines.

With that, I took Zhenya's warm hand inside of mine, and we proceeded through the metal doors, and out on to the bricked top walkway that led to the mighty railway platform ahead. Ancient wooden ramps, that stock cattle had used for years, guided us all up and into the railcars, one by one.

When they jammed us into the train car, so full that you could hardly turn yourself around standing in place, they then slammed the gliding hatch shut.

The latch produced a heavy grinding noise. A clicking sound followed from what I presumed to be the lock engaging.

I took a moment to inhale and hold in the last breath of fresh air I would have for some time.

Our unending journey eastward was just beginning.

§

Those that live within the Siberian taiga will tell you of its trio of seasons. The few weeks of summer, the winter, and the dead of winter. Early February definitely counted as the latter. The frigid conditions and wicked winds were life threatening, and we only had daylight for a mere sixth of each day.

Thankfully, there was a new camp directive that stipulated no outside work could begin if the temperature read minus 40 degrees centigrade, or below. The NKVD guards enforced this directive for the seven consecutive days following our arrival at the encampment. We were experiencing brutal temperatures, even for this part of the country. It turned into a bit of a blessing in disguise, as it allowed everyone to get much needed rest and recuperation from our taxing journey into northeastern Russia.

Not being able to work outside didn't mean that we were idle, not by a long shot. The inside work contingents comprised tasks specifically designed for us—the women. We worked on patching, sewing, and repairs to the men's uniforms and clothing. Making things last in this place was a matter of life and death.

At the same time, we also took stock of our own apparel and made the required mending. The clothes on our backs would have to last us—a long while, in fact. We constantly heard rumours the NKVD guards would issue new clothing for us, however, the matron urged us not to believe in such unsubstantiated talk, until it proved correct.

The indoor work activities were long and mindless, yet it was not too physically arduous for me. The matron took time whilst we sewed to explain about the various outside work details that we'd soon join into.

The most labour intensive enterprise in the entire camp were the timber brigades, and it would involve most of the prison's population. The harvesting of firewood, directly from the surfeit of trees out in the Siberian taiga, was our paramount objective. The trees covered everything around us like a thick carpet.

Our campsite was like an island within an endless ocean of timber. Firewood was crucial because it was the primary source of fuel in the Gulag. Fuel was paramount in the production of heat that the wood-burning stoves provided to keep us all alive. Heat meant we wouldn't freeze to death, and that we'd be able to eat every day.

The trees also produced the shelter we lived in, the bunks we slept in, and the tables we ate from. The currency of wood was as valuable as gold in this wretched place. Thankfully for everyone, an immeasurable deposit waited for collection out in the ancient forests that now surrounded us.

Over the course of the first few days which followed our arrival, the matron also interviewed all of the women in her hut. She was trying to match up everyone's skills and abilities with the duties assigned to her, along with determining everyone's physical assessment. Everyone in the Gulag would be segregated into classification levels based upon their work capabilities: heavy-work capable, light-work capable, or invalid.

That last classification—invalid—was not a desirable one. The NKVD guards assigned it to those prisoner's incapable of producing any meaningful work. They relegated invalids to a half-ration of food each day. Half-rations were an invitation to slowly starving to death, and it became quickly obvious to us that even living on full rations here would barely be enough food to sustain life.

The crushing climate and the expectations of the heavy-work quotas burned twice as many calories as we were used to. My mind contemplated ideas on how we could supplement our meagre rations.

When it was my turn to speak with the matron, we sat at the communal tables near the wood-burning stove, across from one another. The matron carried with her a small ledger where she made notes during all the interviews. She retrieved a small pencil from her pocket that looked well used. She then placed the pair of glasses that hung from a lanyard around her neck, upon her face.

"If you could please give me your full name, family surname first, then given name and patronymic. I also require your Gulag identification number."

I gave her my full name and the personal identity number from my badge as I watched her scribble quickly within the pages of her notebook. Her handwriting looked precise, and she used the space on the blank sheets with much economy by writing in a teeny manner.

"Don't you want to know how old I am?" I asked the matron, expecting her next question.

"No, I don't want to know. Your age is of no importance in here. Only your ability to complete work." The matron, I noticed, didn't like to make eye contact with me. "How would you say your overall health is at the moment, Valeriya Timurovna?"

"Matron, I'm in decent health considering our circumstances. Truth be told, I've been thinking about a secondary food supply for all of us. I'm positive we could get some winter vegetables planted without too much trouble. You know, kale and cabbages—that sort of thing?"

"Were you a farmer back in the world?" The matron tilted her head downwards and looked at me over her tiny glasses. I could see I intrigued her with my proposal.

"I was not a farmer. However, I grew up on a farm. I'm sure we could use all of our collective knowledge within this place. With as many women as we have here, there's bound to be the skills we would require. It might make all the difference between living and slowly starving."

"I'll take it under advisement and talk to the other hut matrons." I could see her as she made special notes in her book hurriedly.

"I must confess Matron, I think I'm now hungry enough to eat a rat." I was only half joking.

But the constant gnawing of hunger in my belly was a nagging reminder of just how dire my situation had become.

"Oh, you can forget about that notion, Valeriya Timurovna."

I looked quizzically at the matron.

"We already ate all the rats when we built this camp last year. I doubt if there's a living rodent within fifty kilometres of this place."

So much for my brilliant idea, I thought.

"Tell me, Valeriya Timurovna, what did you do for a living back in Moskva?"

"I had no formal employment, Matron. I helped the other women with the cooking and cleaning duties within the communal kitchen at our kommunalka. My husband and I, along with our granddaughter Zhenya, only lived there for a short while though. "Before Moskva, we were in Leningrad for twenty years. I cared for my blind uncle there. My husband served in the navy, so naturally he would often be away at sea for lengthy periods of time."

I decided that it wouldn't be wise at all to mention that Sava served in the NKVD. While it didn't save him from being arrested and taken away, I feared for our treatment here if that fact came to light—even though Zhenya and myself were in the same predicament as everyone else.

"I see, Valeriya Timurovna. Can you think of any other special skills or abilities that might be of use to me here?"

"Well, during the Great War, I served as a nurse. I completed three years of service and earned several proficiencies."

"That is excellent! I can think of one place where we may match your skills perfectly." The matron smiled at me.

I took a moment and lowered my voice.

"Matron, you've not yet asked me what they arrested me for."

The matron then took some time and explained to me that inquiring about the reasons of someone's arrest and incarceration were ultimately fruitless. Because we were all women arrested in the wake of the crimes that our husbands, brothers, or fathers had allegedly committed, we were nothing more than collateral damage to the Communist State.

We were guilty in the sense of a greater collective guilt. We were wreckage in a system of terror that was eating its way through the country, like a terrible cancer. We knew we were all innocent, however there wasn't anyone with who we could plead our cases. No one who would listen to us. There was no one to fix our injustices and make us all whole again.

Our captivity painted us with a stain of guilt that would take years to cleanse. The decade-long sentences we all received validated that fact, and the entire enterprise fed upon itself as a snake devours its own tail.

I sat there for a moment and recalled a joke I heard, currently making its way through the camp. The gag perfectly illustrated the absurdity of it all.

"Tell me zek, what is the term of your sentence?" An NKVD guard asked a political prisoner one day.

"Twenty years, Sir." The prisoner replied.

"And of what crimes were you convicted?" The NKVD guard then questioned.

"I promise you Sir, I have done nothing!" The prisoner replied.

"You are a liar! For nothing, they only give you ten years!" The NKVD guard yelled out.

The matron shook her head at me.

"No, Valeriya Timurovna. I will not ask what they arrested you for. In this place we are all guilty. Guilty of being innocent."

§

We'd all come to hear a certain word that the NKVD guards hurled at us—perhaps 100 times each day. I gave it no mind the first few times I heard it—possibly out of sheer ignorance.

However, like an itch that one cannot easily scratch, I noted it more and more. This certain word bothered me. I would shake my head and desperately try to keep my feelings bottled up. Bother turned into disgust and disgust into shame. The feeling was ludicrous when I thought about it. Late at night, and in the privacy of my mind, I knew there wasn't anything to be ashamed for. But in my waking hours, I only could encapsulate these feelings for so long before they boiled over.

The word they used was zek—or when they taunted the women—zechka. It became a blemish and one that we'd have to learn to live with—for quite some time.

Put simply, a zaklyuchennyi, or prisoner, which the NKVD officially abbreviated as z/k, became the vernacular word of zek. A zek referred specifically to those condemned persons within the Gulag apparatus. But, in time it morphed into an epithet. The NKVD guards derisively perverted it into a vulgar slang term and lobbed it at us liberally. Prisoners were naturally guilty. For what other reason would they incarcerate you within the Gulag?

We were second-class citizens—err, correction—no longer citizens even. We were merely statistics in an immense ledger of slave labour now. Zeks had only one purpose in life: fulfilling one's work quota for the greater glory and benefit of the Motherland.

By the time we'd all been in the camp for a few days, the weather improved, and life revolved around a never changing endless cycle of repetitive work—outside. Every woman in the hut, unless outright classified as an invalid, started their work within the timber brigades.

From our time before sunrise, to well after sunset, we followed the same strict routine every day. Routine was essential in maintaining discipline. Discipline was essential in making sure we fulfilled our daily work quotas. And the work quotas, as we soon discovered, meant the difference between eating or not eating.

A Day In The Life Of A Zechka

As the dawn approached, sounds of the other women getting out of their berths within the bunks awakened me. Jockeying for a desirable position in the queue that formed for the latrine quickly became a priority for everyone. Since the hut had only one, being an early bird meant being able to relieve oneself within a few minutes after waking up. If you had the unfortunate luck of being at the rear of the group, it could easily be one-half hour, or more, of waiting—nervously. Until all the women went through, those who remained fidgeted, danced, and implored their fellow hut-mates to hurry with all urgency.

Once Zhenya and I finished relieving ourselves, the premier order of the day was taking part in the camp's morning count. Without fail, all the hut's inhabitants followed their matron as she led them out and into the centre of the camp's courtyard. The NKVD guards would then perform a physical count of all present.

Collectively we called this the first calculation. The only exceptions allowed were those women who had the miserable happenstance to spend the night in the camp's punishment hut.

Our matron informed us that the punishment hut didn't have a wood-burning stove—so there was no heat. Even one night spent inside there —for infractions as slight as not performing an order or task to the satisfaction of your matron—could be fatal to one's health.

Once outside, with the first calculation underway, I saw row after row after row of tired and beleaguered women lined up, standing helpless in the elements. The weather was of no importance, only our bureaucratic routine was. Because the days were short on light during this time of year, the NKVD guards performed this count, and the one at the end of our day, in total darkness. If we were lucky, for a few days each month the light of the moon lit up the campgrounds with such brilliance, that you could almost make out the finer details of the drained faces standing nearby you.

    I always ensured that Zhenya stood close to me and remained quiet and respectful. The NKVD guards would pace up and down the ranks of women, looking for anyone out of line, or missing. Frequently, I spotted women with absolutely no self-discipline remaining get pulled from the lines for administrative punishment. I pleaded with Zhenya to shut her eyes anytime a man approached us. There was no reason to give them any excuses to single us out. As the counts of the women filtered through the matrons, and on to the NKVD guards, and up to the NKVD lieutenant of the day watch, the final tally stood tantalisingly close to completion. Only the additions of the women sentenced to the punishment hut and the subtractions of any women that had passed away during the night remained. This arithmetic would invariably seem to drag on for an extensive period. The wicked winter winds from the north made our waiting more painful, stinging our freezing faces with much ferocity. Rarely, mistakes in the tabulations would occur— which meant the entire process would begin anew. Considerable grumbling and the gnashing of teeth soon followed in that event.

    Immediately after the all-clear was sounded, it was like a mad dash race to get back into the relative warmth of our huts so we could all devour our breakfasts—we were all constantly hungry. Once our morning repast concluded, there would be one additional opportunity to use the latrine before heading out to our work for the day.

All labours performed at the women's camps were naturally segregated into two locations: in situ, and ex situ. On-site jobs within the campground varied from the mundane—shovelling snow and restocking the supplies of firewood inside each hut—to the more advanced services performed at the workshops in the centre of the quad. These were light industrial duties such as brick making, metalwork, and various woodworking projects, just to name a few. The NKVD guards reserved labour inside the camp for any woman placed on a light-duty capability status.

Unfortunately, neither Zhenya nor I qualified for these light-duty positions at the moment. Our work assignments lay off-site. We joined an army of women serving in the timber brigades today. As such, bundling up with many layers of clothing was essential to our survival. Our outermost garment, the balakhon, may have been plain looking, but it was crucial in keeping us warm out in the frozen Siberian taiga.

We swiftly trudged out of the zona—that deadly no-man's-land barrier at the edge of our campground—next to the fencing. Any woman caught inside the zona, without permission, would risk being immediately shot by the NKVD guards manning the watchtowers.

Invariably, the poor corpse would then linger upon the snowpack until late spring, as a reminder to the others.

It didn't take long for our work group to be far enough away from the encampment so that there was no obvious sign of any civilisation around. Only an innumerable cathedral of trees surrounded all of us now.

Fresh heavy snow weighed down these evergreen giants, and they swayed endlessly as if in an eternal dance with the northern gales.

They assigned more than half the camp's inhabitants to these timber brigades, and there were a multitude of tasks for us to perform here. A contingent of bored NKVD guards stood watch as the matrons divvied the women up into mini work-units and then assigned us our collective roles. The men on duty constantly chain-smoked their cigarettes, as they tried to keep warm out here. As I would soon discover, continually moving around proved a good defence against the bitter cold. I'd rather be warm and tired than cold and rested.

A dozen matrons conducted the symphony of work, which would last straight through until the blessed hints of dusk approached, signaling our reprieve. At this time of year, that meant the early afternoon. Because we were all horribly inexperienced in anything having to do with the production of heavy logging, we spent what seemed like countless days just mastering the tools and instruments we'd be using. We practised all the required steps on the smaller trees first. Repetition, as they say, is the mother of all learning. After thrice weeks of preparation, we found ourselves proficient enough to move into the full orchestra of industry.

Harvesting timber is the most physically taxing enterprise I think I've ever accomplished. Logging crews of eight women each would first spend hours just chopping away, with heavy axes swung at right angles, just to fell one mighty pine or white spruce. With a surfeit of logging crews engaged all around us, the bellows and yelling of the words smotrite nizhe would ring out regularly.

A tremendous explosion followed that ominous warning as the dropped tree shook the ground mightily in all directions, like an earthquake. I always looked up, every time, so as not to find myself on the wrong end of the behemoth when it crashed.

Once we completed the arduous task of bringing a tree down, the proper harvesting work would then commence. Other crews of women would descend upon these gigantic wooden corpses to begin the limbing process. Removing all the tree's appendages could take many days to perform by hand—depending on its size. Some women would carry out delimbing, whilst yet others would drag away the remnants—the boughs, branches, and needles.

Next came the bucking process. This penultimate step in producing our life-sustaining firewood that we depended upon is arguably the most labour intensive function for the entire logging crew. The matrons reserved it for only the most physically fit of women. Our supervisors used their proprietary tape measures ensuring cuts to the massive trunks came at just the right lengths needed for the last step in the rendering—the splitting. Measuring out a metre at a time, the bucking crew would start at the far end of the tree, the crown, and work backwards—thin to thick.

Special wooden shims raised the trunk just enough off the ground for the bucking operation. A brace of women would then use what we nicknamed a misery-whip to saw the required lengths clean away from the tree. These large two-man crosscut saws were serious and heavy. They took just the right rhythm to get them going with maximum proficiency. Bucking was a back-breaking toil to be sure, and far beyond my capabilities any longer.

The massive, rounded cuts of wood—known as billets—could easily weigh 100 kilograms, or more. These billets rolled straightforwardly over to the last step in production. Lifting them into the fearsome piece of iron apparatus known as the splitter was another matter entirely. Sometimes it required a quartet of women to guide the billet into the machine.

Working with the splitter required the utmost concentration. Any lapse of attention, for even a second, and you could easily sever a hand or an arm. That error in judgement would deliver you straight to an invalid work status, with a slow death sentence of starving to boot.

The splitter instrument was perhaps the most important one the camp possessed. It saved us a colossal amount of time and effort to produce the perfectly measured and cut cordwood which we needed to fit into our wood-burning stoves. The matrons tasked an entire team with keeping the splitter properly oiled and maintained. If the splitter should break, or suffer any damage, we'd be in for even more back wrenching labour.

Once we completed cutting the cordwood, we'd gather and place it upon special pallets to begin the months-long process of curing—which would transform it into firewood, the fuel source here in the Siberian taiga. A proper curing period ensured the elimination of any moisture within the wood, so that the maximum efficiency in burning could take place.

We stationed these caches of stacked firewood—some as high as ten metres—all around our campground. Secret maps drawn and maintained by the matrons kept track of every cache of wood, and where in the curing process each one was. A curing period of six months was the absolute minimum time required. A full annum of curing proved ideal.

On the coldest of days, and with some cajoling from the matrons to the NKVD guards that watched over us, we would take brief breaks for hot tea. These steaming metal cups of goodness were a lifesaver during this time of the year. I always was especially thankful.

Once the brilliant solntse dipped below the horizon, we had fewer than 15 minutes of ambient light remaining to walk back to our campsite. To satisfy our work quotas, our overseers made sure that the labour continued until the very last moment.

Supper immediately followed upon our return and I regarded it as the best part of my day. After supper came the second calculation by our watchers, which repeated the process we followed from the morning.

During the last hour before the matron declared the mandatory lights-out period, we performed a plethora of activities. Some women would carry out housekeeping and dishwashing duties. Many others gathered for the evening songs, whilst yet more attended a mandatory rotating curriculum known as political reeducation. The matron herself usually taught these insufferable classes. Sometimes her designate filled in. These seminars focused on the finer points of why Communism was the preeminent political philosophy in the world, and what we could do as prisoners if we ever expected to rejoin the citizenry of our glorious Soviet Union.

At the conclusion of every evening, the matron would announce that it was five minutes until the period of quiet, and for us to wish our fellow sisters a peaceful night. Then, 39 women obediently arranged themselves into their respective berths inside their bunks and made themselves comfortable for the interminable night ahead. One soul would always remain awake, performing a crucial role.

§

It was almost always dead silent inside the hut once the lights-out period began. Oh, in the first couple of nights we were here, I heard women crying and sobbing for their loved ones long gone now. Some of them couldn't adjust at all to their new realities and went mad with despair.

They passed away quickly, thank goodness.

Occasionally, the sounds of an internee shrieking would pierce the veil of darkness. No doubt a terrifying nightmare—as she relived a trauma from her past.

These torments would jolt everyone awake instantly, maddeningly, until the blessed silence returned. Now after 90 days into our alternative lives here, everyone was just flat out exhausted at the end of each day for any such nonsense.

Getting our much-needed rest was vital in having the energy to work. Performing work meant being able to eat. And eating here was essential to life. Everyone's needs boiled down to the very basics within the Gulag.

Tonight, I would see us all safely into the dawn, because it was my turn to act as the fireman for our hut. Once the matron ordered everyone to slumber, I bolted the front door to our hut and used heavy canvas sacks to insulate against the gaps at the bottom of the frame. We filled these bags with pine needles, which saved us from ice-cold drafts of air just centimetres away. Were the cracks not plugged properly, our life-sustaining heat would leach unnecessarily outside, and that could prove fatal to us all.

The fireman's chief responsibility was to attend to the wood-burning stove and to never let its life-giving blaze go extinct. Feeding the furnace every half hour did this trick nicely. This meant I'd have to stay attentive right through the entire night. To let the flames go out would surely mean the hut's internal temperature would fall well below the freezing point of water, in short order. Sleeping in such conditions would then prove impossible. Therefore, the fireman's duties were essential to our success.

The towering and neatly arranged stack of dried cordwood behind the wood-burning stove was my fuel source. When in the dead of winter, we would typically expect a fireman to use between 40 and 50 pieces of firewood for an entire night's shift. As it was now just into the month of May, we were averaging closer to 35 pieces a night—depending.

Stalin's Door

As I placed the thick pieces of pine into the furnace, it was always a matter of chance what tuneage I'd hear. Just based upon the pitch the firewood produced when they ignited, I could discern how long, or short, they cured for.

Short curing periods meant I instantly heard a sharp high-pitched hissing sound, as any remnants of moisture inside the firewood were being flash-vaporised.

After a nice long curing period, our fuel always generated the most pleasant sound imaginable. It was akin to a loud popping and crackling sound and meant everything was burning cleanly and efficiently. This always made me feel contented and relaxed.

I made myself another cup of black tea and sat down in the fireman's chair by the hulking iron wood-burning stove. This special wooden chair I'd spend the night in was firm and felt comfortable to me. Our women sourced it from the pine trees out in the Siberian taiga and constructed it in one of the light industrial shops in the centre of the campground. The workmanship of the chair was really first rate. I set my warm drink down and reached over to slide open the baffles near the top part of the kiln. When I opened them completely, they allowed for the dispersal of the vitalising heat throughout the hut.

The orange and yellow flames from within cast a vivid light that danced upon my face. I slowly squinted my eyes to stare inside the furnace. It was like peering at the sun. I blinked my eyes rapidly and then shut them tightly before it became too painful. I saw afterimages of blue and purple colours, which faded rapidly into black on the insides of my eyelids.

I then realised my entire body felt heated now, which was a rare feeling as of late. The punishing and unseasonably low temperatures we'd all experienced over the last few weeks here made me almost forget what being warm felt like.

    I relaxed further into my recliner and took another sip from my strong beverage before resting the cup on the dusty wooden floorboards below. I sighed out loud. This was my favourite part of the day, when I could finally unwind and think.

    I then watched as my empty weathered hands began to dance instinctively, in an all too familiar pattern upon my lap.

    For a few moments I dreamt holding knitting needles, as I imagined myself comfortable at home, waiting for Sava to return from his life at sea. I pretended making him another scarf, which always came in handy during our harsh winters.

    I could really sense the soft working yarn within my grip as I guided and wrapped it over my left pointer finger. With a gentle flick over the tip of the needle, I repeated the purl, hundreds and hundreds of times over. With my right proper tension square, I knew I was on the correct track. After years of practise, I could make these manoeuvres with my eyes closed, and perhaps even in my sleep!

    But there would be no slumber for me this evening. Snapping back to reality, I held my emptied hands out in front for inspection, turning them over, back to front. I held no knitting needles and owned no yarn. This revelation saddened me.

    A curious incident with Zhenya earlier today was still at the forefront of my mind this late evening as I tended to my fireman's commitment. Near the conclusion of our supper, I noticed that Zhenya had her back turned to me as we sat at the communal tables. Each one of her legs straddled the wooden bench, and she seemed to fidget about incessantly. There weren't too many other women sitting near us, as some had gone to use the latrine one last time for the night. Yet some others weren't even waiting for the lights-out announcement to crawl into their bunks—they collapsed in utter exhaustion.

For some strange reason, when I peered over at Zhenya, I could see she had placed both of her hands inside her lap, with them clasped tightly together. Out of idle curiosity, I asked her what she was doing.

Zhenya appeared startled and nervously put both clenched fists into her trouser pockets. She then turned around to face me. Her eyes refused to meet mine, and I knew immediately that something was amiss.

"Show me your hands, Zhenya!" I didn't know what she was concealing, however I felt determined to find out.

Zhenya pulled out her hands quickly and showed them to me, her fists now unclenched, fingers splayed, and hands turning over and over as if to stress their emptiness.

"See, I have nothing, Grandmother!" Zhenya still would not look me in the eyes.

I knew for certain something was afoot here.

I took hold of her right hand inside mine, and then the left one, as I inspected them intently. It startled me to discover that her fingers felt nice and toasty. The ambient temperature of her extremities should have been icy, as everyone's always were. Her palms were also red hot and sweaty. I could see moisture glistening by the light of the kiln, as it evaporated away. I looked her in the eyes and implored her to be frank with me.

"Tell me what is going on. Please honey, I promise I won't be angry with you."

I saw the expression on Zhenya's face as she acquiesced. She reached into her right trouser pocket to retrieve an item. Her head darted from side to side as she quickly scanned the room to ensure no one was looking directly at us. She then placed something small and heavy into my right palm and folded my fingers on top of it. Our hands were below the level of the table, and out of sight now.

She whispered at me.

"Please don't show this to anyone else."

With my hand closed around the object, it felt warm—bordering on hot. When I opened my fist hurriedly, my eyes gazed upon a small spherical golden object—about the size of a delectable plum. This metal prize had a bumpy and uneven surface and resembled a corded entanglement.

Delicately, I used my fingertips to feel all around its edges. I noticed it was hollow throughout its centre, as if its creator scooped it out from each end. Affixed to the front of the orb was the unmistakable emblem of the USSR, a solid shining red star with a golden border. In the middle of the badge lay the golden hammer and sickle, the ubiquitous symbols of the proletariat.

I marvelled at how Zhenya kept this treasure hidden from me and from the thieverous NKVD guards in all these weeks of time. It was a blessed miracle. I knew for a fact that should our captors discover this wondrous bauble, they would confiscate it from her immediately! I closed my hand around it slowly and surreptitiously passed it back to Zhenya for safekeeping.

"Please don't be angry with me Grandmother! It's my Young Pioneers neckerchief woggle. It's all I have left from home." Zhenya peered at me with furrowed brows and a distinctive hint of panic upon her face.

"Oh child, I am not angry with you. Not at all. Keep it hidden and out of sight. Keep it safe." I smiled to reassure her.

Stalin's Door

As I reflected upon our conversation from earlier that evening, I couldn't help but wonder about Zhenya's neckerchief woggle. What made it so hot to the touch? Why, I bet with that magical sphere cupped inside your hands, you could keep warm, even well out into the frozen expanse of the Russian wastes.

I refreshed my brew once again and guessed that it was now just after midnight. The new day was just beginning. I took a long sip of my hot tea. By decree, no one but our jailers had access to clocks or watches inside the Gulag. Not that it mattered anyhow. We had a tightly regulated work schedule, and specific units of time became irrelevant. Meaningless really. The day began in darkness and ended in darkness. Nevertheless, dates were still important to me. Unlike our matron, I cared what day it was. One more day ended here meant one day closer to leaving this horrendous place behind.

I took a moment to contemplate and counted out the days Zhenya and I had been at the camp. We arrived some 12 weeks prior, and if my calculations were correct, this was now the third day of May. I took some joy in knowing that today was my birthday. I was another year older, and hopefully wiser. As I surveyed the backs of my wrinkled hands, I chuckled at the irony. Turning 56 years of age didn't feel any differently than being 55. I was still an old woman.

Year Of Wood

The year 1943 was a gruelling time for all of us inside camp Mytininsk-23. A terrible war had broken out with fascist Germany in the summer of '41—one that would become known throughout the Soviet Union as the Great Patriotic War.

It didn't escape the NKVD administrator's notice that the population of men inside the Gulag camp system declined precipitously. Comrade Marshal Stalin forced Gulag prisoners to join the millions of drafted soldiers already stationed on the front lines, fighting to protect the Motherland in the west.

These men of the Gulag found themselves embedded into special units called punishment brigades. They would undertake the clearing of minefields, or other hazardous endeavours. Inevitably serving on the front lines, like so much cannon fodder, they would meet their fate. Slowly dying in the camps or quickly dying on the battlefields—it all became a moot point. One cannot outrun one's destiny it seems, in Russia.

The NKVD camp guards also joined their countrymen to do their patriotic best, which left only the very oldest men on guard duty here. War is a younger man's game, and not for the aged. This military action was like a giant meat grinder that tore through our beloved country. A veritable black plague that left nothing but death and destruction behind in its wake.

The hostilities affected every family, every city, every farm, and every factory. The Germans meant to wipe us out and take over our lands to augment their own limited resources.

They wanted to establish a living space for their citizenry—what they called lebensraum. Russia was to become something of an auxiliary part of Germany, from where they could expand their burgeoning Reich. The end of '41 saw the invading German horde nearly reach Moskva. They were within just a few kilometres of striking Red Square.

But, just like when Emperor Napoleon tried to invade Russia during the last century, our greatest general then came back out of retirement, and to our rescue. Herr Hitler was driven back from the gates of our capital city. I'm speaking of General Winter. Our infamous Russian season had stopped the Germans—cold in their tracks.

We were precisely 10,000 kilometres away from all the fighting, and news of how the war was progressing was scarce within the Gulag. We were on an isolated island in the great ocean of timber known as the Eastern Siberian taiga. The only time we received any updates at all in the camps was when we received new prisoners.

We would interrogate all the unfamiliar faces for news from the outside, hanging on their every word. If we were lucky, we'd discover that the newly interned had stuffed their clothing with newspapers to keep them warm on their multi-day journey from west to east.

We'd happily take these broadsheets off their hands and dissect them for information. We were keen enough to know that most news was propaganda, yet something was better than nothing.

Stalin's Door

Since late '40, I had ascended in rank, and took over as the matron of hut No. 31 when our old matron left to start construction of a new camp that was even further to the east than we were.

With Zhenya as my trusted assistant, I could get much accomplished as I did my best to take care of the 39 women who depended upon me. One of the greatest deficiencies we faced were the food shortages.

Because there was a dreadful war ravaging the countryside, the very last thing the NKVD senior leadership cared about were feeding some poor pathetic politicals living in a women's corrective labour camp cut off from civilisation. The weekly shipments of food that arrived by train to Mytininsk dwindled, and life in the Gulag descended into pure misery. Had it not been for the planting of winter vegetable gardens that I pioneered when I first arrived in camp, we'd have all long starved to death.

I recalled a rare occurrence. I found myself back inside the hut with two hours until the logging brigades returned for their supper. The days were finally starting to lengthen as we approached summer, which meant it no longer got dark at three o'clock in the afternoon. I said a silent prayer to the Lord in thanks.

My mind then clicked into gear, and I checked on the meal preparation with our pair of cooks. I also ensured the wood-burning stove was in satisfactory working order. Our firewood supply for the week was only half exhausted. We were in fine shape for once. Still, because I was the matron, the inside of my brain constantly swirled with all the dozens of details that would ensure my sisters' care and compassion. They depended upon me, and I never considered my chores really completed until I found myself back inside my berth. And that time was many hours from now.

My old body felt unusually drained today, but I had work yet to do. I sat at the community table, took the pencil from behind my ear and began collating all my outstanding matronly duties and responsibilities. The papers, so many papers lay in front of me. I was drowning in a sea of paperwork. There were checklists, forms, permission slips, work orders, and personnel issues. The administrative management alone crushed my soul. My mood improved when I realised it beat cutting down trees or making bricks. I considered myself lucky the NKVD guards classified me as light-work capable now.

One of the endless tasks I performed was the timber production management for the entire camp. I stumbled into this job two years ago with the onset of the war, partly out of necessity and partly out of self-preservation. Some jobs in the camp needed constant attention to detail, and this undertaking was far too important to leave to chance.

Firewood was our primary fuel for heat and food production within the Gulag. Mytininsk-23 had 40 huts, each of which used 45 pieces of cut and cured firewood each day—for this time of year. Heating accounted for 75 percent of the daily firewood allotment, whilst cooking elucidated the other 25 percent. Then I had to add in another 20 pieces of firewood for each of the guard's watchtowers, the administrative shack, the guard's posts, and the guard's barracks.

The traditional metric unit for cut firewood, the stère, is a measurement of basically one cubic metre. Each stère holds an average of 64 pieces of cut firewood, at just over one-half metre each. They were a perfect fit for the wood-burning stoves in all the huts. A decent-sized pine tree or larch out in the Siberian taiga, with a diameter at breast height of at least naught point six metres, can easily produce 30 stères. Rounding up for errors, Mytininsk-23 was using 2,275 pieces of firewood per day. That's just slightly fewer pieces than the average net production from 36 stères.

Under ideal conditions, it took several logging crews a solid 72 hours of formidable effort to fell, limb, buck, and split each tree from the forest. With a full logging brigade of 100 crews, which was approximately one-half of the camp's full complement of women, we had to work at least 325 days each year just to stay ahead of what we were consuming ourselves—and routinely losing to the NKVD guards. Out of habit, greed, or spite, they confiscated two-thirds of our firewood production for their own uses.

I suspected they traded for better rations, or just to enrich themselves.

When I factored in for sickness, overwork, equipment breakage, maintenance, along with seasonal weather difficulties and curing times, it didn't leave me with much of a cushion each year to ensure our collective survival. If we somehow produced an excess consignment of firewood one season, and secretly squirreled it away, I sometimes could barter for extra food or supplies from within the Mytininsk camp network. It took all my accounting tricks just to keep my head above the water in this area.

Much of our firewood bounty I knew went to supplement the stocks of the Mytininsk men's camps. The incarcerated men of the Gulag focused on mining operations, where lucrative deposits of gold, tin, nickel, copper, and coal—all desperately needed for the war effort—received top priority from Comrade Marshal Stalin.

The Gulag administrators unrealistically set the production quotas for the collection of our country's natural resources to beyond the breaking point, knowing that there was always a limitless supply of replacement slave labour available.

As I sat at the communal table, my mind planned for the coming summer season, and all the challenges presented.

Sometime later, it surprised me to see Zhenya saunter into the hut at this time of day. She made herself a cup of tea from the boiler and sat down beside me.

"What are you working on, Grandmother?" Zhenya was breathing heavily, which was unusual for her.

"Oh, just my matronly obligations. You know the job never ends."

Zhenya nodded at me, however I don't really think she was paying attention. I scribbled some more notes, paused, and then removed my glasses. I always gave my eyes a break in the low light of the hut.

"What are you doing here, Zhenya? Shouldn't you be working with Dasha Yurievna on your nurse's training?"

Zhenya was qualifying two afternoons a week to be a caregiver at the newly provisioned camp hospital hut. I couldn't complain about it much. It relieved her of some stress performing the heavy-work while serving in the timber brigades. Zhenya would turn 18 years of age later this month, and they already considered her an adult by all measures and statutes of the Communist State.

"Oh, she let us go early today. She said something about having to pop over to Mytininsk sixteen for the afternoon."

Zhenya looked excited, as if she was bursting at the seams. What was wrong with her?

"I can see you have something to tell me, so spill it, dearest. I know you're hiding something."

Stalin's Door

I replaced the tiny pencil behind my ear. I raised my left eyebrow along with my curiosity, and I saw Zhenya crack a tiny smile. She looked devious.

"All right Grandmother, however, please keep this between us." Zhenya was positively beaming now.

"I will promise nothing. Now, get to it, I'm swamped today."

I felt intrigued, yes, however I was also way behind in my commitments. I also felt utterly exhausted.

Zhenya pulled an item from inside her blouse and left it covered with both of her diminutive hands. She uncupped her palms, slowly, until I saw something unexpected come into sight. She was holding a medium-sized Reinette Simirenko. This was a wondrous surprise! My Lord! I hadn't laid eyes upon a single piece of fruit for over five years. The colour of this delectable apple was a bright greenish-white, and the skin looked undamaged and firm. I immediately took my own hands and closed them around Zhenya's with frightening speed. I then pulled her hands below the lip of the table, before letting them open again.

"By all that's holy, where in the world did you get that tasty delight?" I whispered frantically, hoping not to attract any undue attention.

My hands were now trembling with excitement. This pome was a treasure, to be sure.

"It's a funny story, Grandmother. I was walking along the edge of camp by the no-man's-land, just outside the zona, and there it was! Sitting on the ground in the muck. I couldn't believe it. You can't miss the tint of them. I remember these from my childhood. I pocketed it swiftly and ran over to the rain cistern to rinse it off."

Zhenya stared wantonly at her prize.

I had a hard decision to make now. What should I do? I won't lie, the thought of devouring it straightaway was paramount inside my mind.

"No one was around then—I mean, did anyone see you pick it up?"

"What do you mean, Grandmother?" Zhenya's voice was cracking. "Don't you like this gift I've brought to you?"

"Very much so, yes." My heart throbbed inside my chest in utter delight.

I stood up from the table and went to retrieve a knife, surreptitiously, from the cupboard over by the wood-burning stove. Returning to Zhenya, I sat down again and held out my right palm.

I looked at Zhenya sternly. Zhenya then surrendered and placed the delectable apple into my hand. I felt its weight for the first time. The skin was firm, and the texture was smooth and inviting. I carefully cut the fruit in half, and then into quarters.

I passed Zhenya her share of the bounty.

For myself, I wasted no more time. I placed one piece up to my nose and inhaled deeply. My olfactory senses became overwhelmed, all at once. I couldn't recall ever smelling anything as lush, ripe, and delicious as this apple slice.

I took a bite of the quarter piece, and my mouth experienced a sensation I'd only ever felt once before—from that first night's meal in this camp years ago.

I felt exultation. The taste of the apple was tart, yes, but not as overpowering as some varieties. Everything on my palate balanced out perfectly. The aftertaste was unusually spicy and rich. No pome I'd ever eaten before was as juicy or mouthwatering as this one was today, though.

I devoured the one quarter piece, and then the other, with dispatch. I noted that Zhenya was right behind me in finishing.

Zhenya had a smile on her face that measured from her right ear, all the way to her left. If she'd been happier before now, I couldn't easily recall when.

We consumed everything. The seeds, core, skin, and stem. The pleasure I experienced from this extraordinary treat was undeniable.

Upon finishing, I said the Birkat Hamazon and turned back to Zhenya.

"I would say this is one of those days we'll remember for quite some time, my dear!" I grinned at her.

"Maybe I'll get another one, Grandmother?"

"Oh, no Zhenya. Surely you know this gift was as rare as a hen's tooth?"

"He might be there again. You never know."

I sat for a minute and looked at my paperwork that I suddenly realised I was ever more behind on. I stared off into space for just a moment when I caught myself.

"Wait, Zhenya. What did you say? He? He who?"

I was barely aware of what I was asking her. I surely hoped this wasn't going in the direction I feared.

"Um, well, Grandmother, I saw a camp sentry standing guard on the other side of the no-man's-land. The nice old fellow smiled at me and asked if I wanted an apple? Naturally, I nodded yes. I didn't speak to him, I swear it! He tossed the fruit into the mud and then said he'd see me later. That's when I collected it and cleaned it off at the rain cistern. I then came straight here."

"Oh, Zhenya, you may not have spoken to him, however you didn't report this contact either. You know that's strictly against the rules. I hope you can appreciate the awkward situation you've placed me into as your guardian and matron."

I glared at her and saw she thought she was innocent in this entire affair. I contemplated what course of action I should take.

Feeling exasperated, and backed into a corner, I deferred judgement until later in the evening.

"Go now Zhenya and help the cooks with preparing supper." She now understood my displeasure and looked distraught. "Go on now."

§

After our collective repast, when all of my sisters finished eating, I surveyed the 39 souls that I was responsible for. I was lucky I had an exceptional group and thankful that any nonsense was minimal. Everyone worked hard and genuinely looked out for one another. This was a blessing.

This hour of the evening was the most festive inside the hut. Once hungry bellies became full, the overall disposition of the women sitting at the tables drifted towards mirth and frivolity. Inevitably the singing of a chastúshka, or two, would break out. These simple peasant folk songs were humourous and inventive. Some were even overtly anti-political.

Still, when one's day contains nothing but work and plight, even 60 minutes to bond and forget your troubles can provide some much-needed relief from the realities of life. The poems were subversive, yes, however living in the Gulag we sometimes just needed to blow off some steam.

Stalin's Door

Our resident poet laureate was Mme Derzhavina, and she was a master at her craft. Back in the world, she held a prestigious literature chair as a professor at Moskva State University.

Frequently her chastúshki were lewd and salacious, and they always drew a loud and appreciative applause. For a few minutes, I even forgot the seriousness of what I needed to do this night. As she rhymed, I could see all the women hanging on her every syllable.

There once was a Georgian young lady
Who courted all the boys from her block
They say she could never be sated
She couldn't say no to the cock

Not even resting on the Sabbath
She worked at her trade with little sleep
The farm boys formed long lines to her door
When they should have been tending their sheep

The entire village knew this lass
Her promiscuity was legend
Men would even come from Tbilisi
The girl's cheeks were always reddened

Stalin's police came knocking one night
"You're under arrest, we made our checks."
"I'll do well in the Gulag, Captain,
I will just pleasure the fairer sex."

A huge boisterous cackling sound then erupted from around the tables. Some younger women held their hands over their mouths as they feigned embarrassment for laughing at the lyrics of the song. I even smirked at that last line. No one missed the seditious dig at Comrade Stalin, having been born in Georgia.

"Ladies, please, please! May I please have everyone's attention? For conscience's sake! Let's have a little decorum in here. Now, before this evening degenerates into total chaos and levity, I have an announcement to make."

I stood upon the speaking crate and cleared my throat. After a few more seconds, with conversations winding down, I continued.

"It pains me to relay this to you, however, we've had a minor violation of the no fraternisation rule."

I heard a hushed murmur descend upon the hut.

"I must deal with this infraction forthwith, lest we invite more transgressions of the same. That would surely jeopardise our collective work quotas, which would then invariably affect our supply of rations, negatively. This cannot happen. We're barely—and trust me when I say this—barely getting enough to eat as it stands.

"While this individual did not initiate contact with the NKVD guards, the mandatory reporting of the incident did not take place, as required. It is with considerable sadness that I now strip Yevgeniya Ivanovna of her full ration bowl. I am placing her on half-rations for thirty days."

I looked at my ward with much heartache for many seconds.

"I hope, Zhenya, that you take this time to reflect upon the seriousness of your transgression."

I then heard the inevitable outburst from Zhenya, as she rose from the table and ran over to her berth.

"I hate you!" Her face was red and slick with tears.

I felt incredible guilt, as I too had enjoyed devouring the apple in secret.

"And just in case any of you are thinking there is any bias in this decision, I will also place myself on half-rations for a month, as I didn't do enough due diligence when I first learned of this offence."

The entire hut now sat in stone cold silence.

As everyone turned in for the evening, I could hear poor Zhenya crying in her berth above my head. Her sobbing shattered my heart into tiny razor-sharp shards, and it took me longer than normal to fall asleep.

§

Out alone in this ancient Russian forest, I always enjoyed the time required to walk between the camps. Hiking in the fresh snowpack always made a pleasing tamping sound beneath my feet.

This time of year, I could just smell the promise of spring in the air. Caught in between the endless dark winter days and nights, we approached the seasonal change that would come and go, almost in the blink of an eye. Before you could get used to the wonder, early frost would set back in, and the crush of winter would be back with us for months.

This was my only time to meditate, a genuine time all to myself. I could breathe out here in the Siberian taiga, and I could think. The air in this place was clean, and it felt good inside my lungs. Truthfully, I had more than my fill of the noxious cerulean exhaust from those damned wood-burning stoves.

My pace today was not immediate, not by any stretch of the imagination. I wouldn't be overdue for a little while yet. I thought to myself, why not enjoy this day? The majestic pine trees in this part of the timberland reached up to impossible heights, kissing the perfect true-blue sky above. I loved to stop and take it all in.

If I listened carefully and really concentrated, I swear I could hear the haunting of the Leshiye, the Russian forest spirit guardians, running about in their packs. As they flitted around, they created a heavy timpani that would elicit feelings of fear and wonderment from those nearby.

One time I thought I caught the faintest glimpse of one up close, before it scampered off. This Leshy had a light green complexion and glowed with an otherworldly light all about his body. I'll never forget those haunting —Stygian eyes—as he looked me over and studied me. These faeries were always surveying the interlopers to their woodlands, probing for weaknesses. And then, as if by magic, he disappeared.

I could feel my heart inside my chest beating briskly at the thought of seeing one again! I knew that they were with me today. Close to me—always there—watching.

As I proceeded on my journey, I discerned an amazing noise produced by the towering trees. The unrelenting winds from the north swirled within a myriad of intertwining branches, and its grinding made a slow, melodic creaking sound which was unlike anything else I'd ever heard. It was as if this symphony of wood came alive in a performance just for me. Beautiful and timeless.

Stalin's Door

At this moment, I was so cut off from any civilisation, that if there was another person within ten kilometres of where I stood, I would feel shocked.

I happily drifted along until I paused, suddenly catching myself, and becoming keenly self-aware of my surroundings. My feet felt light, as if I wasn't even walking any longer—I was just floating there. I was unsure of where I was now. I was, in fact, lost. This was not where I should be. I knew if I didn't get to my nursing duties at camp Mytininsk-14 shortly, then the NKVD guards could very well declare me delinquent. Spending time inside a punishment hut for my transgression would then be the best I could look forward to, as I was already on a diet of half-rations for the incident with Zhenya.

In a panic, I turned around and looked for my bootprints in the snow from where I came. Perhaps I could backtrack to where I was more orientated? I felt myself nauseated when I realised I couldn't find any! There were none! I saw nothing but the undisturbed snowpack on the trail all around me. Stopping and remaining still, I could hear only the heartbeat within my upper torso. Thump-thump-thump, thump-thump-thump. This was not an optimal situation at all.

From out of the periphery of my left eye, I abruptly caught sight of a uniformed man approaching from inside of the rough brush, just off the trail boundary.

Heavy snow limited his progress as he trudged his way over to me. Surely he should be able to get me back on the right path? I had no time to lose and had to get on my way soonest, before they declared me absent without leave.

"Excuse me, Sir! Sir? I need your aid. I am lost and must find my way to camp Mytininsk nine straightaway!" I hollered whilst waving my arms frantically.

I hoped that the stranger had seen and heard me and could render help.

This squat colourful fellow closed the distance to where I stopped and then stepped out on to the trail in front of me. With a quick motion, he tipped the brim of his hat with his forefinger, acknowledging my presence.

"Pleasant afternoon, Comrade."

I studied his uniform in amazement, and for some bizarre reason I couldn't get a cracking good look at his face.

The immaculately dressed man wore the uniform of a senior general of the Soviet army. If I didn't know any better, I'd venture to say he held the rank of Marshal of the Soviet Union. His neatly pressed dark green jacket held a solitary medal just above his left breast pocket. The thick red ribbon of the medal joined a single five-sided gold star dangling below it. This award was the highest distinction anyone could receive. Hero of the Soviet Union. The soldier's shoulder boards featured enormous gold stars and a perfect replica of the Communist State emblem.

As his face came into focus, I noted a bushy black mustache and a greyish, pockmarked complexion. His brown eyes looked dull, and almost completely dilated. I instantly knew who he was, and I became deathly frightened. I felt the blood within my veins pumping overtime as it circulated about my worn-out body.

The premier marshal studied my form for a moment and appeared taken aback by my attire. He knew by the way I was dressed I was a convicted felon, incarcerated within the Gulag.

To him, convicts were nothing but trash, and deserved his utter contempt. In a fit of disgust, he quickly corrected himself, clearing his throat in the process.

"—I mean Citizen."

"Excuse me, Comrade Marshal. Can you please tell me what you're doing here? Shouldn't you be in our glorious capital city of Moskva planning the defeat of the fascist German invader?"

I gawked at the man, not totally comprehending what was happening here. I couldn't help but think he should be much taller. His perpetual portraits, banners, and statues made him appear as if he were three metres in height—and larger than life.

"Oh, I am everywhere. At once. I'm here, I'm there."

The marshal waved his right hand in a slow sweeping motion.

"You never know where I will be next. I'm all knowing and all seeing. Never forget that—Citizen. I can be here with you for a bit, of that you may have no worries."

The fierce fighting in the Great Patriotic War between our heroic Soviet Union and the cowardly Wehrmacht was approaching its third year, with no end in sight. The generalissimo continued his harangue.

"The saboteurs and wreckers of our glorious Revolution are everywhere, so watch out! These vermin infest our Motherland and deserve nothing less than total extermination. I am sorry we locked you up, my dear. But is it not better that I arrest and jail one hundred innocent men than for one guilty man to go free?"

The marshal looked pleased with himself now and smirked.

"I'm sure you can appreciate that. In twenty or thirty years, I'm positive no one will remember all of you riff-raff. Who now remembers the names of the boyars Tsar Ivan Grozny got rid of? No one. One of my former Internal Affairs commissars used to tell me all the time, that when one chops wood, the woodchips will fly. This Communist garden paradise I've created for everyone is fragile and needs regular care and maintenance. Unless you pull out the weeds, entire crops will suffer in ruin."

Being labeled as collateral damage—a woodchip, or a weed—made me take pause for a moment.

I didn't mind being thought of as a weed. Weeds have special properties. They can thrive within harsh environments, they don't require special tending and feeding, and they are exceedingly hard to control. Weeds fight back. Weeds can sting you.

I, for one, wasn't done fighting. I'm a survivor. I left our supreme leader to mutter to himself as I quickly found my way to Mytininsk-14.

§

The men's corrective labour camp of Mytininsk-14 was a huge campsite that dwarfed our own, Mytininsk-23. Once a week on average, I'd be relieved from my matronly duties and make the trek over to this vast base of enterprise for the day. My knowledge and abilities having served as a nurse in the Great War would assist the other doctors in the vast hospital huts that Mytininsk-14 supported. Mytininsk-14 was a mining camp, which produced coal, tin, nickel, copper, and most crucially—gold. Gold was a precious commodity, and our Gulag administrative masters gave it precedence.

Stalin's Door

Besides men and munitions, it was perhaps the USSR's most precious resource. Gold funded the unending war effort, and winning the Great Patriotic War was Comrade Marshal Stalin's highest priority.

Mytininsk-14 had an inmate population of over 16,000 men, which meant it was easily ten times the size of Mytininsk-23. It was a virtual city of its own, out in the wilds of northeastern Russia.

Because the miners relied on electric torches deep within the earth to perform their work, it didn't take the Gulag managers long to figure out that they could maintain a constant 24-hours a day work schedule. Miners would work a 12-hour shift and then hand off their duties to the other half of the camp's population. The extraction of gold ore would then continue indefinitely with no stops in production.

While I worked in the accident and emergency ward of the largest hospital hut, I assisted a brilliant middle-aged medical professional, who'd been a world class internist at a clinic in Stalingrad. His name was Dr Trusov.

Inmates of the Gulag were once thought to be plentiful, expendable, and easily replaceable. A cave-in at a mine shaft just killed 50 of your workers? No bother. Another 500 prisoners just arrived by train yesterday.

And then the Great Patriotic War started. The ceaseless arrivals of new men—young and old—dipped for the first time and making do with the existing population posed a new challenge for the Gulag administrators. Younger men were leaving for the western front in droves to serve within the punishment brigades. The older prisoners left over in the Gulag naturally became more valuable. This meant that unlike in years past, the treatment and rehabilitation of inmates who became injured or disabled whilst slaving away in the mines became a priority.

If an inmate's injuries were anything short of terminal, the doctors would expend all efforts to patch him up and heal him quickly, so he could return to his mining duties. Quotas for these treasured commodities, extracted from the deep earth, would naturally rise with every month. The number of those being arrested and sent into the Gulag apparatus, especially those in the ideal ages for fighting on the front lines, was in decline. Hence why hospital huts, and anyone with any medical experience, became paramount.

I accompanied Dr Trusov as we attended to the newer patients this afternoon. The heavy mining machinery used to extract the precious gold could inflict the most hideous of injuries imaginable. Severed limbs, mangled flesh, horrific burns, and poisonous chemical inhalations reminded me of what I saw when I cared for the wounded at the rejuvenation wards in Novorossiysk during the Great War.

Even with immediate care, our field hospital only had limited services available. Some of these wounded men died slow, horribly painful deaths, with little we could do to relieve their suffering.

These fatals, as they came to be known, mercifully left our ward in short order. Other injuries were more than treatable, and with a little care and tending these men were back to normal in no time. I felt grateful whenever this was the case.

The eternal problems of supplying enough food for the men, especially those working in the mines, where their expenditure of work outstripped their required caloric intake by three or four times, was intractable. Everyone here was consistently on the verge of starvation. The terrible side effects of vitamin deficiencies also ran rampant. Scurvy and pellagra were common and devastating skin aliments, or worse, soon followed. Dr Trusov was in a war of his own with the camp administration to try to improve the situation.

Thankfully any threat to the gold quotas scared the Gulag brass so severely, that for a time food blessedly ceased to become an issue for the miners. Even food from the NKVD guards was used to supplement the prisoners' own. That is, until our jailers themselves started starving, which promptly halted the practise.

One particular class of injuries was painfully obvious to Dr Trusov, and the more experienced nurses like myself: self-inflicted wounds.

We'd treat these traumas just like any of the others, however. The trick for the miners, it seemed, was threading the needle between not injuring yourself enough to get excused from work and injuring yourself so dreadfully that you became a fatal.

In a rare moment when Dr Trusov and I could take a quick break, I asked him about a troubling sight I witnessed in the camp before I started work today.

"Doctor, may I ask you about something?"

"Yes, Valeriya Timurovna. What is it?"

"On my walk over here this morning, once I made it inside the campground, and before I reached our hospital hut, I saw an enormous series of pits freshly dug into the earth, over by the punishment huts. I didn't mean to get too close, however, the walkway over here became narrow as I passed by.

I noticed a few of the NKVD guards with rifles on duty there. I couldn't help notice these deep ditches weren't here on my last visit."

"Oh yes, they were just dug last week by some miners from the punishment huts. A small contingent of essential workers staged something of a work-stoppage strike last week to demand better labour conditions. Well, the NKVD bosses wanted to squash that movement right in its infancy. They threw the ringleaders into the pits until they recanted their demands."

The doctor looked dispirited now.

"I doubt if any of them are still alive considering the weather."

The problems of hut No. 31, and my matronly duties, suddenly seemed insignificant.

Year Of Tin

When we entered 1948, the start of this new year was an occasion of special reverence. Zhenya and I both knew we would shortly leave this miserable place behind us. Our arrest date anniversary was the tenth of January, and upon that day we will have officially repaid our debt to the Motherland in full.

As soon to be ex-convicts of the Gulag apparatus, they would place us upon trains travelling westward, departing for civilisation, and far away from here. As part of our collective release agreements, the government prohibited us from re-settling in any town or village within 100 kilometres of where we came from. We'd not be going back to Moskva to live. This directive was of no matter, because I would travel with Zhenya to Leningrad, and desperately try to put our lives back into some semblance of order.

Zhenya arrived at this encampment with me as a girl, not even 13 years old, and would leave as a mature young woman—with the rest of her life still ahead of her. The last ten years had been terrible for her and cut short a happy childhood. As for myself, I already had lived most of my life before I came to this accursed hole in the Siberian taiga. That I had made it this far at my age was a miracle. I couldn't wait to put as much distance between me and the snow and ice as I could afford to. In four months' time, I would turn 66 years of age. For the days I had left to me, I hoped to fill them with quiet and solitude.

Preparing for an errand today, I put on all of my winter layers and donned my heavy wool jacket and leather boots.

Zhenya urgently pulled on my sleeves. I could see she was dying to ask me a question.

"You're off to speak with the commandant, aren't you?"

"Yes. Yes, my dearest. Our release date is quickly approaching for us."

"Won't you take this then?" Zhenya covertly held out her closed right hand to me. I knew what was inside. "You know it's a lengthy walk into Mytininsk. It'll keep you toasty." She pleaded with me.

"No honey, you keep that with you."

I knew that Zhenya was offering her Young Pioneers neckerchief woggle to hold on to. What I could never reconcile, after all these years, was the fact that the woggle would give off a pure and pleasant warmth which radiated outward throughout my body when I held on to it tightly inside my hands. Even in the punishing sub-naught temperatures out in these northeastern Russian forests, her uniform accoutrement could keep my palms nice and balmy, and thus my entire body felt heated. Zhenya looked disappointed in me.

"Dear, please understand, if the MVD guards should stop and search me. They would confiscate your treasure immediately. We can't take that risk. You keep hold of it now, all right?"

Zhenya politely demurred.

"Besides, we will not be here for much longer now!" Zhenya instantly lit up with a broad smile and hugged me goodbye.

The other women they interned us with back in '38 had already gained their freedom back. Once their decade long sentences expired, the MVD administrators discharged them from the Gulag within a matter of days. I took solace in noticing there weren't many of us remaining from that horrifying train journey eastwards, so many years ago. Death, disease, overwork, and hopelessness had claimed all but a lucky few. If I didn't have Zhenya, I doubt very much if I would have made it this far.

I thought for a moment about the camp garden plots where we grew our supplemental food. Picking crops specifically that thrived in the high winter months came about after much trial and error. Cabbages and kale, leeks and chard did the best for us in these inhospitable conditions. Even so, they were just a mere hobby when compared to the real bumper crop of the Gulag—death. We buried more people than I could remember. The gardens we tended to were gardens made from stone.

§

The walk over to the city of Mytininsk was a pleasant one, despite the frigid temperatures of a typical Siberian winter. What had started out as nothing more than an NKVD train supply depot in '36, had developed into a village, then a minor town, and now was a thriving metropolis in this part of northeastern Russia. The commandant's office was located here. Lt Col Zholdin was responsible for two-thirds of the corrective labour camps within the Mytininsk network, which they laid out more or less in a hub and spoke manner. He commanded four full-strength battalions of MVD soldiers and auxiliary guards units, comprising nearly 2,000 men. Now that the USSR had won the Great Patriotic War, his troop strength was more than supplemented by the returning soldiers from the front lines. I'm positive Mytininsk was just a stepping stone for his lofty ambitions.

Inside my satchel today, I carried a special list of names. The women so named were all the internees in Mytininsk-23 who were due for release within the next few months. I also would recommend who would succeed me as the matron of hut No. 31 and who would be the next camp matron. In the last couple of years, I had ascended to the rank of Camp Matron too. This made me the senior internee within the entire camp.

By law, I alone would liaise with the Gulag camp administration. What this really meant in practise was that I was now the camp spokesman, more or less. I would pass on important adjustments to our work quotas, move work brigades around depending on needs, plead for food supply increases, and argue for better medical care. This rank also gave me tremendous freedom to come and go as I pleased, inside and outside of the campgrounds. The MVD guards hardly even ever looked at my day-passes any longer. They would just nonchalantly wave me through the gates with disdain. I'm sure they all questioned what possible trouble an old white-haired grandmother could make for them.

I didn't assume that everyone outside of the campgrounds knew of my rank, and therefore I always ensured my papers were in order, in case they stopped me.

The lieutenant colonel met me at his open office door and appeared chipper this afternoon. Commensurate with his promotion, he'd only just arrived in Mytininsk a few weeks ago to take on his new duties and responsibilities. This was in fact only the fourth time I'd spoken with him.

Stalin's Door

"Come in, come in Valeriya Timurovna and please take a seat. And how are we today? How are things in the best women's camp under my jurisdiction? You know we dare not disappoint the Boss." The lieutenant colonel had a young-looking face, with eyes that had yet to lose their hope within the system.

The man appeared fit and trim, and in his late 30s in age. His neatly pressed olive-green uniform jacket complemented sharp Prussian blue trousers. I'd never seen the fellow's black boots not polished so assiduously, that if you wanted to, you could see yourself reflected within their blinding sheen. Even with the constant snow and mud from outside, his footgear was always inspection ready.

The lieutenant colonel sat down behind his enormous desk, strewn with paper, plans, maps, briefs, folders, and work materials of every kind imaginable.

On the wall directly behind the lieutenant colonel's head hung a large black-and-white photograph of Comrade Stalin. All of our dear leader's subordinates had the habit now of referring to him as the Boss.

Following an unofficial decree that every room now display his visage, no one missed the message that the Boss was eternally standing watch over us, with his pitch-black eyes everywhere—seeing all.

This specific photograph was the famous one taken back in '37. Comrade Stalin held his fashionable pipe and stared intently off and to the left. Our dear leader was captured wearing one of his signature French jackets, named after the British Field Marshal from the Great War who popularised it, and not after the country.

On the right-hand side of Comrade Stalin hung a smaller black-and-white photograph of the current chief of the MVD, Minister Sergei Kruglov.

The Ministry of Internal Affairs, known by its acronym MVD, was the agency that succeeded the People's Commissariat for Internal Affairs, known as the NKVD. Anyone who landed on the wrong side of Comrade Stalin could surely expect a visit from Comrade Kruglov's ever burgeoning army of secret policemen.

Lt Col Zholdin wore a black bushy mustache upon his face, which was all the rage amongst the senior Soviet leadership these days, and their cult of personality for Comrade Stalin.

"We are doing well, Comrade Commandant. Rather well, in fact. I will leave the camp in expert hands, I'm sure. Since I've been Camp Matron for the last couple of years, we've never failed to complete any of the levied work quotas. My women are dependable, work hard, and cause no problems." I always made eye contact when speaking with him, sat straight up, and spoke in a calm and pleasing manner.

"Yes, yes." The lieutenant colonel looked down now at the excessive amount of paperwork on his desk.

He took hold of a thick, red and black folder within his hands. Across the top of the cover, stamped in large bold lettering, I saw the following words:

MOST URGENT

"You know, I've just received some new orders sent directly from MVD headquarters in Moskva." The lieutenant colonel glanced up at me and tilted his head ever so slightly to the left, referring to the photograph of Comrade Kruglov behind his desk. "With all the post-war rebuilding going on across our glorious country, the work quotas are being increased yet again. We are significantly behind schedule, and I'm here to rectify that deficiency.

Half our returning soldiers captured and interred by the Germans—well, the ones that are still alive—are being arrested and placed within the Gulag. Something about them having too much foreign contact with the enemy, they said. I don't understand it myself. But orders are orders. The new Five-Year plan accelerates our reconstruction processes. The raw materials needed for such an ambitious plan are located right here in the heart of northeastern Siberia."

"I understand, Comrade Commandant. I'm sure that whoever you eventually select to succeed me won't let you down in this endeavour."

"I'm not sure you completely realise it all, Valeriya Timurovna." Lt Col Zholdin looked down at his desk at another pile of papers. "I've also received new directives regarding the prisoner dispositions. Because of the forecasted demands of these new work quotas, my orders are to extend the sentences for all Gulag prisoners, indefinitely. Therefore, I shall defer all forthcoming amnesty. I'm afraid, Matron, that you're not going anywhere—except back to work."

The lieutenant colonel lit up a matchstick and brought it to the chamber of his tobacco pipe. A quick burst of inhalations from his pursed lips rapidly got the brier ignited. He exhaled a lungful of thick white smoke and took the pipe away from his mouth. The smoke smelled acrid, and I found it most disagreeable.

"I'm terribly sorry about all of this." The lieutenant colonel then looked back down upon the mountain of paperwork and sighed loudly. "Was there anything else you wanted to discuss with me today, Matron?"

His meaning was crystal clear. There was to be no debate on this matter. I politely said my goodbyes and excused myself from his office.

For the first time since my incarceration within the Gulag, I cried.

As I made the dreadful walk back to Mytininsk-23 that day, great sadness suddenly overcame me. I thought about those new directives from the commandant's office, and a crushing pain filled my sides. I had to pause for a brief respite. I felt the bitter northern winds—which had been at my back for the trek over to Mytininsk—as they now stung me all about my face. What were to have been tears of joy were nothing but tears of heartache and despair. I felt bad for myself, I won't deny that. Even so, I felt even more unfortunate for poor Zhenya. She was so looking forward to leaving this place behind and getting on with her life. I couldn't bear to think of how to break this crushing news to her, and to everyone else that had survived for this long.

I noted with some irony, that had our arrests occurred only a few more days earlier in '38, I'd be on a train with Zhenya right now travelling westward—to freedom and starting our lives over again. I didn't know how long this indefinite suspension would last. I didn't even know if I'd be alive to see it lifted.

A hard crust of saline now coated my face, where tears had been only moments ago. Standing still in this weather was dangerous. I had to keep moving.

As I resumed walking along the forest path, I tried to remove the frozen tears by brushing my cheeks with my hands. I winced out in pain. My skin felt as if it were being scraped right off. This fresh agony only reinforced that nothing in Siberia was simple. Not even crying.

Stalin's Door

§

That evening back in the camp, I did my best to avoid Zhenya and the other women whose sentences were soon expiring. Everyone was expecting excellent news from me, and I didn't yet have the words, or the heart, to express myself. These new directives that ordered the forced work quotas to increase didn't surprise me. The MVD had been stepping up year over year production ever since the Great Patriotic War ended. We'd have to work it out or die trying. As women passed away here, or with the lucky ones—gained their releases, there seemed to be a never-ending supply of replacements coming in. The mass arrests and purges within Russia ticked upwards again, like the return of a terrible season.

I skipped eating supper and delegated all my matronly burdens away. Tonight, I just wanted to go to my berth early. When my head touched the straw, I fell asleep instantaneously and dreamt.

I dreamt of my first husband Edik, this night.

I found myself in late summer, back in '13. We strolled along the grand boardwalk by the Black Sea, in the quaint resort town of Sochi. The weather was at its most delightful for the entire year here. Like the gargantuan sea out to our right-hand side, tranquillity was the only order of the day here. I saw nothing but an endless expanse of brilliant white waves and cool blue water.

In front of us, I spied scores of couples with their arms locked inside arms. They meandered upon the perfectly maintained wooden planks beneath their feet, not moving hastily at all.

For there was no reason to! I wondered if they were on holiday. Perhaps they were even on their honeymoons, like we were.

With the bright warm sun upon my face, and the crystal-clear azure skies above, I felt as if the passage of time was nearly non-existent. We revelled in the magical golden hours of late afternoon, and the salty sea airs did wonders for my quartet of humours.

But alas, Edik was antsy. His hands were fidgeting, and his concentration fleeting. Edik was always in a rush whilst on land, like a fish out of water. My husband always made sure he was never too distant from any port and constantly gazed out towards the horizon where the water met the skyline in the distance. I'm positive he felt most at ease whilst on board his ship, and when he lost his sea-legs on land, he felt uncomfortable. If my husband could have compressed this honeymoon down to just a day, I think he just might have considered it.

Edik had just rated a promotion to chief petty officer. This terrific honour had been the objective for his entire career whilst serving in the Russian Imperial navy. His tireless work ethic was being recognised and rewarded. I believe he had just broken the fleetwide record of never having taken any time off, nor of ever getting sick, which earned him a special medal of distinguishment. My husband loved his duties aboard ship so much that his new captain practically ordered him to take a post-wedding trip with me!

Edik relayed their conversation.

"Be with your lovely new bride, Chief. Go on now. Once our shakedown cruise begins, it'll be some time before we're back at the naval base. Now don't make me formally put it in writing, Eduard Yegorovich!"

Stalin's Door

"See? You should always obey your captain." I helpfully advised, as I heard Edik grunt in agreement. I continued. "And ever obey me too!" I drew my elbow upwards into his ribs and gently nudged my husband.

I peeked up and detected just the slightest hint of a smile as Edik turned his face away from me. I felt taken aback for a moment. I thought it strange that I could never look upon the face of my husband straight on. This was inexplicable. Edik's face was always twisting, or he had his back to me. I put the thought out of my mind immediately, not wanting to ruin the moment.

Edik's new battleship, the *Imperatritsa Mariya,* would launch in a few weeks' time. This fearsome heavy dreadnought was state-of-the-art and shall be the pride of the entire Russian Imperial navy, according to my husband. Edik refused to stop talking about her and was beside himself at the thought of not getting back aboard soonest. His brand-new obligations as chief of the boat could bear no more delays, it seemed. With some time to spare until they would put his warship to sea, his captain had granted him a leave of absence for the entire month of August. This was a rare occasion, and a treat. Now was the perfect opportunity for a proper honeymoon.

When we hastily married in a whirlwind ceremony only nine months ago, his old battleship, the *Ioann Zlatoust*, was in Sevastopol for emergency repairs. I hadn't even had time to make a formal wedding gown. No matter, Edik was making up for lost arrangements and opportunities now.

A new world class spa recently opened in Sochi, known as the Kavkazskaya Riviera. People would come from all over to take advantage of the healing qualities of the mineral baths there, called balneotherapy. I tried desperately to get Edik to join me in partaking in the waters, but he was having none of it. He said he'd much rather sit in one of the cafés facing the sea and study over one of the innumerable steam-turbine technical journals that he insisted on bringing with him. I swear he packed an entire suitcase full!

I'd never seen the like. Still, I couldn't complain. This honeymoon was like a dream. Even the hotel room that we were staying in was luxurious.

We could only afford the smallest room they offered, yet I wasn't criticising. A comfortable bed and a private WC were all I required.

Today I wore the most elegant evening gown I'd ever laid eyes upon. It surely must have rivaled anything seen in the Romanov court back in the days of old. In fact, I joked with Edik that I might never take it off! I tried to demur when he presented it as a surprise gift upon our arrival here. However, in all honesty I had absolutely no intentions of sending it back. I knew it must have cost my husband an entire months' hard-earned wages.

But I stopped feeling guilty the second I slipped it on—it was a perfect fit! With its exquisite ruffles, delicate lace, and materials sourced from far across the continent, I was absolutely the envy of the entire grand boardwalk this late afternoon on our stroll. Edik experienced some difficulty between staring at me and looking out to his beloved seascape. I never really got a swell look at his face, though. If I turned his way, he instantly shifted in the other direction. This was most awkward.

We made quite the couple. My husband looked spectacularly handsome in his new chief's naval dress uniform. Edik's new rank, badges, and insignias garnered much respect within this compact seaside city. The other couples who walked upon the grand boardwalk with us would politely nod with approval as we passed them by, and the single men would tip their index fingers to the brims of their hats and smile at us. We felt special today.

Stalin's Door

With Edik's extra responsibilities, and his new battleship, I felt as if the entire Black Sea Fleet were in excellent hands. My Edik would see to that.

We promised ourselves a single glorious evening out on the town during our holiday, with dinner, dancing, and a bottle of the finest wine in the house. That's where we were off sauntering to, all dressed up on this late afternoon. We would dine like royalty—if only for a night.

After some polite inquiries, they directed us to the famous continental restaurant, Monsieur LeFrançois, which was situated just down the grand boardwalk from our hotel.

I confessed to Edik I felt nervous about ordering. I didn't speak the language of the Gallic, and I wasn't sure how we'd make do. What if I made a mistake and wound up with some horribly expensive dish?

As always, my husband reassured me that all we needed to say were the following phrases:

"Champagne pour deux, et coq-au-vin, s'il vous plaît."

Our hotel concierge was so kind enough to give Edik a crash course on the finer details and protocols of a carte du jour, just in case we needed them.

Our destination was just off the esplanade, inside another of the fancy hotels that dotted the beachside. Wandering into the cavernous lobby, I noticed the environment was clean, refreshing, and polished. The circulated air felt cool on my warm face, and it instantly put me at ease. I could see there were many plush chairs and couches to unwind in, in here, and the carpeting was thick and luxurious. It felt marvellous underneath my feet, after our stroll on the hard boardwalk decking outside. We continued over to the entrance of the French restaurant, in a quiet corner on the first floor. Edik held the door for me as we walked inside.

Immediately, I experienced delight at the romantic ambiance of the establishment. There was a duskiness to the atmosphere in here, and the air smelled just a little smokey. The dining room held a dozen petite tables, spaced respectively apart. An ornate candelabrum lit up each surface, and I could see fancy, thick white linens, accompanied by sets of fine china and sterling silverware, arranged with care and precision. Leaded crystal glasses of all sizes refracted the graceful candlelight, as if they were performing a perfect tango, just for our benefit.

The restaurant lay deserted, save for two older gentlemen seated along the far wall. They engaged in small talk, smoking their cigars and sipping expensive brandies.

The generous bar anchored this bistro, with its dark ornate wood and a brilliant white countertop made from marble, which ran the breadth of the establishment. I presumed that continental culture dictated that you must eat dinner much later into the evening. It was the only logical explanation for why no one was yet dining.

Edik gently took my hand inside his, and we walked over to the station where the maître d'hôtel stood watch.

The headwaiter, dressed in an impeccable black tuxedo, greeted us in a gruff and aloof manner. He didn't even bother to look up from his lectern. A small crystal electric lamp illuminated the stack of papers he was pouring over. The man used a stubby pencil to scribble away upon menus, table diagrams, and the like. He then spoke to us.

"Bonsoir, Madame et Monsieur. Avez-vous une réservation?" The words were both foreign and sophisticated sounding to me. Edik didn't speak French, so he proceeded as best as he knew how to.

"We'd like your finest table for two, please. We'll be having dinner tonight." Edik then smiled brightly at me.

The maître d'hôtel interrupted his paperwork and placed his writing implement behind one ear. Our host looked over the top of his thick glasses, staring at us both. It shocked me as he took a long, hard gaze at Edik. As if my husband had just offended the tuxedoed man in some manner. A quizzical look formed all about the fellow's face, and he stepped out from behind his post to survey us both now. Up and down, slowly. The maître d'hôtel then shook his head from side to side, briskly. I felt taken aback and didn't quite know what to make of all this.

In a guttural, gloomy voice, the headwaiter replied as best he could, using our mother tongue.

"My regrets, Sir. We have a full dining card this evening. Perhaps you'd be more comfortable eating in the café." The rude man motioned with his white-gloved hands curtly, as if to shoo us away from here.

Edik took a step forward and addressed the maître d'hôtel brusquely.

"Sir, this is a special occasion. We're on our honeymoon. We will easily finish our dinner before most of your guests arrive tonight."

The maître d'hôtel then folded his arms across his chest and snapped back.

"Non. C'est impossible."

I tugged on Edik's arm.

"Oh, bubelah, let's leave here. We can find another restaurant to dine in tonight. I saw several excellent looking establishments on the walk over."

Edik stood his ground, and we both overheard the headwaiter mutter under his breath.

"We don't want your kind in here."

"What did you just say?" Edik could barely get his words out.

"Oh, I think you heard me, filthy zhyd." The maître d'hôtel sounded smug and self-assured.

Edik was furious now at the man's insult and outrage, taking another step forward. He violently grabbed the maître d'hôtel by the lapels on his expensive jacket. Edik wasn't one to back down easily, especially when he had his dander up. I could see he was beyond agitated, as he stared down at the headwaiter in disgust. It was all I could do to assuage his anger.

"Please, dearest, be the bigger gentleman here. Remember, the burden is always equal to the horse's strength. Let us walk away now."

Edik released his hold on the headwaiter, who appeared petrified.

"As you wish, my dear." My husband then brushed his palms over the man's wrinkled lapels to straighten them back out.

Beads of sweat visibly dripped down from the frightened fellow's temples. I then let out of tremendous sigh, feeling relieved.

"I am confident that we can find a better venue." Edik said with a smile as he elegantly took my hand.

We walked out of the restaurant, through the hotel lobby, and back out on to the grand boardwalk. The early evening was gorgeous, with the sun just beginning to set over the horizon of tranquil Black Sea waters. The air was crisp and clean out here, with just the slightest saltwater breeze. Edik approached the railing and stopped, turning his back to the sunset. He then leaned back on the thick metal bar. Edik reached into his pocket to retrieve a cigar.

"I was saving this for later. I think now might be an agreeable time, whilst I figure things out."

"You go right ahead, dearest. I cannot say I'm surprised at our treatment in there. I can say that you handled the situation really well. I am proud of you, and how you conducted yourself, my husband."

Edik ignited his cigar with a matchstick and huffed it five times thusly into the bright flame. The thick white vapour rose above his head, following the sea breeze in a swirling motion.

Edik then twisted his head away from me again. As I followed the torrent of his cigar smoke, I caught sight of an enormous black cloud, low on the horizon, and some considerable distance out on the water. As I squinted my eyes, I could just make out a ship's silhouette underneath the Stygian fog.

"Um, dear, what is that over there?"

"What is what, honey?" Edik murmured.

"I think there's a vessel out there—on fire!"

"What are you saying?" Edik turned himself around rapidly and looked out to the horizon. "Egad! The flames!"

We both stood there for a few moments, watching helplessly as the ship continued to burn, belching angry plumes of inky smoke up into the atmosphere. By this time, many people had joined us on the grand boardwalk, all looking out to sea, and pointing, powerless to do anything about it. Over the course of our scrutiny, the ship closed the distance to the shoreline by more than half.

Everyone could now see clear details of the vessel, and the raging fire aboard her. I stared at Edik, as he was craning his neck forwards, trying desperately to take it all in.

"What kind of ship is that?" I begged Edik.

"B'ezrat Hashem! That's a battleship!" Edik didn't take any time in replying to me. "I can't understand it. What would she be doing here? We're hundreds of kilometres away from any port that could service her."

"Can you make out the ship's name?"

Edik placed his left hand up to his forehead to block out the light from the setting sun.

"It's got a double-headed eagle on the bow! Wellaway! It's one of ours. I—N—three—nine! Nyet! It cannot be! It's the *Imperatritsa Mariya*! How is this possible?"

My husband's entire body shook about now. His hands had long ago dropped the lit cigar to the ground, and he was clenching the grand boardwalk railing with all his strength. Edik desperately leaned forwards with all his might to catch a glimpse. As he stared out to sea, the gigantic fiery battleship was now close enough to the shore so we could distinguish her individual sailors. They dotted the decks of the warship and scurried about as they fought the multiple breakouts of the fearsome conflagration.

A tremendous explosion then erupted from somewhere below the waterline of the vessel, and her entire hull seemed for a moment in time to rise out of the sea, floating effortlessly and silently. I could hear an audible gasp all around me as everyone who witnessed the catastrophe took in the gruesome sight.

As the battleship crashed back into the water, the brashest thunderclap I'd ever heard in my life rang out and continued reverberating within my ears painfully.

Not three seconds later, the heat from the eruption arrived with a rush of air that knocked me to the ground and flat onto my back. I looked up at Edik, who stood motionless, staring out to the spectacle. As I righted myself slowly, I worried that my new evening gown had become damaged irreparably. That thought instantly left my mind as I caught sight of Edik. Edik's uniform jacket was now on fire in multiple places about his torso.

"Edik! Edik!" I shrieked in horror.

I ran over to him as rapidly as I could manage. With my gloved hands, I slapped at the flames using as much force as I could muster. As I tried in vain to tamp the fire down, my mind couldn't comprehend why Edik was just standing there. My ministrations didn't seem to help at all. More than not, the inferno seemed to spread all about his body.

I continued screaming and took off my black scorched gloves, flinging them away from me in disgust. Their off-white shimmer ousted by a black soot colour of char—and now ruined beyond repair. An acrid odour now engulfed my nostrils, and it didn't take me long to figure out what it was. The sickening smell of burning flesh permeated all around me. I cried out hysterically and continued beating my husband's body with the palms of my hands. Perhaps if I could just knock him to the ground, I could find a blanket, or some such cover, and I could smother out the horrible flames. Edik was still clenching the boardwalk railing, and I couldn't understand why.

"Edik! Edik!" It was all I could think of to yell out.

"I could have saved more of them. But there were so many wounded waiting for rescue. Horrible burns and smoke inhalations. If only I had more time? I am sorry I quit you, Lera. Shalom, my love."

Edik spoke to me in a whispered voice, yet I could not comprehend how. His mouth, such that I could still see, wasn't moving. In fact, his entire body was now burning, engulfed by the angry combustion. Thick black smoke was pouring off of his frame and heading skyward. The flames were so brilliant, I could no longer distinguish the colour of his uniform jacket or trousers. Edik's face and hands were alight now. His sailor's cap had long boiled off, leaving his hair underneath aflame. It made a distinct hissing sound as it melted.

I hollered for help, to anyone who would listen. As I did so, I looked up and down the grand boardwalk, desperately searching for someone—anyone. The dozens of people who were here earlier watching the battleship in flames had now disappeared. My mind stopped functioning, and I knew I was powerless.

As I sat upon the ground, I pounded my clenched fists into the hard wood of the planks, crying out. After a moment, I examined my outstretched hands. My palms were badly burned, yet I felt no pain. My fingers, horribly disfigured and gnarled, would knit nothing ever again.

I overheard a voice in the distance—calling out to me, desperately. A youthful woman's voice. I knew it immediately.

"Grandmother! Grandmother! Please wake up!" As I opened my eyes, I saw Zhenya standing over me in the dim light of the hut.

"Please come quickly! There's a terrible fire in the camp!" Zhenya frantically pulled me from my berth.

My mind immediately snapped into my role as camp matron. My Lord, what were my sisters going through?

The camp's fire was fast, devastating, and deadly.

Across the way, in the section where the even numbered huts stood, a blaze had inexplicably broken out in hut No. 18. Within just minutes, the conflagration had spread rapidly to the huts nearest the point of origin. Huts No. 16 and No. 20 bracketed the eruption, as they were each only four metres distant. The flames consumed those three huts almost instantaneously.

Huts No. 14, and No. 12 were further away from the flash point, yet they too caught fire within a matter of a few moments. By the time I arrived on the scene to survey the mayhem, combustion thoroughly engulfed these five huts, burning rapidly in the night. A state of total chaos now reigned.

I shuddered as I heard the panicked shrieks of dozens of trapped women still inside their huts, as they begged us for rescue.

I felt myself helpless as I watched the thick black smoke gushing from underneath the eaves of the hut's metal roofing, rising into the darkness above. As the roaring flames sucked in all available oxygen to burn, it produced a horrifying high pitch shrill, the likes of which I'd never forget. Everything the fire touched was being consumed and turned to ash. Because it was an exceptionally cloudless night, the light of a full moon and the thousands of heavenly bodies above us bathed the campsite in an otherworldly twilight.

Suddenly, the brilliant stars overhead slowly winked out, one by one, as the sky became obscured by the dense smog from the fire. As each point of light winked out, snuffed for all time, I couldn't help but wonder if they represented the passing of another one of my sister's souls. There was no time to lose.

The construction of each of the huts was nothing more than giant cut wooden logs sourced from the same timber we harvested daily in the Siberian taiga. The floorboards, bunks, door, latrine, tables, and practically everything else inside came from this identical wood. That lumber was now well over a decade old and in an over-cured state. The tundra was exceptionally dry this time of year, which meant that the huts were giant tinderboxes, waiting to ignite. As I looked back, it was a miracle that we hadn't had a fire in the camp until now.

I hurriedly surveyed the damage and could see that the huts next to No. 12 were only partially on fire. We could save them with some effort. Getting the blaze out at its terminus would also prevent it spreading to the other parts of the campground.

I endeavoured to get a bucket brigade going with as many able-bodied women that I could round up in a brief time.

Many of the women from the neighbouring huts were awake and ready to help, however it was the matter of getting something with which to put out the inferno.

Since it was in the middle of the night, and in the dead of winter, the frigid temperatures meant any water drawn from out of the wells on the quad would freeze within scant minutes. I ran urgently to the MVD guard post at the front of the no man's land. I begged and pleaded with the camp guards on duty to wake the other men in their barracks next to our campground. Even getting the flames out now would still save many lives. The lieutenant of the night guard was eventually found, and upon assessing the situation, he merely muttered that there wasn't anything he or his men could do to help us.

"I think it best that we let nature take its course, Matron." The MVD lieutenant suggested meekly.

I left disgusted, but not before a final censure.

"You're a worthless human being! I cannot believe you have a mother and sisters! Would you let them burn to death? You—you paskudnyak!" I spat violently into the lieutenant's face, after using the most savage of all Yiddish insults.

For my insolence, I received a vicious slap to the face and stinging rebuke.

"Thirty days on administrative rations for that outburst, old woman! Don't make me put you in the punishment hut too!"

The stinging pain in my cheeks faded quickly and the reprimand was surely nothing when compared to what some women were dealing with.

When dawn finally broke, they assembled everyone still alive into the quad. The fires had finally extinguished themselves naturally.

I informed everyone that five of the huts burned right down to their foundations. Two of the huts sustained major fire damage, yet they were still standing. I doubted they'd be in any reasonable state to live in, however.

We stood there freezing on the ice as the MVD guards conducted their morning calculation. This was the worst part of the day. I hadn't eaten, and I shivered all the way to the marrow of my bones. I awaited the tally—with dread. I knew it would not be pleasant news.

"1,413 prisoners present and accounted for!"

There were 67 women that had taken refuge in the administration shack and workshops in the middle of the campground. The blaze had injured them too badly to report for the first days' calculation. Another 14 women were already recuperating in our makeshift infirmary hut. This meant that by taking the sum of the three counts and subtracting from the evening calculation of 1,589 prisoners made only 12 hours ago, that there were 95 women now not accounted for. I presumed these women perished—victims of the heinous fire.

As camp matron, I instantly began to triage the wounded into the unaffected huts for their recoveries. Most of the survivors now had chronic breathing issues because of their smoke inhalations, along with painful burns that ranged from minor to major. I begged the MVD guard captain to send for any doctors that could come from the other camps, and from the city of

Mytininsk. Once I showed him the level of devastation and the ghastly injuries, he agreed to call for aid. I thanked the captain profusely.

I always made it a point to manage by example, so I urged that all the other hut matrons take in as many of the displaced women as they could. In our hut, No. 31, we could easily accommodate ten survivors. I volunteered to give up my berth, and Zhenya kindly did the same. We could comfortably sleep by the wood-burning stove for as long as it took our guests to heal themselves.

The injured souls we received endured devastating second and third-degree burns, horrible infections, and wicked breathing problems.

Even with the gentlest of care, any handling at all to the afflicted traumatised tissues and skin produced an unimaginable pain. The victims cried out in an agony I'd wish on no one. The doctors that arrived from the town could do little to treat such painful disfigurements, beyond light bandages and salves.

These remedies did nothing to relieve their suffering, and many of the wounded women died slowly—and not until after many nights of torture.

I then heard an abominable cough ring out. I'd heard its pitiful timbre before, during the Great War. The damage to the lungs of a fire victim —from the smoke inhalation—were very much like what I'd witnessed with the wounded afflicted by the poisonous gasses deployed in the trenches. So dreadful were those injuries to the psyche of mankind, that every nation around the globe outlawed gas warfare forever.

The Great War—we now called it World War I. It should have been the war to end all wars. But it was just a starter course to The Great Patriotic War—what everyone else refers to as the fighting on the Eastern Front in World War II. I'd seen plenty of death and destruction between 1914 and

1918. I'd volunteered as a nurse, serving my Empire and doing my patriotic duty. The rejuvenation hospital I worked in at the Black Sea port of Novorossiysk saw thousands of casualties with injuries and wounds that would take months, or even years to heal fully. Of all the patients I'd treated, one stays forefront in my mind to this day.

A young naval officer was recovering from grisly third-degree burns to over 40 percent of his body from some kind of accident aboard his battleship. The left side of his body, from his head down to his thighs, had been scarred badly in the blaze. His body's recuperation lasted for quite a while with painful healing therapies and multiple skin grafts.

How that man managed to fight through his relentless agony was an act of Herculean courageousness. I never saw him complain once. But as the weeks turned into months in his recovery, the lieutenant began to manifest the hidden cost of war. How his mind would heal too.

As he recovered, he began to worry about the visible burn scars about his body, especially the ones to his face. He thought he'd never be able to marry, or even continue with his naval career. Would he be shunned forever, as people recoiled from his hideous countenance? He confessed to me one day in therapy, that he was at the lowest point of his stay. He was thinking of ending it all.

I informed him to put all such thoughts out of his head immediately! I told him I considered him the bravest man I'd ever met, and that he shouldn't let anything, or anyone stand in his way of achieving all of his life's goals. He had his entire lifetime ahead and could do anything he put his mind to. Why, with his indomitable spirit, I assured him he'd even make the rank of admiral one day.

I've tried desperately over the years to remember anything else about that remarkable officer. I cannot even recall his family surname or patronymic. I think his given name was Fridrik.

I wonder what ever became of that young man?

§

In the days that followed the catastrophe, an investigation would determine that many of the women who died in the fire itself were ones who rushed back into the huts. This was not to look for and assist those overwhelmed by the smoke and flames, but to rescue the portraits of Comrade Stalin that every hut displayed, by official decree. Perhaps these deranged women thought that by bravely saving the visage of our dear leader, they would gain special treatment by the MVD camp guards.

I would never learn their genuine reasons.

A week later, I was sitting by our hut's wood-burning stove with Zhenya. I stared into the bright flames and didn't blink until my eyes became dry. I dared not cry here. Not in front of everyone. I needed to be strong for my sisters and set a positive example for everyone to follow.

As the heat warmed up my body, my thoughts wandered aimlessly and by chance I recalled having a dream just before Zhenya woke me on that terrible night of the fire.

Normally I wasn't one who could recall what I dreamt, however I knew that Edik was in it. I knew it had to be Edik in my dream, except that even now when I recalled my long-dead husband, I couldn't recollect any details of his face. I had completely lost the ability to remember what he looked like.

    Edik's smile was just a blur to me and his expressive eyes were closed now. He was a mere shadow of a man. This revelation made me feel doubly sad.

Year Of Crystal

"General Secretary Stalin is dead." The MVD guard captain proclaimed with reverence. The announcement to the entire camp hung over all of us like an ominous storm cloud. No one dared look upon the face of another. No one dared show any emotion at all.

For myself, I stood motionless and stared blankly ahead. Was this another one of my dreams? Was I in fact just imagining all of this? I felt lightheaded, and I attempted to steady my feet in the mud. Was I about to wake myself up and find out that nothing had changed, and that I was merely another day closer to death?

Perhaps I had just died in my sleep, and this was just some kind of afterimage that my brain was producing as the inevitable rigor mortis set in.

The MVD guard captain stood atop the wooden platform on the gallows, looking down at hundreds of scared and confused women. Thankfully, there had been no sentences of capital punishment levied so far this year. His deep voice echoed all around us, as he lowered the small megaphone used for maximum projection, away from his face.

I quickly surveyed the camp's population. The entire camp, nearly 1,600 women, stood dutifully lined up in formation. Each hut of 40 women, with their matrons at the front of each column, assembled in the camp courtyard at midday.

We'd been performing this drill twice daily for the camp guards to count us for years now. In the mornings before work began, and just after supper, before lights out.

I thought of earlier today, when rumours filled the campground. Stories circulated wildly to the matrons that a special announcement for us was imminent. I recognised something remarkable was transpiring, I just didn't know what it was yet. For the next several hours, I could not help answering any of the innumerable questions they peppered me with. Questions from the other matrons about what the subject of the proclamation would be.

I told them truthfully I knew nothing, other than what they knew, and that I'd find out right along with them what it was all about. Chaotic scuttlebutt began circulating around the campground like wildfire. Was the Soviet Union going back to war? Had the capitalistic United States of America invaded our land? Were we being moved to another campground? Anything seemed possible. We just didn't know.

I no longer held the position of camp matron—and hadn't for two years now. I had to relinquish my duties and responsibilities, reluctantly, because of my advanced age. Because I could no longer do any work, the camp administrators now classified me as an invalid. They relegated me to a permanent half-ration of food. It was a virtual death sentence. Had it not been for all the other women around me who felt sorry for the way I was being treated, I would have surely perished. Each of these kind sisters in my hut sacrificed a small spoonful of their own sustenance each day to make up for my deficit. For that generosity, I'd be eternally grateful. Everyone still regarded me as something of an emeritus matron, as I carried a lifetime of wisdom, knowledge, and a penchant for survival. I would happily impart it to anyone that needed my help. I also knew things well ahead of everyone else.

The date was 13 March 1953. A day I'd never forget as long as I could rise every morning. The winter chill outside wasn't that severe today. I doubted if it was much below minus ten degrees centigrade. I could just see the sun as it poked through the impossibly white clouds above.

Was an extraordinary day about to dawn for us in the Gulag? Thoughts of endless hopes raced through my mind. My bones were brittle now, and it felt painful for me to stand for lengthy periods of time.

How ironic it was that the great and powerful USSR still considered an elderly woman like me a terrible threat. Thankfully, I was now in full-time possession of Zhenya's neckerchief woggle. The heat that little orb produced to keep me warm throughout the year was a magnificent gift!

The MVD guard captain started reading his announcement.

"So, it is with great despondency that I report the Supreme Leader of the Soviet people passed away the morning of the fifth of March. General Secretary Stalin died whilst still working at his desk. No doubt he'd been up all evening, and long into the night, as he often would be. Planning our way forward in the world was a onerous task that he alone could tame.

"His enormous courage saved our glorious Union from the fascists in the Great Patriotic War and left us all in debt to his unrivaled steady genius. I doubt if we'll ever be able to repay it all back. He was always rooting out and stamping down the myriad of conspirators and wreckers that would love nothing more than to see us all fail as a united nation.

"He always focused his great thoughts on what was best for our extraordinary Union. I fear that his tireless efforts were finally too much for one man to cope with."

I heard the MVD guard captain's voice crack at that last line.

"He must have known his end was nearing. These were his last instructions to us, written by his own hand, as he gasped his last breath upon this earth."

The MVD guard captain paused for five seconds before nearly shouting out Stalin's epitaph:

"Let no man declare I didn't give my best for my Union."

The MVD guard captain waited a few moments to let our dear leader's words sink in.

"I say again, General Secretary Stalin is dead." The MVD guard captain removed his cap and bowed his head in silence. Everyone around me did the same.

We all remained motionless. No one dared speak. No one dared look anyone else in the eyes either. Eyes can betray thoughts. And thoughts in this place were just as dangerous as words. And words were enough to incite a revolution.

With my head lowered, I jutted my eyes out a little past my brows to peek about. Some women near where I stood were trembling uncontrollably. I could see hands upon hands shaking unrestrained, right down the line. I could hear a low moaning sound emanating from somewhere behind me. Tears began flowing and replaced what was once a dead stillness with crying. Dozens began wailing out, followed by hundreds. Some women must have cried in despair. Some others disguised sadness with what could be nothing short of pure joy. More than a few were stone-cold, emotionless, as if the news of Comrade Stalin's death, and what it might bring, had yet to sink in fully.

For myself, I noted that the news of such an earth-shattering event still took eight days to reach us here, in far northeast Russia. We truly were in a world of our own in this place.

§

A new directive filtered its way throughout the entire Gulag camp system in the months that followed the death of Comrade Stalin. The MVD camp administrators enacted an amnesty of sorts for any prisoner interned from '41, or before. Regardless of their crime or sentence, they ordered immediate parole. I was now finally free, and so was Zhenya.

The date of our liberation was ironically International Workers' Day. Our incarceration inside the Gulag had lasted 15 years.

Zhenya assisted me as I walked through the front gates of camp Mytininsk-23 for one last time that day. We left our internment with nothing more than what we came in with. Oh, there were tearful goodbyes from all the other matrons as we departed. We exchanged hugs and kisses, with many promises to keep in touch. Our friends presented us with a collection of some dry foods, clothing, spare rubles, and kopeks. However, I refused all charity. I merely thanked them and said we'd make our own way now, just as we'd always done before.

This trek to the burgeoning city of Mytininsk was unlike that of any journey I'd made before. With Zhenya at my side, we kept up a good pace through the endless forests of the Siberian taiga. Would I shortly be saying goodbye to them forever? I could still hear the sounds of trees as their singing rang out in this eternal cathedral of wood. Would I ever get to see the Leshiye again?

Once we arrived in Mytininsk, they directed us to find the boarding home of Mme Konnikova. She ran a half-way house for newly released Gulag prisoners. In exchange for work in the laundries and kitchens of various establishments around the city, she'd provide us two meals a day and a cot in the bunkhouse. We could also earn additional funds doing sundry labours like knitting, sewing, and mending.

Because neither Zhenya nor I had any other alternative, we eagerly claimed the opportunity. Working in Mytininsk for a few weeks allowed us to slowly reintegrate into society. I marvelled at the fabric of the inhabitants of this city on the frontier of our great country.

Everyone who lived here had a personal connection to the Gulag machine. Inmates and guards transitioned to former prisoners and former jailers—and all decided to make Mytininsk their home.

The children born here in this frozen abyss would know a better life than we did, now that Supreme Leader Stalin had departed for chert voz'mi. The national shame of the Gulag would surely move into the annals of history, long after I too passed on.

I informed Zhenya of my grand plan. We'd work straight through, 18 hours a day if needed, until we had saved enough for the purchase of tickets for our journey on the mighty Trans-Siberian Railway, from Mytininsk all the way west to Leningrad.

The trip would not be easy and required many steps. From Mytininsk, it would take two days just to travel to the terminus of Nizhny Bestyakh, 888 kilometres distant. From there we would pick up the TSR spur of the Amur–Yakutsk Mainline, which connected to the Baikal–Amur Mainline at Tynda, 1,034 kilometres distant. Finally, we would travel to the main TSR station in city of Tayshet, for another 2,348 kilometres of travel. From Tayshet to Moskva on the TSR, we'd traverse a distance of 4,516 kilometres. Moskva to Leningrad was a measly journey of 650 kilometres in comparison. We'd reverse the hellish rail trip we experienced here, on our way to freedom. In total, from northeastern Siberia, back to our family home in the Baltic seaport, we'd experience a peregrination of 9,436 kilometres.

What would we find there after 15 years inside the Gulag, and a devastating world war in between? Would any of our family still be alive?

The passage to Leningrad would take us approximately 12 long days. The third-class accommodations, as meagre as they were, would surely feel like first-class to us, in comparison to the hellish cattle railcars we journeyed to Siberia in, all those years ago.

We'd also have to put some money aside for the purchase of food and beverages from the vendors we'd meet on all the stops along the way home. Travelling west across 11 time zones a half-a-world away we'd experience and interact with a dozen different cultures of the mighty USSR.

As I soon discovered, I unfortunately wasn't of much help to Zhenya in the punishing manual labour department—washing clothes and cleaning dishes. My 71-year-old body felt beyond useless and worn out. Zhenya never complained once.

Still, I contributed greatly with the various darning and stitching chores that needed done to make my way towards our goal of leaving. And whenever I had the opportunity, I greatly appreciated being able to knit again. My mother used to say if you love riding a sled downhill, you must also love to carry it back up the knoll.

But I didn't think of it as work at all. I adored the feeling of the napped yarn in my weathered hands again, as it soothed and relaxed me.

The day before our excursion west, I purchased Zhenya's ticket home at the rail station office. An entire month's wages barely covered the expense.

§

On the day the mighty TSR train arrived, I stood with Zhenya on the rail platform and looked up at the majestic sun. There was something about the light in the Siberian taiga I never quite could figure out—everything around me seemed to glow. Today was a beautiful day though, and the weather was just starting to show signs of a late spring here in northeastern Russia. The crisp air inside my weary lungs refreshed my spirit immensely.

With all of her earthly belongings tucked inside a small knapsack beside her, Zhenya practically hopped up and down in anticipation. I marvelled at her positivity and upbeat spirit—even after everything that we'd been through. She was now 28 years old—err—well, really 27 years old because of a trick I'd used many years ago. Was that fair to her? To have made her accompany me? I wondered.

I kept her alive, yes, just as I'd promised. But at what cost? She didn't have a proper childhood. Zhenya had seen more death, strife, heartbreak, and suffering to last her a lifetime.

Zhenya stood proudly in the midday sun, wearing the new snood I'd managed to make in secret over the last few nights. I borrowed a pair of knitting pins from Mme Konnikova and was able to procure the most fabulous yarn I'd ever used, dyed in the colour of ultramarine. The result was a stunner of an heirloom piece that would keep her warm for years to come. Zhenya cried tears of joy when I presented it to her at the boarding house over supper last evening.

Zhenya appeared nervous as the fearsome behemoth of the iron road pulled into the rail station, right on time. Only a small window was allowed for the embarkation of passengers, and delays to the tightly regulated timetables were not permitted.

"Honey? Zhenya? Listen to me to me now."

"Yes, Grandmother? What is it? We should get going. We don't want to miss the train."

"I have something to give you my love."

"Da? What is this? Another surprise for me?"

I reached into my coat pocket and palmed an object. With my hand closed around the item, it felt frosty to me—almost as if I was holding a small ball of ice. I found this quite mysterious after relying upon its radiant heat all these past years. I opened my fist and I held it out for Zhenya to see. I gazed upon the golden gadget for one last bittersweet moment in time. The light of the solntse caught the red star of the badge, reflecting it perfectly into my eyes. I would surely never see this wondrous gift again.

I pushed the woggle into Zhenya's open hand and saw a wave of confusion flood over her.

"Why is it so cold, Grandmother? I don't understand. Why are you giving me this now? It belongs to you."

"No, Zhenya, it's yours again. You keep hold of it. I don't need it any longer."

"Wait. What are you saying?"

I stood by her in silence as Zhenya worked out my true intention.

"Wait a moment—you're not coming with me, are you?" Zhenya appeared deathly concerned now.

"No, no I am not, my dearest."

"But why? Please, you must come. We can go together."

"My life is here now."

"Then I'll stay with you."

Zhenya threw down her scant belongings to the ground in protest.

"No, honey, this is not your home. This was never to be your home. You don't deserve to live here any longer. Please go back to the world and make a life for yourself. Remember everything I taught you. Always strive to bring kindness upon this earth—and never turn away from doing the right thing. Do this for me. I'll be all right. I'm a fighter. I'm tough. I'll be fine, I promise."

Zhenya burst into tears and hugged me tight for several moments.

"Thank you, Grandmother. Thank you for saving my life."

"And I'm saving it again. Now get on board, dear. It's almost time for you to go."

I nudged her towards the passenger railcars. I then watched as she climbed aboard the iron horse.

Zhenya quickly found her seat and opened the window. She shouted to me one last time.

"I'll never forget you, Grandmother. I'll come back for you, you'll see. We'll be together again, I just know it!"

"Shalom, Zhenya. I love you."

I then watched as the mighty Siberian transport departed on its 9,500 kilometre journey westward, with Zhenya safely aboard. As the train barrelled along the tracks rapidly away from Mytininsk, it only took three minutes before I could no longer see it on the horizon. Its thunderous whistle echoed out into the Siberian taiga before silence reigned once again.

I knew I would never see Zhenya again—for as long as I lived.

And for only the second time since living in northeastern Russia, I cried.

Zhenya's Allegory

◇◇◇◇

Return To Stalin's Door

A Thursday In April In The Year 2000

A woman's voice suddenly came over the public address system and jolted me awake in my seat. I had dozed off—but only for a moment. The subway conductor spoke in a rapid-fire manner, which perfectly mirrored the speed at which the entire Moskva Metro system operated.

Her tone was professional and no-nonsense. She informed us we were about to enter the Chistyye Prudy station, and to make sure and collect our belongings if we were disembarking. I knew that station's name.

If my memory serves, the original name of the station was Kirovskaya, named in honour after Sergey Kirov. Mr Kirov's assassination in '34 ignited a firestorm within my country. A conflagration of fear, repression, and murder the likes of which engulfed millions of innocent people. Today, historians refer to that period as the Great Terror. Ironically, it was at the direction of Stalin himself, by ordering the killing of his political rival Mr Kirov, that put me on the path to endure 15 years locked up within the Gulag machine.

I took my forefingers and rubbed them firmly on the temples of my forehead. I couldn't comprehend why it was this morning that I should have the worst migraine headache that I could ever recall. Between the noises the subway car made as it barrelled down its tracks, and the station announcements, my skull was pounding.

Unfortunately, I didn't carry any aspirin, which might have given me some relief. This was not my stop. I had one more to go this morning before I reached my eventual destination.

This morning I transited the Sokolnicheskaya line, the oldest one within the entire Moskva rapid transit system. Each one of the original 13 underground through-stations, and the many that followed, used only the finest building materials. Imbued with polished marble walls and floors, which joined magnificent edificial ceilings, these rail terminals were like modern masterworks. Their massive decorative chandeliers so brightly lit up the interiors, one might be mistaken in thinking it was sunlight from above.

The architecture was palatial, and the artwork housed throughout magisterial. These through-stations were the showcases of Communist art and science—melded together. Even just walking through these cavernous temples, inspiration would fill ordinary citizens with splendour.

The Metro was always a point of pride for the city of Moskva, and they maintained it in a state of spotlessness. There was never a hint of anything out of place. The heavily armoured police presence within each station guaranteed law and order, and a peaceful commute. The Metro was not the place to act foolishly. When the Moskva Metro had its grand opening in '35, I was there too. But that was another time and place.

The subway car I was riding in this morning was clean, modern, and differed vastly from the original ones I remembered years ago. As I looked around, people young and old filled this carriage to capacity. The atmosphere in here was agreeable, albeit I felt a little claustrophobic. Warm fresh air circulated about me, and the lighting in here was bright. I sat comfortably on

Stalin's Door

one of the blue-coloured padded plastic benches that lined each side of the car, perpendicular to the direction we were travelling in.

I felt nervous because I found myself wedged in between a middle-aged man and woman—who I assumed to be regular commuters.

As the car rocketed along the underground tracks, I felt my shoulders gently bump into theirs repeatedly. Now and again, I apologised to them for my incursions. My seatmates just smiled at me and told me not to worry about it. I said a silent prayer for receiving a seat at all when I boarded ten stops ago. This time of day was still within Moskva's general rush hour, and the plethora of people crowding the aisles as they stood in place was reminiscent of another journey I once took long ago.

I watched as their bodies swayed back and forth with inertia when the subway car would suddenly brake. Everyone tried desperately to hang on to something and not to encroach into another's personal space. For those who were tall enough, the car contained metal handholds anchored into the ceiling. I imagined that successfully reading one's newspaper, whilst holding on by one hand, would be more of an art than science.

The underground train was without conversation this morning because most of the commuters were introspective. I discerned from their faces many feelings of boredom and sullenness as they made their way to work. Hardly anyone around me smiled today. An inordinate number of folks listened to what I assumed to be music. Their personal headsets were as diverse as the individuals themselves. Some headphones looked large and bulky, whilst others were sleek and stylish. Oh, to have choices like that now, I thought to myself. I was certain they didn't realise how lucky they were!

I peeked around the car at the people seated near me. Many of the commuters wore suits and ties, whilst some dressed more casually. I counted professionals, labourers, students, mothers with their children, and older folk like myself who were just making their way about the day. It was infinitely simple for me to spot the tourists—as they held on to their giant maps, unfurled and unwieldy about themselves. There was a complete cross-section of society represented here.

I didn't mean to, and I knew it was rude, however I couldn't help but overhear a spirited conversation that was taking place right beside me. The professionally dressed gentleman and lady, who bracketed my old and frail body, were engaged in a heated debate surrounding national politics.

They chatted over my diminutive frame, as if I wasn't there at all. They presented both of their cases, and the argument was passionate. They were quarrelling over the results of the Russian presidential election that took place two weeks ago. I detected a hint of familiarity between them that told me they were a couple.

"Well, at least I voted for a winner. All you did was throw your vote away by supporting that lamentable weakling Yavlinsky. Even a fool could see he stood no chance of winning." The fellow next to me said forcefully towards his companion.

His gargantuan hands waved all about animatedly as he spoke. He kept tapping his chest with his forefinger as if to reinforce his position.

"Pah! You think yourself so enlightened, do you? Do you really think Putin will bring about all these promised reforms he campaigned on? Who do you think owns all the television stations that backed his presidency? Who do you think paid for all of those incessant election advertisements? It's the oligarchs, stupid!" The lady retorted.

I realised she wasn't backing down at all to the position of her partner. I could see the man's face turning bright red as he thought of his rejoinder.

"Keep your voice down, Yuila. Putin's ascension brings strength, and this country needs that after ten years of corruption and decay. You'll see. Mark my words! Putin is an eminent man!"

"Glupyy!"

By now, the woman clearly had her fill with the argument and turned away from the man, sulking down into her seat in disgust.

Mr Putin had served as acting president of Russia since New Year's Day, commensurate with the resignation of President Yeltsin the day before. Mr Putin's formal inauguration would be in just a few weeks, on May seventh. I wasn't certain how I felt about our new leader. Mr Putin was not the man I voted for either.

We all sat in silence for a few minutes more until I felt the subway car decelerating again as we approached the next stop. The conductor announced the through-station we were arriving into—Lubyanka—which lay directly underground of the famous Lubyanka Square that bears its name.

The principal Lubyanka building housed in the centre of the square was the headquarters for the Federal Security Service, known today as the FSB. During the latter Communist years of the USSR, this organisation bore the infamous initials of KGB. In the time of Stalin, its name was the NKVD and then the MVD. I had arrived.

Being an elderly woman didn't do me any favours commuting inside a metro famous for its speed and efficiency. It took me a moment to stand up and comport myself. I knew that I only had a few seconds to disembark, so I begged the kind gentleman standing by the doorway to hold it for me—if only for a moment. I smiled at him as I stepped onto the stone platform in the station, just as the subway car doors slid shut behind me. That was a close one. I must endeavour to be more vigilant.

As I ambled towards the exit, I discerned a contrast of how this station's architecture differed extensively from the others in the original 13. All the other primary stations had an elaborate décor: the arched cathedral-like ceilings, the polished marble floors and walls, and bright chandeliers. This station, in comparison, appeared downright bleak. Everywhere I looked I saw plain, cold, brown stone floors that met stark, white marble walls, with neither classic artwork nor any decorations. The station was clean, as all stations were, just empty and mute. The recycled air in here was slightly antiseptic. This stop reminded me more of a mausoleum than a modern metro station.

Just before the exit to the escalators that would take me up to the street level, I took notice of something I remembered from my childhood. In a tiny vestibule along the side of the inner wall lay a simple pedestal, with an ornate metal bust of a man directly atop. The visage of the man was Felix Edmundovich Dzerzhinsky. His was the name used for the original station's moniker, Dzerzhinskaya. Mr Dzerzhinsky was famous for creating the very first Soviet secret police force, named the Cheka, during the time of the Revolution. The sculpture looked well maintained and cared for, and it wouldn't surprise me to learn that they constructed it from iron. Mr Dzerzhinsky's nickname had been Iron Felix, given to him by Vladimir Ilyich Ulyanov himself, better known by his alias of Lenin. It honoured Mr Dzerzhinsky's creative talents, albeit pure ruthlessness, at his job.

Once I found myself above ground and outside, I felt much better. My pounding headache receded, if only into the background. Wide open spaces had a positive effect on my soul. I could finally breathe again, and I deliberately gulped deep lungfuls of the chilly spring air. Even the pollution of the diesel exhausts from passing commuter buses and motorcars didn't spoil my refreshment.

At this time of year, our capital would still be brisk in the mornings, however it was mostly pleasant during the day. Warming temperatures were on the horizon. One could feel the turning of the seasons as winter finally departed, if only for a while. The sky was a perfect bright blue colour this morning with not a hint of clouds.

My thick winter jacket, wool hat, and snood might have appeared a little out of place compared to these fast moving, city dwellers all around me —who were rushing about from this place to that in just their shirts and skirts. Everyone here looked serious and no-nonsense going about their business. It was a shame that nobody made time anymore to take in the day. My bias against this modern life was 60 years out of date. I felt like a relic, a grandmother out of time.

I took great care when I crossed three busy intersections, and I soon made a 90-degree turn to walk down a wide alley directly off the Novaya Ploshchad thoroughfare. This area was sizeable enough to accommodate some street parking but was closed off to through traffic. I could see it dead-ended half a block inward. The building I was travelling to today was a large five storey affair that faced the street and took up an entire city block. The exterior was unmistakable, as it was sporting a distinctive brick-red paint job. The architecture was classical, and I could tell that these premises carried out many functions over the last century.

My destination this morning lay on the second floor, office No. 21-A. I opened one of the glass doors and proceeded inside.

I sauntered up the side staircase, being sure to hold on tightly to the polished wooden railing. I assured myself that now would not be the time for a fall. Thankfully, the carpeting on the stairs made my footing firm and sure.

The outside metal door to room No. 21-A looked unremarkable, save for the pair of prodigious men from the Capital Police Force standing guard outside. Adorned with automatic weapons and body armour, they seemed fearsome. I noticed both their forefingers were near, but not resting, on the triggers to their rifles.

I double-checked my watch and proceeded forward—slowly. I was right on time.

"Can we help you, Madam?" The policeman's radio crackled on his utility belt and I could hear updates from a dispatcher speaking rapidly.

I stood there for a fraction of a second before I heard the other sentry speak up.

"Are you sure you're in the right place?" The fellow's demeanour looked like someone who was more bothered and annoyed than one of who showed genuine concern. It seemed that guards, in any century, never ever changed.

"Oh, yes, I think so." I quickly reached into my coat pocket to produce the forms showing my appointment for today.

I unfolded them with care and handed them over to one officer.

"Let's see some identification." The officer snapped his fingers twice at me.

I found my government issued social insurance credential and handed it over for him. I never liked the photograph of myself embossed inside the card's corner.

Stalin's Door

"One moment, Madam." I saw the one constable lower his chin so he could whisper into his shoulder.

He murmured a few coded words. After a brief delay, I could hear a loud buzzing sound from around the thick metal door frame. The policeman shoved my papers and identification towards me.

"Go right in, Madam."

I collected my things and proceeded inside the lobby, with one man holding the door open for me. Both fellows then smiled at me as I passed by them.

"Spasibo." I replied.

Today, I was visiting one of the many auxiliary office buildings used by the FSB in and around their Lubyanka headquarters. Office space inside the principal building was no doubt exhausted years ago, and the FSB were slowly taking over real estate within walking distance to the Lubyanka.

I beamed at the strikingly beautiful receptionist sitting in front of me as I approached the front desk. An enormous replica of the FSB insignia hung on the wall behind her, with colour photographs of two gentlemen. One I presumed to be the current head of the agency, and the other was our acting president, Vladimir Vladimirovich Putin.

"I have an appointment to see Doctor Zavyalov." I said confidently to her.

I took the time to remove my winter jacket, wool hat, and snood, folding them over my left forearm.

The youthful-looking woman nodded at me, and just as she was about to pick up the handset of her telephone, I glimpsed a gentleman who was rapidly walking towards me from the hallway behind the lobby.

"It's all right, Maya Alekseevna." The gentleman announced to the receptionist as he caught his breath. "She's my nine o'clock appointment. We won't need any visitor badges today. I'm already all set up over in conference room Beta."

The gentleman extended his weathered right hand out to me.

"So sorry to keep you waiting. I'm so happy to meet you, finally, in person, Madam Komolova."

I shook his tepid hand tenderly.

"Doctor Zavyalov, may I presume?"

It shocked me to discover that the gentleman was far older in age than I was expecting. I had spoken with him many times via the telephone, and I had imagined a fellow just into his middle ages, not one who looked past the mandatory age of retirement. In fact, it wouldn't surprise me if he turned out to be even older than I was.

The doctor towered over me, and I noted his rail thin physique. His skin was pale, and he kept his white hair trimmed neatly short. A pair of ancient reading glasses dangled around his neck on a braided lanyard. His clothing passed for professional, yet they were drab. He wore brown trousers and a white button-down shirt.

What fascinated me most of all was his manner of speech. With all of our previous conversations on the telephone, I still couldn't place his accent.

"Indeed. I am." The doctor replied, smiling at me. "Won't you come this way?" The doctor motioned his hands towards an open door that led to a compact room in an adjacent corner of the lobby.

A brass placard affixed to the wall next to the door contained a single word. Beta.

"Here, let me take those things from you." The doctor insisted.

Stalin's Door

As we approached the room, I handed him my outerwear.

"If I may say, Madam Komolova, that's a colourful snood you're wearing. I don't think I've ever seen that shade of blue before."

"Why thank you, Doctor. My grandmother made it for me." The wool felt soft and reassuring about my neck and head, like a security blanket.

Once we were inside the sterile conference room, he guided me to a seat near the head of the economical meeting table. I sat down into the faux leather upholstered chair and scooted myself up to the edge. The room could easily accommodate a dozen people and was brightly lit. Because we were in the building's interior, the room was windowless.

Stock photographs of various famous landmarks from all about Moskva adorned the walls. The doctor neatly placed my jacket and hat on an empty chair and took his seat next to me. Dr Zavyalov glanced down at a series of brightly coloured folders placed methodically in front of him. A modern office telephone was also within his reach.

I decided many months ago to take advantage of a Russian government programme, inaugurated in the following year after the collapse of the Soviet Union a decade ago. The vast and innumerable archives of the NKVD, the Communist State secret police organisation in the time of Stalin, would open its archives to the public for the very first time. The Russian authorities convened a formal Truth and Reconciliation committee to declassify all the countless abuses and murders that took place in the period known as the Great Terror.

However, the FSB wasn't about to just turn loose anyone from off the street to go rummaging throughout the basement level annals of the Lubyanka in search of the truth. Not a chance. In true Russian governmental bureaucratic fashion, they established a strict protocol to follow.

First, the public inquirer would fill out request forms detailing the information that they were seeking. Then, they would assign an archivist to research their case. This archivist, an employee of the FSB, would extract said information from the NKVD repositories, collate it, and then present it to the public inquirer far from the secret inner sanctums of the Lubyanka. They hired a legion of archivists initially, and for the first time in history our people would learn the hidden truth of what really happened during the Great Terror.

My case's archivist was a gentleman named N. N. Zavyalov. Over our previous correspondence and telephone conversations, I learned he had been a physician for decades and worked in the city of Volgograd before retiring. I was uncertain how he wound up in the employment of the FSB in his current capacity.

Dr Zavyalov opened the first folder, a red coloured one, and slowly began speaking.

"I have all the information you requested, Madam Komolova." His gnarled hands gently patted the papers within. "Truth be told, we don't get a lot of inquires these days. In fact, you're only my second case this year."

I sat quietly for a moment before asking him a question.

"Why do you think that is Doctor?"

"Oh, in the nascent days of the programme, my caseload was enormous. Many cases were direct from the survivors themselves. Even fifty years after the Great Terror, many of the victims—well—the ones who were still alive, could come calling in person. They would look for loved ones, or closure, or answers to mysteries decades old now. The descendants of the victims were more plentiful, and researchers from academia and so forth, kept us busy. I must say, I'm honoured to meet a primary. There aren't many of you left."

A primary was the term used for anyone who'd lived through the Great Terror, but especially ones that also spent time inside the Gulag.

As if from out of nowhere, my migraine headache came roaring back with a vengeance. I cried out in pain and used the palms of my hands now to massage the sides of my forehead, vigorously.

"Madam Komolova? Are you all right?" The archivist exclaimed, bolting upwards from his chair. "Please let me help you. Tell me what's wrong."

"No, no, I'll be okay, Doctor. Just give me a moment. It's my head. I've had a terrible headache all morning."

"My God! Where are my manners? I am terribly sorry. It must be my senility kicking in. May I order you something to drink, Madam Komolova? They have this new machine in the back office that can brew you an individual cup of whatever you like in a matter of seconds. Coffee, tea, hot chocolate? What's your preference?"

"Tea would be lovely, Doctor. Oolong with lemon, if you have it."

The archivist nodded as he picked up the telephone handset and placed the order, speaking in a low tone that imparted some authority.

"I think I'll join you. It'll just be a moment. Again, I'm so sorry! Are you sure you're feeling better?"

"Yes, and please don't mention it. I am fine."

Within only a minute, the pretty looking receptionist from the front brought us each a steaming beverage before departing.

Raising the searing cup of goodness to my lips, my tongue probed the liquid hesitantly. It was almost too hot to drink right away—almost. I could see a solitary slice of lemon floating on top of the black, orange liquid. After a few seconds of gently blowing the steam away, I took a big sip. The tea was invigorating and chased away the remnants of the frosty air still left inside me.

"Mmmmmm. This is delicious, Doctor. Spasibo. I'm feeling revived." I nodded my approval.

After a couple more moments of studying the document in front of him, and sipping his own drink loudly, the doctor started up again.

"You spent fifteen years in the Gulag? That's almost unimaginable." He was shaking his head slowly, as if to show astonishment with my personal ordeal. "What a tale you could tell!" The doctor continued, just speaking under his breath. "My own experience pales in comparison."

"What was that you said, Doctor? Were you in the Gulag too?" I could see that his advanced age made that a distinct possibility.

The doctor pursed his lips and took a moment. He then looked me in the eyes and spoke slowly.

"No, no. Oh, no. They interned me inside another type of—camp. It's not important." He then sat solemnly and looked downwards at the table.

With my curiosity piqued now, I pressed him on the matter, knowing that I shouldn't have.

After another moment, and sensing that I wouldn't let the matter drop, I noticed that the doctor as he unbuttoned the cuff on his right shirt sleeve. As he rolled up the fine material of the white oxford cloth, he revealed small tattoos on the underside of his forearm. The tattoos were a series of six numbers, which were no doubt originally black, but had faded to a pale green colour over the long decades of time. The doctor quickly pulled down his shirt sleeve and re-buttoned the cuff.

Instantly realising the answer to my question, all I could do was mutter a quick apology.

"Oh, I see. I am so sorry, Doctor." I suddenly felt embarrassed for insisting, and my face felt warm as the blood rushed into my cheeks. "Your experience must have been horrific. My apologies. You're Polish then?"

"Yes, I was born there. I'm a dual-citizen now."

Abruptly, I placed his accent.

"Madam Komolova, let us however return to your case, shall we?"

"I concur, Doctor."

"Now, I've prepared a summarisation of the five individuals you inquired about here." The doctor pointed to the red-coloured folder that was open. "In these other folders, you'll receive a copy of any information I could find in the NKVD archives about each person. Some folders will have more information than others. If the NKVD believed someone was important, then they produced extensive documentation, and kept it on file. In other cases, I could only find a few pages of intelligence."

The doctor ran his hands over the stacked folders beside the summary one. Just as he had explained, I saw some folders were thick and appeared stuffed full of materials, whilst yet some others were pitifully small and thin.

"Was there somewhere in particular you'd like to start? Can I help you interpret anything? I am completely at your disposal for this morning." The doctor smiled at me assuredly.

"Would it be agreeable if I just studied all of this by myself for a little while and ask you if I need something explained?"

"That is completely acceptable, Madam Komolova. You go right ahead." With that, the doctor gently slid over to me the materials piled in front of him.

I reopened the red-coloured summary file and quickly scanned it. This record was like a ship's manifest. It contained all the top-level information, but hardly any details. It would point you at other files and acted like the key to deciphering their cryptic data. I thought of its usefulness, much like a legend on a map.

The manifest presented the names of five individuals, straight at the top, with a brief paragraph description of each person below.

The first two people listed were the names of my parents, whom I last saw on that fateful night in December 1937 when I left them. It was the night Stalin's secret policemen came to arrest them.

By the thickness alone of the black-and-gold coloured jacket on the file stacked neatly next to the red summary one, I could easily tell that it had to be my father's record. It contained the most documentation from any of the five persons I inquired about.

Because my father was a loyal Soviet government commissar with daily access directly to Stalin himself, the all-powerful NKVD apparatus would naturally have scrutinised, catalogued, followed, and documented him with the utmost excess. As a general rule of thumb, the closer one was to Stalin's orbit, the greater the perceived threat he thought you might be to him. So, Stalin dealt with threats to his absolute power, real and imaginary, in the only logical way he knew how: the summary execution or exile of said threat.

As I read the case summary, I experienced a feeling of numbness. I found it was difficult for me to engage in any emotions towards my parents after 62 years apart from them. I felt nothing for them any longer.

I quickly scanned the text of the synopsis.

~~MOST SECRET~~

Kanadin Avksenty Yemelyanovich. People's Commissar For Water Transportation, 1935-1937.

Arrested: 30 December 1937.

Found guilty of counter-revolutionary crimes** against the Communist State.

[**Articles No. 58-7 and No. 58-14, counter-revolutionary sabotage and wrecking.]

Executed: 14 March 1938.

Rehabilitated: 02 June 1956.

Kanadina Aleksandra Vasilievna. Wife of the Commissar.

Arrested: 30 December 1937.

Found guilty under the authority of NKVD order No. 00486.

Sentenced: 06 January 1938.

Transported: 10 January 1938.

Died: 1941.

A word I was not familiar with immediately jumped out at me.

"Doctor? What does rehabilitated mean?" I turned the summary case file around and pointed to that specific word on the page.

The doctor affixed his reading glasses to his face and peered over the table towards me.

"Oh yes, that's the novel guidance that came about after the famous speech that Premier Khrushchev gave back in 'fifty-six. Premier Khrushchev's speech widely condemned Stalin for the abuses that took place during his regime, and the insatiable cult of personality he wielded. It also paved the way for thousands of individuals falsely condemned, tried, and then executed by the NKVD, to return to a state of acquittal."

The doctor looked up at me now and continued.

"In effect, legally the government found your father not guilty of any crimes against the Communist State, posthumously. I know that must be a cold comfort to you now, decades after the fact."

I sat serenely for a few moments and let all of this recent knowledge sink in. I then reached over to the stack of folders and took hold of the widest one, sporting a distinctive black-and-gold coloured jacket. This one was my father's. I hastily opened the thick dossier. I skipped some black-and-white photographs affixed with paperclips to the inside front cover of the file folder.

These no doubt showed my father's visages throughout his years of service in the commissariat, culminating with his arrest and execution photographs.

As I leafed past them, I saw most of the file contained page after page of typed correspondence on faded yellow typing paper—hundreds of pages long. There were times and dates on the left-hand side of each page with reports of persons, conversations, and movements on the right-hand side.

This area of the file obviously contained the transcriptions from the NKVD surveillance we were all under. It started the day we moved into our flat at the House on the Embankment. The sheer amount of detail of what they recorded astounded me. Day after day, and night after night. Every day. They missed nothing. Every argument my parents ever had with one another —and there were plenty of them—they reproduced here in perpetuity. Every conversation, every word, every complaint, and every compliment. It was beyond my understanding how this was even possible.

One particular typewritten and initialed name, recorded at the bottom of every other report, conspicuously stood out: S. Y. Komolov. I knew this name to be that of Saveliy Yegorovich Komolov, the mysterious cigar smoking officer that worked on the other side of the Stalin's door, in the drawing room of my flat. After the NKVD arrested my parents on that horrible night late in 1937, I only lived with the fellow for two weeks at the start of 1938. When the NKVD came to arrest one of their own, Mr Komolov, I felt utterly numb. He faced summary execution, like so many hundreds of people a day did, during the time of the Great Terror.

I can still see Mr Komolov's serious face the night he rescued me in that dank sub-basement in the House of Secrets. I found it satisfying when I read that the man in charge the night of my father's arrest, a Major Chernobrovin, took a demotion for losing track of the Commissar's young daughter, Yevgeniya Avksentyevna. That used to be my name.

Going by the dates from the daily NKVD reports, our overseers recorded nearly three years of our activities. The entire period I lived at the Government House. My mind boggled at the complexity involved to even attempt such an operation. The NKVD carried out this surveillance—by law— on every resident within the House on the Embankment. That must have involved hundreds of officers. Stalin had an insatiable appetite for paranoia, and his secret police network fed him a steady diet of all he could eat.

The last part of my father's file was perhaps the hardest to read, and I asked Dr Zavyalov to help me sort through and interpret it for me. Contained within the dossier were the typed transcriptions from my father's interrogations, following his arrest for treason.

For six weeks the NKVD held my father captive inside the cold catacombs of the Lubyanka prison. Because he was a High Value Interrogation Detainee, they subjected him to the most intense and hideous torture techniques practised by the secret police. The doctor disclosed that one goal was to have my father confess to a litany of crimes, real and imaginary, to satisfy the needs of the system.

The establishment of a guilty verdict always came first. It was then up to the NKVD interrogators to prove that guilt by extracting a confession from the accused—by any means necessary. The truth, however, was just a little more insidious. A signed confession was not even of any real importance. It was merely just a check box to fill in. Everyone knew that the NKVD only arrested the guilty, so an admission of guilt was merely procedural.

While most prisoners confessed quickly to end the brutal pain of their interrogations, the real prize the NKVD sought were more names. Lists of accomplices, confidants, accessories, and so on. Questioning under the pain of torture could yield dozens of new suspects and uncover fanciful new plots not even dreamt of by the most seasoned secret policeman.

The NKVD, armed with this additional evidence, could then expand upon the investigations of treason, wrecking, and assassination conspiracies. Names begat arrests, and interrogations begat more names. The cycle was incessant.

Dr Zavyalov further explained that following standard NKVD protocols, they would use a series of ever intensifying cross-examination techniques to break down, systematically, any resistances a prisoner had. They subjected prisoners to sleep deprivation, starvation, and a constant barrage of rapid-fire questions by an interrogation team which left their subjects dazed, confused, and ready to sign anything put in front of them.

If by some miracle the interrogators still didn't have what they were looking for, then a genuinely mediaeval array of what they euphemistically called special methods would then come to bear against the prisoner. In written orders, Stalin explicitly authorised these special methods himself. The typed transcriptions compiled of the gruesome tortures that my father endured for weeks made me feel sick to my stomach. After finishing just one page, I couldn't read them any longer. I gently closed the jacket to my father's file and pushed it away from me.

The second file I explored was my mother's. I discovered, unfortunately, that it was not very complete, and contained just the barest of details. Included inside were copies of her NKVD dossier, including her biography. There were various profiles of her observed behaviours and estimates on her political reliability. Dr Zavyalov discovered that the NKVD only briefly questioned her following her arrest with my father. Her guilty verdict guaranteed passage on a train to serve out a 20-year prison sentence at the Akmolinsk Camp for Wives of Traitors of the Motherland—in what is now the northern portion of Kazakhstan. The doctor could find nothing else on her except a brief note explaining that she died in 1941. The NKVD recorded the cause of her death as acute typhus.

The third file I studied contained two names labeled on the front: Komolov Saveliy Yegorovich and Komolova Valeriya Timurovna. The first was the NKVD officer who rescued me the night of my parents' arrest. The second was the woman who I called grandmother for 15 years, whilst incarcerated within the Gulag in Siberia.

Digging into the file, I read that the NKVD interrogated Lt Komolov for nearly three days following his arrest, before they summarily executed him in the basement of the Lubyanka on 13 January 1938. The transcriptions described a litany of his alleged capital crimes. The death warrant contained his neatly typed name at the bottom of the page, presumably prepared beforehand, but I noticed his signature was missing. I didn't see any indications in his dossier that Saveliy Yegorovich confessed to anything, nor did he give up the names of his supposed accomplices.

Regrettably, there wasn't any information the archivist could find about the disposition of my grandmother—except for her name, her identification tag No. 069033, her arrest date, and the date that they sentenced her to serve out a ten-year term in the Gulag under NKVD order No. 00486. Next to my grandmother's name I noticed a big red coloured circle around my name, <u>Komolova Yevgeniya Ivanovna</u>.

The doctor noticed where I had stopped in the notes and interjected.

"Oh yes, I was hoping to ask you about that. I discovered in my research that you're actually the daughter of Commissar Kanadin. You also used to live in the House on the Embankment. So, can you please tell me how you came to use another name—one taken from a lieutenant that served in the NKVD? This is all very curious to me."

I briefly explained the story of the cigar smoking man, my rescue, his arrest, and the arrest of my grandmother. I informed him of my grandmother's suggestion to pretend to be 13 years old, so they wouldn't separate me from her.

Would I have been better off in the State orphanages? I don't know. To throw off the NKVD men still looking for me, I changed my name and purported to be her son's daughter.

"Oh, I see the logic of it now. That's brilliant, really." The doctor smiled at me, however, only for a moment.

I suspected he realised that in deciding to go with my ersatz grandmother, I would spend years incarcerated within the Gulag. He quickly bowed his head again.

The final folder I'd look at today was also disappointingly brief. The name on the label read <u>Zykin Tikhon Stanislavovich</u>. The doctor explained it for me.

"You see this individual died just before the dawn of the Great Terror. His heart attack spared him from the horrors of the arrests, executions, and deportations. I think he was lucky, in a way. Had he lived, Stalin would have killed him too. I couldn't find much personal information on this individual. Did you know him? Perhaps he was a family friend?"

"No, Doctor, I only met the gentleman once—for a few hours one evening. He hosted a glorious reception-dinner for my father, my mother, and me."

"I understand."

Before I closed his file, I noticed a particular number and street name at the bottom of the last page. It was the address for the old commissar. I took a scrap piece of paper and jotted the information down for future reference. This is what I needed. This is what I came for today.

"One last question, if I might trouble you again?"

The doctor nodded his head with approval.

"When I was inside the Gulag, on the day we found out that Stalin had died, they gave us all a big lecture. Long-winded praise, and a laundry list of his achievements preceded the proclamation of his last words to the nation, apparently written by his own hands after a marathon session of working at his office.

"Allegedly he knew he was dying, so with the last gasp of air leaving his lungs, he wrote out his commemoration. If I recall correctly, Stalin's message was something to the effect of him having given the best for his country, to which no man could say otherwise. Do you know anything about that?"

"Oh, yes. After working as an archivist for nearly ten years, I'm something of an expert in Soviet history. It's an established fact that Stalin had a habit of working well into the night. However, what you described is a fallacy. He never wrote his own epitaph. Speaking as a medical professional, Stalin suffered a devastating intracerebral haemorrhage. In layman's terms— it was a severe brain bleed that expedited his departure from this earth. Severe hypertension is usually the root cause of an ICH."

The doctor paused for a moment to think, before starting up again.

"The dictator often worked alone, you see, and as such they didn't check up on him until many hours into the next morning. No one dared disturb him—including his personal guards posted just outside the office door. No one had the courage. Because of the paralysing fear he instilled within everyone, Stalin lay collapsed upon the floor, in a puddle of his own cold urine, unable to speak or move, for hours. I think he may have lived on for a few more days, after they found him, in a nearly vegetative state. Certainly this wasn't the heroic ending you just described."

I then asked what time it was. The doctor looked at his watch and told me the time. I had been in this conference room for three hours. I needed to get going.

I politely said my goodbyes to the doctor as he escorted me through the lobby to the front doors. He made me promise to come and visit him again, because he was quite interested in hearing my stories after having lived through the most turbulent time in our country's history.

I told him I would consider it. I'd already lived through it all once, and honestly, I wasn't prepared to live through it all over again.

I made my way outside of the FSB offices and caught my bearings. My next stop today would be the place I called home for three years, so very long ago: the House on the Embankment.

§

The nearly three kilometre amble over to the former Government House took me past storied landmarks within the heart of downtown Moskva. I proceeded down Nikolskaya street and then cut over to the Kremlevskly Proyezd thoroughfare and crossed into the heavily touristed Red Square. The sights and sounds within this world-famous landmark were virtually identical to the time when I lived near here as a girl.

I then strolled over into the Moskva Kremlin and could plainly see the majestic Cathedral of Vasily the Blessed in the near distance. Better known today by its popular name, St. Basil's Cathedral, the old church's vivid coloured domes looked as if they twisted their way up into the brilliant true-blue sky above. Millions of people from around the world visited and admired this cultural national treasure, a de facto trademark of our country.

Once I left the vicinity of the Moskva Kremlin, I made a beeline for the bridge which would take me over to my former home.

As I proceeded however, I couldn't get past a dreadful feeling within my gut. From out of nowhere, I suddenly knew someone followed me. Like a sixth sense, my intuition informed me I was not alone. An old man trailed behind me, speeding up when I increased my gait, and slowing down or stopping when I rested.

My tail always stayed just out of reach, and just further back so I couldn't get a proper look at him. This was most peculiar. Why on earth would anyone want to follow me? I'm an old pensioner with nothing left in this world.

For a brief moment I thought it might have been Dr Zavyalov, trying to catch up for a follow-up question. Perhaps he tried to return an item I'd left behind.

Still, I knew it couldn't be the good doctor. My shadow wore a distinctive bright white jacket and dark trousers. How he expected to remain inconspicuous, dressed in that manner, escaped all comprehension.

When I finally reached the bridgehead of the Bolshoy Kamenny, the familiar odour of the Moskva river below returned to my nose for the first time in 62 years. The river was exactly as I remembered it. Murky and muddy, with subtle hints of sewage. That scent was not unlike that of any other river within a major metropolitan area, however the olfactory feedback I was receiving here triggered a flood of memories from deep within my subconscious.

As I peered over the ornate wrought-iron railing, I could see the surface of the water today was actually quite clean—with no signs of debris or garbage floating about.

Commuting upon the river this afternoon, I spotted pleasure craft, commerce boats, and ferries carrying all sorts of people.

The Moskva river perfectly bisected the metropolis. The bridge's concrete footpath I strode upon received regular maintenance and appeared spotless. Enormous grey lampposts, spaced every 15 metres, brightly lit the bridge at night. The pedestrian route was wide enough for three or four folks to stand shoulder to shoulder, if they wished.

Most of the span however contained motorised traffic, with six dedicated lanes of black asphalt, split between opposite directions. Modern cars, mopeds, and trucks of all types raced back and forth beside me as they went about their daily business.

These are my memories. Today, I stand upon the famous Bolshoy Kamenny bridge, my gaze descending to the storied Moskva river. This is where I left you, dearest reader, at the beginning of my story only a moment ago.

Won't you accompany me just a little way further?

I have two more calls to make this afternoon.

I thank you for your continued camaraderie.

Quickly traversing the bridge, I approached the hulking House on the Embankment which lay off to the right—at the end. I remembered that once I crossed over, I'd be standing on what the Moskvichi colloquially called the Island, which lay in the metropolis' heart.

Taking in the view of my former home, I couldn't help but notice a mammoth advertising logo affixed to the top of the building's southern tower. The symbol must have been visible for many kilometres all around downtown. Everyone in the world knew of this German trademark, a distinctive tri-pointed star surrounded by a circle—on sight.

My, how times had changed.

Walking into the main first-floor entrance to the former Government House was simple now. I stepped up a half flight of concrete stairs and pulled the right side of the heavy glass double doors open, and then proceeded inside. There were no military guards to present one's papers to, no forms to sign off on, and no checkpoints to cross. Just an uncomplicated primary entrance you might find at any office building these days.

I hurriedly made my way over to the lobby's side, to not block the way of any individuals coming or going. This hall reminded me of a modern shopping mall. Bright and airy, with tall ceilings, and plenty of places to sit and relax.

From where I stood, I could spot various sundry shops upon this level—from banking, to clothing, to electronics. A travel agency, a dry cleaners, coffee and tea shops, restaurants, and two mini-markets also were available. I thought for a moment that this was not unlike what was available years ago. For a random Thursday afternoon, it appeared busy with happy patrons.

A formal building directory and map lay affixed to the wall directly behind me. Good. I could now acquaint myself with where I needed to visit next. According to the guide, commerce dominated the entire first floor and the now totally enclosed courtyard beyond. No one lived there. The remaining space inside this former compound contained modern business offices and luxurious private residences.

Stalin's Door

With the building's centralised location within the hub of Moskva, I imagined that the premium for living here must cost tens of thousands of rubles a month. That price was far beyond the means of most, but for those who could afford it, surely they lorded it over their peers.

As I continued to scan the directory, I came across the name and location of where I needed to be. My destination? The House on the Embankment Museum. According to the map, the museum was on the first floor, at the far western side of the building. The gallery contained its own entrance, accessible from the street. I exited the shopping mall and made my way around the corner.

A distinctive red-coloured door lay inside of a tiny alcove, with an eight-step walk up. Had it not been for the large brown sign affixed to the portico, I would have surely missed it. I climbed the stairs slowly and then made my way inside.

The interior of the House on the Embankment Museum was like stepping backwards in time across 60 years. According to a poster just inside the vestibule, this used to be the flat the chief of the Soviet Army guards lived in—which was quite a prestigious honour back then.

The museum space appeared cramped, with two principal rooms and a private restroom. The flat served as the headquarters of a working non-profit foundation that aimed to preserve history and teach about life inside the Government House in the '30s and '40s.

A placard informed its visitors that there was a nominal admission fee, which they waived for children under 12, and all pensioners. I could immediately see that I was the only guest in here, at the moment. The air smelled stuffy to me, and not at all agreeable.

Formal displays of period-correct furniture, paintings, photographs, books, and other household items, arranged with much care, dotted this first chamber, and it was comparable to a life-sized diorama. Affixed to every item, a small, printed placard of information explained the finer details of its form and function. The museum staff did a respectable job imparting what life in one of the Soviet government's elite flats used to be like for the period.

I could see small posters, placed upon easels, scattered about the place which contained the photographs and biographies of some of the more famous residents of the House of Secrets from over the years. A dedicated television screen in the room's corner ran a short ten-minute film on a loop showing the history of the building and its cultural heritage and significance.

As I read from a pamphlet, I learned that the museum unofficially started in '89, when some older residents took up a collection of items and looked for a dedicated space to display them in. Testimonials from anyone that had lived here during the time of Stalin's purges in the Great Terror became highly sought after. Funding through the Moskva museum directorate was solicited and secured in the Russian Federal Assembly. After a few more years, and some large donations from private individuals in the '90s, the museum opened officially in '98 inside this space.

Without warning, I dropped the brochure onto the floor and stopped myself for a time. I inhaled deeply. I abruptly noticed that I could not see properly. Everywhere that I looked around, things were blacked-out, blurry, and unfocused.

I felt a severe pain in my head, worse than the migraine headache I suffered from earlier today. The shock made my skull feel as if it were being crushed inside a vice.

I sucked in another lungful of air and then felt a sharp stabbing sensation coming from behind my eyes. I knew that I could not stand up for much longer, and I grabbed the sides of my head in my hands as I helplessly fell over. When I felt myself hitting the floor, I lost consciousness.

§

"Excuse me, Madam Komolova?" I heard a voice say as I opened my eyes and looked upwards. "My name is Emma Danilovna. Do you remember me? I'm the assistant museum curator."

The woman gently applied a cool, damp washcloth to my forehead. I was still laying down, with my head elevated by a small pillow.

"You took a nasty fall there. How do you feel?"

I felt weak, and I was desperately trying to get my bearings. I felt as if my mind had turned to mush as I grasped for clarity.

"How—how long was I unconscious for? Who are you again?" I still couldn't see perfectly, and the brightness from the desk lamps hurt my eyes.

A blinding light painted everything around me, as if I wore a white halo.

"Oh, you were out for about a minute. Don't you worry though, I've already called for an ambulance. They'll be here any moment and will take good care of you. See if you can remember today's date and tell it to me again."

The middle-aged woman was dressed professionally and had short blonde hair. She wore those stylish, black-rimmed glasses, that seemed all the rage today.

I forced myself to sit up with some effort.

"Nyet, nyet. Please don't. I just need to catch my breath. I'm not sure what happened there. It's the strangest thing. I've had this terrific headache all day and coming in here just seemed to overwhelm me. I'll be fine. Please, don't let them take me to hospital. All right?"

I then stood up as I felt my legs strengthen in place, with some redoubling of my will. I answered the woman's question.

"Today is Thursday the twenty-seventh. I'm sorry, but have we met before?"

"Yes, we have. Are you certain you're better now?"

"Da, I am satisfactory again. I skipped eating lunch today. My low blood sugar, don't you know?" I did not fully understand why I passed out just then, but that excuse was as good as any I could think of.

I heard the sounds of an ambulance siren approach outside.

Just then I saw a brace of lanky men, presumably the paramedics called by the museum curator. They charged through the front door to the museum flat with their medical gear in hand, and their two-way radios blaring out dispatches.

"Who called for us? Where's the emergency?" They both looked at us, with their hearts pumping and eyes wide.

After more than a few minutes of begging and pleading with the EMTs to let me go, I agreed to their demands for a health and wellness check. They recorded my blood pressure, shined a brilliant light into my retinas, took my temperature, and so forth.

I was more than a little relieved. I still needed to get one more thing completed today and had no time to sit in an antiseptic emergency room clinic whilst doctors probed and prodded at me. I was feeling much healthier now.

Stalin's Door

The young men reluctantly went away without taking me to the emergency room after I signed a waiver. Once the courteous EMTs released me, I approached the museum curator to thank her again, before I departed.

"Emma Danilovna, thank you again for all that you've done for me. Truly, I am feeling fit and will take my leave now."

The woman took my hand and shook it gently three times.

"It was an honour to meet you Madam Komolova. I hope that we can continue our conversation at a future time. There's so much I would like to learn from your time living here at the House on the Embankment."

Abruptly, I felt awkward. What did she mean? I don't remember talking to her at all from before, and I certainly wouldn't have told her I used to live here. I remember that I was reading a pamphlet when I suddenly passed out in great pain.

"Excuse me, Emma Danilovna. Did we speak earlier?"

"Oh, we did. Do you not recall that? You came into the museum and I introduced myself. I inquired about showing you around. You struck up a conversation about how the Government House was your home, a long time ago. This excited me greatly. There are so few of you originals left now that I ran over to get my binder to make some notes. I was only away for a minute.

"When I turned from my desk to come back over, I saw you suddenly collapse. I'm positive I saw you hit your head. Are you sure you're all right, Madam Komolova? You know you senior citizens need to take it easy. May I bring you some tea?"

Her demeanour was pleasant and disarming, however I felt positive we'd not spoken at all. It mystified me how she knew my name, and that I used to live here.

I hadn't planned on revealing that on this particular visit because I wasn't prepared to speak about my experiences here.

"You know come to think of it I'm not feeling that well after all. If it's all right, I think I'd just like to depart. In fact, I was hoping to swing by the apartment I used to live in. You know? For old times' sake. I used to live at flat number one three seven."

I hesitated for a moment, quickly realising I needed her assistance.

"Do you think you can tell me how to get over there, Emma Danilovna?"

"That would delight me immensely, Madam Komolova. And I'll even do you one better. I'll escort you over there myself. Just let me grab my purse and we can go there right now."

§

I'm grateful that I didn't decline Emma Danilovna's offer to tag along with me. Fancy electronic security key cards protected the new residences and business offices of the old Government House from unwanted visitors. To gain entry, you had to possess these credentials, and only the tenants and business employees carried them.

Thankfully, because my new friend worked here, she could get me access. We made our way through the busy shopping mall area and over to the eastern side of the compound. Once we proceeded through a set of heavy glass doors, we approached an elevator bank that would take us to the fourth storey.

That's the floor where I used to live.

Stalin's Door

Emma Danilovna continued to explain to me that there was no guarantee that my old flat would even still be there—intact as I remembered it. Over the decades since I'd lived here, there'd been countless turnover in residency and many periods of building renovations and improvements. Some apartments that once housed families, now contained fancy spaces for commercial enterprises, complete with a prestigious mailing address and centralised location within the metropolis. Some flats underwent a complete remodeling and now enjoyed ultra-modern amenities. For a kingly price, they combined several smaller units into one larger one. Was flat No. 137 even still there? We wouldn't know for sure unless we looked for ourselves.

Once we reached the fourth floor, I took a familiar left turn and walked down the carpeted hallway deliberately. I didn't see doors for flats No. 135 or No. 136 any longer, which was not a good sign. Perhaps my home was long gone. But just then, right where I remembered it, stood a well-known door. Precisely 13 metres distant from the stairway, on the left, was No. 137. I turned around and looked across the hallway. Missing was No. 140 where my old childhood friend Zina used to live, before she disappeared.

"This is it, Emma Danilovna! This is where I used to live, during the time of Stalin. I can't believe I'm actually here, standing at my old front door." I felt overwhelmed with emotions as I stared at the freshly painted black door.

It had taken me decades to make the journey back.

"That is wonderful Madam Komolova! I cannot imagine what remarkable circumstances you endured just to be here today. When the time is right, I hope you'll tell me the story of your life spent here. Your first-hand anecdotes, as an original survivor, would prove invaluable to our foundation."

"I will give that my honest consideration, Emma Danilovna. In the meantime, I know it might be a little unorthodox, but do you think the current resident who lives here now would mind if I asked to poke my head inside for a minute or two? I would keep the visit brief."

"Oh, Madam Komolova, I don't think that's a good idea at all. The modern folks that live in Moskva today don't take to trusting strangers so quickly. They're much more reserved than when you lived here. Besides, everyone works these days and I'm guessing there's no one at home. If you like, I could try to make a discrete inquiry when I get back to the museum. Perhaps we could arrange something for a later date?" Emma Danilovna checked her watch surreptitiously. "You know, I've got to be getting back soon."

"You're probably right."

But then I abruptly felt an urge that I had to get inside the apartment, no matter the cost, so I reached over and depressed the doorbell. I repeated pressing it three times in short order and heard a distinctive buzzing sound coming from the other side of the door. I then perceived a child wailing away from the inside, as if I had woken him up from a slumber.

"What are you doing? This is crazy!" My companion appeared panicked and tugged on my arm desperately, showing that we should leave immediately.

Before she could pull me away, I heard a series of locks being disengaged from behind the steel door. In a moment, it swung half-open and I could see a young-looking woman glaring at us. She held a crying and squirming toddler inside of her arms. She desperately tried to calm him down.

"Da? What is it you want here? Why are you bothering me?" Obviously, the annoyed mother was not at all happy for visitors.

Emma Danilovna spoke up instantly.

"We are so sorry, Miss. Pay us no mind. We were just leaving."

I felt that now was my only opportunity, so I took a chance and spoke up.

"Please listen, young lady. I apologise for disturbing you. I wasn't aware you had a little one with you. I am sorry I have awakened him. Let me explain. I used to live here a long time ago, and I was just wondering if I could come inside for just a moment to look around. It would mean so much to me."

The new mom stared at both of us and shook her head from side to side in disgust. She then slammed the front door to the flat directly into our faces. The closing sound made quite a racket, and I could hear the toddler start up again with his sobbing, even from out here in the hallway.

"Well, I am sorry Madam Komolova. Perhaps there will be another time for all this. Today is not your day. Let's get you back to the museum, shall we?"

"Nyet! I am not giving up. I didn't come all this way just to turn around now." I really didn't know why I said that.

What was this inexplicable feeling? Relief could only come by going inside my old flat, it seemed.

Emma Danilovna studied me for a minute and realised I would not take no for an answer.

"I regret to hear that Madam Komolova. Please understand that I need to return to the museum now. I hope that we'll have another chance to chat. Please come and see me again when you have time. It was so good to make your acquaintance." I watched as she hurriedly excused herself, sprinting down the hallway.

Within a moment, she disappeared from my sight.

I took a few steps down the brightly lit corridor, stepping over to the other side of the hallway. I then stopped myself to think. What was I doing? I didn't feel quite myself. I turned so I could lean up against the wall and waited for a few moments for my head to clear. I was not well. This was highly unusual.

Time seemed to both simultaneously slow down for me and speed up. I was aware of where I was, however, I did not understand what I was really doing here. I watched the front door to flat No. 137 with much intensity. My gaze was so acute that my eyes burned and felt dried up.

Now and then I would see an ever so tiny crack appear by the frame, as if someone on the other side was covertly opening it to take a peek. Then the gap would disappear as if the door was closed tightly again. Hours could have been passing me by, or perhaps it was only just a few minutes. I wasn't sure which was the case because I didn't wear a watch. My mind felt like cold molasses.

I was catatonic, and my legs wouldn't move themselves when I commanded them to. With nothing else to do, and feeling paralysed, I stood there along the wall. I couldn't tell you for sure how long I remained.

From within the corner of my eye, I spotted a well-dressed man approach me. He was young, perhaps in his early 30s, and he wore an expensive-looking dark suit. He carried a leather briefcase inside his left hand, and a brown paper grocery sack inside his right arm—presumably from a store in the shopping mall downstairs.

Stalin's Door

The fellow studied me for a moment with a quizzical expression upon his face. He shook his head about and then turned to approach the door to my old home. I could hear a set of keys jingling from inside his trousers as he juggled the provisions around—he no doubt preferred to gain entry by putting nothing down first. Before he could disengage the lock with his keys, the door opened, and I saw a pair of lissome hands reaching for the groceries. I heard both voices whispering to each other frantically.

"Lena, do you know who that old woman over there is?"

"No, my husband. She's just been standing there like that all afternoon. She rang the doorbell a few hours ago and woke poor Jora up. She said she used to reside here and wanted to come in for a moment to look around. I didn't know what to do, so I just shut the door on her. She's been there ever since."

The couple then went into the apartment and closed the door. I continued to rest where I was, and still couldn't move myself about. I should have felt panicked, yes, however a remarkable feeling of calmness radiated all about me.

More time passed by and the entryway to my old home opened once again. I could see the father as he stood in the doorway. He was now without his suit jacket and tie, and had rolled his shirtsleeves up onto his arms. He stared at me for what seemed like five minutes. The fellow must have been keenly aware that I had no intention of leaving now. The man then walked over to me deliberately and introduced himself.

"Hello there. My name is Berngards Zimnyakov. What's your name?" His intonation was calm and non-threatening, and a smile now formed upon his face. I took note that he used his given name and family surname only, which was a growing modern trend of which I did not approve.

"You may address me as Madam Komolova, good Sir." I insisted with him.

"Of course! No offence intended." The fellow pantomimed the slapping of his head with his palm. "I'm delighted to meet you, Madam Komolova."

"Likewise." I waited for a moment, and then apologised. "I am so sorry, I didn't mean to intrude upon you and your family."

A tingling sensation now diffused throughout my legs, as if blood was rushing back in through the veins. My feet experienced that uncomfortable pins-and-needles sensation.

"Could you please tell me something, Madam Komolova? You told my wife you used to live here, at number one three seven. A long time ago, yes? When exactly was it—can you remember?"

"Oh, let's see. I know we moved into the flat in early 'thirty-five and moved out late in 'thirty-seven."

"I understand. My, that was so long ago. What exactly do you want from us?"

"Please, gentle Sir. I would just like to come inside for a time. I haven't lived here in so very long, and I was just wondering if I could visit my old home again. I wouldn't put you out for over five minutes. I pray it would mean so much to me."

"Agreed, but only for a moment, and only because you remind me of my own grandmother Svetla. I can show you the living room only. Would that be acceptable?"

"Oh yes, Sir! Thank you very much!"

My legs and feet were right as rain again.

When we approached the front door, I instinctively crouched down and took off my worn-out shoes.

"What are you doing, Madam Komolova?" The fellow had a puzzled look upon his face.

"I'm removing my shoes before I go in. Where are your tapochki? I don't see any slippers here."

"Oh, don't you worry about that. We don't use them any longer. Please, just come inside as you are."

The good fellow extended his hand and watched me as I walked through the doorway. I had finally come home.

§

The spacious living room was located off of the foyer, just like in my old flat, and was slightly smaller than the same footprint of our old drawing room. Instead of Persian carpets, the room now contained an exquisite polished wooden floor. I could see many modern pieces of luxurious furniture in here, all covered with grey, white, and black patterns of expensive fabric. The wallpaper was bright and elegant and replaced what used to be the rich wood panelling from before.

They had installed a gas fireplace along one wall. The low flames flickered within, bathing the room in a constant wave of warmth. The chamber still contained great airy windows, which looked down upon the Moskva river below. The space was brightly lit with many lamps that cast a soft yellow-white light all around us. At the back of the room, where the entrance to the dining room used to be, I could see they erected a new facade.

A contemporary décor dominated this living room, with its avant-garde artwork and expensive sculptures worthy of admiration. In order to afford the exorbitant rent that such a flat commands, and with a young stay-at-home mother to boot, I guessed that Mr Zimnyakov must be a partner at an expensive downtown law firm, or perhaps he was a successful business owner.

Feasibly he was in Russia's nouveau riche class. Maybe he was even connected with the Russian mob. But that was none of my business.

I declined Mr Zimnyakov's offer of anything to drink and begged to sit down for just a moment. Being in this room after so much time left me with feelings of anxiousness, almost beyond any description. My kind host stood nearby me and sipped on his own dark coloured alcoholic beverage in a short thick glass. Two large artisanal ice-cubes made a distinctive clinking sound within the leaded crystal with every one of his sips of the expensive whisky.

Mr Zimnyakov's wife made a brief appearance and looked none too pleased to see me sitting here. Her attitude remained standoffish, and she soon departed the room no doubt to attend to their son in another area of the flat.

"So, tell me Madam Komolova, you say you lived here in the 'thirties? That was during the time of Joseph Stalin, wasn't it?"

"Yes Sir, it was."

"Why, that's just incredible! You know they don't teach the kids these days much about Stalin. Oh, yes, when I was in secondary school there were the requisite parts about how his political policies led to the deaths of millions in the Gulag and at the Holodomor—you know all that stuff. He was a dictator and a killer for sure. However, he helped defeat the Germans in the second world war and saved all of Russia. But today, he's not even hardly mentioned in our history books. It's as if kids should just think of him as some kind of enfant terrible. I just don't know what to make of all of it. I believe we're losing sight of something very important."

"He was an utterly cold, cruel, evil man who ended up taking everything away from me."

"Oh, I am so frightfully sorry. I didn't know. I suppose, I guessed—maybe. Please, I must apologise for bringing him up. I know it's a sensitive issue for some people. People of your generation, I mean, to talk about."

"You know what? He was here. He was here in this very room. Right where you're standing."

"Joseph Stalin? Joseph Stalin was here in this room? When exactly was this?"

"It was in the fall of 'thirty-six. My parents were hosting a reception-party along with the couple that used to live across the way at number one four naught. It was late, probably after midnight, when Stalin appeared with his bodyguard entourage in tow. I can still remember that he commanded the room with such a presence that no one dared speak unless spoken to first. All the adults were deathly afraid of saying the wrong thing around him."

"Incredible! That's an unbelievable story! The man was actually—in here. Here. In my living room." My host then refreshed his drink. "What else can you tell me Madam Komolova?"

"Did you know that the residents who lived here were under constant surveillance from his secret police force, the NKVD?"

"What do you mean? I've heard of the NKVD before, of course. But what do you mean by surveillance? Do you mean the residents were closely being watched here? In their own homes?"

"Oh yes. They were being watched all the time. All of them."

"Now wait just a moment, Madam Komolova. That's just an urban legend, right? When I moved in here last year with my wife Lena, we heard wild rumours about that kind of thing going on from back in the day. I never gave it a second thought. It just sounded like Bogeyman type stuff. You know, tall tales to frighten little children with late at night."

"It was all very real, Sir. In fact, I can prove it to you."

I stood up from the comfortable sofa and ambled over to that familiar corner of the living room. The corner where I used to smell the cigar smoke.

"The taynyye politseyskiye worked in here." I pointed to an area on the wall, just before the two edges met. "We used to call this a Stalin's door."

"What was that about a door? I don't see a door there, Madam Komolova. Do you mean to imply secret policemen would watch you from the other side of the wall? How could they possibly do that?"

"This wall is actually a panel that slides—that way." I motioned with my hands. "Inside there's a little room where they could watch us and make notes. Notes of our conversations, movements, guests, and anything that even hinted at disloyalty. All the apartments had one of these chambers back then."

"I am sorry, Madam Komolova, but this is pure nonsense. Are you telling me that Joseph Stalin used over five hundred men just to listen in on all the people that used to live here? Was that man so paranoid?"

"Have a look for yourself if you don't believe me."

I began tracing my fingertips along the rich, expensive wallpaper, and was searching for a seam. This took me many moments. My host was just watching with feigned amusement, whilst he tried to process what I had told him. Just then, I found what I was looking for. I forcefully pressed my fingernail into a small depression that ran the length of the wall.

By tearing the wallpaper back, a little, I could use all of my fingers to get a handhold onto the gap in the wall underneath. With a giant tug using all my strength, I could move the wall panel to the right, seven and one-half centimetres. I now revealed a dark blank space behind the wall.

I peered assuredly over my shoulder at my host. The eyes of Mr Zimnyakov were as wide as saucers, and in his confusion, he dropped his whisky onto the polished wood floor below. The stout crystal tumbler shattered into a myriad of tiny pieces with a loud thunderclap.

"What in the world are you doing?! Have you gone crazy, Lady?" The gentleman rushed over to me, sounding incredulous.

He came right up to the wall and stared into the blackness within the gap.

"Well, are you just going to stand there with your mouth gaping, or are you going to help me out?"

With the fellow's help, we got the wall panel slid all the way over, so that a 60 centimetre opening unveiled itself. Without hesitation, we both stuck our heads in to investigate this hidden space.

"This is fucking astonishing!" My host was all but beside himself with excitement. "Lena! Lena! Come out here and look at this! You'll never believe it!"

I could see that it was dim in the antechamber we uncovered. Through the opening, we observed a chamber inside that was no larger than 16 square metres. Along one wall was a small working desk, which looked ancient. I could see no chair sat behind the desk, nor could I see anything placed upon the bureau.

The wooden surface was in a pristine condition. This seemed so bizarre to me, because the desk and everything else in here should have had a layer of dust some decades old. No one could possibly have been inside this area for a very long time.

Above the desk were two small framed black-and-white photographs. The one on the left was obvious to everyone, it was Stalin. The other was a man who I didn't recognise. The air inside the place was cold and stale. I coughed for a moment, trying to catch my breath.

I stepped just a little way inside the mysterious room. It was 62 years ago on that fateful night that they arrested my parents and took them away. I remembered seeing this room from a distance, and then only for the briefest time. However, I never forgot about this place.

Except for the desk and the two photographs, the room was vacant. A partition lay on the opposite wall. If I didn't know any better, I'd say it resembled a primitive door or hatchway. I knew I now stood where the man who rescued me worked for all those years, as he watched and reported on my family. The man who smoked his cigars.

I walked completely into the antechamber and my host followed me inside. I could see him shaking his head in disbelief.

"This is just surreal. Can you believe this? Wait till Lena looks in here! How did you know this room was here? This—this Stalin's door. This is where the secret police watched you, huh?"

I affirmed the story again and examined the desk in more detail. Because I could see nothing on the surface of the desk, I checked all the drawers. One by one I opened them and heard nothing but creaking dry wood that made a distinct sound as they rubbed together. There were three drawers on the left-hand side and three drawers on the right-hand side. All were empty.

I then checked the little slide out pencil drawer that was located right beneath the top of the surface. As I dragged it open, I could see a small pristine white envelope appear. I quickly reached for the curiosity and held it inside my hands. The paper felt thick, and appeared in flawless condition, as if it were brand new. I could detect no discolourations, nor attacks by moths, nor any spoilage. A seal closed the envelope on its backside. I flipped it over to reveal a name, written in a dark-coloured pencil, and in cursive. The name read:

Lera

My companion looked at me and tried to examine the envelope.

"Hey there! What did you find? Let me see that!" The fellow tried grabbing the correspondence from my hands.

"Nyet! This is not for you!" I insisted. I turned my body to protect it from him.

"What's it say on there? On the front? I saw a name. I think it said Lena! Yes, it said Lena, didn't it?" My host was resolute now and was desperately trying to yank it away from me.

"It didn't have your wife's name on it, I swear to you! Now, let me go!"

"I saw Lena's name, I know it! I demand that you hand that letter over to me right now! Are we being spied on? Who is writing to my wife? Are you a part of this?"

I turned to see my companion running back into the living room, calling out frantically.

"Lena! Lena! Come out here now!"

I exited the antechamber and was in the living room again. My host then turned to me and pointed his forefinger.

"You! You wait right here."

I carefully placed the envelope into my coat pocket and decided that now would be a good time to leave. While Mr Zimnyakov went to fetch his wife, I walked as quickly as I could to the front door of the flat and saw myself out. Within a minute I was already on the staircase and descending rapidly. I had one more call to make today.

§

Once outside, I made my way over to the edge of the boulevard to hail a taksi. As I waited, I noticed that the old man who followed me earlier had now returned, albeit he was a bit closer to me this time. He stood motionless, like a statue, about ten metres away from me near the entrance to the old Government House. I couldn't make out any features upon his face, save for his jet-black hair and moustache. This infuriated me. Well, let's see if he can keep up with me now! An off-yellow coloured sedan screeched its tyres, as it came to a sudden halt to pick me up. I hurriedly climbed aboard.

"So where to today, good lady?" My driver inquired.

I told the young man where I wanted to go, after consulting the scrap piece of paper I made notes on from the archivist's office.

"Oh my! Why do you want to go there, Mother? I heard ghosts and spirits haunt that place. Terrible luck, if you ask me. Are you sure about it?"

I was positive. This was my final destination for today.

Stalin's Door

The taxicab I rode in was dingy, well abused, messy, and smelled horribly. Even with the windows rolled all the way down, I couldn't escape the awful feeling that something had recently died in the backseat. Thankfully, my trip was only seven or eight kilometres from the House on the Embankment and passed quickly for me.

We sped through the busy downtown traffic of modern Moskva and arrived in fewer than 15 minutes. I was let out near the front gate, with my driver still shaking his head in disbelief. I visited the Novodevichy Cemetery this afternoon.

The cemetery grounds were expansive and arranged in a grid-like structure with three major sections segregating its residents: old, new, and the newest. As I wandered through, it immediately struck me at how peaceful everything inside appeared. For a major cemetery in the heart of a capital city, it was like being within a sanctuary.

The 20,000 grave sites here ranged in size, as varied as their occupants. Some gravestones were simple carved affairs with scant information and tiny burial plots. Yet others were mausoleums of some renown, dedicated to men and women long departed. Some monuments had their own iron railings which encompassed the burial plots with fancy metalwork, stone carvings, and intricate busts that bordered on artwork.

The cemetery's most famous residents, like Anton Pavlovich Chekhov, Nikolai Vasilievich Gogol, and Nikita Sergeyevich Khrushchev had their own stone statues, which would surely outlast mankind by centuries.

The cemetery was pleasant to stroll through and included trees and bushes of all types—it was almost like visiting a botanic park. I could see flowers everywhere, and I knew that this metropolis of the dead received regular care and maintenance.

I took hold of the scrap paper where I jotted down the notes that Dr Zavyalov had given to me. I was to go to the old section, Division II, subsection IV, plot number 187.

I located the gravestone in under an hour of searching about. I stared at the simple black rectangular polished stone, about a metre high, a metre long, and several centimetres thick. This was where they buried the fellow I came to see this afternoon. Intricately carved upon the face, I read a name and two dates. Distinctive silver paint highlighted the text:

Zykin Tikhon Stanislavovich
1890-1935

The headstone recorded no other information.

I stood for a moment in solemn silence. This was the gravesite of the old commissar I met all those years ago on my very first visit to the House on the Embankment. I can still remember being driven in that fancy black ZiS limousine and all the rich food and drink my family enjoyed that evening.

I reached into my coat pocket and retrieved a diminutive item. I held it inside my open palm and gazed upon it for one last time. A beautiful golden paint bathed the object's surface, and I could perceive little ridges twisting and turning on the bulbous gadget—as if it were the centre of a great knot of cords. The article was hollow throughout its middle and was approximately the size of a champion walnut. Attached onto the front of the device lay a large brilliant five-pointed red star, outlined in gold. Its ruby colours radiated out in all directions from the shiny and reflective centre. I could discern two common tools embedded within the crimson symbol. A gilded hammer and sickle.

Stalin's Door

I was holding my neckerchief woggle that I wore upon my uniform when I was a member of the Young Pioneers organisation so very long ago. But that was in another time and place. The woggle glowed brightly, catching my eye and looking just as new as the day I received it from the old commissar as a birthday gift.

It shocked me however to discover the temperature of the woggle felt cold. It was almost freezing inside my hand, as if I was holding on to a sphere of solid ice. I could bear this frigidness, but only for a time. I had endured much colder things in my lifetime. I clenched my fist around the woggle tightly, however it refused to grow warm inside my hand, as it had always done for decades. I knew then that the woggle wasn't mine to possess any longer. I knew I needed to return it to its original owner.

In one slow motion, I gently placed the woggle on top of Commissar Zykin's gravestone.

When I pulled my hand away, I abruptly experienced another light-headed sensation for a brief moment. I wondered if I would pass out again. What was happening to me? I remained conscious for the time being and inhaled and exhaled rapidly. As I exchanged the old stale air inside my lungs for the warm afternoon spring air outside, I felt better and stronger. The interior of my bronchus now felt pleasant and invigorated. For the first time in quite a while, a sensation of refreshment radiated throughout my entire body, and I breathed effortlessly. I could get used to this! What a change of fortune!

Ever skeptical, I wondered aloud. What had transpired just now? I couldn't quite put my finger on how to interpret my new mood.

A voice in the distance called out to me, breaking my trance. I turned around to see who it was. No one knew I was here. Why was that elocution suddenly familiar to me?

"Zhenya! Zhenya! I'm so happy to see you again!"

A handsome middle-aged woman rapidly approached me on foot from the pedestrian path I walked in from. As she drew closer, her form passed from a complete blurriness, to sharp and crisp.

My interloper dressed herself in what they would consider vintage clothing—outdated by today's modern standards. A plain white headscarf adorned her head, covering her long silver-grey hair.

The woman grinned at me and could hardly contain her excitement. She appeared to be breathing rapidly. Her radiant skin glowed in the rays of the April sun, looking natural. For a time, I just stared in amazement at her. It took me more than just a moment to recognise who my visitor was. And then it came to me.

"I cannot believe it! Grand—is that you—Grandmother? How—how can this be? Where did you come from?" I couldn't trust my eyes. Surely I was imagining all of this. Was this her spirit sent to haunt me?

"Yes. It's me. Hello darling, Zhenya. Oh my, don't you look beautiful today?"

"How did you get here?" I gawked at this woman in complete and utter disbelief.

"I arrived here the same way you did, my dear."

"I don't understand. What is happening to me?"

"Why don't you look at your hands?"

I stared down at my unclenched fists in awe. My old, weathered hands—gnarled with age—were now youthful looking again, smaller than a moment ago, and in perfect condition. I inspected the rest of my body and saw that I was noticeably shorter now and wore a fancy young woman's dress. I took my fingers and felt all around my face and forehead. Everything felt soft. A smoothness replaced my old and wrinkled skin. My hair was lengthy, well below my shoulders now, and blazed the striking blonde colour from my youth. I honestly did not comprehend what was transpiring. I closed my eyes tightly shut and screamed out in fear.

"Stay calm, my dear Zhenya. Do not worry. You're exactly as you were—the first time we met each other. When my Sava rescued you after they arrested your parents. Don't you remember? That winter night he brought you to our kommunalka? And I am exactly how I appeared on that fateful hour when you first met me. Albeit I resemble a woman twenty years younger than you used to be a few minutes ago, give or take a year."

"Am I—am I—deceased?"

"Certainly not, Zhenya. Honey, please understand, you're exceptionally vital—well—you're in a higher plane of existence now. Mortal death is merely just a stepping stone for where we're headed to. I know it must confuse you, so please just concentrate on what you feel right now. You're talking to me, I love you, and it's a beautiful spring day. The sun is shining upon your face, and you're breathing warm, clean air. Shall we not enjoy it together?"

I suddenly burst into tears. My grandmother reached her arms around and pulled me in close. Her powerful hug consoled me in an instant. It was exactly what I needed. It had been so long since I last saw her. It had been 47 years, in fact.

I remembered when I departed from her, alone at the train station in Mytininsk, half a world away from here. Everything was happening too fast now. I needed time to process all of this. I couldn't rightly figure anything out in my present condition.

"There, there. It's all better now, Zhenechka." My grandmother then gently released me.

An odd feeling of something now within my right hand's grasp, seized my attention. I peeked down to see a pristine white envelope. The very one I had retrieved from the desk in that antechamber of my old home—only an hour ago. I stared at it again and studied the beautiful cursive handwriting in pencil, with her name upon it. It was Lera's name.

"Grandmother? I think I'm supposed to give you this." I handed her the special letter.

My grandmother examined the envelope within her grasp, taking particular note of the addressee. She then beamed at me again, with the most perfect smile in the entire world.

"Why thank you, Zhenya." She tucked the correspondence into the waistband of her pleated skirt, so that the top of the envelope was poking up onto her tucked in blouse. "I will have the pleasure of reading this later."

"Grandmother, please. I still don't know how I got here. If I'm no longer the person I used to be, then how did all of this come to pass? Please, you must tell me."

"Take my hand precious one. I will show you now."

"Grandmother? What about him? Will he be coming with us too?" I pointed at the figure of a man standing very near us now. In all the excitement, I failed to notice that the fellow who'd been following me today had finally caught up.

We both studied this squat fellow, dressed in a bright white uniform jacket with large button-down pockets over each breast. Fastened black buttons on the coat ran from the bottom of his throat all the way to his waistline. His dark-coloured trousers and brown riding boots looked immaculate. A full head of pitch-black hair, and a thick moustache were unmistakable.

His most striking feature, however, were his eyes. The man squeezed both of his eyelids tightly shut, which left his mouth ajar in a grimace. I could see his head twitching violently, as beads of sweat dripped from his temples. Our intruder said nothing and remained paralysed. Of course I now recognised who it was who'd been stalking me. I wondered if he knew that we were even there.

"Oh, him? No, honey. He's staying here, in the land of the lamented. He's not been invited. Where we're going to—it's only for the righteous. Please put him out of your mind, forever. He cannot hurt us any longer."

I took hold of my grandmother's hand in mine and suddenly blinked out for a second.

§

I found myself instantly back inside the House on the Embankment Museum. I stood next to my grandmother, and we watched Emma Danilovna as she talked to a plainclothes policeman, likely an inspector from the Moskva police force. The two of them were having a discussion, and we listened in.

"Grandmother! How can we be here again? How did we arrive? What is going on? You promised to tell me!"

"Shhhh! Zhenya, just listen and they will reveal all to you."

"That's correct, Inspector Domnin. It's like I said—when I came back from eating my lunch in the mall cafeteria, I discovered this poor old woman collapsed upon the floor. I ran over to see if I could help her and saw that she—she wasn't breathing any longer. I immediately dialed one-one-two to call for an ambulance. When the paramedics arrived here five minutes later, they administered CPR. But I am afraid it was too late for her. She had passed on. I never saw this lady before today."

"And you didn't speak with her, Ms Karaulina?"

"Of course I didn't! She was no longer with us. Who was she, by the way?"

The police inspector looked through his mini-notebook, at his record entries.

"According to her identification papers, her name was Komolova Yevgeniya Ivanovna, a resident of Sankt-Petersburg. Aged seventy-six. Interesting. Today was her birthday, in fact. Poor ancient gal—dying on the day you were born. Do you think she used to be to be a resident here?"

"She could have been. A lot of the older residents used to stop by occasionally to reminisce. There aren't too many original ones left nowadays. You know? If you give me a moment, I can check for you."

The museum curator went to retrieve a large ledger from her desk in the room's rear. She returned and leafed through it with the inspector.

"Do you have a record of everyone that lived here then?"

"Yes, yes, I do. It's all alphabetised. Here—look in the K section. I see no one with the family surname of Komolova that used to live here at the House on the Embankment. In any year. Sorry about that, Inspector. Perhaps she knew someone that lived here instead."

"What do you make of these items, Ms Karaulina?"

Stalin's Door

The police inspector retrieved a small clear plastic evidence bag from his pocket and unfolded it for the museum curator to examine.

"Well, let's see. What I am looking at here?"

"These were the only items on her person. Do any of them look familiar to you?"

The museum curator picked up the sack and turned it around many times, focusing on the items inside.

"I can see a few kopeck coins in here. I see poor Madam Komolova's social insurance identity card. There's an unfolded piece of paper with an address written on it. I think it says two Luzhnetskiy Proyezd, Moskva, Russia, one one nine naught four eight. If I'm not mistaken that's the Novodevichy Cemetery, yes? But this last item. Whew! What a beauty! Why, I've not seen one of these in a very—very long time. Do you mind if I take it out for a closer look?"

"Well, I suppose that can't hurt now. Go ahead. I couldn't figure it out myself." The police inspector looked slightly puzzled.

Emma Danilovna opened the clear plastic bag and palmed a small, rounded object.

She held it out in between her forefinger and thumb so it would catch the light for her examination. I could see as she moved the bauble all about, gazing at it with much affection within her eyes.

The object was about the size of succulent plum—and painted in gold —which had lost most of its lustre from over the decades.

"This is a real stunner, Inspector. I think I've ever only seen one other exactly like it before. But this one is first-rate! It's a neckerchief woggle for a Young Pioneers uniform. You see, it would hold their distinctive red neckerchiefs cinched about their necks. This beauty is a rare find. Is there any way we could place it into our collection here? That's a museum piece if I ever saw one!" "Well, Ms Karaulina, I can't just give it to you today. However, if no one from the deceased's family comes to claim it in the next six months, then I can't see why it wouldn't be able to take up residence within your museum in perpetuity."

§

My grandmother and I now found ourselves outside on the sidewalk, right across the street from the behemoth House of the Embankment.

We just stood there for a short time, revelling in the late afternoon spring air and sun. Young and old alike were making their way around, enjoying themselves down by the banks of the mighty Moskva river.

Further out, pleasure craft and commuter boats of all kinds plied their way through its muddy waters. As I looked up, the most perfect cloudless azure sky imaginable filled my eyes in awe. I inhaled deeply and relished the warm breezy air within my lungs. Everything now felt alive, new, and vibrant to me.

In the far expanse ahead of us on the horizon rose the most alluring cityscape I ever beheld. This wasn't downtown Moskva that I stared at, this was something else entirely. Something strange, yet something wonderful.

Made entirely from silver, the metropolis shimmered in the sunlight and nearly blinded my eyes. I desperately squinted, so I could steal a better look at this miraculous vista.

Gigantic metallic buildings, impossibly tall complexes, and superlunary architectures beckoned to me with an allure I'd never experienced before. This was perhaps the most gorgeous sight I'd ever witnessed.

Urgently, I pulled on my companion's arm to inquire further.

"Grandmother, what is that—over there?" I pointed frantically at the majestic grey-white gorod that rose into the sky-blue ether in the distance beyond.

"Oh, that?" My grandmother smiled at me. "That's where we will live now, my dearest."

"Is that—is that heaven?"

"No. No, we don't call it that. However, it is our new home. Hold my hand and let me take you there."

The End

Glossary Of Transliterated Russian Words

Alfa — Alpha.
Babushka — An old married woman or grandmother.
Balakhon — Loose rugged outerwear.
Bol'shoye spasibo — Phrase which means, "Thank you very much."
Blin — A pancake. Also slang for "Damn it!"
Buran — Snowstorm or blizzard.
Chashki — Plural form of kruzhka.
Chastúshka — A traditional type of short Russian humorous folk song with a high beat frequency, that consists of one four-lined couplet, full of humor, satire or irony.
Chastúshki — Plural form of chastúshka.
Cheka — Name for the original Soviet secret police organization.
Chert voz'mi — Slang for "Hell."
Da — Yes.
Ded Moroz — Grandfather Frost. A figure similar to Father Christmas and Santa Claus.
Dyadya — Uncle.
FSB — Federal Security Service of the Russian Federation. Successor to the KGB.
Glupyy — Slang for "Stupid."
Gorod — A town or city.
Grozny — Fearsome, formidable, menacing, or terrible.
Gulag — Glavnoe upravlenie lagerei. Informal name for the NKVD bureau of prison-camp administration. Synonymous with Soviet prison labor camps in Siberia.
Kasha — Breakfast porridge.
Kaleydoskop — A kaleidoscope.
KGB — Committee for State Security. Soviet secret police organization from 1954 to 1991.
Khvorost — Thin twisted ribbons of pastry, deep-fried and sprinkled with powdered sugar.
Kommunalka — Singular form of kommunalki.
Kommunalki — Communal apartments.
Kopeck — A monetary unit of Russia, equal to one hundredth of a ruble.
Kosovorotka — The traditional long-sleeved Russian peasant shirt.
Kremlin — A citadel within a Russian city. The Moskva Kremlin is the de facto seat of government.
Kruzhka — A cup.
Leshiye — Russian forest spirit guardians.
Leshy — Singular form of Leshiye.
Litso — A face.

Mamushka — A more endearing term for mommy, mom, or mother.
Matryoshka Dolls — Also known as Babushka dolls, stacking dolls, nesting dolls, Russian tea dolls, or Russian dolls. They are a set of wooden dolls of decreasing size placed one inside another. The name matryoshka, literally "little matron," is a diminutive form of Russian female first name "Matryona."
Moskva — Moscow. Capital and largest city of Russia, USSR.
Moskvichi — A Muscovite, a native or citizen of Moskva.
Mudozvon — Slang for "A bugger."
MVD — Ministry of Internal Affairs. Follow on agency to the NKVD.
NKVD — <u>N</u>arodnyy <u>K</u>omissariat <u>V</u>nutrennikh <u>D</u>el. People's Commissariat for Internal Affairs. The primary secret police organization in the time of Stalin.
Nozh — A knife.
Nyet — No.
Okhrana — The Department for Protecting the Public Security and Order. The Russian Tsar's secret police force.
Pelmeni — Dumplings that consist of a filling wrapped in thin, unleavened dough.
Pirozhki — Baked or fried yeast-leavened boat-shaped buns with a variety of fillings.
Pirozhok — Singular form of pirozhki.
Poklonnik — A fan.
Politicheskiye — Political prisoners.
Psikh — Slang for "madman" or "psycho."
Rassolnik — A traditional soup made from pickled cucumbers, barley, and pork kidneys.
Reinette Simirenko — A variety of apple, native to Russia.
Rezidentsiya — A residence.
Ruble — The currency of the Soviet Union.
Rukavitsy — Mittens.
Ryba — A fish.
Samovar — A metal container traditionally used to heat and boil water.
Sankt-Petersburg — St. Petersburg. Also known by Leningrad in the time of the USSR.
Shakhmaty — The game of chess.
Shershni — Hornets.
Siberia — An extensive geographical region spanning much of Eurasia and Northern Asia. Siberia has been part of modern Russia since the latter half of the 16th century.
Smotrite nizhe — Phrase which means, "Look out below."
Solntse — The sun.
Solnyshka — Diminutive form of solntse.
Soviet — Derived from the Russian word sovet, meaning council, assembly, advice, harmony, and concord.
Sovnarkom — The Council of People's Commissars.
Spasiba za padarak — Phrase which means, "Thank you for the gift."
Spasibo — Thank you.
Struchok — A pod.
Tapochki — House slippers.
Taksi — A taxicab.
Taynyye Politseyskiye — Secret policemen.

Telnyashka — An undershirt horizontally striped in white and dark blue, worn by the Navy.
Tetushka — A more endearing term for aunt, or grand-aunt.
Tetya — Aunt.
Troika — A group of three people working together, especially in an administrative or managerial capacity.
Tvorog — Cheese curds.
Ulitsa — A street.
Ushanka — A Russian fur cap with ear flaps that can be tied up to the crown.
USSR — Union of Soviet Socialist Republics, was a federal socialist state in Northern Eurasia that existed from 1922 to 1991.
Voda — Water.
Vodka — A clear distilled alcoholic beverage.
Voronki — Black ravens, a metaphor for the windowless trucks used by the NKVD.
Vnuchka — Granddaughter.
Zaklyuchennyi — A prisoner.
Zechkas — Feminine version of Zek.
Zek — Russian condemned person in a prison or labor camp.
Zhenshchina — A woman.
Zhyd — An anti-Semitic pejorative term.
ZiS — Zavod imeni Stalina, a major Russian automobile, truck, military vehicle, and heavy equipment manufacturer that was based in Moscow, Russia, USSR.
Zona — No man's land.

Colophon

Production

Hardware: Apple MacBook Pro (Retina, 13-inch, Early 2015)

Operating System: macOS Big Sur v11.1

Word Processing Software: Apache OpenOffice v4.1.8

Text Editing Software: ProWritingAid v2.0.48

Cover Art Hardware: Apple iPhone 7 (128 GB)

Cover Art Software: You Doodle v7.8.3
Pixomatic v2.10.0
Adobe Photoshop v22.1.1

Cover Art Typeface: BEBAS NEUE

Inside Typeface: Georgia

Statistics

Novel Word Count: 107,468

Novel Page Count: 401

About The Author

John St. Clair lives with his wife Nancy in the northern Virginia suburb of Reston, Virginia. This is his debut novel.

Made in United States
North Haven, CT
18 December 2022